VIRAGO MODERN
CLASSICS
577

Rumer Godden (1907–98) was the acclaimed author of over sixty works of fiction and non-fiction for adults and children. Born in England, she and her siblings grew up in Narayanganj, India, and she later spent many years living in Calcutta and Kashmir. Several of her novels were made into films, including *Black Narcissus*, *The Greengage Summer* and *The River*, which was filmed by Jean Renoir. She was appointed OBE in 1993.

Also by Rumer Godden

The Lady and the Unicorn
Black Narcissus
Breakfast with the Nikolides
A Fugue in Time
The River
Kingfishers Catch Fire
An Episode of Sparrows
The Greengage Summer
China Court
The Battle of Villa Fiorita
In this House of Brede
The Peacock Spring
Five for Sorrow, Ten for Joy
The Dark Horse
Thursday's Children
Coromandel Sea Change
Listen to the Nightingale

CROMARTIE v. THE GOD SHIVA

ACTING THROUGH THE GOVERNMENT OF INDIA

RUMER GODDEN

A VIRAGO
MODERN CLASSIC

VIRAGO

This paperback edition published in 2013 by Virago Press
First published in Great Britain in 1997 by Macmillan
Published in 2013 by Virago Press
This edition published in 2026 by Virago Press

1 3 5 7 9 10 8 6 4 2

Copyright © The Rumer Godden Literary Trust 1997

Lines from 'Childhood' from *Poems 1906–1926*
by Rainer Maria Rilke, translated by J.B. Leishman

The moral right of the author has been asserted.

*All characters and events in this publication, other than those
clearly in the public domain, are fictitious and any resemblance
to real persons, living or dead, is purely coincidental.*

All rights reserved.
No part of this publication may be reproduced, stored in a
retrieval system, or transmitted, in any form or by any means, without
the prior permission in writing of the publisher, nor be otherwise circulated
in any form of binding or cover other than that in which it is published
and without a similar condition including this condition being
imposed on the subsequent purchaser.

A CIP catalogue record for this book
is available from the British Library.

ISBN 978-0-349-01760-0

Typeset in Goudy by M Rules
Printed and bound in Great Britain by
Clays Ltd, Elcograf S.p.A.

Papers used by Virago are from well-managed forests
and other responsible sources.

Virago Press
An imprint of
Little, Brown Book Group
Carmelite House
50 Victoria Embankment
London EC4Y 0DZ

The authorised representative
in the EEA is
Hachette Ireland
8 Castlecourt Centre
Dublin 15, D15 XTP3, Ireland
(email: info@hbgi.ie)

An Hachette UK Company
www.hachette.co.uk

www.virago.co.uk

ACKNOWLEDGEMENTS

I should like to give my most sincere thanks to those experts who have so generously helped me with the plot and writing of this book, extraordinarily difficult and intricate as it was.

To Mr and Mrs Talbot, Rina and Rupert of New Delhi, and their colleague Mr Reddy of southern India, for their constant advice on location and custom.

To Robert Knox, Keeper of the Department of Oriental Antiquities at the British Museum, London, who, by happy coincidence, was one of the experts called in by the Government of India to identify the dancing Shiva. He not only taught me a great deal and gave valuable advice but actually lent me his book containing an account of the statue and trial *and* let me keep it until my writing was done.

To Andrew Henley, barrister, for his long and patient help on matters of law, and his wife Kris who acted as a 'go-between'. Also Fraser Barber, film sound recordist, for many practical suggestions. To my brilliant editor at Macmillan Publishers, Hazel Orme, and friend and typist Sheila Anderson, whose patience never seems to wear out.

And to my long-suffering family and staff. Once someone asked my elder daughter Jane if she too wanted to be a writer when she grew up. 'No thank you,' was the candid answer. 'One in the family is enough.'

R.G.

1997

LONDON

'Cromartie versus the God Shiva. No, thank you,' said Sir George. 'Walter, I really don't think I can take this case.'

Sir George Fothergill, QC, was head of one of the most prestigious sets of chambers in London's Inns of Court. Walter Johnson was its head clerk.

The Chambers, though not in Lincoln's Inn, were nearby in Lincoln's Square. In the tall old house, Sir George and his deputy head of chambers, Miss Honor Wyatt, QC, had the two panelled first-floor rooms. The rest of the barristers in the set worked two or three together while Walter was in the spacious basement, which he liked because it opened on to the narrow terrace of garden. His 'snug', as he called it, not only had his desk, filing cabinets and shelves of law books on every wall, but his armchair by the fireplace – in winter the flickering gas fire was always lit – with a fine Persian hearth rug and above, on the mantelshelf, his collection of toby jugs. Next door was a large office for the deputy clerk – Walter's son, Johnny – Johnny's own assistant, Jeffrey, and his accounts clerk, Elizabeth. Ginevra, the perky young receptionist, had her desk with its telephones above in the front hall.

'It's always the head clerks who really run chambers,' Sir George would say. 'Walter's family have been in the set longer than any of us.'

'Yes,' Walter agreed. 'John Johnson my father, then me, Walter Johnson, and now Johnny, my son, who's only been here five years, and he's just had a baby son. Perhaps he ... I like continuity,' said Walter.

Now Sir George was going on: 'I don't want to oppose you, Walter – when have I ever?' he asked. 'But this is too fantastical – a Hindu god going to law.'

'Acting through the Government of India, sir, which seems solid enough to me.'

'It can't be solid if it's a spirit, which I don't believe is active. No, I can't bring myself to do it. We should be a laughing stock.'

'Ask Miss Wyatt what she thinks.' Walter was a diplomat.

'A laughing stock? Why?' asked Honor Wyatt. 'I find it piquant.'

'*Piquant?*' Sir George was outraged.

'Yes. It seems to let in another air – a fresh one. It

could become a sensation, which would extend us. And, George, think too of the fee.'

'Yes, indeed,' said Walter, and he was soon justified. When the Government of India heard rumours that Sir George Fothergill was hesitating, the fee was immediately doubled.

'It's a plum,' Honor said. 'We can't let it go. I wish I could take it.'

'I wish you could, Miss Wyatt, but you're on the Huntingdon case.'

The Huntingdon case was exciting wide and horrified interest. Lord Ian Huntingdon, eldest son of one of the country's oldest and richest aristocratic families, had learned he was to be disinherited for deceiving his father over the estate and an attempt would be made to strip him of his title, but before this could be implemented the old Marquess had been found dead. It might have been a heart attack but the 'young idiot', as Honor called him, had also killed his mother the Marchioness. Honor was briefed for the defence – and this case had brought a great deal of notoriety. 'There's nothing, except the royals, that can excite British public sensationalism more than the aristocracy,' she said regretfully. 'It may take weeks, even months. I wish I *were* free but I'm not.'

'Then who?' asked Sir George.

Walter knew he had to say what had been in his mind all along. 'Sir, I've been thinking of Mr Dean.'

That took Sir George by surprise. 'Young Michael?'

'He isn't all that young, sir, and doing remarkably well. His handling of that awkward Gibbons case was masterly – if that's not too strong a word. Old Gibbons was so crafty he'd have defeated most of us. And it seems to fit, sir. Mr Dean was born and brought up in India.'

'Only until he went to school,' Sir George cavilled. 'As far as I know he hasn't been back.'

'No,' Honor intervened, 'but if you've been in a country as a child, it is, as it were, in your bones, and I think he's still attached.'

At thirty-one Michael Dean was the senior of all the junior barristers at 2 Lincoln's Square. There were sixteen of them and Michael had recently been made a Leading Junior, able to lead another barrister in a case – 'For which normally you need ten to fifteen years' call,' Honor had told his parents, 'unless you're exceptionally able and confident, which Michael is after only seven, and we would never hold back such talent.'

Honor knew his calibre: in his early days, when he had been a pupil, she had taken him for six months' training.

To repay her he had done all her paperwork, as was customary in chambers, 'And learned and learned,' he often said, 'by grace and favour and luck.'

'Not luck,' said Honor. 'Brains, hard work and determination from the very beginning.' That was true. 'It's as difficult to get into a set of chambers like Sir George Fothergill's as it is to climb Everest without oxygen,' she would say. She knew: she had had to do it. 'And I had influence. Michael did it all himself. I've often wondered how he can afford it.' Every barrister in the set had to pay his or her own way: rent, services, telephone and fax, electricity. 'His parents couldn't help him much,' Honor told Sir George now. 'They're teachers, quite ordinary – except that his father is a teacher poet. Michael has poetry in him, too, so this case may not be at all a strange idea to him. Though he's astute, there's something undoubting in him – you would call it credulous.' She smiled. 'Why not call him in and talk to him?'

Sir George opened the proceedings. 'Michael, you have undoubtedly heard of the case concerning a Mr Cromartie and the Hindu god Shiva, acting through the Government of India.'

'Of course, Sir George. "Versus the God Shiva" – that's

caught people's attention. The whole of Chambers is buzzing with it.'

'And that is just what I find too fantastical. The case has been offered to us but—'

'Sir George, you're not going to refuse it?' Michael was so alarmed that he forgot to whom he was speaking.

'I think I must. A Mr Bhatacharya has just come to see me from Delhi. He's a high-ranking official if not a minister.'

'He's a minister,' said Walter.

'Obviously he wants us – hasn't his own government chosen us? – but I confess I feel out of my depth. If it were a case of a valuable antique bought or stolen and taken to another country with the idea of selling it there for profit, of course I could understand and sympathize, but this! Candidly I'm afraid of it. We could be brought to ridicule.'

'I think it might enhance us,' Honor put in. 'Don't you see, George? The inclusion of the god makes the charge more serious.'

'Mr Dean, sir,' Walter was steering skilfully, 'you remember something of India, don't you? Wouldn't you agree with that?'

'Completely,' said Michael.

'Then can you tell us why?'

'Because in India the gods are alive, living as well as sacred, so anything to do with them is sacrosanct.'

'But to go to law!'

'Well, Indians can be fanatical – just like us,' Michael admitted. 'Of course, I don't know a great deal about India now, but I do know that most Hindus live their religion. To them it's not something apart as it so often is with us, but the core of every day, so much so that to us it is almost shockingly everyday. The Hindu gods eat and drink, fall in love, marry just like us. For Hindus sex, too, is sacred. The symbol for Shiva is the *lingam*, the phallus, the male generative organ, while, for the various manifestations of his goddesses, it is the *yoni*, the vagina.'

Sir George's expression showed that this was distasteful to him, but Michael was so carried away that he had almost forgotten him. 'They're found in every Shiva temple. This bronze, I understand, is a little Nataraja Shiva, in his cosmic dance around the universe, extremely sacred. In India, to steal a Nataraja denigrates it, which is blasphemy.'

'Blasphemy!' Sir George was shocked.

'The worst crime of all, the only one that can't be forgiven,' and Honor quoted, '"He that shall blaspheme against the Holy Spirit hath never forgiveness." It is, to some extent, in every religion.'

'In India it's law,' said Michael. 'Oh, Sir George,' he was on fire, 'I do so hope you'll take this case.'

Sir George looked from one to the other. 'Cosmic dance. Sex. You'd better tell me who or what this Shiva is. How does he fit in?'

Michael did not answer at once. He won't hurry, not even for George, thought Honor, pleased. She always liked to look at Michael: not tall, he was slim, quick in his movements; dark-haired, he had hazel eyes, which were oddly penetrating when he was fighting in court, but they could light up with fun and laughter. Although she was his senior not only in rank but by several years, Honor liked going out with him. 'And he seems to enjoy it, not just politely – he really does.'

'Hasn't he got a girl of his own age?' Sir George had not meant to cast any slur on Honor, who was not at all perturbed.

'Dozens, I should think, but nothing serious. He seems adept at avoiding that.'

'Wise man.'

'No,' said Honor. 'He's clever but not wise – and he's so consistently steady in court that it's as if nothing touches him deeply. I think Michael has a lot to learn. Perhaps India will teach him.'

Now Michael began: 'Hinduism is an old, old religion, going back to the elemental gods – Surya, the sun, Indira, god of storm and rain, Agni, fire – and they still, in a way, remain. A good orthodox Hindu wife will hold a kitchen *puja* – prayer. It's a holy day when all the pots and pans are scoured, cleansed and tidied. The shelves are freshly papered, marigold garlands hung along them, vases of fresh flowers brought in. Finally a new fire is lit. Anyone can recognize the elements in that simple festival, but as the Hindus became more educated, less simple, they wanted something not as abstract as the elements, close but still powerful, and deeper than themselves, mystical, and so the individual gods manifested themselves.'

'It seems to me they have hundreds of gods,' said Honor.

'Only three. Most are aspects, male and female, of the great Hindu trinity: Brahma the Creator, "who has made all things visible and invisible", as Christians say, Vishnu the Preserver, who holds all things together, and Shiva the Destroyer who, because he brings death, is also resurrection. To Hindus, death is simply a stage in the cycle of creation, so Shiva in his dance around the world is god of all movement, especially in time and all life. That is why he is so often shown as a Nataraja – *nata* from dance, *raja* meaning king or royal, a great king against whom one must not trespass.' He paused. 'He must be deeply insulted now by being stolen, which is why the Government of India is so outraged.'

There was a silence until Sir George said, 'Thank you, Michael.'

When he had gone: 'I thought Michael got by on his charm. I didn't know he could speak like that.' Sir George blew his nose.

'He usually does, but that was the real Michael. George, let Walter give him the brief.'

'I had half a mind to when he was speaking, but we have to be careful. However fantastical, this is an important case and Michael is still a junior.'

'Senior Leading Junior,' Honor reminded him.

'But, still ... will they accept him?'

'If they're told he's one of the most brilliant of the oncoming young barristers in London,' suggested Honor.

'Isn't that putting it rather high?'

'No,' said Walter, 'and he's greatly in demand. I could do with more Mr Deans.'

'Well, if you can't spare him to go to India – obviously

as we are for the defence someone must go – we could send a solicitor.'

'Sir, something tells me Mr Dean should go in person.'

'It's Michael who's telling you that.' Honor was insistent. 'Michael himself.'

Sir George capitulated and picked up the telephone. 'Ginevra, please ask Mr Dean to come back.'

'Michael, the Lord God Almighty and Our Lady want you in His office.' Though Ginevra could be impertinent she was efficient and loyal – as were all the staff. As a matter of fact, 'lord' and 'lady' suited Sir George and Honor well: Sir George was imposing with his height and well-trimmed beard – 'Though not half as well tailored as Walter,' he used to say, because there were several expensive young Fothergills. Perhaps Walter, with his Savile Row suits and hand-made shoes, was trying to mitigate his own thickset stubbiness and grizzled hair. 'Well, even head clerks have their weaknesses,' said Sir George in sympathy. But no one could challenge Honor Wyatt, with her own height and imposing carriage, her fall of blonde hair – Michael remembered it drawn back into a knob, to hide it under the white barrister's wig, which seemed to make her features more clear. Her eyebrows were level, her grey eyes, too, although in court they could be as sharp as gimlets. She had an authority, a wit, that struck even Michael with awe: there could be no pretensions when he was with Honor. Now she, Sir George and Walter were waiting for him as he came in.

'You wanted me, Sir George?'

Sir George did not answer at once: he was looking at Michael as if he had never seen him before – Which he probably hasn't, thought Honor. 'Michael's made for this,' she had told Sir George, and added, as if she were thinking more deeply, 'He has hazel eyes.'

'What can that have to do with it?'

'Hazel eyes are mixed brown and grey, brown for earth and grey for—' she broke off. 'I'm only guessing but I think he can see further than we can.'

'With this case he'll need to,' said Sir George.

Michael, though he tried to restrain himself, was growing fidgety. 'You wanted me, Sir George,' he said again, and then as if he could not contain himself any longer, 'Oh, Sir George, I do so hope you've reconsidered.'

'I have reconsidered but not for myself. Michael, you'd better go and get your jabs. I gather you need a good many for India – typhoid, tetanus and I don't know what.'

'India?' Michael was almost speechless. 'You mean—'
'I mean go to your doctor at once.'

The first thing Michael wanted to do was see the Nataraja, which was still, for security reasons, in Sparkes's, the famed art dealers', strongroom. 'Of course I will get you a pass,' Mr Bhatacharya had said. 'You can use it whenever you want, because I expect you will need to study the Nataraja closely.'

'As soon as I can,' Michael told him, 'but first I need a session with our head clerk.'

'The redoubtable Johnson? I wish I had someone like him in my office.'

'There's nobody like him,' said Michael.

'I know you prefer finding things out for yourself,' Walter began, 'but you'll need a few facts. How much do you know about this Shiva?'

'I know it has at some time been taken out of India – been certified here as eleventh century. Finding it is surely a triumph after it has lain buried and undiscovered for all those years.'

'Not quite all,' said Walter. 'For some ninety years now, many people have known exactly where it was until it disappeared again. Mr Bhatacharya has told me the story as far as it goes and he had it from the woman, Mrs McIndoe – they call her Miss Sanni – who owns the hotel on the South Indian coast where the Shiva was housed.'

'An hotel?' Michael was surprised. 'How on earth – or should we say in heaven and earth? – did it get there?'

'If you'll listen,' said Walter severely, 'I'll tell you.'

'From where?'

'I'm coming to that, but I have to go back to the beginning as far as we know it. It may take time. I'll be as short as I can.'

'Not too short,' pleaded Michael. 'It's fascinating.'

'Very well, but I've warned you. In the early nineteen hundreds, say nineteen five or six, an Englishman, Henry Bertram, had made a fortune from indigo. All sailors' livery used to be dyed with it – all blue cloth. It grew like a weed in Bihar. But Bertram was an astute businessman. Chemical dyes were coming rapidly on the market and he sold his factory and fields just in time. He wanted to stay in India, so went to the east coast and built a luxury hotel – the only hotel in a most beautiful spot between the low hills and the beaches.

'He was even more astute than he knew, as it isn't far

from the Sun Temple at Konak, the most beautiful in the world, in a region of temples. In the hills behind it there are rare ancient cave paintings and it made an ideal tourist centre, especially for the scholarly, while the beaches, too, are wonderful. As if he knew its future, he insisted on having what was rare in hotels at that time: a wine cellar and an ice-room in the basement, so that the workmen had to dig deep, so deep that they came upon the ruins of still another small temple.

'They refused to go on, begging Henry Bertram to choose another site. Like most English businessmen then, he knew nothing about Hinduism but he did know how to manage a workforce: he doubled their wages. But they had another reward. They found the little image of the Nataraja, lying face down, his hoop of flames unbroken. To propitiate them even more, when the hotel was finished Bertram had a niche built above the drawing-room-cum-ballroom door. I believe the Hindu servants and the villagers came to worship there and bring their offerings.'

'And he allowed them?'

'Always.'

'He must have been a remarkable man.'

'Yes, and he must, too, have had an affection for Bihar.

He called his hotel Patna Hall – Patna is the capital of that state. The hotel is run now by Henry Bertram's granddaughter, Samantha.'

... 'Now?' she always said. 'I have been its manager since I was nine.' ...

'Henry Bertram brought her up,' Walter went on. 'There's no mention of parents. Though she married a Colonel McIndoe, Bhatacharya says everyone calls her Miss Sanni or, if you are close to her, Auntie Sanni. Colonel McIndoe, who does the business side, firmly installed electricity, telephones and a fax machine, but except for that Miss Sanni insists on keeping Patna Hall exactly as it was, in full old-time panoply, which must be very expensive. Indeed, Mr Bhatacharya thinks she finds it hard to keep it going, especially as he says India now has a chain of hotels, the Uberois. "They are in every province," he told me, "with high standards, comfortable and excellent service, quick, which Patna Hall is decidedly not." Yes, there's no fault to find with Uberois except that all over India they're exactly the same – public rooms, furnishings, even the menus. Most people stay at them, but visitors say that if you've once been to Patna Hall you want to come back again. An archaeological group has been coming every October for the last twenty years. It's led now by a Professor Ellen Webster who, I believe, is well known in America. When she took it over the tour was only for women, a mixture of holiday and sightseeing. Mr Bhatacharya told me that the Patna Hall servants called them the "cultural ladies", but now it's for men too and it's considered a privilege to be accepted on one of these tours – students get grants for them and people book them from as far away as China.

'Professor Webster is meticulous,' Walter was appreciative, 'and each year she comes to Patna Hall a week or so in advance to check on every possible arrangement. Mr Bhatacharya says this is very wise as there is a proverb that Indians are so anxious to please that they tell you things not as they are but as you would like them to be – and now we come to the point. On every tour there are evening lectures in the ballroom. One is always on the Hindu deities and, though no one else was allowed to touch it, Miss Sanni let Professor Webster use the Nataraja, lifting it down and putting it on her table. Last year the genuine statue was in place, but at some time during the last twelve months it has been exchanged.'

'And no one noticed?' Michael marvelled.

'The fake, they say, is exact,' said Walter, 'and remember, at Patna Hall everyone was used to seeing it in its niche. No, it took an Ellen Webster and she took the precaution of writing her discovery down.' He produced a page or two of manuscript and handed them to Michael.

> As soon as I lifted it I knew it was a fake. The first thing was the weight. It was too light. Next the surface of the bronze was too smooth – no patina – and though it was so expertly made, something was missing, an ambience of calm, I can call it nothing else, a calm in spite of the dance. Of course I raised an alarm. I remember shouting, 'Auntie Sanni, Auntie Sanni! Come here at once. Call the Colonel. The Shiva's gone.'
>
> 'No. He is here.' Auntie Sanni had come, not hurrying.
>
> 'He's not. This is a fake. Someone's stolen yours. We must get the police at once.'
>
> 'There's no need for the police. He has not gone.'
>
> 'He has. He's gone! Gone! Gone!' I was trying to hammer it into Auntie Sanni. 'Gone.'
>
> The confidential servants, Samuel the old butler and Hannah the housekeeper, his wife, had come running. 'Aie! Aie! I get the police. I, Samuel.'
>
> 'No, Samuel,' said Miss Sanni. 'No, Ellen, let things be.'
>
> 'I can't. The Nataraja is not just yours. It's a national treasure, worth I don't know how much.'

Auntie Sanni was suddenly stern. 'I know what it's worth and I know the value, but not your kind of value or worth. Police, money, everything that disturbs. I forbid you, Ellen, absolutely forbid you to tell anyone. We still have our Shiva-ji.'

Michael read it closely. He looked up: 'What happened next?'

'Nothing for twenty-four hours, but the next day was the day when Mr Cromartie, a Canadian art dealer, arrived in London. He took the statue straight to Sparkes's. Soon there were mentions of it in some of the better English newspapers and the Indian ones immediately picked them up. Patna Hall's telephone rang incessantly. An enterprising journalist announced that he was coming. Miss Sanni had to give in: her prohibitions were no longer valid. "Do as you like," she said. Professor Webster had already written her formal testimony and lost no time in sending it to London.'

'Thank God for faxes,' Honor had said, when it arrived.

'It was certainly timely,' Walter told Michael. 'The Professor even offered to come to London as soon as her tour ended. The police made over the testimony at once to Mr Bhatacharya, who gave copies to everyone concerned. One is probably on its way to you. He told me he even gave one to Mr Cromartie, hoping he would drop this ridiculous case. But no. He's set on it.'

Michael came down to the snug again. 'Walter, have you a few minutes?'

'No,' said Walter, 'but I'll make some.'

'Thank you. Something has struck me about Cromartie versus the God Shiva, and I have a feeling that you know more than you let on about this man Cromartie.'

'Yes.' Then Walter was silent for a few moments. 'I was going to tell you when it seemed ripe but I don't think I behaved very well.'

'*You?*'

'Yes. Yet it was well before we were involved in the case. The Indian government and Mr Bhatacharya had not even approached Sir George, but when Mr Cromartie – Sydney Carstairs Cromartie, to give him his full name – had decided on litigation, he took action at once to find himself a lawyer. He seems not to have any friends or advisers in London, which doesn't surprise me, so he asked around. He said he wanted the best – and it appears that he's got plenty of money. Someone told him of us and he didn't wait a minute but came straight here demanding to see Sir George. Of course, he ended up with me.'

'What's he like?'

'Crass,' said Walter, without hesitation. 'Unbelievably ignorant because he's so cocksure he's always right. "I go my way and my way goes with me as it damn well has to" was one of his sayings. Ginevra didn't stand a chance – he was in the hall, had shut the door behind him and was flourishing his card at her before she could say a word. She still did her best. "Have you an appointment?"

'"Don't be silly, girl. I don't waste time making appointments. I have to see Sir Fothergill at once."'

Michael could not help laughing.

'It wasn't funny,' said Walter. 'Ginevra thought it better not to argue, but she's quick. She gave our invariable excuse, "Sir George is in court" and before Cromartie could speak she said, "If you'd like to leave your telephone number I'll get someone to call you as soon as possible." She got up to show him out but he stood between her and the door. She told me later she didn't like the look of him – well, he's certainly the reverse of attractive – and she really thought he might push straight past her so she showed him in to me. I expect he thought she'd capitulated and followed her quietly. "Someone to see you, Mr Johnson," she said, but one look at my snug and he was on the defensive. "You're not Sir Fothergill!"

'"Certainly not, Mr Cromartie." Ginevra had put his card, too flashy, on my desk. His name was in big letters but below, in smaller print, was "Ye Olde Oriental Treasure Chest" and an address in Toronto.'

'Ah!' Michael put in. 'Oriental Treasure Chest. That's the connection.'

'Obviously. The newspapers said the same. Anyway he attacked at once. "Sir George Fothergill's in court and, however urgent, he can't possibly be got out for me. That's the long and short of it, isn't it?" I had to agree, and he went on, "I'll tell you what I don't like – the way you English treat people from overseas as if they were bloody foreigners. I'm Canadian, mister, and Canada is part of the Commonwealth so we should be compatriots but I'm beginning to think that for us you're the bloody foreigners."

'Like Ginevra, I thought it better not to argue and there was a pause. Then Cromartie asked, "If I can't see Sir Fothergill who are you?" I told him my name and that

I was head clerk to Sir George Fothergill's chambers,' and Walter added, 'I couldn't bring myself to call him sir.'

'"You don't look like a clerk," he said, so I told him again, head clerk. "I think you'll find, Mr Cromartie," I said, "that in chambers, even the heads work through their clerks, and so, Mr Cromartie, if you wish to see one of our barristers—" He interrupted me. "Sir George or no one. I won't have the girl."'

Walter, for once, had been moved to fury. 'The girl as you call her is Miss Honor Wyatt QC.'

'What in God's name's a QC?'

'Queen's Counsel, a very high rank of barrister. Anyway she couldn't take you. She's on an important case but, Mr Cromartie, to return to what I was going to tell you, if you want to see a barrister – certainly one of our barristers – your solicitor should make the appointment and accompany you.'

'Solicitor!' Cromartie exploded. 'So they told me but I'm not having any of that! I have no solicitor, Mr J., nor do I intend to have one. It's just another of your law-wallah's ruses to get money from a gullible public!'

As Michael heard that, he gasped. 'He said *that* in our chambers? Outrageous!'

'Yes, I nearly pressed the bell for Johnny and we would

have propelled him out on to the street, but it wouldn't have been seemly – especially with all the notoriety of Miss Wyatt's Huntingdon case – so I let him go on.'

Cromartie had ranted, 'Well, I'm not gullible and you'll never make me have a solicitor.'

'Then you'll never see any of our barristers, nor, I can guess, any decent barrister,' had been Walter's response.

'That silenced him for a moment and I knew a struggle was going on in the man until he burst out, "Bloody blackmail!" Again I nearly pressed the bell for Johnny but Cromartie was evidently near the end of his tether and, sure enough, he almost wailed, "I must talk to *someone*. I wish I'd never seen that damned statue."

'It was pitiful. He was in such a state, his suit was crumpled – he was so paunchy it looked uncomfortably tight. His face was red with anger and he'd forgotten to brush his hair, which was ginger and clashed with the suit, which was a blatant bright brown – but there was no mistaking that he was genuine and I thought if I let him talk, asked him a few harmless questions, it might get rid of some of the spleen.'

'You're a kinder man than I am,' said Michael. 'I should have got Johnny at once, no matter what.'

'You'd have been right, but it seemed best at the time.

I knew that the spleen was not only of rage but disappointment, not to say worry. Cromartie feels the whole world is against him and he doesn't know why, and he really *is* genuine. In fact, Michael, if this case does come on, I don't think you'll make mincemeat of him. He could get round a jury just as he nearly got round me.

'I began with what I thought was a safe question, "Do you have to travel a great deal for your Treasure Chest? To India perhaps?" but it made him even more belligerent.'

'I've never been to India in my life, and I don't want to!' Cromartie had bellowed. 'I bought the statue right there in Toronto where I do my business – successfully I'm glad to say. Mister, I run this small shop – exclusive, mind you – for which I buy Oriental goods. I have my sources. What's wrong with that?'

'Nothing, as long as you know where the goods come from, but do you always?'

'How could I? In my trade you don't ask questions. Anyway if you did you wouldn't be told the truth. A chap came to see me, bringing the statue. You people treat me as if I were an idiot but I tell you, the moment I saw it I knew it was different, though I didn't know how different. He said he'd bought it in India from a workman who'd found it buried.'

To Michael, Walter added, 'Well, as you know, that happened to be true.'

Mr Cromartie had gone on, 'The fellow called himself Narayan Gupta. Of course, he haggled over the price, but I couldn't get him below twenty-five thousand dollars – more than I ever paid for anything in my life. Of course I never saw the fellow again.'

'We could trace him through the cheque.'

Mr Cromartie had given Walter a pitying look. 'I paid him cash.'

'Cash? Twenty-five thousand? Didn't that make you suspicious?'

'It's the custom. How Mr Narayan Gupta keeps his accounts is nothing to do with me.'

'It was convincing,' Walter told Michael, 'but somehow I felt I must persist so I asked him, "You are sure, Mr Cromartie, that the Shiva is yours to sell?" and for the first time, there was a moment's hesitation until he said reluctantly, "Granted there was some hanky-panky."

'"Dishonesty," I told him flatly.

'"Not on my part. Didn't I get a licence to bring the statue over? Declared it to customs. It cost me a bomb, I can tell you, but I had to get it valued."'

Michael interrupted, 'Toronto has the Royal Ontario

Museum with a wonderful oriental department. Why didn't he go there?'

'He did, but only to ask them if they'd tell him who were the best dealers for oriental antiques. To give him his due, Mr Cromartie doesn't do things by halves. Of course they said Sparkes's. He booked the next flight to London.'

Michael had been brooding as he listened. 'Cromartie said, "Damned statue." I don't like to think of him with the Shiva.'

'Neither do I, but it wasn't for long. As soon as he was free of Customs, even before he'd found an hotel, he put the Shiva into a taxi and took it to Sparkes's and, in Cromartie fashion, demanded a table or a stand, took the statue out of its case, set it there and told the dumbfounded salesman to fetch the manager who, surprisingly, came – I expect the salesman had said something to him. Soon two or three others were summoned, and a young woman. Cromartie saw they were deeply impressed.'

'Of course I was gratified,' he had admitted to Walter, 'I told them how and where I got the statue, but not, of course, what I paid. Then I asked them straight out, "How much do you think you could get me for it?" In this country it seems no one can answer a question directly. They hummed and hawed. "It will take time, Mr Cromartie" ... "We'll have to be sure" ... "Get expert advice" ... "Maybe consult the Indian government" ... and finally, "If you leave it with us ... "

"'No way,' I told them.

"'It would be safer than in an hotel – we have a strongroom,' they said. 'Of course you would have a receipt.' Oh, they went on until I said, 'I'll leave it with you for two days, no more.' And what did they do?' Mr Cromartie had burst out in fury again. 'They called in the police, without a word of reference to me.'

'That was a bit hard,' said Michael.

'I thought so too,' said Walter, 'but I said, trying to smooth things over, "Perhaps they thought if they'd told you, you'd have taken it away."'

'God's truth I would!' Mr Cromartie had been emphatic. 'It's mine, isn't it? Yet they treated me as if I was a receiver of stolen goods.'

'Perhaps you were – unwittingly.'

'There you go. You too!' Mr Cromartie said bitterly.

'I said *unwittingly*,' Walter reminded him.

'And so you should. Haven't I told you and told you? From the day I first saw the statue I have behaved with complete openness throughout. *Throughout,*' Mr Cromartie had emphasized again. 'That's more than can be said for Mr Bhata— I can never remember their names. The man they sent for from India.'

'Mr Bhatacharya. We know of him. He's a senior official.'

'He may be. I thought at first he was trustworthy, but he's glib as hell. He was sent here immediately the British police informed the Government of India. He told me he'd been authorized to reimburse me for the money I'd paid and the same again, and all in pounds not dollars, as a thank-you for bringing the statue so openly to London. A "thank-you", I don't think.'

'But you accepted it,' Walter had demurred.

'Then, not now. Then it seemed quite good to me. Fifty thousand pounds is not to be sneezed at – pounds not dollars. But I'd put nothing in writing. We Cromarties are not fools, mister, and, sure enough, I found the Government of India had tried cheating me. The experts, especially that Sir Lennox from the British Museum, valued the little piece at at least a quarter of a million pounds. Two hundred and fifty thousand, mark you. And said he'd be glad to pay even more to have the statue in his museum.'

'Of course he can't. It's got to go back to India,' Walter said.

'So it will, if they pay me for it – the proper price which, mind you, they knew all along, not a paltry fifty thousand. They're trying to cheat me. You can't deny it, though I think you're trying to persuade me that I have no case. Of course I have. Haven't I checked and rechecked?'

'Beyond all doubt?' Walter had asked, and said now to Michael, 'I felt I had to drive that in and I said, "Mr Cromartie, you're not on certain ground. If at any point the Shiva had been stolen it wouldn't be yours to sell. You've read Professor Ellen Webster's testimony, which is beyond all doubt, so maybe fifty thousand was generous."'

'Was it?' Mr Cromartie had snapped. 'What if I told you I know something that you, smart Mr J., her and even Mr Bhata don't know.' He had come so close that Walter could smell his breath – 'And himself, ugh,' he told Michael. 'It was very disagreeable.'

'A young man came to see me.' Mr Cromartie had been almost whispering. 'He had read in the papers about my bringing the statue to London. His name is Kanu and he's much closer to Mrs McIndoe – Miss Sanni of that hotel – than any visiting professor. He was practically brought up at Patna Hall. He says Miss Sanni was like a mother to him. Kanu is now nineteen and has been working at Patna Hall as barman and receptionist – staff there have to double up, these days. His great ambition, though, is to be a barman at one of the Uberoi hotels, and to help him Mrs McIndoe sent him to London for a short intensive training course.

... "For an Uberoi you need it," Kanu had said. "All Uberois first class, modern, not like running-down old hotel..."

'It seems,' Mr Cromartie went on, 'that Patna Hall is in financial trouble and he swears that the stealing of the Shiva statue was only a pretence. In fact, it was carefully planned, and by whom? This Mrs McIndoe – good old Miss Sanni herself. She had the fake one made – Kanu says she knows every image-maker or sculptor in the region. It was she who switched the statues and – I guess under her colonel husband's advice – sent it to be sold. Kanu says he understands: "She did it to save Patna Hall."'

'Hm,' Walter had said. 'Who told him that?'

'I assume Mrs McIndoe.' Mr Cromartie was haughty now.

'In a court case,' Walter said, 'we can't assume. We have to prove.'

'Isn't it proof?' Mr Cromartie had argued. 'Kanu was privy to everything. She treated him like a son.'

'So he says, but mothers don't tell their sons everything, nor sons their mothers.'

'But don't you see? You all seem to set such store by this Professor's testimony but Kanu's story explains why Mrs McIndoe wouldn't let anyone call the police and wanted it all to be kept hush-hush. It fits like a glove. You can't deny that.'

'I don't, but from what I've heard of her it doesn't fit Miss Sanni.'

'Why?'

'Kanu himself says the hotel is in financial difficulty yet she finds the money to send him on an expensive course – they always are expensive – just to help him further his ambitions. That sounds beneficent to me and not like someone who would make the statue vanish and blame it on someone else. As for Kanu, if she did tell him in confidence, he took the first opportunity to betray her. Mr Cromartie, why do you think he told you?'

'For money,' Mr Cromartie had said, as if that explained everything.

'Then,' said Walter, 'for money he would betray you

too. No, Mr Cromartie, I'm sure Sir George Fothergill would advise you not to proceed with this case.'

'Drop it? When I've just discovered—'

'It's too tricky. You might lose a lot of money.'

'That's my business, so don't bloody well try to talk me out of it. I have a watertight case. The statue was *not* stolen and I am *not* a receiver of stolen goods.'

'I had one more try,' Walter told Michael. 'I felt I had to.'

... 'Mr Cromartie, I admire your courage but you will have the whole weight of the Government of India against you, and they've brought in an added power, the God Shiva.'

'I don't listen to that sort of crap.'

'No, but a jury might if it comes to it. In law, we're taught to respect other people's beliefs, and the God Shiva has great influence.'

'Balls!' ...

'And he left as suddenly as he'd come,' Walter finished.

'I think he ran away,' said Michael, and cried, 'Hail, Shiva, *Jai Shiv Shankara.*'

Now, to see the Nataraja Michael had to be provided with an official pass. 'They have to know exactly who you are,' Mr Bhatacharya had told him. The police had left the Shiva in Sparkes's strongroom, 'Where it couldn't be more safe, and we have given them a security guard round the clock.'

Michael's arms ached from the inoculations and one had swollen, but with every prick he had felt more alert, expectant.

He made his way to a high old building in the quiet of St James's Place. Premises seemed the right word for Sparkes's. Michael knew it was one of the world's chief specialists in oriental sculpture, paintings, *objets d'art*: Cromartie chose well, he thought. A commissionaire in a braided uniform was standing outside.

Michael was early, and spent the time looking in the windows. Though they were high and of plate glass, they were almost empty. In one was a sixth-century bronze incense burner. But for the card Michael would not have known what it was. The next window held only a Chinese ivory fan lying spread in all its delicacy on a length of crimson brocade, but another had a vast Tibetan banner with flowers, demons and flames in brilliant colours. Michael stood, trying to take it in, until the commissionaire beckoned him.

Inside it was more like a salon than a shop. He was met

by a polished and poised young woman. 'Mr Dean? Good morning. I'm Julia Macdonald and I look after our smaller artifacts.' She offered him tea: 'China or herbal?' Out of curiosity Michael chose herbal. It came in small, handleless jade cups and he could not help thinking, Miss Julia, you're showing off.

'You're the barrister for the defence?' she was saying. 'Have you met Mr Cromartie?'

'No, but I gather he's not the kind of client Sparkes's would enjoy.'

'Well, I felt we were a bit high-handed. I'm surprised he isn't suing us. There was quite a scene.' Julia Macdonald laughed then sobered. 'And he did bring us the Nataraja, but here I am wasting your time when you must be longing to see it.'

Michael got up with alacrity – the herbal tea had been disgusting.

She called to the commissionaire and he brought in another man, who led the way down a flight of steps to a narrow passage without windows – Michael guessed it was below the shop. Then, in a small hall or vault, they were faced with double steel doors which the man opened with a combination of keys. The room behind was instantly lit, flooded with light by inset rays from overhead and along the walls. In the centre, set on a high table that fitted its plinth, was the Shiva, dancing in his hoop of miniature flames. Michael caught his breath.

The Nataraja seemed far larger than it was, dominating the room. The dancing limbs were naked in eternal energy. 'The drum in his upper right hand makes the primordial sound of creation,' whispered Julia Macdonald. 'His left upper arm holds a flame, the flame of destruction, while the left points to his dancing left foot, which means release, and he is treading on a dwarf who lies prostrate, the dwarf of all ignorance and prejudice. Shiva wears men's and women's jewellery because although he had wives, his attachment to the world is without gender.'

Michael nearly said, 'Hush.' He wanted only to look. '"Statue" is too still a word for this. He's living,' he whispered, as if to himself but it stopped Julia.

'Shiva *is* life,' she whispered back.

'Yes, look at his face, utterly detached, yet there's something in-dwelling.' Michael stopped in surprise. 'That's an odd word for me to use.'

'It's exactly right.' There was no trace of the polished, poised, a little pretentious Miss Macdonald. 'I come in here every night before I go home to find out what it is, but of course – it *is* in-dwelling. Yes, I might even bring him marigold garlands.' She had recovered herself, and as Michael left, she said, 'Mr Cromartie swears he bought the Nataraja in good faith. Maybe he did. Anything may happen but I know I wish ...'

'Wish what?'

'That Shiva should go back to where he belongs. India.'

'I can only try,' said Michael.

'So you leave tomorrow?'

'Yes,' said Michael. 'I still can't believe it.' He had come to say goodbye to Sir George and Honor.

'Have you all you need? Walter given you your papers?'

'Everything, sir. I think he'd quite like to come.'

'I can't imagine that!' Honor laughed.

Sir George got up – he did not believe in protracting things. 'Well, goodbye and good luck. I'm sure you'll do well.'

'If I can have a free hand.' Michael was Michael to the last.

'Good God!' Sir George expostulated, when Michael had gone. 'There's conceit for you – laying down conditions!'

'George, he has to. He has no idea what he'll find. Nor

have we, but to do your best you have to believe in your case. I'm sure Michael does and will fight for it, no matter what it costs him. Isn't Michael the fighting angel?'

INDIA

In his hired car, an Indian-made Ambassador, Michael drove from the airport at Ghandara, Patna Hall's nearest small town, along a dusty golden plain where white oxen were ploughing small fields and the road was filled with people, rickshaws and little black-and-gold three-wheeled taxis he did not remember having seen before. Then he came through a pair of great open gates, under a tall portico.

The first thing he heard as he got out of the car was the sound of the sea, although the portico faced inland. There seemed no one about so, taking his briefcase which he always kept with him, he walked round the house to find the beach.

The hotel stood high on its plinth of basements, which Michael knew held Henry Bertram's wine cellar and ice room. The house itself was painted blue, now faded, a tribute to the indigo, and a wide flight of steps led to the lower veranda – as he looked up there seemed to be two, one on each floor stretching its full length. The flat roof was parapeted but he could see more rooms up there.

As he walked round, he discovered that Patna Hall was quite a demesne. There were domestic quarters, and, though he did not know it then, a separate house for the two head servants, Samuel and Hannah. There was a gatehouse, a side court with a row of offices, a large vegetable garden, a poultry yard, even a private cemetery. Behind the hotel was the village, but all Michael could see of it were palms and a few thatched roofs.

On the other side of the house, facing the sea, was a garden with a wide lawn, beds of English and Indian flowers and a path of stepping stones bordered with shells that led down to the hotel's private, netted beach. As he walked down towards it the sound of the surf was a roar. He followed the stones and came on to dry white sands that stretched away on either side into dunes of feathery trees. Tamarisk, he guessed, and behind them were what he thought must be mango groves.

Beyond the sea had lost its sunlight and was beginning to glimmer. On the foreshore of hard wet sand, the great rollers of the Coromandel coast rose – he was amazed at their height – and crashed down, sending ripples far up the sand almost to his feet.

'Sahib, I think you get your feet wet.'

It was a man's voice, deep toned and speaking English;

a giant of a man. It was too dark to see clearly but even in the fading light his skin was brown gold. He wore nothing but a loincloth and a short white *chaddar* shoulder wrap, and hanging from his hands were local fishermen's helmets, made of woven wicker, immensely strong with a pointed peak, to break the waves – otherwise they stun you, Michael learned. The man was hanging them on a rail to dry. 'For hotel bathing guests,' he explained. 'I Thambi, Patna Hall lifeguard.'

He spoke English slowly, as if he had by heart what he needed to say. 'If Sahib swim tomorrow I help him.' He gestured towards a high diving tower and a stack of surf boards.

'Thank you, I will,' said Michael.

There was a pause until Thambi said, 'I am thinking you must be legal gentleman from England.' He laughed. 'And I thinking, too, that he will be important, older, with spectacles and perhaps a beard.'

'I'm sorry.'

'No, I like, and pleased to see you. Miss Sanni very not happy about it at all.'

'So you know about the case?'

'Everybody know it. How not?'

'But you have no idea who did it?'

At once Michael sensed a caginess. For all his impressive presence, a lifeguard was a servant at Patna Hall. It isn't a cliché, thought Michael, to say that no one knows more about their masters than those who serve them, but he was sure that if Thambi knew anything about the Shiva he was not going to tell.

The sun was now completely gone. A little chill wind blew. Thambi gave a shiver. 'I think better I take you to hotel.' They walked up the stone path, then he showed Michael round to the portico and opened the car boot, took out the suitcase and brought it into the hall. 'I put car away. Reception is there. Salaam, Sahib.'

The hall was panelled, as was the staircase leading up from it. Doors opened into the ground-floor veranda and the dining room. There was a fine grandfather clock, two carved low chests, and behind a long counter a young Indian waited with his telephone and ledgers. He was formally dressed, wearing a collar and tie – there was nothing casual about the service at Patna Hall. Kanu, Michael guessed.

'Good evening, Mr Dean. We are expecting you. If you would just sign here, and I must have your passport, please. May I say welcome. Please call me Kanu.'

To Michael, there was something too glib – as if Kanu was copying what he had learned on his course in London. He was very good-looking, in a childish way – the thick hair that must have been curly once, long eyelashes, the charming smile, which vanished as a door opened. 'Auntie Sanni is coming. She always like to welcome guests herself.' He sounded a little peevish.

Kanu should not have said 'Auntie Sanni'. To her staff and most guests she was Miss Sanni. 'Auntie', in Eurasian parlance, is the title given by children to any grown-up female, but with Mrs McIndoe not everyone was allowed to use it, and before she spoke to Michael, she said sharply, 'Kanu, you should be at the bar. Go and put on your jacket at once.' Then she advanced. 'Mr Dean, we are so very glad to meet you.'

Michael saw a massive old woman wearing what he was to recognize as one of her usual voluminous cotton dresses that hung like a tent to her feet; she called them her Mother Hubbards, from the garments missionaries used to hand out to make the native women what they called respectable. 'Well, I am a native,' she would tell Michael. She had country sandals: 'They suit me and are very comfortable.' She said 'very' in the Eurasian way so that it became 'veree' with a little lift. 'Well, I expect I am Eurasian. I expect my mother was Indian, maybe her mother. I never knew them. He didn't marry my mother.'

'Did you want him to?'

'Why? That's men's business.'

To Sir George she would have been illegitimate, but to Auntie Sanni it was 'natural'. Her skin was of the mixed-race complexion, the pale yellowish brown of old ivory and unwrinkled which, though she was old, made her look young. Eternally young, thought Michael, with her head of short curls, still auburn and glossy, while her eyes looked curiously light, sea-colour, now green, now blue. Mixed, like mine, thought Michael, but set wide like a child's, although again he was to learn, as every perspicacious person who came to Patna Hall and every business person with whom she dealt soon learnt, while, above all, every servant and villager knew, that Auntie Sanni was no child.

'And so you have come about this unfortunate case.' Michael knew that the sea-blue eyes were taking him in – not only from head to foot, but heart and soul. He had not thought, until this case, that he believed in souls.

'I hope I can help,' he said, 'but I've come really to help me understand.'

'There could be no greater help,' said Auntie Sanni, 'no greater,' she said. It was mysterious that at once he had ceased to think of her as Miss Sanni, certainly not as Mrs McIndoe. 'Mr Dean, I have to confess that this case is very objectionable to me, but come, we will not talk of it tonight. You must be tired. Hannah, our housekeeper, will show you to your room. We have put you in a bedroom on the front where you can catch the sea breezes. Then perhaps you will join me and my husband, Colonel McIndoe, at our veranda bar and have a drink before dinner. Ah! Here is Hannah come to show you upstairs. She and her husband, Samuel, are the pillars of Patna Hall.'

Hannah was a big woman, though not compared with her mistress. She wore a crisp white cotton sari, bordered with red, and an old-fashioned red bodice high on the neck. Her scant grey hair was pinned in a knob at the back of her head, but in spite of this simplicity she was laden with silver jewellery: the lobes of her ears hung down with the weight of earrings, she had several necklaces, bracelets, finger rings, and toe rings on her gnarled bare feet. She beckoned to a houseboy in white trousers and brass-buttoned tunic, with a small round black embroidered hat on his head, who ran down the stairs to carry Michael's suitcase. Once again Michael did not let his briefcase out of his hand.

They showed him to a high-ceilinged room off the top veranda, with a mosquito-netted bed, wardrobe, dressing-table and stool, a comfortable wicker chair, a table, flowers, a newspaper. Everything, thought Michael. 'Give Kancha your keys,' suggested Hannah as Michael stepped outside to look at the view. Before he came back, filled with it, Kancha had unpacked, putting things orderly in drawers, hair brushes on the dressing-table, ties on a rack, jackets and trousers on hangers; he was already laying out on the bed a clean shirt and the fine linen suit Michael had instinctively brought. 'As I had guessed,' he wrote later to Honor, 'at Patna Hall we dress for dinner.'

When he had bathed and changed he did not go straight down but stopped again on the high veranda outside his room and looked far over the garden to the dark sea, quiet now, only the rollers glimmering white in the starlight. He stood there a moment, feeling cleansed and fresh, letting the breeze blow cool through his hair. It brought a scent of flowers, strong and sweet, and the hours of travel, closed in the small plastic world of aeroplanes, dropped away. Then, A drink would be nice, and he turned to the stairs, but at their foot he paused. Why not explore?

The rooms were all high and floored with red stone. Michael looked into the dining room, where it was evident that a ritual was going on: tables being meticulously laid by white-clad waiters, vases, each holding a single rose, brought in. The stone shone: indeed, every morning a posse of village women came in to sit on the floor, moving slowly backwards as they pushed empty wine bottles, their bases wrapped in waxed cloth, until it gleamed.

'One electric polisher could do the work of twelve women,' said Kanu.

'I know, but I like to employ as many villagers as I can.' Auntie Sanni was quite comfortable.

Now, a humble woman, her sari drawn over her head, was giving the floor a last sweep because, to Samuel's grief, if the wind were high, sand blew in over it. Of the great Samuel himself there was no sign: he, too, was changing into a fresh white uniform for dinner.

There was a billiard room with a good table, empty now; it had a bar in one corner. Perhaps, thought Michael, gentlemen, chiefly Indians, would come in from Ghandara to play, have a few drinks or perhaps bring their ladies for dinner, but the veranda bar, he imagined, was reserved for residents.

The drawing room-ballroom was away from the rest, an immense double room. Its floor was green as, though paler, were the walls, lit by crystal-beaded candle sconces – Henry Bertram certainly didn't stint himself, thought Michael. A matching chandelier hanging in the centre of the room bore this out. Auntie Sanni had chosen a rather naive sweet-pea chintz for the sofas and chairs, and there were small brass-topped tables on carved ebony legs. Over the ornate marble fireplace was a not very good painting of a young girl – plump even then – in a 1920s ball dress, pale blue with sequins. The auburn curls were held in a circlet of small pink roses and she had a bouquet to match. A coming-out ball? wondered Michael. It was plain that Henry Bertram had been proud of his granddaughter.

It was a room that was evidently used for occasions. Did Patna Hall host weddings? Receptions? But he guessed, Seldom now, and when he dared to turn on the electric fans they creaked, yet he could see it filled with people in elegant dress, dancing or chattering and laughing. Then, as he turned to go, he saw the Shiva Nataraja.

In a niche above a side door that opened onto the

veranda steps to the sea, the Nataraja danced, a votive light burning before him with offerings of flowers, fruit and rice. As Michael looked he was transported back to Sparkes's strongroom and saw again the beauty and strength of what he had come to call 'the real Nataraja'. At first he saw no difference between that and this but exact as this Shiva was, to the last little flare in the circlet of flames around His head, and although there was still a feeling of steadiness, well captured, there was no aura of that inward strength of detachment, that indwelling. Well, this Shiva had been made by a craftsman, but no more than a craftsman, and Michael's thoughts went to that true artist-sculptor of centuries ago.

'You are looking at the Shiva.' The voice made him jump. Auntie Sanni was standing beside him.

She, too, had changed, into a clean Mother Hubbard, white scattered with bright blue flowers – Auntie Sanni loved colours. She wore her pearl necklace, the pearls real and beautifully matched; the curls had been brushed hard and her toenails polished. Hannah, he was to find, was not only housekeeper but Auntie Sanni's personal maid. Every evening when she was dressed, Colonel McIndoe in his heavy silk dinner jacket – in the hot weather a silk cummerbund – came to fetch her and escort her to her swinging couch on the bar veranda, 'Her throne,' mocked Kanu. Michael guessed this was, like so much at Patna Hall, the evening ritual, yet now she was alone. 'I still say, "Our Shiva-ji",' she told Michael. 'I'm the only one who does.'

'You still say it?'

'Every morning. Every night. He is still Shiva.'

'Auntie Sanni.' Then Michael remembered he was still a newcomer. 'May I call you Auntie Sanni?'

'If I may call you Michael.'

'Of course. Will you tell me what happened?'

'You have read Professor Ellen's testimony?' she asked.

'Yes, but underneath …'

'Ah! Underneath. There are things she doesn't know. My grandfather, Henry Bertram, was a wonderful man. When Shiva-ji was found buried and the workmen refused to go on my grandfather did not double their wages as has been told but sent for their priest to unearth the little statue and turn it round. The men did not dare to touch it but most Englishmen then would have stepped in and got it. After prayers the priest turned it gently and then lifted it up. Usually statues which have been long buried – and this had been so for centuries – are crusted with soil and stone, particularly by the sea, and there could have been termites, but the Nataraja came up as clean as on the day he was buried, the limbs still dancing, each flame intact. Above all, His face was serene and smiling.

'The workmen prostrated themselves and my grandfather promised that this little shrine would be made in our most important room to which not only the house servants but all the villagers could come and worship. The workmen refused to take another *anna* for their work to build the hotel which, of course, meant,' she added laughing, 'he had to keep their families for months.'

'He must have been a remarkable man,' said Michael, for the second time.

'He was, and what would he have said now to this horrible Cromartie case?'

'It must be horrible to you too. Walter Johnson, the head clerk at our chambers, saw Mr Cromartie and tried to persuade him not to bring it.'

'He deserves to lose. He must lose. I have no pity for Mr Cromartie,' said Auntie Sanni. 'He says he bought the Shiva Nataraja in good faith. That is not true. Good faith would mean he bought it to love and revere. Oh, no! He bought it to make money, *invested* in it, and now, because he has not made the profit he expected, he is prosecuting, and so denigrating the god even more. Also he is a fool. My grandfather always said, "Beware of litigation."'

'So beware of me,' said Michael.

Auntie Sanni looked up into his face, then took his hands with both her own. 'I think I need not beware of you, Michael. I know now we are in this together. Now, come. You must meet my husband and the few others who are staying here – old friends except the policeman.'

'The policeman?'

'Yes. I'll tell you later.'

But Michael stopped for a moment. 'Auntie Sanni, don't you mind about the fake?'

'It is not a fake. It was time for our Shiva-ji Nataraja to move on. He had other work to do, but very kindly he left himself behind, for us. Come,' said Auntie Sanni.

The veranda bar was the residents' sitting place, with cane chairs and tables, cane stools, old-fashioned steamer chairs with extended arm boards on which feet could be comfortably put up. There was a bar at one end, well stocked. 'Well, we get visitors from all parts of the world,' Auntie Sanni would say, and halfway down was her swing couch, with its bright chintz cushions and canopy. It was true that before lunch, which she called 'tiffin', and before dinner she liked to sit there and reign. Now a small group of people were sitting round one of the cane tables near Auntie Sanni's throne. All old, thought Michael, with a touch of dismay. One of the oldest, the lights shining on his bald head, got up at once, came to Michael and shook hands.

'I am Samantha's husband,' he said, no one else used that name, 'Colonel McIndoe. We're glad to see you here. Kanu,' he called, 'get the sahib a drink. Whisky, gin, vodka, a glass of wine?'

Kanu, transformed by a striped cotton jacket, came at once.

'Whisky, please. Thank you, sir.'

Kanu looked at him surprised. Perhaps because I called the Colonel 'sir', thought Michael, as Auntie Sanni began, 'Alicia, this is Mr Dean come to help us over this miserable affair. He wants us to call him Michael. Michael, Lady Fisher is one of our oldest friends.'

'You must be tired,' Lady Fisher said gently, but then, 'No. You young people are never tired.'

'Not when we're on the scent, I suppose,' said Michael. 'I'm so glad it has brought me here.'

'Patna Hall has brought us every year, hasn't it, Sanni?' There was clearly a deep friendship here. 'My husband

and I. John, this is Michael Dean,' and Michael knew there was some familiarity about Sir John, his height, the silvery – cliché or not he could not help thinking it – 'silvery' hair. He's like someone I know. Sir John immediately confirmed it. 'You're from the chambers of Sir George Fothergill? I'm glad. Good set. I have a niece there.'

'Honor Wyatt.' Michael was certain.

'Yes, in fact I was able to be instrumental in bringing her to your chambers. I used to know Simpson well and, of course, that wonderful head clerk, John Johnson.'

'We have his son Walter now, and Johnny, Walter's son, has just joined us. Walter's a great advocate for Honor.'

'I don't wonder. She's an outstanding young woman.'

'John,' Lady Fisher interposed, 'Mr Dean hasn't been introduced to Ellen or Chief Inspector Dutta. Professor Ellen Webster,' and 'Ellen, I think you've been expecting Mr Dean?'

'Indeed I have.'

She was a small, over-thin woman – Probably works too hard, thought Michael, and is too intense. Michael could never help analysing everything. The Professor was pale, her hair cut into neat shortness, grey eyes behind steel-rimmed spectacles, an almost anonymous blouse and skirt. She doesn't care about superficial things, thought Michael.

'You're going to help us save our Nataraja.' She held his hand, looking up at him closely, and he knew that here was a heartfelt passion, though she had learned how to keep it cool. 'Mr Dean, this is Chief Inspector Dutta of the Indian police.'

'I didn't know that they had been called in,' said Michael, as he shook hands.

'I am always called in.' The Inspector chuckled. Younger than any of these guests, he was still middle-aged and plump and genial, but Michael sensed at once that Inspector Dutta was not a chief inspector for nothing. Though dressed for the evening, he still seemed to be in uniform, thin trousers and a tunic jacket, both khaki, and a red scarf round his neck in lieu of a tie. 'I am necessarily here,' he explained. 'Our government has decided that we must outface Mr Cromartie and must have positive proof that the image was stolen. Forgive me, Professor Webster, if I say that your testimony, though so valuable, is still not positive proof, besides which it was written so long after the theft. We must discover when, how and, above all, by whom the Bertram Nataraja as it has begun to be named, was taken.'

'I should think very difficult after all these months,' said Sir John.

The Inspector laughed. 'Set a thief to catch a thief. I am an accomplished one, stealing shreds of evidence wherever I can and weaving them together until I understand fully.' There was a hint of menace in the way he said that; then he was jovial again. 'I'll catch him.'

'Michael,' Auntie Sanni obviously wanted to end that conversation, 'you must be thinking our hotel is over-quiet and empty but tomorrow it will be much better as Professor Webster's group will be arriving.'

And to Michael's surprise the Colonel, Sir John and Lady Fisher chanted, 'The cultural ladies, the cultural ladies.'

'Don't be alarmed, Michael,' said Auntie Sanni. 'Before Professor Ellen's day that's what Samuel and Hannah used to call them, not mockingly – they have a great reverence for learning.'

'Since Ellen took over it has completely changed, with many men now, and it's considered a privilege to be accepted for a tour – students get grants. I believe we shall have a Chinese girl on this one,' said Lady Fisher.

For the first time Michael looked, really looked, at Lady Fisher. When she spoke it was with authority but most of the time she sat quietly, her eyes alight with interest as she listened to what everyone was saying. He guessed that was her greatest asset, listening, and a rare talent. Sir John had a sun-tanned, wrinkled skin from years in the tropics, but Lady Fisher, who had spent all of them with him, had a complexion that looked as if strong sun or a rough wind had never touched it. 'Alicia prefers not to go on the beach or bathe, or lie in the sun,' Auntie Sanni said to Michael, who was sitting on the swing couch beside her.

'Then why does she come to a seaside hotel?'

'To be with John. Has it never occurred to you, Michael, that some eminent men, with pressures of work, tangles of worries, disappointments and horrendous surprises, need a calm, steadfast and highly intelligent wife? Sir John thinks he is taking care of her but she is really taking care of him.'

'Well, Ellen,' Sir John persisted, 'when they come, I'll leave.'

'Nonsense, John.'

Lady Fisher said, 'I grant you that, in the old days, the ladies were a bit of a bore but Ellen's here now and Artemis has flown out from London to bring them from New York. The tours always begin and end in New York. Artemis is Ellen's assistant.'

'Assistant! She's my star. No wonder, John, you always fall for her,' Professor Ellen teased him.

'Artemis is a witch,' admitted Sir John.

'I've never known a girl called that,' said Michael. 'Isn't it a bit fanciful?'

'I think it's a lovely name,' said Lady Fisher.

'And she's a lovely girl,' said Professor Ellen.

'So, John, you're not to forget how things have moved on and call the women old tabbies.' Lady Fisher turned to Inspector Dutta. 'They're such inspiring tours. I wish more young people could get grants for them. I think your government ought to support them. Can't you use your influence?'

'I have no influence. I do only what I am told.'

'That I don't believe,' and Professor Ellen went on, 'In fact, since you came to Patna Hall I am sure, over the Nataraja, you're on the same side as Michael and all of us.'

'This detestable case!' Auntie Sanni burst out. 'It was you, Ellen, who told me – and everyone else – what our Shiva-ji was worth in value of money and that seems to me the beginning of the trouble. Since then everything has gone wrong.'

'It seems so,' Professor Ellen said miserably.

Auntie Sanni was shaking, tears running down her face. Lady Fisher got up, went to her and put an arm round her, holding her close. At the same moment Samuel sounded the gong.

'I'll tell him to hold dinner back a few minutes.' Colonel McIndoe was up, but nothing could have revived Auntie Sanni more.

'No. No, Giles. You can't do that to Samuel. Nor can I.' She stood up too. Lady Fisher had given her a handkerchief and she dabbed her eyes. 'Dinner is ready,' and she and the Colonel led the way to the dining room.

That was always a proud moment for Samuel. He stood at the entrance, regal in his flowing white tunic, full trousers, and red and gold cummerbund. His white turban, with its fan of white muslin, was held by a narrower crossband, red and gold to match, with a glittering Bertram crest. His whiskers and upturned moustache were white too, his eyes alert to every least movement.

It was understood that they went to different tables. Professor Ellen was with Auntie Sanni and the Colonel, the Fishers had their own corner and Inspector Dutta turned to Michael. 'We are both alone. Shall we eat together, Mr Dean?'

'I'd like that, but please call me Michael.'

'Then I am Hem.'

Samuel had anticipated this, and led them across the room to a table already laid for two.

'Now you must want to pump me,' the Inspector said, as they took their seats, 'but you will be wasting your time. The food here is too good to think of anything else.'

The table itself was inviting: the single rose was a fine one and, in china soup plates with the Bertram crest, a chilled raisin soup waited, rich brown and refreshing.

'I am, I admit, impressed,' Inspector Dutta said, 'particularly because I have seen how it is all achieved. Miss Sanni does not believe in change. In Patna Hall's pantry there are packing cases lined with zinc, a small brazier burning red to keep food hot and an army of boys to run with dishes between the kitchen, which is outside, and the house.'

Hot plates were slipped in front of them and Samuel himself waited on them. 'Koftas,' he explained to Michael, 'little batter rolls of fish. Crayfish. Very good.'

Michael discovered he was starving while Hem Dutta said, 'I should very much like to give you some wine but, Michael, you choose. Europeans know much more of wine than us ignorant Indians.'

'Ignorant! Hem, don't put me to shame. It's we who are ignorant of your great country.'

'Choose,' said the Inspector, and when the wine list came, Michael was careful to find something good but among the less expensive – he had no idea how much an Indian policeman, even a chief inspector, earned. Then his dilemma was solved: Samuel brought a bottle of cool white wine, already opened – 'From Miss Sanni.' He poured it.

Michael stood up to thank her. 'To Miss Sanni and Patna Hall.' Everyone drank.

The hotel served a menu of both Indian and European food. The koftas were followed by partridges on toast, then Auntie Sanni's exquisite apple meringues – she made them herself. Afterwards there was cheese and Samuel brought round a perfect port – 'With Colonel Sahib's compliments.'

'Coffee served on the veranda, Sahib.' Deep in talk they had not been conscious that, though the other waiters had gone, Samuel was still there.

'I'm sorry, Samuel,' said Michael.

'Sahib is welcome.'

Nor did they want coffee. 'I think,' said Inspector Dutta, 'I shall take a stroll in the garden and go to bed.'

'What a good idea.'

They walked in silence across the lawn, avoiding the beach. Michael was still flying but not in an aeroplane. The surf thundered even in this peaceful garden, full of shadows with only gleams of light from the house. From a bush near the steps there was a scent of such sweetness and strength that it wafted far over the lawn. He could see its small white flowers and stopped. 'Isn't that...?'

'*Raht ki rani*,' said the Inspector.

'Queen of the Night. Yes, I remember.'

'They say its perfume is so strong it can make you giddy.'

'I am giddy.'

But the Inspector was not listening. He sighed. 'It is on nights like this that I miss my wife,' and, as Michael was silent, he asked, 'Michael, have you a wife?'

'No, thank you. I am very well arranged as I am.'

'Poor Michael! Good night.'

On impulse Michael went to have a last look at the Shiva, and this time it was he who made Auntie Sanni jump. She was in her dressing gown, standing below the niche where the small lamp burned. He saw that her lips were moving, her eyes rapt, although she put out a hand to stay him. When she had finished, she turned to him and smiled. 'I am making my night prayer.'

'To Shiva?' He could not help being slightly shocked: he had taken it for granted that she was a Christian until, once again, as if she had divined his thinking she said, 'Why do religions feel they must have edges? To me they are all one, as in this house. Our Goanese cook and Samuel and Hannah are Catholics.'

'As Hannah told me. She said Thomist Christian.'

'She would. St Thomas is supposed to have come to Madras. She is very devoted, but works happily with all the others. Colonel McIndoe's personal valet is Buddhist, as are the houseboys. Or perhaps they are Hindu – they come from Nepal. The table servants are Muslims, our gardeners Brahmins, the highest Hindu caste of all, and the sweepers, men and women, are Hindus too but rank so low they have no caste at all. They are outcasts and called "untouchables" yet they all work together happily at Patna Hall.'

'And revere the Nataraja.'

'Yes.'

'But this one? It doesn't rival the true one for beauty and feeling. Auntie Sanni, I went to see it in London.'

'So,' she said, 'to you this is not the same?'

'Not quite. This is a wonderful copy made by a craftsman who has a touch of the artist, but I can't help thinking of that complete artist who carved the other so long ago. The power ...'

'Shiva's power.'

Michael's instinct made a sudden leap. 'Auntie Sanni, I think you have known about the changeover all the time.'

Auntie Sanni looked at him severely. 'I am not saying anything. Good night.'

Michael felt he owed himself a morning on the beach and, after a Patna Hall English breakfast – bacon and egg with mushrooms, toast, home-made marmalade and coffee – he changed into his trunks and a beach-robe that he found in his cupboard with a wide towel. He followed the stepping stones across the white sands, already warm with sun, until he came to the foreshore strewn with shells and flotsam brought in by long ripples from the waves. Crabs scurried across it, there was an occasional starfish and blue jellyfish. All along was the barrier of tossing white, higher than his head, as the waves swept in, rearing up before crashing down; he had not realized last night quite how gigantic they were. Beyond them the open sea was calm and azure blue.

Patna Hall's beach was forbidden to the local fishermen and had its own security guards in Thambi and his assistant Moses.

'Ours is not a gentle sea,' Auntie Sanni had told Michael, as she told all her guests, when she saw him in his bathrobe. She always said, 'Please remember it is dangerous to go in alone to bathe, even for strong swimmers. You must take a guard.'

Michael went in with Thambi, who brought him one of the wicker helmets he had been carrying last night and helped him to adjust it tightly. Michael felt the pointed peak and knew how strong it was. Thambi also had a light surfboard so that Michael, having dived through the surf, could ride in on the height and speed of the wave, Thambi swimming alongside.

Once Michael went down to the seabed, he would have felt the full thud of the wave had he not been wearing the helmet but its peak pierced the water and he was borne up again, in the exultation of riding to be tumbled over and over on to the open sand.

Afterwards, peacefully exhausted, he lay on his towel in the sun and Thambi brought a beach umbrella to shade his head. I must make plans, he thought, but the peace, with the light breeze bringing not fragrance as it had last night but sunshine and saltiness, began to overtake him and he felt sleep steal over him. After all, he had been working with Mr Bhatacharya and Walter up to the last moment, then had had the long flight. There had been, too, this strange inner excitement and an elation he could not suppress. All this is quite normal, he told himself. If you work in law you go anywhere, anytime. Yet it still felt anything but normal. You must let go, he told himself.

'You didn't come out here to let go,' an inner voice seemed to say.

Only for an hour or two, he pleaded, but before anything more could be said, he was asleep.

Thambi shook him respectfully. 'Sahib. I think time to wake up. Twelve o'clock. Tiffin – lunch served soon.'

Still half asleep, Michael put on his robe and went up to the house. Lady Fisher, on the veranda, was quietly sewing – he had seen her embroidery last night. He went round to the portico, thinking he would go in by the hall, and his sleepiness was immediately banished.

A coach was standing there; houseboys were unloading suitcases and grips while, from the hall, came a hubbub of voices, chattering, laughing, exclaiming. The cultural ladies – cultural group! He almost said it aloud.

He dodged back into the garden, up the veranda steps – not disturbing Lady Fisher – but there was a dilemma. To reach the stairs and get to his room there was no other way than up the staircase from the hall, and it was crowded with men and women, still in their travelling clothes and carrying their impedimenta: handbags, shoulder-bags full of books, notebooks, papers and maps; cameras, binoculars, radios; some of the older people had walking sticks. Kanu, full of importance, had a queue for registering, a pile of passports, and was handing out keys.

Professor Ellen was in the midst of it, introducing the group to Auntie Sanni one by one, with a few married pairs, always breaking off to produce others: 'Mr and Mrs Horn, Dr Sidney Duncan and Miss Susan Carmichael' – Not married, thought Michael – 'Madame Duvivier who joined us from Paris,' *soignée*, elegant. 'Ian Macpherson, and you must meet our Chinese student, Ansie Lee. Ansie, where are you? Ansie.'

One young woman had not waited but introduced herself: 'I'm Marcia Barclay, my husband Eric. We work at Sussex University. I'm so glad we came. Ellen has told us so much about you. Your marvellous mulligatawny soup.'

'Marcia!' Her unmistakably English husband tried to curb her.

'Well, I'm starving. Could we be having it for lunch?'

Auntie Sanni had been caught by somebody else but, 'Mulligatawny on lunch menu' – Samuel had come, in full regalia, to help receive the group, while Hannah was on the stairs, which was just as well. Already there was a complaint.

'I hope I'm on the first floor,' wailed a voice. 'It seems there is no lift.' It was one of the more elderly ladies, cross-looking. 'A hotel with no lift!'

'Memsahib is on first floor.' Hannah had immediately come down. 'Stairs easy. See, Hannah help you.'

Pillars of the house, Michael remembered Auntie Sanni saying, but already the group were calling the woman Mrs Moaner. 'There's one on every tour.' Professor Ellen was back.

Michael tried to flatten himself against the wall. He knew Auntie Sanni had seen him, but she had a policy at Patna Hall that one guest should never be introduced to another unless both wanted it. Professor Ellen had no such restrictions: 'Oh, Michael, there you are. Come and meet Mark and Millicent Erle. They're so interested in—' but she broke off to speak to another guest and Michael never learned what Mark and Millicent were interested in, nor when she came back with a younger woman,

'Ann, meet Mr Dean. Michael, Ann does all our—' did he discover what Ann did.

As Lady Fisher had said, there were plenty of young, standing a little apart; they wore jeans and T-shirts, their hair cropped short or for the girls let loose and streaming. One large boy had his tied in a pony-tail and wore an earring. A girl, obviously waiting to go upstairs, still carried her rucksack on her back. Independent, that one, thought Michael.

Professor Ellen came over with especial quickness to introduce them. 'Maria, Jacky, Di, Marilyn, Morgan, Tom.' The names swirled round Michael. 'Duke, Charlie.'

'Hello. How do you do?' That was a girl, while the young man called Duke asked, 'You here for the archaeology, like us?'

'I wish I were,' said Michael, 'but no, I'm on other business.'

Duke was well-mannered and did not ask further questions. 'This seems like a nice place,' he had begun instead, when Auntie Sanni came over to them.

'Wouldn't it be nice if you found your rooms?' Half the crowd had already gone. 'I expect you want to wash and then come down to our veranda bar and have a cool drink.'

'It sounds heavenly,' cried Marcia Barclay, 'and then lunch, and you promised us mulligatawny.'

'Marcia!' But Samuel made her a small bow. 'Memsahib quite right. One of Patna Hall's famous soups. Wait till you taste, Sahib,' he said to Michael, but Michael was not listening. He was looking beyond them. 'I saw her,' he always said afterwards, 'I can never forget it.' A young woman, not talking but leaning on the reception counter. There was a coolness about her as she looked on at the flock she had brought so far, watching with a gentle tolerance as if they were, indeed, a flock and she their shepherd.

Michael, though, was surprised at himself because she was dressed in a way that usually would have alienated him at once: an Edwardian-length, draggle-tailed black cotton skirt and a white muslin blouse with a frilled neckline. Nothing more unsuitable for travelling could be imagined; it seemed almost wilful. Her dark hair was up, with rat-tails, which he particularly abhorred, but perhaps it was the poise of her head, proud, the grace with which she leaned on the counter. Forgetting his bathrobe and skilfully avoiding Professor Ellen, he wove his way through the remaining crowd, who were moving towards the stairs. 'Good morning.'

Her gaze immediately came to him. Her eyes were blue – but the dark blue of sapphires. They lit up when she saw him; evidently she approved. 'Hello, I'm Artemis.'

'I knew that the moment I saw you. I'm Michael.'

'Ellen told me the lawyer was coming for the defence but you're too young to be a lawyer. We all thought he would have spectacles and be cagy and wise.'

'I think I'm very wise. I saw you across the room and came straight to you.' But Professor Ellen had come too. 'I see you've found each other, but I must help Auntie Sanni.'

Auntie Sanni was talking to the young people, who were the last to be shown upstairs. 'I hope you won't mind sleeping in Paradise,' she said. 'That's what we call a line of rooms on the roof, simple and small like cells.' She did not tell them that, in Patna Hall's grander days, they had been kept for the ladies' maids, valets and chauffeurs who came with Europeans, Americans, ambassadors or merchant princes.

'Yes, sleep in Paradise,' Artemis called. 'Up there you are almost in the sky. You can see this whole world, land and sea, and at night you will be close to the stars. If any of you don't want to sleep there I will.'

'No, dear, you won't.' Professor Ellen had drawn her aside but although she whispered, Michael could hear every word. 'Artemis dear, if you do that, fraternize completely, you won't keep your authority.' To Michael she explained, 'Artemis Knox, I hope, is going to succeed me. You can't imagine what she has done for us, or how serious she is, coming every year for the last five, the only person I have ever had who hired a car and went into the hills on her own. She has even learned Telegu, and last year she brought a film unit with lights and camera, which showed us so much we didn't know about the cave paintings.'

But Artemis was still rebellious. 'I hate authority.'

'All the same, you'll find it your greatest asset.'

'I know, and I use it all the time.' Artemis was suddenly wistful. 'That's what makes me so sad. Before I had it – or have I always had it? – I was free.' She looked so forlorn that Michael felt a strange pull.

Is that what they call heart-strings? he wondered. He had not known he had any – his affairs had always been light-hearted. And to feel it so quickly? It isn't possible. But the answer was that he did feel it. He put out a hand to touch her, but she had darted across the hall – empty now that the young people had gone upstairs – and she was hugging Auntie Sanni. 'At last I have a chance to kiss you. Oh, it's so good to be back!' She was smiling and there was a dimple on each cheek.

The dimples finished Michael.

When he came down, changed for lunch, he found that Auntie Sanni had been right: the veranda, which had been so quiet, was filled to overflowing with people, voices, chatter and laughter, as the hall had been. She had Mark and Millicent with her on her throne and seemed to have taken over the Chinese Ansie; the other young people had carried their drinks to the garden steps, but most were gathered round the bar where Kanu, in his striped jacket, was a little repressed by Colonel McIndoe helping him; it was he who had suggested a John Collins, gin and ginger beer taken long with plenty of ice. 'I expect you've been warned about ice in India. It's often made with water that hasn't been boiled, but our butler, Samuel, sees to that himself so you're safe.' Some had mango juice or iced tea. Kanu was further depressed by being asked if he could make mint julep, of which he had never heard, and to his chagrin he had to consult Samuel. Michael took up a position by the bar where he could listen and watch while Professor Ellen went from one cluster to another, asking if they had settled in.

'Indeed we have,' said Marcia, 'it's lovely.' Her Eric was drinking with the other men so she could be as exuberant as she chose: no one would have believed she was a serious archaeologist.

The group had landed in Delhi, gone to Calcutta and Dacca. 'So we've had hotels, and after that Uberoi chain, all exactly alike, I never expected anything like this. Sheer bliss.'

There was an echo of agreement until, 'Bliss? You call it bliss.' It was Mrs Moaner. 'I certainly didn't expect anything like this – no telephone in the room, no television or room service. That nice young man at the desk says that this Miss Sanni, as we are expected to call her, refuses to modernize.'

'Oh, come,' said Artemis, who had slipped in quietly. 'Patna Hall has air-conditioning and electricity.'

Michael was glad to see she had changed into a sundress with a poppy red skirt and brief bodice; its white straps over her shoulders and across her bare back showed off her skin – surprisingly not sunburned but as petal fine as Lady Fisher's. It had a glow he had not seen in girls he had met in London. I suppose it's energy and health. She wore the lightest of sandals and her hair was tied with a red chiffon scarf. She doesn't have to look a mess, thought Michael, with relief.

Though the veranda was in shade, the air was warm and balmy, and the sunlight from outside made patterns on the floor. The garden basked in midday brightness but a soft breeze brought the fragrance of flowers. There was a chatter of parakeets – their bright green and red could be seen in the trees – the harsh caw of crows, and mynah birds, brown with orange beaks, hopped on the floor looking for the crumbs Marcia threw for them. Michael had never felt more content and peaceful.

There's something about this place and about that girl ... he thought, but Mrs Moaner was grizzling on. 'And what about the bathroom?' she demanded. He could understand that, particularly to an American, Patna Hall's plumbing arrangements were primitive. 'Never did I think I should have to sit on a stool in a little room divided by a kerb, with one tap, and *that*'s cold, and pour water over me with an outsize zinc mug.'

'Lovely warm water, just as you want it, plenty of it, standing in *gharras*, those big earthenware pots freshly filled ready for you.' Artemis tried to soothe her.

'And should we not, if we come to a country, do as they do?' asked Madame Duvivier.

'And isn't it part of the fun?' asked Dora, a small twinkling brunette who sat on one of the wicker couches with her Jamaican friend, Kate.

'It's this sort of fun that makes this place so different.' Marcia grew more enthusiastic every minute.

'Fun! Downright cheating and not even hygienic.'

Artemis lost patience. 'It's odd you should say that, when the Indians think it is we who are unhygienic in having a bath, lying in the water of our own dirt.'

'*Dirt!*' Mrs Moaner was truly shocked. 'How dare they? I've never been dirty in my life. Oh, I wish I'd never come.'

'We can easily fly you back tomorrow if you like,' said cruel Artemis.

At that moment, fortunately, Samuel sounded the gong.

'Whoops! Mulligatawny soup,' cried Marcia, as they all sprang to their feet, but now Michael saw a completely different Artemis.

She had gone to Mrs Moaner. 'Come,' she said, with all her charm. 'I'm sure you'll feel much happier when you've had some lunch. The food here is truly good. Oh! You haven't finished your drink. Never mind. Take it with you. I'll bring it. Let me help you up.' And Mrs Moaner went with her, smiling.

'You see? She can manage them.' Professor Ellen was at his elbow.

'Sure as God made little green apples.' Her earnestness made Michael flippant.

'There's nothing green about Artemis,' she said at once.

The group had two long tables. Professor Ellen was at the head of one. She tinkled a knife against a tumbler to make an announcement. 'This afternoon you will probably like to rest or go on the beach. This evening Miss Sanni is kindly giving a reception and supper to welcome us.' Artemis was at the head of the other table; again, she had that look of authority though she laughed and talked. Michael found himself watching her all through luncheon while he carried on an absent-minded conversation with Inspector Dutta, who said, at last, 'Michael, you are not listening to me at all!'

'I'm sorry, Hem.'

'I am asking if you would like to come with me this afternoon to the village and bazaar?'

Michael was jerked back to his own world.

'If you don't want to come, never mind.'

'But I do, of course I do, especially as I must as soon as possible. Thank you, Hem.'

'I long to see a bazaar again,' said Michael, as they set out. Inspector Dutta had two of his men with him, a sergeant from his home town, who spoke Hindi, and a young trainee who spoke Telegu, which was why he was given this opportunity. Both knew English. In the garden Auntie Sanni had turned a hut into an office for them; she did not want police work in the house.

Now they went out past Patna Hall's big double gates and its lodge where Thambi lived. His handsome, big-breasted young wife, Shyama, was supposed to be the gatekeeper but as they were always kept open she had nothing to do and did nothing but wash her hair, spreading it on her shoulders to dry as she lazed in the sun. If Thambi happened to come home – he did the shopping and cooking – he would pick up a tress, run it through his fingers and kiss it.

At dusk, though, Shyama would come out and light the little oil lamp below the sacred small *tulsi* tree they kept in their courtyard. When the flame was steady, she would blow on a big conch shell, 'Ulla-la, ulla-la, ullah.' To Thambi it was a call home.

'Well, Shyama is very lovely,' said Auntie Sanni. 'Plump and sweet.'

Michael thought that too when, although she had hidden her face in her sari, she opened it a little to smile at him.

'When I was a child,' Michael told the Inspector – and he felt he was a child again – 'I was not supposed to go into the bazaar alone, but I got over the wall of our garden and went wandering.'

'Has it changed very much?'

'Not really, except for all the plastic, plastic everything. *Gharras*, water pots, plates. They used to use banana leaves but now plastic tumblers, toys, even bangles.'

Plastic and electricity – usually a single bulb hanging on a cord – and radios blaring, yet the bazaar had not changed. There were still the lines of shanty shops, all open booths showing their wares: sacks of grain or rice, vegetables piled high or floating in water; saris hung up or carefully folded on shelves; baby jackets on tiny hangers, flat as paper. There were cookshops where samosas and puris sizzled in open pans, and the smell of hot mustard oil mingled with the stench of urine from the gutter. A barber was shaving his client in the open while a letter writer had his floor desk on the pavement, his paper, ink and stamps ready. There were the inevitable crows with their harsh voices, pigeons, mynah birds, some in cages, and nanny goats, with their udders shut away from their kids in muslin bags. There was even a sacred bull, helping itself unhindered from a grain bag or vegetable stall; its hump was covered by a cap worked with beads. And there were, of course, the people, walkers, shoppers, children running loose, babies crawling and, in the road, bicycle rickshaws, their hoods patterned with flowers, their bells ringing, and a swarm of small black-and-yellow three-wheeled taxis hooting incessantly. 'Those are new,' said Michael. 'I've never seen them before, but I'm back.'

They came to a kite shop that could have been the one where he had bought his kites, made of the thinnest paper in pink, green, red, white stretched on the lightest cross-bars of bamboo. He seemed to feel the wickerwork spool turning as he flew them. 'We used to pass our thread through a mixture of ground glass and glue so that it would cut.'

'So did we,' said Inspector Dutta.

'Then challenge another kite by dipping ours. If it dipped back we crossed strings, which was where the skill showed. I was a mighty kite fighter.'

'So was I.'

Michael cajoled him, 'Hem, let's forget about the case, fit ourselves out and go down to the beach for a kite fight.'

His companion looked at him severely. This was another side of the genial Inspector Dutta. 'Mr Dean, we are searching the bazaar, not playing but looking for the slightest clue. Also I have my sergeant with me. What would he think? And the trainee, who is here to learn. It seems you, too, need to learn.'

Still Michael found it difficult to pay attention. The front of the money-changer's jewellery shop had bars across it, with the man sitting behind them on a red cushion quilted with black and white flowers. Although this was South India, Michael knew he was from Marwar in Rajasthan: the Marwaris were renowned as businessmen and financiers. He had a small black cap on his head and many ledgers in front of him.

There was apparently nothing in his shop but a safe, a pair of scales and a table a few inches high on which he displayed the items that he brought out from the safe. In India jewellery is sold by weight and often made of silver threads, woven into patterns and flowers. While Inspector Dutta talked to the man, Michael bought a pair of his filigree silver earrings for Honor.

Then he saw a small temple and went across to it. The outside walls and floors were tessellated with broken china, countless pieces set in concrete. Its pointed roof was covered in beaten-out kerosene tins which shone silver in the sun, but the painted plaster gods of his childhood had been replaced by two large, jointed Western dolls. They were dressed in gaudy muslin, tinsel and paper flowers, but Michael knew that the priest put them to bed every night, got them up in the morning. 'Hindus worship round the clock,' he had told Honor, and, true, before these doll-gods was a low table with offerings of sweets and flowers. As he watched, a woman came to pray; on the brass tray she put a little powdered sugar making with her thumb a pattern on it for luck. 'But what a shame to have those dolls,' Michael said to Inspector Dutta. 'They used to have wonderful home-made images.'

'They still do,' said the Inspector. 'You must come and meet Veeranna, the potter. His name means "one who is brave and good in his work", which he is. A fine modeller.'

Michael had already smelt the kiln. 'That smell makes me remember that every village has a potter.'

'Often more than one, but for how long can they last

now that we have plastics? Of course, plastics are far more sensible.'

'Ugh!'

The Inspector laughed. 'You can cheer up. We still need potters. Festival images cannot be made of plastic because at the end of their *puja* or feast they are taken to the nearest water – here it is the sea – and they are immersed and have to disintegrate. Veeranna is busy now because the feast of Vinayak Chauthuri is near, when Ganesh, the elephant-headed god, is worshipped. Most of the time he finds it hard to make a living out of clay but, being gifted, he has been trying to do metal work. I believe he went on a course to learn.'

The potter's workshop was away from the village. 'But villagers, even though they are converted to plastic, revere their potter if he is an image-maker as well,' Inspector Dutta told Michael, 'because it seems to them that out of the air, or earth because he works in clay, he can conjure up any god they need, from the little household gods kept in a house's prayer corner, to the life-size ones that are the central figures in a feast when they stand in a *pandal*, a sort of arbour, in the village square or street to be worshipped. Any god or goddess. The people think that marvellous. Veeranna, though, is not sociable, never married and lives a lonely life, immersed in his work.'

His house had the same earthen-clay walls and floors, the same thatched roof as any in the village but it was bigger, having two rooms and a more spacious courtyard shaded by trees. The larger room was for living as well as work, with an open fire for cooking in one corner, a low wooden bed held together by a web of strings, its quilts tidily rolled up. Veeranna evidently believed in order: lines of clay bowls, some little and others as big as *gharras*, stood in the courtyard, largely unsold, but the centre of the room was taken up by his wooden wheel which he spun while sitting on the floor. Beside it was a hole dug wide in which he mixed his clay.

The kiln was outside but so near the threshold that the room's upper walls and inside roof were blackened by the fumes. 'He lights the kiln with coal and cakes of cow dung, which he collects and dries in pats on the house wall outside. But see,' said Inspector Dutta, 'those are jars of glazing made out of local rock, powdered and mixed with soda ash.' Shelves propped on bricks held 'Pigments of all colours,' said the Inspector, 'especially gilt. He has to paint his images.' On another, wider, shelf were the properties needed for the gods: musical instruments –

flutes and, especially, little hand drums – swords, arrows, beads, even a stuffed snake or two, crowns, jewellery, bolts of gauze cloth, some patterned with gold stars or silver crescent moons, or woven with gold thread and with gold borders.

'He must have a good trade,' said Michael.

'He says, enough.'

When they had come in – without knocking, Michael noticed – Veeranna had been sitting on the floor painting in the finishing touches of gilt on the crown of a Ganesh, already complete, even to his short gleaming tusks. For a moment the potter did not lay down his paintbrush, then abandoned it and stood up reluctantly, salaaming.

Veeranna was almost as big as Thambi but modelled more finely. As if he had modelled himself, thought Michael, who looked particularly at his hands, large, long and strong-fingered, the thumbs spatulate and bent wide, almost double-jointed. As he faced the policemen, his hands were never still – Nervous, thought Michael. Unlike Thambi's golden brown skin, Veeranna's was as dark as only a Dravidian's can be: when he dived into the room's shadows – he seemed to think it necessary to show Michael this or that piece of pottery – he almost disappeared and only the whites of his eyes glinted. When he stood in the light, Michael saw that the irises were brown not black as he had expected, and that Veeranna had unusually long lashes. He is proud and sensitive, thought Michael, yet childlike in the way he treats me, this stranger sahib, even though he was obviously frightened by the policemen: 'Police mean trouble.' Michael could have said it for him.

They went into the inner room. 'This is where Veeranna says he will do the metal work that so inspires him.' But the room had nothing in it except a wooden turntable and a bright neon light on the ceiling.

'Nothing else?' Michael was disappointed.

'I expect it is as far as he has got,' said the Inspector. 'The tools are most expensive but Veeranna is determined. I am sure he will get them in time.' But now Veeranna was beckoning.

'He says he have something to show Sahib,' the young trainee told them.

As they watched, Veeranna went to a wall where finished images stood. Because of the coming feast, most were of Ganesh, but one figure, taller than the others, was carefully swathed in muslin and, with something like triumph, Veeranna took off the coverings, lifted it and put it down before Michael, who was astounded. He whispered, 'Saraswati.'

'Yes. Goddess of all learning.' Inspector Dutta was intent on his information.

'Goddess of pen and ink,' Michael remembered, 'and music too, of course. She always holds a *vina*. On her *puja* day I remember they used to set up a *pandal* for her in the street and the students and poets, and schoolchildren, used to bring their books, manuscripts and instruments and lay them at her feet. I always thought she was beautiful, but this is lovely. Tell him so,' he told the young trainee. Veeranna had given her a gauze sari, patterned with little gold stars, a crescent moon in her hair, even the holy little red henna spot that marks devoted women's foreheads. Her smile was so gracious she seemed alive. In English so quick that neither of the young policemen could follow it, Michael said in the Inspector's ear, 'Don't you think Veeranna could have made the new Shiva?'

Inspector Dutta gave a loud guffaw. 'Dear Michael, how you do get carried away! As I have said, Veeranna is a good craftsman but don't forget the Shiva is bronze and he has only just started working in metal – if he has. That needed an artist, someone approaching that old master sculptor. No village potter could possibly have made it.' As Veeranna was standing looking puzzled, the Inspector said to the young trainee, 'Translate for him.'

Veeranna listened, said nothing, only picked up the Saraswati to put her away, but Michael had seen a gleam of resentment in his eyes.

When they came back to Patna Hall the sun was still hot. 'I think I'll go in for a dip,' said Michael. 'I'll fetch my things.'

He came back to find Inspector Dutta at the head of the beach watching Artemis: she was standing at the top of the high diving board built far out into the bay with the surf sending up a turbulence of white against it. In her wicker helmet and turquoise bikini, she was wet and her body glistened. She stood taut, her hands held high and joined ready. Thambi was beside her but not touching her as they dived, she in a perfect curve far out beyond the waves, swimming ahead of him. They were clapping her on the beach as Inspector Dutta said, 'Is there anything that young woman cannot do?' Then, unexpectedly, 'I'm glad I haven't got her for a wife.'

Michael did not answer; he was too intent. She went down – he caught his breath – but came up and rode in on the surf, Thambi holding her on a gigantic wave that, as it fell, rolled them far up the shore, spreading ripples round them as they lay panting but laughing until Artemis staggered up the sand and fell on her swimming towel, spread ready.

'She best of all,' Thambi told Michael, who had dared to walk over.

'Thambi says that to everyone,' said Artemis. 'Don't you, Thambi?'

'This time true.' Thambi laughed. 'Sahib want to go in?'

'He can't. He's going to talk to me,' and Artemis patted the sand beside her. 'Come on, sit down,' and as Michael obeyed, 'Tell me something nice and nothing to do with people. People, people, people!' She was vehement. 'Tell me something innocent as if we were children.'

Sitting on the warm sand, scooping it up to let it trickle through his fingers, by some magic Michael was inspired to begin:

> 'And then with hat and ball and hoop go playing
> in parks where the bright colours softly fade,
> brushing against the grown-ups without staying
> when ball or hoop their alien walks invade . . .

*And hours on end by the grey pond-side kneeling
with little sailing-boat and elbows bare;
forgetting it, because one like it's stealing
below the ripples, but with sails more fair;
and, having still to spare, to share some feeling
with the small face caught sight of there:–
Childhood! winged likeness half-guessed at, wheeling,
oh, where, oh, where?'*

Artemis turned on her side and looked at him. 'I didn't know brilliant young men could quote poetry.'

'I'm not brilliant.'

'Auntie Sanni says you are and she knows.' The teasing stopped. 'Perhaps knows too much,' she said. For a moment she turned away, then back to look at him again. 'Do you write poems, Michael?'

'I have.'

'Say one.' It was a command, and something in Michael told him to rebel.

'No, thank you!' he said, got up and walked away.

Artemis did not come for drinks or dinner: she was busy helping to arrange the drawing room-ballroom for Auntie Sanni and the Colonel's supper reception. Samuel was there too, and the dining room was almost empty. Only the Fishers, Inspector Dutta and Michael were having dinner, waited on by the head waiter. Professor Ellen had a bad headache so that after dinner the four of them were alone on the veranda while from the ballroom they could hear music.

Michael showed Lady Fisher the earrings he had bought for Honor. 'These are really good ones,' said Lady Fisher, 'beautiful. It's amazing what you can find in a village bazaar.'

This led to talk of Honor. 'To us, she's just a young girl,' said Sir John. 'We can hardly believe she's a QC.'

'What is that?' asked Inspector Dutta.

'Queen's Counsel. A very senior barrister. Apparently in her year there were over five hundred applicants and perhaps seventy were admitted. There's a huge waiting list.'

'Of whom only eight were women,' said Lady Fisher.

'Honor has been a QC for five years which, of course, has led to her high status,' and Sir John explained to Inspector Dutta, 'It's all deeply traditional. As a QC, in court you have to wear a full-bottomed wig, gloves, buckled shoes and the traditional black silk gown, which is why it's called taking silk.'

'Taking silk. I like that,' said Inspector Dutta.

Professor Ellen came down: 'To have a little fresh air, and a brandy if I may?' she asked Sir John. The music had changed, dancing had begun. 'I find this the hardest work of all.' She had collapsed into a chair. 'Thank God for Artemis but I shall have to go in soon.'

'And I have just come out.' Auntie Sanni had appeared. 'A brandy for me too, please, John. Ellen, you look very pale.'

'I feel it, but Artemis is there.'

'It seems strange,' said Michael, 'noisy dancing in a room that has a shrine in it.'

'They have dancing girls in temples,' Sir John pointed out.

'But not for this sort of dancing.'

'That reminds me.' Inspector Dutta's thoughts were never far from his work. 'Professor Webster, in your experience, since Henry Bertram's time, did the Nataraja ever go out of the house?'

'Yes. I'd been worried about it. The sea air and saltiness were beginning to erode it. Of course, it should have been kept under glass.'

'Under glass!' Auntie Sanni was indignant. 'That would have defeated its purpose.'

'You see?' Professor Ellen shrugged. 'But Artemis is bolder than I. In her explorations she had come to know a renowned old sculptor, Sri Satya Narayana, who specialized in antiques. He himself used the centuries-old ancient methods, carving in wax. The season before last, Artemis had arranged not to fly home but to spend the summer, the hot weather, researching in Kashmir, and offered to take the Shiva to Sri Narayana on her way there, picking it up on her way back.'

'She went by car?'

'Yes,' Auntie Sanni confirmed.

'With an escort, I hope?'

'Escort? What escort?'

'The Shiva is very valuable, Miss Sanni.'

'Well, Artemis just took it but it was no good. When she got to Sri Narayana's house-studio to collect the Nataraja on her way back, she found he had died two months before without touching it so she brought it back.'

'And you are sure, Professor, that it was the same?'

'Of course it was, there was no mistaking it, and that was last year. It was only this year that I knew at once that what we now have is a fake.'

'Long after Miss Artemis brought it back?'
'Yes.' Professor Ellen was firm.

'Well, if you'll excuse me I'll go up. I want to write to Honor,' Michael told the Fishers.

He could hear Indian music now. What will Mrs Moaner have to say about that, he wondered. For him it conjured up the magic of Veeranna's Saraswati and the *vina* in her hand. The hall, though, was deserted until the drawing-room door opened and Artemis came out, closing it quickly behind her.

She was dressed in what Michael guessed she had adopted as her uniform. Another long black skirt and white frilled blouse, but these were fresh and clean, while her hair was up in a knot tied with another red chiffon scarf. She looked what she was, a leader, but she leaned back against the door and gave a wide yawn.

'Tired?' Michael's voice was tender.

'Michael!' At once she was poised again, as she said, 'You were so cross on the beach I thought you would never speak to me again.'

'Silly! You know I'll always want to speak to you, Artemis...'

He had come closer but before he could touch her she was gone – back to the other side of the door.

'Today is your day for the Sun Temple at Konak.' Although it was early, Sir John was up and had found Professor Ellen with her list waiting for the group to come downstairs.

'Yes,' she said, 'we're just getting ready.' The coach was waiting under the portico as the group gathered, carrying their usual paraphernalia. Samuel was taking on board freezer bags of iced mineral water, orange juice, biscuits and tea-making things.

'It's a long way,' said Sir John. 'They only arrived yesterday and I see Artemis is giving a lecture tonight.'

'Yes, on the sculptures. She really has become an expert.'

'I'm sure, but, my dear, how you do drive them.'

'That's what they came for. They wouldn't be satisfied with anything less.'

'I don't know if I want to go or not.' Mrs Moaner had come downstairs with Hannah.

'Memsahib try,' Hannah encouraged. 'I'm sure if you get tired Professor Miss Sahib send you back by car.'

'They say it's dreadfully erotic.'

'That's why I want to go.'

Duke's eyes sparkled, but Madame Duvivier said, perhaps in gentle rebuke, 'It's the beauty and majesty we go to see.'

'Michael.' He had just appeared and Professor Ellen came eagerly up to him. 'Why don't you come too? It's such a chance.'

'I'm afraid there are things I have to do.' He did not want to hurt her feelings but, as he told Lady Fisher when the coach had left, 'If I can get to Konak I shall go by myself, not in a group with a guided tour.'

'You're right,' said Lady Fisher. 'It's truly the most beautiful temple in the world, built like a vast stone chariot with huge carved wheels and drawn by gigantic stone horses that seem alive. No one has ever fathomed how men – ants by comparison – got the great slabs of stone in place. To see its full beauty you need to be there at the moment when the risen sun touches the entrance, which is guarded by two stone lions crushing elephants, where Surya the sun god sits on his charger as if in welcome. His face has a wonderfully beneficent smile for all who come to pay tribute at his temple. I can't tell you how beautiful it is but you must get up at three or four in the morning. We always did, didn't we, John?'

In her own quiet way Lady Fisher knew even more about this vast country than Artemis.

Artemis! Be sensible, Michael had told himself that very morning. She has things to do and you have things to do, so get on with it.

Samuel had given him a note. It was from Inspector Dutta.

> Shall be away for about twenty-four hours.
> Colonel McIndoe has my telephone number but I shall be moving about. Think I am on to something.

So am I, thought Michael.

He had not forgotten that gleam of resentment in Veeranna's eyes and knew he had to go and see him – with someone to translate.

Instinctively, he did not take Thambi – he was too senior – so, 'Moses,' he said, 'I want to explore the village but I don't speak Telegu and you speak good English.' A little flattery, he had learned, goes a long way. 'Will you come with me?'

'I very pleased, Sahib. I not needed here this morning.'

Quiet lay over Patna Hall. Auntie Sanni and the

Colonel were busy at their desks; Sir John had gone for a quiet stroll along the beach; Lady Fisher was, as usual, on the veranda. There was, of course, no sign of Inspector Dutta, nor had he been at breakfast.

'I come now,' said Moses.

Michael and he set out. As they walked through the gates, Michael smiled again at Shyama, who was in the courtyard sitting on a rush mat dreamily shifting chillies, which were turning scarlet in the sun. She could not hide her face in her sari, which was hanging down her back, leaving her brief bodice and bare midriff showing plump, but this time she smiled back boldly. Out of respect for Thambi, Moses ignored her.

There was a telephone call for Michael. It came to Colonel McIndoe's office – to Kanu's indignation the Colonel did not allow direct calls to reception. Now he pressed a buzzer which Samuel, who was nearest, answered. 'Fetch Dean Sahib. There is a call for him. It's from London so be quick.'

Michael was not in his room, or on the veranda. Samuel sent a boy running to the beach but he was not on the beach. It seemed he was out with Moses. Why Moses, Samuel wondered. Michael was usually with

Thambi. After a moment he went to the gatehouse. 'The young English sahib,' he asked Shyama in Telegu – she was too indolent to pick up even a few words of English – 'did he go out?'

'Yes,' whispered Shyama. She was in awe of Samuel, who clicked his tongue in annoyance.

The Colonel was irritated, too. 'Think of the expense. Why didn't they send a fax?' But Samuel's annoyance was not at the telephone call: he had a deeper dismay.

'The young sahib. Was he alone?' he asked Shyama.

'No. With Moses.'

Now Samuel was truly alarmed.

'What I really want,' Michael told Moses, 'is to go and see the potter.'

'Him Veeranna.'

'I know.'

'Very good potter. Most clever. He make beautiful god and goddess.'

'I know.'

Veeranna was making one now, working on still another Ganesh whose elephant trunk was almost completed. He was absorbed, a lump of clay in his left hand, which he took, scrap by scrap, working it in with his thumb. He did not notice them until Moses touched his shoulder, almost reverently, but as soon as he saw Michael he was up, letting the clay fall back into the hole on the floor.

Copying Inspector Dutta, Michael said, 'Veeranna *bhai*,' and made a *namaskar*, his hands held together finger to finger in the Indian greeting he had learned as a little boy. 'Tell him, Moses, the Ganesh will be very good.'

Veeranna's face cleared as Moses translated and he returned the greeting.

'Ask him if he has ever made a god in metal.'

There was quite a conversation during which Veeranna was obviously proud. 'Him say yes. He take many lessons . . .'

'Where?'

At that Veeranna withdrew. All Moses could get from him was, 'Far away.'

'Ask him for how long.'

More talk with Moses, then, 'He say two years. Not all the year. He go and come. He has his work here.'

Michael wasted no more time. 'Veeranna, you made the second Shiva Nataraja, didn't you?'

There was no need to translate. For a moment Veeranna shone. 'Sahib has eyes! *Ji hah!* Yes, I made him and fool all those clever sahibs.' Veeranna threw back his head and laughed, a deep, throaty, delighted laugh.

Michael's instinct was to stop there – 'If only I had,' he said afterwards, 'but I felt bound to go on.'

'Veeranna *bhai*, you must have had help. Tell me ...' But the delight was gone. Veeranna's face was stern, his lips shut tightly. 'Please tell.'

'I not tell,' and suddenly Veeranna turned to Moses with a torrent of words.

'He say he promise not tell. Sacred promise. If he break promise, Shiva punish him. Shiva punishment most terrible, Sahib.' Moses' eyes showed he had caught some of the terror and awe. 'Perhaps kill.'

'I not tell. Never. Go away.' Veeranna turned his back, sat down before his Ganesh on its plinth and picked up a ball of fresh clay.

Michael had given Moses a handsome tip, then shut himself in his room at the desk Auntie Sanni had sent up for him, his pad in front of him, as he went over the scene in the potter's house.

'Why? How? Who?'

How? Michael knew little about sculpture but enough to realize that, even granted much skill, such an exact replica could not have been made from memory or even photographs. Veeranna must have had the Nataraja before him every moment of his work, but if he had visited it in its niche, or openly borrowed it, everyone would have known.

Why? Michael felt sure he knew the answer to that. Veeranna, by bone, blood and brain, was an artist, and someone, though Michael could not imagine who, had given him the chance to show it – he a poor potter. He had been taught, elsewhere, thought Michael, been given tools. Someone had paid for all these.

That brought him to who, and here he was lost.

There was a knock at the door. It was Samuel. 'Dean Sahib, your call, in reception. It from London, so quick.'

It was a repeat call from Honor Wyatt. 'I could have faxed you but I wanted to hear your voice. Are you still alive and well?'

'Never been more alive and well.'

'Good. How's it going?'

'Inch by inch ... at least I hope it is.'

'Of course I know,' said Hannah.

What had made Michael go to Hannah and not

Samuel he could not say, even to himself. He found her on the top veranda, superintending the gardeners – sometimes with a sharp tongue – as they arranged vases of flowers they had brought freshly in; as each was finished a houseboy came and carried it away to a different room. Hannah would have broken off but 'Let them finish,' Michael said. 'Then when you have a few minutes ...'

As soon as they were alone he began – not with Veeranna but with the little Nataraja. 'Hannah, I think you knew the Shiva had been changed.'

'Of course I know. Miss Sanni say I not to let the houseboys touch it ever. The shelf, yes. I tell them clean carefully, take away flowers and food, but it is I, no other servant, who lift Nataraja to dust it. That how I know, soon as I lift. It not as much heavy.'

'Did you tell Miss Sanni?'

'Indeed I tell and I say to her, "Professor Miss Sahib always telling it very valuable. What should we do, Miss Sanni? Call police?" And I say to her, "What shall I do?"'

'And?'

'"Dust it," she say.'

'And what did you do?'

'As Miss Sanni say,' said Hannah, as if that was the only thing anyone could do.

'Did you tell Samuel?'

'Of course, and Samuel say to me, "You hush."'

Michael went in search of the old butler. 'Samuel, where is Chief Inspector Dutta?'

'He gone away, Sahib.'

'I know, but where?'

'I not know, Sahib. He say back tomorrow night,' and Samuel went on, 'Sahib, I think you take Moses and go to see Veeranna.'

'Yes, I did.'

'Will you tell Samuel why?'

'Because I knew Veeranna had made the new Shiva.'

'Who told you, Sahib?'

'I guessed when I went yesterday to see Veeranna with Inspector Dutta. Veeranna's face told me and this morning he told me in words.'

The bushy eyebrows under the white turban bristled. 'I think you very clever, Sahib, far more clever than police.' Samuel looked at Michael with distrust. And fear, wondered Michael.

He tried to conciliate. 'Samuel, you know I came to help Miss Sanni.'

'Then go away.'

'Samuel!'

'Yes. We all liking you very much, Dean Sahib, but, please, go back England. Do what Miss Sanni say, "Let things be."'

'It's too late. This taking of the real Shiva has become even more serious since your government called in the police – and remember there is Mr Cromartie. Do you want him to have your Shiva?' Samuel shuddered. 'I am afraid, Samuel, that my knowing that Veeranna made the Nataraja is only a first step. I am bound to find out how and why, if I can.'

'But you are on wrong side, Sahib.'

'The wrong side?'

'Yes. I tell you, we know, I Samuel, Hannah, Thambi, but we not say anything ever, not for a thousand thousand rupees, and never to Inspector Dutta. Never. Never.'

There was another telephone call for Michael. 'Inspector Dutta,' Kanu told him, as he handed him the receiver.

'Kanu, please go away, right away.' Michael was sure he would try to stay in earshot.

The Inspector began, 'I was sorry to leave you without warning but I had to leave early. I had a hunch, a feeling that I must go by myself, check about the sculptor, Sri Satya Narayana.'

'I knew you weren't satisfied.'

'No, it sounded somehow too convenient.' The Inspector's voice was excited. 'But it was all exactly as Miss Artemis had said. The Master, as they call him here, had died two years ago but his widow is still living in the studio house – it was easy to locate as he was famous. Mrs Narayana did not know anything about the Shiva. He had so many statues here but she was quite certain he could not have done any work on it. She did not seem to remember Miss Artemis taking it away. "But she very well may have," she told me. "She knew us and knew I was still in mourning and she may have thought it best to have come and gone without troubling me. A charming person."

'I asked her,' the Inspector went on, 'if her husband had lately had any unusual contacts with the outside world, and she said there had been some strange things neither he nor she could explain. A few years ago a letter had come. A printed letter, which she showed me with pride, and certainly it was uncommon, being from what seemed to be a worldwide centre of art, the Presidential Central College of Art, Ancient and Modern, with headquarters in New Delhi but offices in London, Paris, New York and Tokyo, their addresses given as post-office box numbers. The letter was most respectful, asking if Sri Satya Narayana, as master sculptor, would take one of their outstanding male students and teach him the original, centuries-old method of making images of the gods in metal, bronze, silver and gold, first carving them in wax. Sri Narayana had not taken apprentices for years but such a truly magnificent fee was offered "that I'm afraid," the widow said almost regretfully, "it made him accept", so he wrote agreeing. There was no reply but suddenly the money arrived. To her amazement it was in cash, quite a bundle, without even a registration or request for a receipt, and with it the pupil. The young man said he was from Bengal, giving his name as Gopal but, she told me, "He was no Bengali, nor did he want to be an apprentice, saying he had his own work to attend to, but for two years he came for six weeks at a time. He seemed to know nothing of the arts centre but someone supplied him with tools. He never told us who. He had great reverence for my husband, who said he was the best pupil he had ever had. He came for two years, then vanished."

'Michael,' the Inspector went on, 'I tried to contact this arts centre in New Delhi. It seemed not to exist. I tried also London, New York, Tokyo, through the police. This is why I have been so long. Yet there is the letter, the money and, above all, the young man. Michael, I believe I am on to something at last.'

'And so am I,' Michael began, but the Inspector was too engrossed in his own story.

'Tomorrow I am going through the statuary with Mrs Narayana to see if there is anything resembling the Shiva.'

'Hem, wait. I must tell you.'

'I'll be back tomorrow. You can tell me then.'

'Hem!' But Inspector Dutta had rung off.

'Michael,' said Sir John after dinner, 'I have a mind to drop in on Artemis's lecture. I always enjoy listening to her putting it across. She really is very good because she knows her subject so well, yet has a light touch. Come and see.'

Considering the long day at Konak, a surprising number of the group were there, and all the young people.

'Konak!' Duke had said, when they came in. 'I'd expected those statues to move me, which was why I went, but they were ... tremendous. I'm still speechless, and tonight Artemis is going to tell us more about the gods, and how these wonders were made.'

Artemis was in mid-speech, standing before a table on which was a small collection of images, small because, like all experienced lecturers, she never said too much. These, Michael knew, were the household *puja*-corner gods, probably borrowed from Veeranna. On a pedestal was the niche's Shiva, and as Sir John and Michael came in, she drew it to the centre, saying, 'I should like to tell you how ten, eleven, twelve centuries ago, this little dancing Shiva was made.'

She was in her uniform, long black silk skirt and frilled blouse, her hair tied with the usual chiffon scarf but tonight it was of a flaunting emerald green. She loves colours, thought Michael, and knows how they fit an occasion.

On the table various tools and photographs were laid; her voice was as clear and natural as a bell. 'The master sculptors of that time were not primitive as, for instance, early African art is primitive. In its very simplicity, their art has a remarkable sophistication, as has that of the Greeks. They put us to shame with our modern sculptors and their technical appliances from such amenable things as plastic-covered wire with which they can make a structure, the brilliant lights on stands which can be heightened or lowered and moved. These old masters worked by daylight on the floor of, probably, an open-fronted hut – no trace of a studio – or at night with a small oil lamp. This particular method is called *cire perdu*, or "lost wax", but thank God, there are still a few artists left who can do it.

'To begin with the god is carved in wax, hard, yellowish in colour, the texts say, beautiful to behold, because it is now that the master shows his greatest skill as each line, each expression will eventually be reproduced exactly, and it has to be in proportion with the things the god carries, such as a sword, a drum or *vina*, maybe a reptile, all attributes given by the ancient scripts. The carving takes a long time. When it's finished it's given a light coating of clay, carefully mixed with charred husks, tiny bits of cotton and salt, all ground by hand on a stone until they are powder. Then the god is left to dry in the shade. This coating of clay is done three times, at intervals of two days, and each time it is heavier.

'Long tubes with a flared mouth resembling the *kusa* flower are added through the wax on the back, the shoulders, on the nape of the neck and crown of the head and have to be kept open, not blocked by the clay.

'The weight of the finished image has been decided by the weight of the finished wax figure, eight times heavier for bronze, twelve for silver, sixteen for gold. This Shiva is bronze. On the chosen day when the clay mould is hard enough, it is put in an earthenware crucible to withstand great heat and set in a fire. The wax melts and runs out. Meanwhile the metal has been heated until it is liquid. Then, holding its container with a pair of tongs, the artist pours the liquid quickly into the mouths of the tubes until they are filled to the brim. The figure now has to cool. Then the master breaks off the clay mould bit by bit. When the whole is revealed he will know if he has succeeded, and if he can cut away the mouths of the tubes making them level and give his god or goddess its finishing touches.

'The text ends,' said Artemis, 'with a royal instruction. On an auspicious day the King should install it where it can be worshipped every day with offerings, flowers and a light, which our Shiva is,' said Artemis.

'But, Artemis,' said Eric Barclay, 'isn't that Shiva the one which was stolen? The trial is coming up in London. It's made such a sensation.'

'Yes.'

'Then what *is* this one?'

How, wondered Michael, with her deep regard for Auntie Sanni and her own wishes, would Artemis field that?

'This is the one that was not stolen,' she said, and went on too quickly for Eric to say anything more. 'You have listened so politely to me that we'll change the subject and Ellen will show you a film I had made last year of the Ghandara hills' cave paintings.'

'Professor Ellen has a headache,' Sir John whispered to her.

'All the same, she'll have to do it. I've had enough,' Artemis whispered back, and went on, 'We had only a small unit, the cameraman and one soundman, but it came out quite well. You'll see. We're going to the caves tomorrow.'

When the film ended and the audience came out, it was plain they were not only interested but exuberant. There were congratulations, tumultuous questions, drinks, talk, laughter.

'I've already learned so much I can't take it all in,' confessed Duke. 'I'll have to come back.'

'I've learned so much I shall never forget,' said Madame Duvivier. But Michael was in no humour for any of it. His mind was seething with problems as he went further up the veranda, past Auntie Sanni, and leaned on the rail hoping to become part of the calm of the garden until he felt someone beside him. Artemis. She was so close they were almost touching, but as he turned to her, she drew away. She was angry.

'Michael,' she said, 'when we came back I didn't want to rest. Konak always has that effect on me, it's too exciting, so I went into the village to see some of my friends. I have been coming here for a long time. Patna Hall and the village have been very useful to me – they are why I learned Telegu. Of course I went to Veeranna – he's a very special friend – but as soon as he saw me he burst into tears. He says you tricked him into telling you he made the new Shiva.'

'I didn't trick him. When I saw him with Inspector Dutta I guessed. This morning I asked him outright and he admitted it – with delight, Artemis.'

'Then he was lying.'

'I don't think Veeranna lies.'

But Artemis argued, 'How could he have made it? He hasn't any tools. You didn't use your senses, Michael.'

'You're right. I'm supposed to be a barrister and at this stage barristers are never allowed to cross-examine witnesses – that's a solicitor's job, and here I am behaving like a solicitor. What's come over me? It's as if I'm under a spell. You all tell me that Veeranna couldn't have made the Shiva, but I know he did. I know, too, he won't tell me how or why.'

'No. He won't ever.'

'But I have a nasty feeling that Chief Inspector Dutta and his crew have ways of making him.'

She looked at him in horror. 'Must you tell Inspector Dutta?'

'Artemis, I have a professional duty.'

'Prig.'

'That's not fair.'

She came closer. 'Michael, please don't tell the police – for Veeranna's sake. He's such an innocent, and didn't dream he was doing anything wrong. Just for once, Michael,' and she gave him a kiss, light as a butterfly's wing on his cheek. 'Promise.'

'I can't,' said Michael. 'I must tell the Inspector as soon as I see him.'

'Then I hate you,' flashed Artemis, and left him.

The group had to leave Patna Hall at seven to get to the caves.

'We'll get up at five and walk,' said Duke.

'If I were you I don't think I would,' said Artemis. 'It's

sixteen miles. The coach will take us as far as it can, which is twelve miles, then there are four miles of steep rough walking. There will be ponies for those who would rather ride.'

'Perhaps it would be better if I don't come,' said one of the older members. 'After all, we saw the beautiful film last night – but I hope you don't think I'm a coward.'

'I wouldn't think of coming.' That was Mrs Moaner who, for some reason, had got up. 'Not after yesterday. I don't want to see any more of this horrible Indian art. Filthy. Sex crazy. I felt sick, and they call them gods. I was too ashamed to look at them.'

'Then you didn't see them,' said Madame Duvivier.

'The cave paintings are of animals, not humans,' Artemis interposed quickly.

'Animals might be worse. Oh dear.' Mrs Moaner was ready to weep. 'We never seem to do anything nice.'

'Wait for tonight,' said Artemis. 'Professor Ellen will make an announcement at lunch. There's an invitation I think you will like.' She could have added, 'I hope,' but not very hopefully, and returned to the cave paintings. 'Those ancient masters were marvellously gifted. They could draw and paint so that the creatures seem to breathe and live.'

'On rough walls?' Mrs Moaner sniffed in derision.

'That is the wonder, and they had no choice. Remember, there were no canvases then, no paper, indeed no houses. Besides, the paintings were of the utmost importance. To those cave dwellers, animals were far more important than humans because they lived by their hunting, and the people in their innocence believed that if they could catch the likeness on their walls of those birds, wild oxen, bison, wolves, even tigers, they would catch them in reality.'

'Judging by the film, they have been caught,' said Madame Duvivier.

Marcia Barclay enthused, 'Artemis, you make everything so interesting. Will you go through it again?'

'I think Professor Ellen will. I have to go and see a little temple I've heard of higher in the hills.'

'I wish she wouldn't,' Professor Ellen said to Michael, who had got up early to see them off – and also because this was the time when the gardeners came in to decorate the shrine. 'Michael, it isn't safe for a girl to go alone into the hills. I wish you'd speak to her. She might listen to you.'

'Artemis and I are not very good friends just now but I'll try.'

He managed to catch her just as she was leaving for the coach. 'I hear that when you get to the caves you're going off on your own.'

'What business is it of yours?' She was still hostile.

'It's the business of anyone who cares about you.'

She looked up into his face. 'Michael, I think you do care.'

'Haven't I shown it from the first moment?'

She relented. 'Well, don't worry. I don't go alone. I go with a friend and his servant.'

After breakfast Michael went to find Auntie Sanni, who was in her office. 'May I have your permission to ask all your staff a few questions?'

'Inspector Dutta did that the day before yesterday without asking.'

'Inspector Dutta and I have different ways. I'd like to see them one by one, but it will have to be through Moses. May I?'

'Do you really need to?'

'I mustn't leave any stone unturned.'

'These are people not stones.'

'I'll be very gentle, Auntie Sanni.'

*

Michael saw the gardeners first and had Moses ask each one the same question. 'You come every morning to bring fresh flowers for the god. Are you sure you never noticed that he was not the same?'

The answers varied.

'No.'

'He always there. How could we think he not the same?'

'I not look at him very much.'

'I busy with the flowers.'

But they all added up to 'No.'

The Muslim table waiters, Abdul and Karim, both wearing off-duty clothes, were unhelpful, even scornful.

'He Hindu god,' said Karim. 'I never look.'

'I not want to look,' said Abdul.

The Nepali houseboys, Kancha and Jetta, seemed always on duty, yet cheerful, but they said, 'Shiva statue. We not even dust it. Hannah not allow us. How can we know?'

Colonel McIndoe's valet, a servant with a position below Samuel and Hannah's but above the other servants, was contemptuous. 'It great fuss. How can Hindu god be so important? As for me, I never go into drawing room unless there is reception or ceremony when I go in charge of drinks and I far, far too busy to look.'

The sweeper women were more observant, chanting hymns to him as they bumped along the floor with their bottles – but they were too many to interrogate separately. 'Of course he our Shiva, always is, always same,' they all agreed.

'That's a morning wasted,' said Michael, downcast.

'Try Kanu,' said Hannah. 'He say anything for money.'

Michael thought she was mocking him.

He did not have to go to Kanu. Kanu came to him. 'Sahib Michael. How much will you give me if I tell you what I tell Mr Cromartie in London?'

'Nothing,' said Michael. 'I happen to know what you told Mr Cromartie.'

Kanu's mouth fell open in dismay and puzzlement. 'How you know?'

'My business,' said Michael, 'but I'll buy you a drink if you'll tell me that what you told him in London is true. Don't forget, I'm investigating. Gin and tonic?'

'Samuel, he skin me.'

'Not if I give it to you.'

'You so nice, Michael, but you not know Samuel. He

not let me drink one glass. I not stay here. Michael, I going to be barman at Uberoi hotel, Mr Cromartie he say so. He pay me very well. You know why?' Kanu came closer. 'Not only information, I think, but because I am so very pretty.'

Pretty? thought Michael. Yes, if you like that sort of thing.

'Long, long ago when I was small boy I got into trouble here – trouble that for me fine but Hannah make it bad and ever since,' he took a gulp of gin, 'no one trust me. Ten o'clock, I must go home – my people live in the village. If I late my father come to fetch me. But, Michael, I not little boy now. I grown up, Michael, for little money if you want?'

'Kanu, I am not Mr Cromartie.'

Kanu grew spiteful. 'You wrong. I not only pretty. Kanu know who took the Shiva and why.'

'You know why?'

'Yes. Kanu put two and two together.' He was getting excited. 'The Colonel, Auntie Sanni, they get old. My father and mother think Samuel and Hannah like gods, everything good, but Hannah, she there when Professor Ellen took first Shiva figure down for lecture and Hannah she hear what Professor tell Auntie Sanni how much it was valuable – millions of rupees,' said Kanu, his eyes wide. 'Hannah, she tell Samuel.'

'So you think ...?'

Kanu put his finger one side of his nose and winked in glee. 'Aha! Now you listen. Auntie Sanni, she old, soon die. Without Auntie Sanni, Patna Hall die too, or else so few people coming, Patna Hall close. What Samuel and Hannah do then? They also old, too old to get other job. What they do then?'

'I'm sure the Colonel would look after them.'

'Maybe, maybe not, and maybe Samuel and Hannah want – how do you say? Nest ...?'

'Nest egg.' Michael put down his glass.

'Where you going?'

'To ask them.'

'*Ask!*' Kanu was startled. 'I think better you tell Police Inspector Dutta.'

'I don't think Inspector Dutta will be interested.'

'Then you don't believe me.'

'I believe you are a nasty little liar,' but Kanu did not know the meaning of the word nasty.

Michael found Samuel in the pantry behind the dining room having a tumbler of tea before starting to get ready for luncheon. He was in a loose shirt, his impressive turban laid aside, but as soon as he saw Michael he stood up, set down the tumbler and put it on.

'Samuel, have your tea. I only want a few words with you.' Michael sat on a stool.

Reluctantly Samuel sat too. 'Tea for you, Sahib?'

'No, thank you. I had a drink with Kanu. If that was wrong it's my fault, not his.'

'Not easy boy. Hannah and I, we fear for him. His father and mother most nice people.'

'Miss Sanni will help him. Samuel, may I talk to you a little about Patna Hall?'

Samuel was relieved. 'Ah, the hotel. If I can help you ...'

'You can if you will. I know it had a great heyday.'

'Heyday, Sahib?'

'A time of great success. What has changed it?'

'Patna Hall not changed, not one i-o-ta.' Samuel was proud he knew that word. 'Not us. It is visitors. They want quick, quick, quick, airflight everywhere, they not stay. Business people, schedule. Tourist hurry, get so many things in one package. Patna Hall not like that at all so not many people come.' Samuel spread his hands helplessly. 'And we getting old, Sahib.'

'Yes,' and Michael said gently, 'Miss Sanni and Colonel McIndoe too.' Then, he quoted Kanu. 'If they close Patna Hall, I think you and Hannah are too old to get other work.'

'Other work? Never, never. They look after us.'

'If the hotel is losing money, they may be too poor.'

'If they poor, we poor. We be proud to share. Hannah, me and Thambi.'

Michael could only say, 'I beg your pardon, Samuel.'

'Sahib ask pardon of me!' The old man was plainly gratified. 'Sahib—' He stopped as if some thought had suddenly struck him. 'Michael Sahib, you London lawyer, very clever. The Nataraja, is it of so great value as they say?'

'The experts think so. They valued it at more than two hundred and fifty thousand pounds.'

'Ah!' Samuel shuddered, and Michael seized what he was sure was an opportunity.

'May I ask you a question myself? You needn't answer if you don't want to.'

'Ask, Sahib,' but Samuel was bowed down in distress.

'You seem so unhappy and worried,' and Michael dared to go on, 'Is it because you and Hannah believe that what Kanu says is true?'

There was a silence. Then, 'Yes,' said Samuel, and he seemed to brace himself and stood up. 'All these days Hannah and I, Thambi too, not tell you because we so frightened for Miss Sanni. Yes, we not saying anything, anything at all. We so much afraid. The one who took the Shiva for to sell it was Miss Sanni. Of course, Colonel Sahib help her. Michael Sahib, she only do it to save Patna Hall, but now ... oh, what happen to Miss Sanni? Now there is Inspector Dutta, London lawyers, our government. What happen to her?'

'It couldn't have been Miss Sanni.'

'Couldn't? I tell you, Sahib ... '

'I know, but you are wrong.'

'How?'

'For the best of reasons. Because she is Miss Sanni. She would never have sold the Shiva, not even for Patna Hall. Miss Sanni believes in reverence for everyone else's gods, and her own – that before anything else.'

'Then who?' said Samuel uncertainly.

'We don't know, but not Miss Sanni.'

Light broke on Samuel's face. He got up and rushed through the dining room. 'Hannah! Hannah!'

She came quickly. 'Michael Sahib know,' Samuel told her. 'He so much more clever than us. He say Miss Sanni she never never sell the Shiva.' And he repeated what Michael had said.

As she listened the same light came on Hannah's face, tears too. 'Samuel, Michael Sahib right. He completely right. Me, I know it now. I know it in my bones, but we in so much fright. Not thinking properly. God bless you, Michael Sahib. God bless you.'

Michael felt he must try to clear his head so he went down to the beach for a swim – and did not swim.

Back from the caves, some of the young were there too, ready to go into the sea when Moses and his fishermen could take them. Thambi was up on the diving board with Artemis.

Although most of the day had been wasted, Michael, now susceptible, had this unaccustomed happiness in his heart and he stood to watch her, her body wet and ready poised, until there came another spectacular dive far over the others in the water who clapped. But Michael did not want to be drawn into chat just now, not even with Artemis, and he went back to the house.

Auntie Sanni was on her swing couch as he came up the steps to the veranda and he felt he must thank her for letting him interview the servants.

'Well, did you find out anything?'

'Not a thing towards a solution but I didn't expect to.'

Auntie Sanni laid her hand on his arm and said what Samuel had said: 'Michael, we have all come to like you – honour you, too – but please, Michael, give this up and go back to London.'

'It's what I came for.'

'Still, go back. Michael, I see nothing but pain, sorrow and hurt.'

'Auntie Sanni, if justice is done someone has to be hurt.'

'That will be terrible.'

'Not for me. I can't go now.' And, with a sudden rush of the confidence that people felt with Auntie Sanni and a flood of happiness, 'Because this work is not all. Through you and Patna Hall, I know something now that has never touched me before.'

'Artemis,' said Auntie Sanni.

Michael got up. He still did not want to talk about it, but as he went down the veranda he thought he heard Auntie Sanni say, 'Oh dear! Oh dear! Oh dear!'

At the end of lunch Professor Ellen stood up and waited until a hush fell on the cleared table. 'This evening we come to what I hope you will find the highlight of our tour. Our brochure simply lists "evening visit to the old town of Konakpur and its palace, the Gul Mahal", which gives little inkling of what that means. The old town is fascinating. It has a whole street of carved house fronts, an inland lake and overlooking it, high on a steep hill, the Maharajah's palace, the Gul Mahal, which means Rose Palace in honour of the thousands of roses on its terraces. Of course, the Maharajah is not a Maharajah now. He lives on the French Riviera, but the Government let him keep the palace on condition that he opened it to the public. But we do not go as the public. By his special command, his steward invites us every year to a banquet. First you will see the State apartments. They include a famous room where the furniture is made of glass.'

'Glass!' Marcia interrupted.

'Yes, chairs and tables, and there is jewellery. Then the banquet, and afterwards a display of dancing in the pavilion built on the roof. The way up to the palace is by three paths, the chief being the central one which has stone steps with ramps where fountains used to play. On one side is the elephant path. There is a high archway at the top to let them go in but, sadly, there is only one elephant now.'

'Oh dear! I'll never get up,' moaned Mrs Moaner.

'You will, because on the other side there is a smooth path between the ramps. It was for the court ladies' light rickshaws, which needed two men each, one to pull, the other to push behind. The rickshaws are still there – they are inlaid with mother-of-pearl.'

'I've never ridden in a rickshaw.' Mrs Moaner was beginning to sound mollified.

'The banquet will have Indian and European food, drinks and wine, and afterwards we go up to the pavilion for coffee. It really is an enchantment – so high it seems to be in the sky, to which it is open. Its walls are ivory, carved and latticed, its floor has marble squares with silk-covered couches along the walls for the watchers of the entertainments given there almost every night.

'We shall see a display of classical Indian dancing, the famous Bharata Natyam on which the Maharajah doted. Before it begins, Artemis will explain it to you, as she does so well. I know you have had a long morning, but I hope you will all come. It really shouldn't be missed, so please be ready at five. Thank you.'

After lunch, when they were having coffee on the veranda, Artemis came up to Michael and, linking arms with him, drew him apart. 'Michael, why don't you come?'

'I thought you hated me.'

'That was what my mother used to call "temporary temper". Please come.'

'I shouldn't – I've got work to do – but it sounds so tempting.'

'Then be tempted. Auntie Sanni says Inspector Dutta is not coming back until late. I purposely asked her and there is nothing you can do until he comes. Samuel says you have been working hard all morning. Besides... Oh, Michael, I have been back and forth on the coach listening to the chatter, never getting away from the questions, and I have to give quite an important talk tonight. I really do need time to think. Wouldn't you drive me? If you will, we needn't go to the city. Shall we say four o'clock? And you can see the Gul Mahal before the others come. It really is magical.'

'I think I'm ready for a little magic,' said Michael.

The way led first along the seashore then left the feathery trees and dunes for the hard sand and palms that ended in a road through the foothills, planted with what Michael thought was coffee. Soon the hills grew steep.

'Have you ever been to Konakpur?' asked Artemis.

'Nowhere near this coast. We were in Peshawar at Pindi.'

Artemis was wearing a short sleeveless dress, brilliant orange – for this occasion she was out of her uniform – but her hair was still up in a knob with a matching chiffon scarf; its ends fluttered in the breeze from the car window. Michael was in rhythm with it and he began to sing: *'Take a pair of sparkling eyes, / hidden ever and anon, in a beautiful eclipse ...'* The light rollicking tune filled the car.

'Oh, Michael, I do so like being with you.'

'And I love being with you.'

He stopped the car, turned, put his arm round her and kissed her. This time she did not pull away but returned the kiss. Her lips were warm and he found her tongue between the pretty little teeth until, 'Michael, we must get on.'

As they drove, Artemis said, 'To me Konakpur is the most beautiful of any Indian city I know. They call it the Rose City. You'll see why.'

Now they began to pass hamlets and villages where there were only a few stone houses or modern bungalows; small bazaars, almost empty now – the people were still in the fields – then, rounding a corner, looked down on the town. Set in a valley with a lake, it still had its walls, built of the pinkish local stone. 'Seventeenth century,' said Artemis. 'One of the great maharajahs built it, laying it out like a map, which is why its streets and boulevards are so wide, with the narrow streets of carved house fronts between. He must have been fabulously rich, and had a great eye for beauty. At sunset I have seen the stone turn to rose, especially the Gul Mahal.'

They stopped at a wide platform at the foot of the three steep flights of steps, built of darker, almost red, blocks of stone; the parallel elephant and rickshaw paths were smooth to the palace walls high above, crowned with what Michael guessed was the pavilion Professor Ellen had described.

He stood gazing until Artemis said, 'I want you to meet a friend of mine. It's partly why I brought you.' Turning, she made a call towards a building like a barn beside the platform, a call that sounded as if it were blown through a conch: ulla, ullalah, ullahh. There were immediate commands and the sound of a soft heavy tread, tread, tread, until an elephant appeared. Even for an elephant he was a giant, his grey wrinkled skin glinting in the late-afternoon sun, the big tusks banded with gold, the huge ears gently flapping so that the spotted undersides showed as his great feet moved steadily forward. Michael had forgotten how large an elephant's toenails were. Don't elephants' eyes see multiple aspects? thought Michael. These eyes, surprisingly small, black and bright, were looking expectant.

The elephant had a howdah on his back, with red padded seats and curtains, rather frayed, and on his neck sat a wizened little man who, as they neared Artemis, prodded the great forehead with his *ankus*. 'Salaam,' but the elephant had already salaamed, raising his trunk to his forehead three times in joy.

'This is Natram, the friend I told you about. Natram means precious jewel,' said Artemis, 'and Mahdhoo is his mahout and servant, though Mahdhoo drives him and Natram obeys. Mahdhoo looks after him, day and night,' and she said to the elephant, who was shifting his feet, 'Just have patience,' as she patted his trunk. Then she went back to the car, opened the boot and took out a whole stem of bananas. She stood breaking them off, three at a time, peeling them, then putting them into the pink-nozzled trunk, held out before Natram stuffed them into his mouth, pink too. When the last of the bananas had disappeared, she said, 'You see why I feel utterly safe with them when I go into the hills. I only have to send a message and Mahdhoo meets me.'

'*Khachitamuya*,' said Mahdhoo. 'Yes, indeed.'

'Will they take us up?' asked Michael. 'It's years since I've ridden on an elephant.'

'Of course. That's why I called them. If I hadn't, neither of them would forgive me. Come. He'll kneel and we'll get up on to the howdah.' Then Artemis stopped, her hand clapped to her mouth in dismay. 'Michael,' she wailed, 'I've forgotten my notes.'

'Notes?'

'I told you, I've got to give a talk tonight.'

'Couldn't you improvise?'

'You don't understand. It's on Bharata Natyam, which is perhaps the highest of India's four classical dance styles, terribly difficult to explain to an audience whose idea of Indian dancing is the *nautch* girl, almost akin to a belly dancer and who can usually be had for money. A Bharata Natyam dancer is the echo of the *asparas*, or celestial dancers of heaven, who dance for the gods. You'll see. Before each begins she makes a deep obeisance to the god, and never turns her back on him. More than that, every least movement has a meaning –

the hand movements, for instance, have names like Lotus Bud, Deer's Head, Swan's Neck.'

'Who is to know if you make a mistake?'

'The dancers would know and it would be blasphemy. They would never dance for us again. They have been through years and years of strict training and most of them speak English. I must have the notes. If you would lend me your car I'll whiz back and fetch them and still be in plenty of time. You go up on Natram and explore. I don't want you to miss the banquet.'

'I'm coming with you,' said Michael.

As they drew up under Patna Hall's portico, Artemis had the car door open and was out. 'I'll try not to be too long but I must make sure I have everything. Perhaps twenty minutes.'

'I'll wait,' said Michael.

It was peaceful under the portico. Patna Hall seemed silent. I expect they're changing for dinner, he thought. The servants will be having theirs and Kanu is at the bar. The hall was empty. Thambi's lodge was lit inside but he himself had gone with the party, chiefly to help pull the rickshaws up the hill. In the village beyond the palm trees, where points of lantern light had appeared, smoke was going up from cooking fires for the evening meal.

Outside, dust was rising from the paths as the last of the cattle were driven home. 'Cow-dust time', he remembered from his boyhood.

He was peaceful and filled with a happiness that no one, not Auntie Sanni, not even himself, could gainsay, and he began quietly to hum.

'I know where I am going,' but instead of 'Dear knows who I'll marry', he hummed, 'I know where I'm going and I do know who I'll marry. I've found her.' But the minutes were ticking away. Twenty? More like forty.

When Artemis appeared she seemed out of breath. 'I'm sorry, but there were bits I had to reread. Oh, Michael, you're so patient – and hungry too by now, I'm sure. I hope you don't miss the banquet.'

'I'll drive like the wind.'

Artemis settled herself and said, 'In Hindi, to go fast in a car is called *howa khana*, which means "to eat the air". You eat the air but I think I'll go to sleep.'

She lay back and closed her eyes but he knew she was not asleep. Is she fending me off? he thought, in a moment's anxiety, but as if in answer, she smiled and patted his knee.

When he pulled up on the platform, Natram and Mahdhoo were waiting, ready to take them up.

Although he was voraciously hungry, Michael tasted little of the banquet. Innumerable dishes were offered to him: small balls of lamb in an apricot coating, koftas, tandoori chicken, fish, every sort of rice, there was even a side of beef, all on platters that were silver, though they were more than a little stained. There were knives and forks but some of the young or more enthusiastic, like Marcia Barclay, ate with their fingers – to Eric's disgust. After the main course, shallow silver bowls filled with rose water were passed for the guests to wash their fingers. Then came heaped stands of Indian sweets: the edible silver paper on the *sandesh* toffee glittered, and there were *jilipis*, rings of spun sugar dripping with honey, and sliced fresh fruit. Wine was served, and sherbet, orange juice, whisky, yet Mrs Moaner was heard saying loudly, 'It's all very well but the Indians have no standards – tarnished silver, chipped plates.' Michael, who prided himself on assessing everything with a cool head, ate and drank as if he were in a dream.

Afterwards when everyone had finished, they trooped up a marble staircase, led by Professor Ellen, for coffee and liqueurs in the pavilion, which was lit only by torches. A wide space was left in the centre but all round were divans and daybeds on which the guests could recline as they watched. 'It's not always like this,' Professor Ellen told them. She was astute enough to make the point for her tours. 'This is only for us. I think you must agree we are privileged.'

There was a chorus of 'Yes.'

The musicians were already seated on a carpet, all dressed alike in white silk tunics and flowing *dhotis*: a *tabla* drum player with two drums, a flautist with a silver flute, two sitars and, as a concession to a Western audience, a violin.

When everyone was seated, coffee and liqueurs over, Artemis stood up, and the excited chatter fell to a murmur as a single dancer came in, an older woman, beautiful in her brilliant gauze silks, her sari looped up into a pleated fan from her waist to her ankles on which she wore circlets of golden bells that tinkled as she moved. The short bodice was of silk showing her midriff bare. She had many necklaces, earrings and flowers bunched close in her hair, with a pendant on her forehead above her *tika* mark of red henna. She wore only one bangle, however, on each upper arm, because her hands had to be free; they were so supple that they seemed almost to double straight backwards and forwards as she illustrated in movement everything Artemis described, beginning with the deep obeisance to her god. She did not smile but spoke with her eyes.

As Michael knew already, Artemis had a way of making the most technical lecture into a talk that was vividly alive but tonight she seemed incandescent, perhaps catching it from the dancers. And I have found her, Michael marvelled in his deepest heart.

As the first dancer reached her finale the others came in, taking up their positions; the musicians went straight into the long elaborately exquisite dance. When it ended, the dancers repeating their obeisance, the applause was deafening. Everyone seemed lit with enthusiasm. This night will never die, thought Michael.

It was not over yet. When the dancing was finished, and the applause had petered out, cold drinks were served and, for those who wanted it, whisky. The dancers had disappeared. Professor Ellen announced that the coach was ready. Several ladies took advantage of the rickshaws – 'I wish I could,' said Eric Barclay, as he stumbled down the steep steps. Mrs Moaner had fallen asleep, and was carried down tenderly in a rickshaw by Thambi and the palace servants. Last to go was Professor Ellen.

'I'll follow you with Michael,' said Artemis.

They stayed in the pavilion where the torches had

been doused so that the court was lit only by starlight. Although corners were dark, the marble floor glimmered and the ivory lattices were slanted with light. 'Why do stars seem bigger in India than at home?' asked Artemis, and put her arms round his neck. She moved her cheek against his; it was as hot as if she had a fever. She left him, went to a corner and drew back a heavy silk curtain to show a canopied room with a wide divan, covered in brocade. 'This is where the Maharajah used to end his entertainments, picking anyone he fancied that night. Do you fancy me, Michael?'

For answer Michael caught and held her, and carried her to the divan.

'Come, my Maharajah.'

It was like fire, rockets. 'Oh, Michael. Again.'

They were late reaching home. The watchman of the Gul Mahal, plainly accustomed to this, had left them as long as he could. Then, 'Sahib, Memsahib' – Artemis had been elevated to Mem – 'we must lock up or police come. Very sorry but must.' As he had hoped, Michael gave him a mighty tip.

Natram and Mahdhoo had not waited but Michael

and Artemis made their way down, she dancing on every ramp, Michael catching her to kiss her again. The starlight gave them just enough light to see. 'I expect everyone else will be asleep,' Artemis said in the car, as they came near to Patna Hall.

'Well, we don't want anyone else,' said Michael. Then, 'Hush! What's this?'

Thambi's lodge, the hall and portico, the servants' quarters were lit, as was the village where a crowd of people was standing. A drum was beating a long, steady sound. 'Something's happened.' As Michael pulled up under the portico, opened the door and got out, Samuel, who evidently had waited up, came to meet them. His face was grave. 'Sahib, thank God you come. Missy Sahib, be brave. Veeranna, he dead.'

'Veeranna!' Artemis's cry rang through the hall. She had gone white.

'But how?' Michael, stunned, could hardly speak.

'Evening time. A woman passing heard scream, noises, a commotion, and ran to fetch her husband. Veeranna on floor, twisting, doubling up and retch, retch, retch. Husband try to hold him but Veeranna too strong. Woman run for village barber.'

'Barber?'

'In villages no doctors so barbers are only medicine men. He try everything. No use. Veeranna, he die. Barber say poison.'

'Poison!' Artemis screamed. 'Michael, hold me! Hold me tight.' Michael was already holding her, trying to stop the shaking, stem the screams between the dry sobs, no tears, but Hannah came down the stairs.

'Now, now,' said Hannah. 'That enough.' She took Artemis from Michael, who stood helpless. 'It shock, Sahib,' Hannah told him, 'and maybe too much exciting today. You tired out, *baba*. Hannah put you to bed. I just put Miss Sanni to bed,' she told Michael over Artemis's head. 'Now, *baba*, come with Hannah.'

To Michael's surprise, Artemis went.

Samuel looked after them. 'Missy Sahib, she friend of all the village, most of all Veeranna. I think all of us in shock, Michael Sahib.'

'Yes. What did they do when he died?'

'They send for Miss Sanni – always they send for Miss Sanni – but it was Colonel McIndoe Sahib who came. He turn everyone out of the workshop and made them keep distance. He find Inspector Dutta by telephone, who say he come quickly as he can. Meanwhile no one must go in or touch anything. Colonel put Thambi – he just back on the coach – in front, village headman behind, young policeman to patrol. People must go back to their homes.'

'If they will,' said Michael.

'I think they watch,' Samuel agreed. Michael turned away from the portico steps. 'Sahib, they let no one in.'

'I won't go near. I only want to see what is happening now.'

As he came close the drumbeat sounded louder, and he was right: the crowd of men was still standing under the trees; women were wailing in their houses. When he saw Michael, Thambi, who had been sitting on his haunches, stood up. 'It's all right, Thambi, I know I mustn't go in. I just came to see how things were.'

Thambi averted his head so as not to show Michael his grief. 'Sahib very good. Good night.'

'Not a good night now. This is bad,' said Michael. A great weariness was overtaking him as he went back.

'Samuel, is Missy Sahib in bed?' he managed to ask.

'Hannah say, soon as she lie down she asleep, tired out.'

'Me too.' Michael tottered as he spoke. 'I'm sorry to desert you but I think I'll have to go to bed.' He could hardly reach the stairs and had to hold on to the banisters, but Samuel was beside him and steered him to his room.

He fell on his bed and was only just aware of Samuel taking off his shoes and covering him with a blanket before he slept.

'Michael! Michael, wake up.' It was a fierce whisper in his ear, and someone was shaking him firmly. 'Wake up!'

'But I've only just gone to sleep.'

'It's morning.'

He sat up, trying to fight off layers of sleep. 'It's dark.'

He was about to turn over, back into sleep again, when he realized it was Artemis. 'Artemis. What's happening?'

'Ssh!' She pulled off the blanket. 'Thank God you're dressed. Find your shoes and come on. There's something I want to show you.'

'Now? It's still dark.'

'Not outside. It's dawn. Hurry, before anyone is up.'

Still half asleep, he put on his shoes, smoothed his rumpled clothes, ran a comb through his hair.

'Never mind that. We need to go before anyone's awake, and it's quite a way.'

But Michael had recovered his senses. 'I can't be long. I have to see Inspector Dutta as soon as he comes.'

'There's plenty of time to do that. Come on.'

At the foot of the stairs he turned towards the portico

but she stopped him. 'Not that way. We'll go along the beach – then the village won't see us.'

'Us?'

'You and me. Natram and Mahdhoo.'

'They're here!'

'I ordered them. You see, I planned this yesterday.'

They went through the garden, still wet with dew – soon the gardeners would be flailing the lawns with long bamboo rods to stop the sun scorching the wet grass – and, as Artemis and Michael came on to the beach, there beside the high diving board, the great shape of Natram stood waiting and ready.

Mahdhoo and Natram salaamed, then the elephant knelt down. There was no howdah, only a pad fastened with ropes. Mahdhoo stretched down to give Artemis a hand but she was so lithe that she swung herself up easily. Michael was more clumsy: he put his foot against Natram's side to lever himself up on a rope, and slipped back. Mahdhoo spoke. Natram turned his head and his trunk came round: Michael felt its enormous strength as he was lifted up so that he could scramble on to the pad. Artemis laughed. 'Sometimes Natram just picks me up and puts me on his back.'

Natram stood up and began to walk along the beach.

It was beginning to be light, with the sky brightening over the sea, the surf in the waves shining white. Natram walked through the ripples, which he seemed to like, spraying his legs as he went. Do elephants get footsore, Michael wondered. He was surprised, too, at how fast Natram went with a half-rolling, half-swaying gait. It almost lulled him to sleep again.

As soon as they were far enough out of the village, Mahdhoo turned Natram inland. They went through a patch of jungle towards the hills. Natram was a well-trained elephant: if a branch overhung their way, at a command from Mahdhoo, his trunk came up to break it off, in case it hit his passengers. When they came out from the trees on to a swampy patch he tested the ground with a cautious foot before he would venture. Presently they began to climb into the cooler air of the hills. Again, Michael would have gone to sleep but he was aware of Artemis, sitting upright. She seemed oddly tense, her face, in the growing dawn light, resolute and stern.

'Artemis?'

'Ssh.'

'But where are you taking me?'

'You'll see – and see why.'

*

'It is something that, of us all, only Auntie Sanni and I know.'

Natram had begun to go downwards instead of climbing and there, in a cleft of the hills, inset so that it looked across higher hills to a vista of the sea, was a little temple. As the elephant went steadily down an old path and they came nearer, Michael saw that it was walled with small bricks, perhaps made of natural earth, baked in the sun; in the growing light they were already touched with faint gold. The roof had a dome of tiles that matched, and there was a small portico of stone in which hung a bell. 'No one but I has rung it for years. No one comes here now, not even a priest,' said Artemis.

Natram had knelt to let them get down and Mahdhoo took from the pad a bundle of sugar cane. 'Natram's breakfast,' said Artemis. 'I wish I could have brought tea for us but I didn't want anyone to see us go.'

'*Kachiyundu*, stay,' Mahdhoo told Natram, as he stood up.

'Mahdhoo loves this temple,' said Artemis. 'Come and look.'

The courtyard was small, and had in its centre a statue of a bull carved from local stone. It stood looking into the temple, and its eyes, as if in awe, were strangely eloquent. 'He seems to see something there,' said Michael.

'He does,' and Artemis explained, 'He is Nandi, Shiva's emblem. Hindu gods love their animal representatives, and as Shiva is new life, women pray to Nandi for a son.'

'Would you like a son, Artemis?'

'If it could be with the person I love. Yes.'

He would have taken her in his arms and kissed her but she said, 'No, Michael, not here,' and she told him, 'Auntie Sanni, when she was younger, used to come here to make her *puja* and so do I.'

'To Shiva?'

'Shiva and God.'

Artemis swung the tasselled bell, sending its deep note far over the hills. 'Go in, Michael.'

The temple was almost bare: there was only a low shelf with a tray holding *dipas* – little lamps of clay shaped like a leaf – but there was no oil in them, no tiny floating wick. On the floor was a small fireplace made of bricks and full of cold ash; by it a poker and a pair of bellows were covered with dust. Then Michael saw a small inner door. 'What's in there?'

'Nothing,' said Artemis, 'which is why it is so sacred.

There is room only for the god and you, and if you go in you have to lose yourself and find Him. If you take as much as a notebook in, you cut yourself off. And you don't kneel or pray, you simply stand and take *darshan*, which means "look". Hindus believe that if you look for long enough, something will come deep into you from what you look at. This little room is called the womb-house because, as only God is there, with His power of life, you can, as it were, be born again.'

'Even me, an outsider?'

'There are no outsiders here.'

'Come in with me.'

'I don't go in. I have never particularly wanted to be alone with God,' and she said, 'Michael, come outside now because I must tell you why I brought you here.' Outside, sitting on the grass, she said, 'When you win your case against Cromartie, and I'm sure you will, will you use your influence and ask the Indian Government to do what Auntie Sanni and I so much want them to do, which is to let the Shiva come home here, and the temple be made fit for him?'

'I wish I could.' At that moment he truly did. 'But, darling, I have no influence.'

'I was afraid you would say that. Oh, well. It will

probably be put into a museum. A pity, when you seemed to understand so well,' and she was gone, back into the courtyard where she stood, looking at the far line of sea showing in the cleft; one hand was stroking the little Nandi bull and she seemed to be struggling against tears.

Michael had followed her with determined steps. Now he took her by the shoulders and turned her to face him. 'Artemis. You didn't bring me here simply to see the temple and talk about Auntie Sanni.' He gave her a gentle shake and felt her trembling. 'There's something else, isn't there? You brought me here because?'

It came with a rush. 'I thought it was a good place to say goodbye.'

'*Goodbye!*'

'Yes, I'm leaving.'

'*Leaving?*' He was dazed.

'Yes, and I want to thank you. It has been lovely, Michael. For me it was love for the first time in my life.' Her eyes were lit to an extraordinary blue as she said, 'Perhaps the first time in yours too?'

'Yes.' He tightened his arms.

'But I have done all I had to do here.' Artemis broke away. 'Ellen understands. I have to go.'

'Go where?'

'I don't know yet. Anywhere but here.'

It sounded so forlorn that he wanted to hold her close again but he felt he had to keep to practical things.

'When?'

'Now. Today. As soon as we get back.'

'And where are you going?'

'I don't know. Anywhere. Just go.'

'You're not.' Michael took her even more firmly into his arms. 'When you leave here, you leave with me.'

'With *you*? Today?'

'If you insist.'

'I must.'

'Then there's no point in my staying here, is there?' asked Michael.

'Inspector Dutta?'

'With poor Veeranna dead?'

'Don't.' She hid her face.

'I have to. Inspector Dutta is not going to get any further. He can't find out any more from Sri Satya Narayana. The Government will have to accept that the case must be a straightforward battle as to who gets the Shiva. I can deal with that in London better than here. Say goodbye to Nandi because we must go.'

'If only we could.'

'We can. I'll just have to see Inspector Dutta and, of course, Auntie Sanni. You pack. We'll drive to the airport – it only takes half an hour – catch the one o'clock flight to Calcutta. I'll have to drop the car off. In Calcutta, madam, I'm going to buy you a ring – an engagement ring, Artemis. We'll catch the night flight home to London and as soon as possible we'll be married and I'll never let you out of my sight again.' He stood up, 'Mahdhoo! Mahdhoo! Bring Natram. Be quick.'

Natram brought them back the way they had come and put them down on the beach, but when Michael turned towards the garden, Artemis caught his hand. 'I feel so dirty. Let's have a swim before anyone comes down.'

'Without Thambi?'

'I'll take care of you,' she teased, 'or you can stay in the shallows. We can go in just as we are – there's no one to see.' But there was. Samuel was hastening down the garden. At the same moment, Auntie Sanni appeared on the veranda, Professor Ellen beside her. Ellen looking after her ewe lamb to the last, thought Michael, but she was not smiling, neither did Auntie Sanni wave and, as

Samuel with Thambi came nearer, he saw consternation on their faces.

'Missy Sahib,' Samuel said. 'Inspector Dutta, he want to see you in his office soon as you come in. At once.'

For a moment Artemis did not move.

'Missy Sahib.'

Then Artemis dropped Michael's hand and stood clear. 'If Inspector Dutta wants me, tell him I am here in the garden,' and when Samuel had gone, 'Michael, please stay. I think I'm going to need you.'

Unusually indulgent, the Inspector came. 'Well, I wanted a full story and I thought she would tell it better here,' he told Michael. He brought his two policemen – the sergeant with his notebook. They stood at a respectful distance. 'Miss Knox, you went last night with your group to Konakpur and the Gul Mahal?'

'I didn't go with the group. Mr Dean kindly drove me.'

'I gather it is an important evening in your itinerary so it was necessary you should be there. Why did you come back?'

'I had forgotten my notes. I was to give a talk on Indian classical dancing and had to have them.'

'Is that really why?'

'I've told you. I had forgotten my notes.'

'Very convenient.'

'*In*convenient,' Artemis corrected him, 'but Mr Dean kindly came with me and drove like the wind.'

'Yet you found time to go to the village.'

'The village? Of course I didn't go to the village. Ask Mr Dean. He'll tell you. He was with me all the time.'

'All the time?'

'Yes. Weren't you, Michael?' As she looked at him her eyes held not only a plea but a challenge that said as clearly as if they had spoken, 'I thought you loved me. Well, show it. Show it now.'

"*All* the time, Mr Dean?"

The Inspector was like a hound on the scent and Michael was forced to say, 'Except when you went upstairs to get your notes.'

'Coward,' said Artemis's eyes, but aloud she said, 'I was only a few minutes.'

'How long is a few minutes? Ten? Fifteen? Twenty? Half an hour? Mr Dean?'

'Perhaps half an hour.'

'I had to check the notes through, be sure I had them all.'

'But you have just said—'

'Listen, Hem,' Michael interrupted, 'I don't know what the hell is in your mind but stop heckling. I was waiting in the car under the portico the whole time. The hall was lit and I could see right into it to the stairs. If Artemis had come down before she got the notes I should have seen her.'

'Patna Hall has a back staircase,' said Inspector Dutta.

'That doesn't mean I use it.'

'No? Then if Mr Dean did not see you how is it that someone else did?'

'But there was no one about.' Always quick as mercury, Artemis realized she had betrayed herself.

'No? Shyama, I think, has no need to tell lies.'

'Shyama?'

'Remember Thambi had gone on the coach to help at the Gul Mahal with the ladies' rickshaws. You were wearing a scarlet coat and a headscarf but she knew you and was surprised to see you and, being curious, followed when you went, she says, to Veeranna's house.'

'It's her word against mine.'

'Shyama, as I think I told you, does not tell lies, and she is discreet. She did not tell anyone what she had seen until Thambi came home.'

'I can explain.'

'Good. There will have to be more than a little explanation. Can you, for instance, explain why, when you were in such a hurry, you found time to go and see Veeranna? Shyama says you were having a drink together.'

'So? Veeranna loves whisky but can only afford palm-tree toddy so I often take him a bottle and we have a drink together.'

'But not, I think, *that* drink. Tell me what this was doing hidden in Veeranna's house. Isn't it part of the equipment of the film unit you brought over two years ago, a small tripod?'

'Yes, to do with the lights. They call it baby spider's legs. Oh, Veeranna, you promised you would sell it. Poor, stupid Veeranna.' Holding herself tightly, Artemis was rocking backwards and forwards in an agony of grief.

'Miss Knox,' said Inspector Dutta firmly, 'I think the time has come for you to tell me what you have been planning and doing at Patna Hall these last – it seems – three or four years, but I must warn you that everything you say will be taken down.' The sergeant, with his notebook, came nearer. 'Then I will ask you to read it through and sign it.'

'No need,' said Artemis. She was calm now. 'I won't tell *you*,' she was still scornful, 'but I want to tell Michael,

Professor Ellen and Auntie Sanni, although I'm sure Auntie Sanni knows, and tell Samuel, Hannah and Thambi – all the people who matter. I should very much like to tell them. Then I should feel clean, and you,' she flung at the Inspector, 'can listen and take down anything you choose, but here in the garden. None of your offices. Michael, would you call everyone?'

When they came she said, as if she was a hostess in her own drawing room, 'I have to begin at the beginning so this may take a long time. Wouldn't you like to sit down?' Auntie Sanni sat on the low wall that edged the lawn. The rest stood tense.

'Up to now, I have been very clever and ambitious.' Artemis's look was on Michael. 'Almost up to now, when it's too late. That's ironic, isn't it?' She gave a hard little laugh. No one else laughed.

'I was an only child, which is just as well for everyone.' She was standing facing them, wearing the orange dress she had worn last night, crumpled now. Her hair had come down, dishevelled, and she had a smudge on one cheek, but to Michael she had never seemed more beautiful. 'My father was an archaeologist, quite well known. Professor Arnold Knox.'

'Brilliant,' said Professor Ellen, 'and so good-looking.

I knew him quite well but not that he had a wife and child.'

'Nor did he most of the time. You didn't know him as we knew him, my mother and I. When I think of the contrast between his life and ours, I boil with rage. He was usually away on one of his digs, making quite spectacular discoveries – I have some of that gift. He spent all he had on himself. It was Mum and her ordinary job who kept us going in our miserable little house. "He must have somewhere to go when he needs us," she used to say. He never sent any money and she, of course, never took her difficulties to the social services.'

'Why not?' asked the Inspector.

'Because she loved him. I hated him – and a child's hatred is a terrible thing – though in a way, I suppose, I too was under his spell, so I should be grateful. He did at least call me Artemis, which was outside her sphere. Hers was a very little sphere, but, oh, how faithful and forgiving. He was cruel. I expect I got that from him. Yes, I'm cruel too. I see now that she maddened him. If only, I used to think, she would round on him just once! When I was about ten, after he had hit her – oh, yes, he used to beat her up and then sit covering his eyes in remorse, he always had remorse until next time – I got a chair and hit him over the head with it as hard as I could. After that he began to show an interest, even pride, in me, but all the same I made a vow – and it wasn't a childish one – that I would never let a man be in a position where he could treat me like that, and never trust one. Until I met you, Michael. But it's better not to talk about that now.'

After a moment, she went on, 'My mother was an outstandingly pretty girl – otherwise he wouldn't have married her – and I inherited their looks. I determined, again not childishly, to make myself fit for what I meant to do. I went in for athletics, running – I won races and was particularly good at swimming. They said I was a natural – I have silver cups and shields but they were only a means to an end. Mum helped. She never let me go out to work as I demanded – it had to be school, the university. Luckily I got grants – but we were always poor, going without things, hardly able to buy what we needed. All the same, she was proud of me. I got a first in archaeology, the only subject we knew anything about, yet she wanted to send me to drama school, knowing I had a secret ambition to be an actress.'

'You would have made a very good one,' said Professor Ellen bitterly.

'Oh, Ellen, I'm so sorry, I truly am. Soon, there was no question of my being an actress. My mum,' her voice quivered, 'was worn down. Being an actress was too uncertain: I had to earn a salary. But luck came my way – I believe in luck if you give it plenty of help. I gained a post. There were twenty other applicants but I got it. I used my father's name as a footstool and perhaps that helped. The post was as a research assistant in the Oriental Antiquities department of the British Museum, which I knew well. In fact, it was there that I saw my first Shiva Nataraja – they have a fine one. The keeper, Sir Richard Crewe, said he noticed me, a student, standing there gazing at it. Maybe it was that which made him take me.

'He was extraordinarily kind, taught me from his own wide knowledge, put books my way and, more importantly, believed in me. It was he who first told me I ought to go to India. I couldn't because my mother was so ill. Then she died – just when I could give her a little comfort and joy.' Again Artemis was silent, biting her lip. 'One day I saw an article on Professor Ellen's tours. I showed it to Sir Richard. "It sounds the very thing," he said. "South India. That's the cradle of art. By all means go. I'll try to get you a grant," and he gave such a glowing testimonial of me to Ellen that she offered me the trip free of charge if I would act as her assistant. You see, it all began to fit in.'

'I trusted you,' said Professor Ellen.

'I know you did. Sir Richard was pleased. He said, "It will be of great help to you in your career." He didn't know that all the time I wasn't aiming at museums, no matter how prestigious, but, to me, the far more interesting and lucrative world of buying and selling. He unwittingly helped me in that way too. "I go to India whenever I can," he told me, "and send out my spies," but they looked in temples, burial grounds, far villages. They never thought of looking in Auntie Sanni's drawing room where I found the little Shiva Nataraja, alone, unprotected and accessible.'

'And I told you how valuable it was,' mourned Professor Ellen. 'God forgive me.'

'It still needed three years. I had to think how to take the statue, make its replica and, more difficult still, how to smuggle it out of India. It would have been easy to lift it, but with Ellen there, a hue and cry would have been immediate. Every way out would be watched, airports, railways, docks, ships. There had to be another way. Anyway, I didn't waste that first trip. I hired a car and went exploring. I found quite a few small antiques – bowls and vases, an ancient cooking spoon, a ninth-century amulet that Sir Richard bought. "You do have an eye!" he said. I went to the Gul Mahal and met Natram and Mahdhoo. I learned some Telegu. I can have infinite patience when I want something badly enough, like a cat waiting for a bird. Yet I think I must have been as blind as you were, Inspector. With all my explorations I had never explored our village. Now I began to make friends here – real friends. Then, when I went to visit Veeranna, I found the solution. Like you, Michael, I saw at once what an artist he is – was,' she corrected herself, and she told the Inspector, 'Unlike you, it took Michael to see that gleam of resentment in Veeranna's eyes. Oh, Michael!'

'Never mind Michael. Go on.'

'Veeranna's father, grandfather, great-grandfather had all been potters and image-makers so it was in his blood and I guessed he could copy anything exactly, and, given the means, could do it in metal. Somehow I would find the means but I still had to go step by step. First I had to get his trust and liking.'

'And how did you do that – you who can do everything?'

'All too easily. Veeranna loved whisky but could not afford it so I got him some. He was ambitious and knew he could work in metal if he were trained. I told him I would arrange it because he had been chosen by Shiva himself to do a great work. He positively shone.'

'Poor, unfortunate Veeranna.' Professor Ellen was full of pity but Artemis disregarded her.

'I still had to take it step by step but they were firm steps. I knew Sri Satya Narayana long before you heard of him. While I was at the British Museum I had written letters to him from Sir Richard and I went to see him. I had hoped he would tell me if there was a potter or sculptor in the district, but now there was Veeranna. I wrote anonymously to Sri Satya Narayana, as if from a college of art centred in Delhi, asking if he would take Veeranna – under another name, of course – as a pupil and teach him the age-old *cire perdu* method on six-week courses, three times a year, and offering what I knew was an exorbitant fee. Then I sent the money in cash and with it Veeranna, who called himself Gopal. I paid his air fares, and it all went as I planned. Veeranna told me that Sri Narayana had told him that he was the most promising pupil he had ever had. Veeranna did three courses with him before the old man died. Then he worked at home, secretly in that little room off the big one where he hid the Shiva. You will remember I was to take it to Sri Narayana for rescue treatment but I took it instead to Veeranna – just as well because Sri Narayana died.

'Veeranna had the Shiva for about four months,

working on the copy. I provided materials, wax, clay, another kiln, tools. The villagers were so used to him drying his images in the shade that they never noticed that this one was different, and over and over again I told him that if he let out a word Shiva would punish him. I also had to manipulate you, Ellen.'

'*Me!*' Professor Ellen was indignant.

'Yes. Talk you into telling Auntie Sanni the Shiva needed treatment for salt and you got her to let me take it supposedly to Sri Narayana when I went to Kashmir for the summer and pick it up four months later and bring it home. I had calculated that that was the time Veeranna would need.

'Then I, with Auntie Sanni and the household, put the Nataraja back in its niche. Only it was not the real Nataraja. That was securely hidden behind the rafters of Veeranna's house. The niche had been made ready with flowers and lights as all the household came to worship. You know already that it was Ellen who eventually discovered the fake. What you don't know is what I had to do next.

'I had been perplexed, because when I had the Shiva how could I smuggle it out? Then I hit on the idea of the film unit, and engaged the two men to do a short film of the caves. I had worked with them before and knew that among their lighting equipment was a small cylinder made of black fibreboard that held the baby legs tripod, which would just fit the Nataraja. Late on the night before we left, when the crew had packed and put all the equipment ready in the hall, Veeranna and I removed the baby legs – he promised he would sell them – and put the Nataraja, well wrapped in soft rags and paper, into the cylinder, sealed it and put it back, because if you want to smuggle anything through an airport, the baggage of a tour or film unit is almost always untouched, especially if there is someone there in authority. As you were, Ellen.'

'You mean *I* brought the Shiva out!' Professor Ellen sounded faint.

'You certainly did. All I had to do in New York was quietly take the cylinder and get in a taxi as fast as I could. It was clever, wasn't it?'

'You're a devil.'

'I agree. There was one thing more I had to do, perhaps more cruel than anything else. On our last night I had to take away everything I had given Veeranna for making the Nataraja – tools, materials, wax. I couldn't risk anyone finding them. I promised him I would send him money so that he could buy what he needed gradually, which would have been believable, but I shall never forget his look of agony as he helped me pack it all into the car to the last scrap of wax or shredded clay.'

'You forgot about the baby legs.'

'I didn't know about them. First thing in the morning I drove to our little sea port, hired a boat and dumped the rest of the tools far out to sea. I didn't take Veeranna with me – he might have tried to retrieve them. No one will ever find them. There, that's all.'

'By no means all.' Inspector Dutta came nearer. 'Miss Knox, I put it to you that yesterday evening you came back here from the Gul Mahal, not to fetch your notes but to visit the potter, Veeranna.'

'Of course, and to have a drink with him. As I have said before.'

'But this was a very different drink.'

'Yes.'

'Now, Miss Knox—'

But Michael could bear no more. 'Artemis. Why, oh, why, did you come back to Patna Hall? You were safely in New York.'

'Yes, but I couldn't keep away. It was like a call. You see, it wasn't finished.'

'You had the Shiva.'

'I didn't.'

'You *didn't?*' It was like a chorus.

'No. It all turned bitter, bitter. Hasn't it ever happened to you? You set your ambition on something, plan for it, work for it and when you attain it you don't want it. In New York I kept the Nataraja hidden for weeks. I dared not look at it. At last I gave it to a good needy young dealer I knew, Narayan, on condition he didn't mention me. I didn't want money, though he tried to make me take a share. Like you, Auntie Sanni, I couldn't take money for Shiva, and Narayan sold it to Mr Cromartie.

'I thought it was finished and I could come back and it would all be the same. Instead, I found you, Inspector Dutta, and Michael. Oh, Michael. If you hadn't come with your insight, everything would have been all right, but you saw – and said you must tell Inspector Dutta. You would never have guessed on your own,' she threw at the Inspector. 'Veeranna held out against you, Michael, because he liked and trusted you, but with Inspector Dutta's "methods".' She shuddered. 'At least I saved him from that.

'Veeranna was the only one who could tell the truth. At first I thought I would tell Inspector Dutta myself. I thought that was why I had had that call. I forgot that everywhere you go you have to take yourself with you. I have never been afraid to do things, but now I was afraid of what I had done. You are quite right, Inspector, that that drink was a different one. I poisoned it and you needn't trouble yourself to find out with what, I'll tell you. It was the sap of the *kaosi* tree, quick and deadly. I should have taken it myself.'

Her eyes looked at Michael. 'You gave me a chance when you made me that wonderful offer. You don't know how wonderful it was. For a little while I let myself believe, but one mustn't tamper with the gods. It's your duty to arrest me, isn't it?'

There was silence, shock and infinite dismay. Then Inspector Dutta spoke almost reluctantly, 'Miss Knox, theft and murder are the gravest of crimes.' Artemis had taken a few steps backwards as if she recoiled. The sergeant came closer. 'My man will have taken down everything you have said. I shall ask you to sign it. Then, yes, Miss Knox, I shall arrest you.'

'If you can.' Eluding the sergeant, she had turned and was racing to the beach, running as only Artemis could.

'After her. After her!' the Inspector screamed to his men. The younger one shot away but the sergeant stopped to lay down his notebook.

Auntie Sanni, though, had risen in anticipation,

'Thambi, come back,' and she laid her hand on Michael's arm. 'No,' she forbade him. 'It's better this way. Let her go.'

Michael shook off the hand and ran, but not to the beach, only as far as its entrance, and stopped.

Artemis was already on the high diving board, wearing the usual wicker helmet – she must have snatched it up from Thambi's row. 'She not risk to be stun.' It was Thambi's voice beside him. 'She know just what she doing, Sahib,' which, at that moment, was stripping off her dress, standing erect, naked. In the full glare of the sun she held her hands high in her pose and waited.

'She judge when the waves roll back,' Thambi whispered in admiration. 'Ah!'

The dive took her far over the panting policemen's heads, far over the surging surf. They saw the head go down, then come up again, as she swam to the protecting nets, dived under them and swam on out to sea.

'There are sharks.' Professor Ellen covered her eyes.

'Please God, no,' said Auntie Sanni.

Inspector Dutta stood furious and thwarted as Thambi, who had come back from the beach, said in defiance, 'No one catch her now. She gone.'

LONDON

'Is it true, Mrs McIndoe – or may I call you Miss Sanni?' asked Sir George Fothergill, '– that you have never been away from Patna Hall, not even for a night?'

'Never,' said Auntie Sanni.

'Didn't you ever want to see the world? Meet people?'

'The world comes to us, Sir George. People, too, or they used to.'

When Mr Cromartie had dropped the case – he could not do anything else as the Nataraja had clearly been stolen – and gone back to Canada, the Government of India had decided that it would be only fair to offer it back to Auntie Sanni as Henry Bertram's granddaughter. 'We will build you a temple.'

'Please no,' said Auntie Sanni. 'We could not use a temple.' Nor would she take a penny. 'A gift is a gift,' she said. 'I only ask that it stays in this country where it belongs. There is a little temple in the hills ... '

The Government had still brought her over to London. 'We need you as we must have an official declaration of your wonderful gift of the Nataraja to India.

Mr Bhatacharya and our London lawyers will see to that, and they are arranging for you to meet all the experts at a celebratory reception in your honour.' To Michael's surprise she had accepted, though nothing would stir the Colonel. She had had an official escort on the plane but Michael had been deputed to meet her and take her to stay with Honor Wyatt.

Auntie Sanni had made few concessions for London and still wore her Mother Hubbards, but she had shoes instead of sandals and was wrapped in a large *paschmina* shawl, its fine pure wool intricately embroidered.

'Auntie Sanni,' Michael had asked her, 'is there anything you would particularly like to do or see in these three days?' She would not stay any longer.

'Shops?' suggested Honor.

'I never shop.'

'Would you come and visit my museum?' That was Sir Richard Crewe.

'Thank you, but no museums.'

'A visit to the Houses of Parliament and lunch on the terrace?' asked Mr Bhatacharya. 'The foreign secretary would be delighted.'

'No, thank you.'

'The Tower and the Crown Jewels?'

'I know jewels.'

'Then what?'

'Ordinary things. I should like to take a day just to see this city, if Michael would come with me. I suppose it would have to be by car – it is too big to walk. I should like to drive all round it, not to beauty spots or sights but everyday streets, homes, parks and especially the Thames.'

'Why the Thames?'

'It flows out to sea. That will bring me back to scale and I can go back refreshed.'

'And you can really stay only three days?'

'That is enough. Besides I have much to do at home. We are closing Patna Hall, Sir George. It has had its time.'

'Sad,' said Sir George. 'I was hoping I could come and stay with you.'

'We shall still have spare rooms for our friends and we shall still be there, the Colonel and I, Samuel our faithful butler and his wife Hannah, our housekeeper. Thambi, our lifeguard, will stay in his lodge but we shall demolish most of the main house. The sale of the land will pay for it.'

'This is where we should help,' said Mr Bhatacharya. 'At least let us give something towards the cost.'

'I can take no money for Shiva-ji.'

Honor had drawn Michael away. 'This must be very painful for you.' Michael had told her everything. 'Poor Michael, you look five years older.'

'But I feel richer not poorer. I had her.'

'And will have, for ever.'

'To the end of my life,' said Michael. 'Artemis.'

Mr Bhatacharya was still trying to persuade Auntie Sanni. 'After all, you and your grandfather sheltered the Nataraja and let him be worshipped for close on a hundred years.'

'That is why I can take nothing for him.' Then Auntie Sanni stopped. 'There is one thing I should like you to do.'

'Of course. No matter what.'

'That first offer you made to the man Cromartie. Michael told me about it. Wasn't it fifty thousand pounds?'

'Yes, and at first he thought it generous.'

'Please make it to him again – pounds not dollars.' Auntie Sanni smiled – Walter had told her the whole story of his meeting with Mr Cromartie. 'Fifty thousand pounds – not dollars. After all, he did bring the Nataraja home.'

AFTERWORD

This book is a twin; more than that, a Siamese twin, in that places, people, even phrases are taken from another of my books.

A few years ago I wrote a novel, *Coromandel Sea Change*, set in an old-fashioned hotel, Patna Hall, on South India's Coromandel coast. The sub-continent of India is shaped like a vast pear-drop and this is on its eastern side.

When the novel was half-way through, my attention was caught by a newspaper article in *The Times* of such interest to me that I immediately became aware that I had two plots for the same novel, something most uncommon and inconvenient because they were both so strong that I could not blend them. I had to choose and so went back to my original one which, I am glad to say, met with a measure of success.

In 1994 I had to spend some time in India to make the BBC's documentary programme *Bookmark* which, in the course of its journeyings, took me back to that eastern coast again. Perhaps it was this that made my second plot erupt into life.

As I have said, the book is based on truth – as can be seen by the newspaper cutting that first caught my eye.

MUSEUMS FEAR FOR THEIR TREASURES
Bronze idol must be returned to Hindu temple

By Andrew Billen

A High Court decision to return to India a twelfth century bronze idol worth more than £250,000 may have put under threat other art treasures in the possession of British collectors and museums.

Mr Justice Kennedy ruled that the Nataraja, a statue of the Hindu god Siva, belonged to a ruined temple in Tamil Nadu and said that similar ownership claims could be made.

'Many will fail but some will succeed, particularly if the criminal character of their taking could be proved,' he said. The judgement ends a legal battle that began in August 1982 when Scotland Yard seized the Nataraja as it was being examined in the British Museum.

The Nataraja had lain buried in the temple grounds for centuries when it was dug up in 1976 by a labourer while he was building a cowshed. He sold it for 200 rupees (£12).

By 1982, it had come into the ownership of a London antiques dealer who sold it for £50,000 to the Bumper Development Corporation, a Canadian company controlled by Mr Robert Bordon, an oil magnate, art collector and philanthropist.

It had been handed to a conservator at the British Museum for advice on its transportation to Canada when police intervened.

The judge ruled that while Mr Bordon's behaviour could not be faulted, the labourer from India, Mr S. Ramamoorthi, was guilty of criminal misappropriation under local law.

The case was complicated by some recondite issues, including whether a consecrated deity such as the Nataraja can be regarded as property. The Indians who wanted its return claimed its divine properties did not prevent its remaining a lump of stone.

The judge also had to decide which of the co-plaintiffs was the rightful owner. Rejecting the claims of the Union of India, the local state, a public official of the Temple and Siva Lingham, a cylindrical piece of stone representing a Hindu god, he decided the ruined temple itself was a legal entity capable of suing.

He said: 'I am satisfied that the pious intention of the twelfth century notable who gave the land and built the Pathur temple, remains in being and is personified by the temple itself, a juristic entity.'

Yesterday, a spokesman for the Indian High Commission applauded the ruling. He said: 'The judgement is very welcome encouragement for us. As a result we may be able to open the way for others of our things to come back to us.'

Both the Victoria and Albert Museum, which has a collection of 33,000 Indian paintings, sculptures and textiles, and the British Museum, which owns hundreds of religious objects from India and Asia, have followed the case keenly.

The two museums said yesterday that they did not believe that any of their exhibits were in immediate danger, but that they would need to examine the judgement in detail.

The Times,

20 February 1988

Through an experienced researcher, I managed to collect several other articles and then, by tremendous luck, was lent the documentary book of the trial, which opens with an account of a writ issued by a Canadian antique dealer against the State of Tamil Nadu in India for the return of an eleventh-century Nataraja, which he had brought to London to sell and which had been impounded by the British police.

The Union of India & Others v Bumper Development Corporation Judgement

INTRODUCTION

0.1 The issue which I have tried arises in an action brought by Bumper Corporation Ltd ('Bumper') against the Commissioner of the Metropolitan Police and two of his officers to recover an antique Indian bronze sculpture. The Police interpleaded between Bumper and the State of Tamil Nadu, who had asserted a claim to the bronze. On 10 February, 1983, by consent, Master Waldman ordered that the following question and issue should be tried:

> 'Whether the State of Tamil Nadu can prove that it has a title to the Bronze which is superior to the title of the Bumper Development Corporation to the Bronze, and that meantime all further proceedings in this action relating to such other questions or issues be stayed until the trial of the said preliminary issues or until further order.'

This account of the trial goes on for 145 closely typed pages and is unutterably tedious, confusing and complicated; so many claimants followed Bumper that the

Government of India launched a counterclaim in which the god Shiva became the plaintiff.

I decided finally to keep to the Judge's opening – its first two paragraphs – and let my story be almost completely imaginary.

APPENDIX

SHIVA NATARAJA

Shiva Nataraja – S. India AD 1100. Shiva manifests five aspects of eternal energy: creation, preservation, destruction, concealment, favour. He is seen here as Supreme God and Lord of the Dance. In his upper right hand he holds a drum representing the primordial sound of creation. The upper left hand holds a flame of destruction: indicating the overcoming of opposites in the nature of this great god echoed by wearing both female and male ear-rings. He makes the gesture 'have no fear' and points to his raised left foot, symbolising release. He treads upon the prostrate dwarf of ignorance, 'Apasmara', and the diminutive figure of the Goddess Ganga appears in his flowing hair. The God maintains an exquisite poise and equanimity at the centre of the whirling cycle of cosmic activity.

Plaque from the glass case holding the great Nataraja in the Department of Oriental Antiquities in the British Museum.

By permission of the Keeper, Robert Knox.

LET'S TALK
Romance

For exclusive extracts, competitions and special offers, find us online:

- **f** MillsandBoon
- **X** @MillsandBoon
- **◉** @MillsandBoonUK
- **♪** @MillsandBoonUK

Get in touch on 01413 063 232

For all the latest titles coming soon, visit
millsandboon.co.uk/nextmonth

OUT NOW!

Available at
millsandboon.co.uk

MILLS & BOON

OUT NOW!

Available at
millsandboon.co.uk

MILLS & BOON

TWO BRAND NEW BOOKS FROM
Love Always

Be prepared to be swept away to incredible worldwide destinations along with our strong, relatable heroines and intensely desirable heroes.

OUT NOW

Four Love Always stories published every month, find them all at:

millsandboon.co.uk

FOUR BRAND NEW BOOKS FROM
MILLS & BOON MODERN

Indulge in desire, drama, and breathtaking romance – where passion knows no bounds!

OUT NOW

Eight Modern stories published every month, find them all at:

millsandboon.co.uk

COMING SOON!

We really hope you enjoyed reading this book.
If you're looking for more romance
be sure to head to the shops when
new books are available on

Thursday 21st May

To see which titles are coming soon, please visit
millsandboon.co.uk/nextmonth

MILLS & BOON

'Okay.' She nods, blows out a harsh breath. 'Okay. What do we do.'

'We get engaged.'

Continue reading

MY FIANCÉE PROMOTION
Emmy Grayson

Available next month
millsandboon.co.uk

Copyright ©2026 Emmy Grayson

MILLS & BOON®

Coming next month

MY FIANCÉE PROMOTION
Emmy Grayson

Sera stares at the newspaper with horror etched onto her face.

'What...who took that?'

'One of the event photographers. Once they realised who I was, they decided to make a quick buck.' I toss the newspaper down on the coffee table on top of a stack of books.

She sighs, her hands coming up to her temples. 'The damage is done. I'll submit my resignation on Monday.'

Knots form in my chest, tighten. 'No.'

No, only something drastic will repair this.

A frown draws her dark golden brows together. 'Then...I don't understand. What can we do?'

Something stirs inside me at her use of the word *we*. I may not know the woman standing in front of me like I thought I did, but her dedication to Hawke Financial is one thing I don't doubt.

The one thing I'm counting on.

'I do have a proposal.'

hadn't been so far gone that he'd forgotten the things she'd whispered in the night after his father's death.

Sometimes he thought those words haunted him.

But of all the possible responses he'd imagined, it wasn't the way she smiled at him.

Her lips curved gently. Even kindly, he thought.

And then she rose.

The fabric cascaded off her and slid in heaps of shimmering color to either side of her, landing on the tiles at her feet.

But Tadeo forgot all about that. He couldn't take his eyes off her.

Because the Esme he had last seen five months ago had been lean and lithe and in some way resembled the ballet dancer she had once told him she would have liked to have become, in a different life.

She stood, the fabric fell, and she placed her hand on the shelf of the belly—*her belly*—that had swelled up to enormous size. A great deal as if she had a ball beneath her shirt, when, of course, she did not.

It was impossible. It was inconceivable.

It was a disaster of epic proportions and she was *smiling*—

"About that divorce," Esme said, as if they were discussing the weather. Or what to have the staff prepare for a snack. As if she was not very obviously *pregnant*. "I wonder if you might want to rethink."

Copyright © by Caitlin Crews 2026

mouth open while sounds of desire poured out, and how she writhed beneath him, taking more and more until he wasn't certain if either one of them would actually survive—

But that was not the point of this visit.

"My father has been dead for five months," he told her curtly.

"Five months and thirteen days," Esme replied. Oddly specific, to his mind, but she said it so calmly. Her lips curved. "I am aware, Tadeo."

If he could go back in time, he would not have given her access to his family name. By the end, only his father still called him that in person. Most of his friends from school called him variations on his title. Or other nicknames of one sort or another.

The press, of course, used all of his names as they pleased.

He could have had her call him by his proper first name and he often thought that would be easier, because he wouldn't feel this tug of undeserved familiarity. Maybe the name alone would have done it. Maybe then he would never have become familiar with her at all.

But he couldn't go back to that first dinner in a quiet restaurant overlooking the Charles and fix what happened.

He could only do the necessary damage control now.

"I told you long ago that we would remain married only as long as necessary," he told her, no longer caring how dark he sounded. It needed to be done. It didn't matter *how* it was done. "I've come here to let you know that I intend to begin our divorce proceedings. Immediately."

Tadeo didn't know what he expected. For her to cheer, perhaps? Sometimes he convinced himself that she was no more interested in continuing this marriage of theirs than he was. Perhaps he thought she might cry? After all, he

Tragically, she also remained the most beautiful woman he'd ever encountered.

This had been true when she was but a sophomore at Wellesley. It was even more true now. It was an outrage on every level, but she still looked like the model of the perfect woman, should he have been asked to draw such a creature.

Should *drawing* be one of his talents.

It was not that she was the most beautiful woman in the world, he supposed. But it was a cruel trick of fate that she managed to hit every single one of the buttons Tadeo had not entirely realized he had until he'd met her. She was elegant. She was graceful in everything, from her smallest gestures to the way she laughed—a sound that came from her belly and transformed her whole face. She had the sort of exquisite manners that were necessary for the circles they moved in, but Esme always made them seem as if they were innate.

As it was not something she was *doing*, but something that was simply a part of *who she was*.

She had been kind to his father, who had been less enticed by the *fairy-tale* argument and had been largely chilly in return. She was always kind to their subjects, no matter what sort of questions they tried to ask her while she was shaking hands and playing her part. It was his cross to bear that she also looked equally as stunning when she was in jeans and flats as she did in a bespoke gown made for ceremony and circumstance.

Today, she had her dark, glossy hair piled casually on the back of her head. It looked like she was wearing a simple T-shirt, which seemed to hug her curves more than usual. And yet she still simply emanated sophistication from every pore.

Only Tadeo knew that there were ways to touch this woman that lit her on fire. Only he knew what she looked like, her dark eyes glazed over with sex and longing, her

He waited. Esme didn't look up. She was talking animatedly to one of the women dressed in black beside her. They were both moving their fingers over the fabric that was swaddled all over as if they'd been draping it over Esme on purpose, but he couldn't hear what they were saying.

It was possible he had stood there a long while before a different woman altogether looked up, met Tadeo's gaze, and gasped.

"Your Majesty!" she cried.

He watched the ripple effect as it happened. First everyone froze. Then, as if lit by the same flame, all of the servants leaped to their feet—pushing back their chairs so there were loud scraping noises against the tile patio, then dropping into deep, deep curtsies.

His queen, Tadeo noticed—his *wife*, though hopefully not for much longer—did not rise, though it was protocol that she do so. Esme stayed where she was, draped in so many different shades of billowing fabric that he could barely see her body beneath it.

"Leave us," Tadeo told the staff, and did not watch them as they all fluttered off, like so many dark-feathered birds. He kept watching Esme. He studied her maddeningly perfect oval of a face with her dark flashing eyes and that lush, impossible mouth that he absolutely could not feel all over his body, because that was insupportable.

"Have you taken up sewing?" he asked her, not convinced he was entirely in control of his voice. He blamed her for that, too.

The proverbial straw on a camel's back.

"I'm redecorating a room," she replied.

In that same serene voice of hers. Brimming with that same abominable confidence that he found both atrocious and wildly compelling.

Tadeo half expected to find the vines torn up and discarded in favor of an amusement park or something equally hideous, but they were still there. Waiting for the summer to ripen into grapes suitable for wine.

He heard voices again and strode toward them, feeling more and more like a storm cloud as he went.

Then he walked up through the vine-laden path to the pergola and found his wife at last.

She was sitting at the long table in the shade there with what appeared to be her own staff members. There was food and drink on platters, but there were also swathes of fabric, and Esme herself seemed to be wearing half of them.

It took him long, heart-pounding moments to realize that he was reacting to two things at once. One, he had no idea what they were doing, and no one seemed to look at his direction or even notice he was there, which was unusual. Two, and more concerning, it was impossible not to notice that Esme looked...well.

Very well.

Glowing, in fact.

And his body, his temple that he preferred to keep completely under his control at all times like a bit of marble that he alone could sculpt, betrayed him yet again.

The way it had from the start where Esme was concerned.

Because every time he laid eyes on this woman, it was like he was burned alive. She was a poison in his blood, a curse upon his soul, and a great lamentation in the cock that he otherwise ruthlessly controlled. If *a great lamentation* was what to call it when he was nothing at all but hard and needy while the woman was doing nothing but sitting in a chair across a table from where he was standing, with very little of her visible aside from her face.

Damn her.

with no thought whatsoever for the lines of the garden or its pathways or its internal logic, apparently.

He stood still in the not precisely warm air of the late February morning, generating more than enough heat on his own. The sun was already warm, hinting at the fairer months to come. The chill of winter almost felt like a memory when the sunlight moved over his face.

Tadeo needed her excised from this house, and the kingdom, and his life before another season passed. If he allowed himself the sort of dramatics he felt only when he was in Esme's vicinity, he would be tempted to think his own life depended on it.

"But I do not allow it," he growled out at himself. As a reminder he should not have needed, yet clearly did. Another reason this long, torturous chapter of his life needed to end.

He thought he heard a sound in the distance and he made himself walk toward it, scowling at the once-orderly flower beds everywhere, now showing no restraint or any evidence of planning. It was all too bright. Too out of control. As if someone had spun around in a circle like a child with bubbles, flinging seeds about.

The image he had then, of Esme doing exactly that, did not help his mood any.

Tadeo battled his way down an overgrown pathway where vines had been encouraged to do as they liked, making his way out toward the far end of the gardens, where a pergola sat between the garden proper and the start of the vineyards that some enterprising queen had insisted be grown here some while back. They did not produce a lot of wine, but every year, the queen's vintners produced a specialized run of limited-edition bottles of the queen's Pinot Noir. It had long been seen as something of a status symbol among certain sets in the kingdom's society.

At last.

On the other side of the ruined house, he stepped outside onto one of the back terraces and surveyed the gardens as they stretched out toward the horizon and the Pyrenees in the distance.

It did not take a degree in landscape architecture to realize that the gardens, too, had been changed.

In seven years, Esme had completely transformed the sophisticated, manicured gardens that previous queens who had lived here—excluding his mother, of course, who had never set foot on this property while the gleaming shores of the Côte d'Azur existed—had enjoyed. They had all taken pride in overseeing the tending of these gardens, always passing the torch along to keep them quiet, contemplative. A fitting place of respite for a queen. A place for meditation and relaxation.

There was nothing the least bit *relaxing* about the gardens greeting him now.

They were a deafening bugle of early spring exuberance.

There were daffodils and crocuses and cherry blossoms, and they were everywhere, bright and bold. Unseemly and overwhelming, Tadeo thought darkly, and he could not understand why he could not find a single, solitary soul to explain to him what was happening here.

He knew that Esme had not gone on a trip of any kind. Her schedule went through his office, for his review. The palace had only just begun taking on their outward-facing duties again as mourning for the late King had only this week come to an official end.

Esme should have been here. Doing whatever it was she did with her time.

Which was, he reflected now, wrecking heritage sites with the wanton application of tawdry colors slapped about

No servants appeared at the door, or responded when he knocked, so he opened it himself and went inside. And in case he'd imagined that the exterior of the building was the only place that his wife had allowed her creativity free reign, he was quickly disabused of that notion.

The color scheme—though that word, *scheme*, suggested some kind of a plan, which Tadeo doubted very much had been used here—continued inside. He walked through, finding that his jaw was tense and that he was grinding his teeth as he looked from one ruined room to the next. There was nothing in the whole of the historic house that she had not changed.

Nothing.

It felt like a metaphor for the way she had laid waste to Tadeo's own principles and self-regard.

Tadeo hated fucking metaphors.

Though as he walked through one atrium that bled into the next, with more floral theatrics at every turn, he knew that he could not lay that solely at her feet. The woman could be as wicked as she liked, but it was the wickedness in him that had met hers.

He was the one at fault. He accepted that.

Now he wished to be done with it. There was no doubt a sweet, unassuming, deeply boring heiress somewhere that he could marry and never think about again. She would do her job and leave him to his. They would have a pleasant, comfortable, smooth sort of life, marked by nothing but the milestones of their children and the peaceful prosperity of the kingdom.

He could almost taste it. All that was needed was the quietly amicable divorce he had planned, with tasteful statements to the press about going their separate ways with no acrimony and the best of wishes for the other's happiness, etcetera, and he could have peace at last.

friendship in advance, so that the years they would spend together as husband and wife could only be better for it.

Too well had he understood the point of the stories King Hugo had told about his own courtship of Tadeo's mother. Lady Marisol had not been his family's first choice. She had not been a choice at all. She had been impetuous, bright, and bold. The King had fallen hard and had insisted that he would marry her or he would not marry at all.

But soon enough, Marisol had grown bored of royal life. Just as everyone had warned the King she would.

What had followed had haunted his father for the rest of his life, and now haunted Tadeo too. The ghost of Marisol was what lay beneath every decision and every plan Tadeo made for his life and his reign. He thought about the scenes she had made, the extramarital affairs she had flaunted, the contempt with which she had treated the kingdom in general and his father in particular, and vowed to do whatever was necessary to protect the kingdom from a repeat of such embarrassment.

He had married Esme because their kingdoms were invested in their wedding, a choice he would make again if necessary. Just as he would divorce her now because she could never be an appropriate mother to his heir. She was too difficult. Too...problematic.

Back in Boston, Tadeo had possessed absolutely no desire to repeat history. He'd had no intention of ever allowing the kind of passion that had blindsided his father and made him turn his back on his kingdom for the pleasures of the flesh to level him as well.

He had been completely and totally unprepared for Esme, in other words.

Another familiar feeling he very much wished to banish from his life entirely.

he trusted not to sell him out to the papers. This meant that he was significantly less of a player than many of his boarding school friends, but he would not be the one to put the family's name into the mud again.

He had vowed it after his mother's funeral. It was the first, last, and only time he had ever seen his father cry. Or, more precisely, allow his eyes to look damp. For the smallest moment.

Tadeo had learned over time that there were warning signs when a woman he might have been interested in was the wrong choice. Bright red flags that would indicate when a woman was appropriate for him or not, and it was his duty to look for those flags and react accordingly. He liked the women he dated, very privately, to be circumspect in all things. Modest, practical, and smart enough to think twice when it came to exposing him.

He had never chosen wrong.

If it had been up to him, he would never have chosen Princess Esme.

Tadeo had been the one to initiate their meeting in Boston. He'd been in graduate school across the river in Cambridge and even though he did not go out of his way to keep up with the Princess's every move, he could not avoid knowing that she was attending nearby Wellesley College, a very highly selective women's college with an august reputation.

His palace handlers—now his team—made certain he knew.

They were both far away from the intense press interest that surrounded them in their own countries. They were both still immersed in their studies, so there would be no chance of accelerating the march toward their wedding. Tadeo had thought it would be safe. Easy. A smart move to build a

wrong way. You might find this onerous. But it is excellent practice for your future. His craggy face, with the blue eyes Tadeo had inherited, had been somber. *I expect there to be no scandals, Tadeo. Not one, not ever. Do you understand?*

Tadeo had always understood.

He had only been eleven when his mother had died, off in a boating accident in Italy with one of her many lovers. Some had claimed that Tadeo was too young to understand what was happening then, but they were mistaken. He had understood completely. And even if he hadn't, he certainly would have heard every sordid detail at school, where his status as crown prince had long since lost its luster.

Even if he'd wished to avoid his mother's exploits, he'd been unable to.

For years at that point, it had been impossible for Tadeo to avoid the sordid details that his mother seemed to have no shame sharing with the whole world. Everybody knew the story of the selfish, unsatisfied Queen of Bellaza who had provided the kingdom with its needed heir and then declared her duties and responsibilities completed.

The rest of my life is mine, cries the Queen! the headlines screamed.

Tadeo had understood completely and totally that he could not, as that queen's son, create that kind of scandal. No matter what.

Even if he hadn't been told exactly that by his father, repeatedly, he would have come to the same conclusion himself. The kingdom prized its calmness. Its peace. Scandals were for other, more volatile nations.

It was Tadeo's duty not to become a scandal. He took that seriously.

He had therefore enjoyed himself, but always with women who understood his position. And who, more to the point,

And to Tadeo's way of thinking, their entire relationship had already been entirely too prolonged.

He had known that he was betrothed since he was a child. He was five years older than Esme and had been shown pictures of her over time. She had been raised in Clarebonne, which was even smaller than Bellaza and had always enjoyed favorable relations with it, dating all the way back to the time in antiquity when the kingdoms had been joined. Their betrothal had been speculated about in the press all throughout their teenage years because it was not a formal, legal betrothal in the old style. It was an understanding.

An understanding between two kings was as good as law, in some places, but the two kings in question had been very deliberate about the way they'd handled Esme and Tadeo. The two of them had not met. They were deliberately kept apart, in fact.

No one expects you and Esme to molder on shelves, at least until you meet, Tadeo's father, King Hugo, had always said. *You can enjoy yourself as you wish, as long as you remain* ever-conscious *of your duties and* scrupulous *about your reputation.*

Yes, sir, Tadeo had murmured. He had been all of fourteen and did not wish to think about his duties any more than necessary, given he had already found them crushing. Much less his spotless reputation, though that part he was admittedly more concerned with.

King Alain and I are agreed that you and Princess Esme should meet when she is finished with her studies. What that means, his father had said, perhaps more sternly than before, *is that you may do what you wish, but you should never be linked in public with another woman. Neither one of you must ever be seen in any kind of amorous situation, or in any questionable position that could be interpreted the*

kingdom. She had been an undergraduate in the same city. A city that seemed like a long-lost daydream to him now. The Boston of his memories was always covered in towers of snow to mark its bitter winters. There were no mountains to speak of, when Bellaza was ringed with them. More, the wild Atlantic was forever seething about at the end of streets and in the distance, as if keeping watch.

He liked to tell himself that he had been happy to leave that strange, small city—but he still woke up from dreams that smelled like the salt marshes of Cape Cod on a quiet spring morning, or sounded like the rattle of the T, or had him remembering walking along the Charles River on a picture-perfect fall afternoon.

Tadeo exited the car outside the manor house, shutting the driver's door sharply behind him. Then realized that he was standing about because he wasn't used to arriving anywhere and not being immediately greeted by staff. He was quite certain that there was staff at the manor house. What he did not understand was why none of them made themselves known as protocol demanded.

Thoughts of Boston felt like a reprimand, but then, he had known at the time that those years were an indulgence. That he was permitted to indulge in a kind of freedom there—the independence to walk where he pleased and live a life with far less scrutiny in a country not his own. He had known he never would again.

Still, he found himself shaking off unwanted memories yet again as he started for the main door, painted in a revolting shade of pink. If he was a vindictive man, he might have been tempted to make Esme pay to restore the house to its traditional state before releasing her. But that would only prolong this.

He rolled to a stop only centimeters from crashing into the insufferably bright magenta wall before him. He continued to stare out through the windshield, not able to accept that he was truly seeing the ornate, excessive, and expansive palate of too many colors before him.

He wondered if it was possible that he was, in fact, having a stroke.

At least that sensation was familiar.

It was much the way he had felt the morning after his father's death five months ago, when he had woken to find that it wasn't a dream. Not only was his noble and admirable father truly dead, when the old man had always seemed so invincible, but Tadeo had actually gone and done the one thing he'd vowed he would never, ever do.

He had allowed Esme into his bed. Or rather, a couch in his father's study, but it was the same regret either way.

Tadeo knew better.

God help him, did he know better.

He could recall that morning perfectly. How he had lain there on the couch in the study where she'd found him after the funeral, feeling as if he was fracturing into a thousand shards of jagged glass as she curled up at his side. She was so peaceful. She looked like an angel as she slept, the way she always had.

She still fit against his body perfectly.

It seemed impossible, after all those years, and yet there was no denying it.

Tadeo had felt as if his chest was cracked wide open, and she was to blame for it.

Just as she had been the first time, years ago, when they'd finally met each other on the other side of the world. He had been doing his graduate work in the sort of business, economics, and public policy issues that could only serve the

Because he would finally be able to *breathe*.

He would not let her damned flowers get to him, reminding him of too many things he did not wish to think about. All of them involving Esme and that recklessness only she conjured up in him. He would see to it that her gardening additions were summarily removed as soon as she left the manor house and replaced with a tidy hedge. There would be no sign of Esme's disruptive presence once she left, and that was what mattered. This chapter of his life was finally ending.

And not a moment too soon.

The drive wound around at last to the house itself, which was a fine old Bellazan structure made in the late medieval period, then renovated time and again in the centuries since to suit the whims of a succession of queens. When Tadeo had handed it off to his brand-new queen on their wedding night, it had been a sturdy, quietly elegant monument of the kingdom's history. He had not been here since.

An oversight, clearly.

Tadeo was not certain that he could entirely believe his own eyes as he gazed out at the monstrosity that loomed before him at the top of the drive.

She had...painted it, if that was what it could be called. What she'd done was gaudy. It was an *assault*.

In place of the expected white walls and red-tiled rooftops that nodded toward the kingdom's Spanish neighbors, plus the hint of the nearby French countryside in the sprawling gardens that would not look out of place surrounding a chateau, the Queen's Manor House—once considered the refined jewel of the royal estate—now appeared to have been vomited upon by an intoxicated rainbow.

Tadeo was so aghast at the tasteless horror show in front of him that he almost forgot to step on the brake in the car.

because he did not intend to leave the royal estate. Now, still on the garish drive, he slowed the vintage Rolls-Royce that had been a part of his grandfather's collection and ordered himself to find his center. To remain calm.

Something that was normally not the least bit difficult for him.

Only Esme disrupted his equanimity. Only Esme forced him to confront the distasteful evidence that he truly was his mother's son, made of all the wild, impossible parts of her that had led her to make such a display of herself for all the world to see. He loathed that he possessed such depths inside himself and had spent most of his adult life doing all that he could to keep them locked away.

He could not be the king his country deserved unless and until he removed Esme from his life. He had known this going in, but there had always been so much investment in the fairy-tale notion of the Prince of Bellaza marrying the Princess of Clarebonne from the neighboring kingdom. Not least because the two kingdoms had been one, long ago, and this only added to the fairy-tale mystique. After the scandal his mother had wrought on her marriage and therefore also on Tadeo's father's reign, a fairy tale had seemed like a gift. A gift that could fix what his mother had broken.

But the fairy tale had run its course. Now was the time to act, and Tadeo was ready. He was more than ready.

Their marriage would end quietly. There were no children after seven years of living completely separate lives in private, so there was no claim to the throne to worry about. Esme could go off to make a mess of whatever she wished, wherever she wished to do it, without it having any bearing on him.

Just so long as she left Bellaza and Tadeo never laid eyes on her again, he would be happy.

with his team plotting out the details. Once the divorce was handled, after a suitable period of reflection, Tadeo would find a far more suitable queen and set about making the heir the kingdom required.

He had spent seven years making certain that he saw Esme only when required to for the work they did, never in any private capacity that could lead to complications in his plan in the form of the child he adamantly did not want with her.

Well, a voice in him chided, *you managed it for almost all of those seven years, anyway.*

Tadeo did not wish to think about that one slip, five months ago. There were other, more pressing things at the moment, like the fact that the condition of the manor's grounds appalled him. More than that, the sight seemed to dig beneath his skin, as if she—and he knew it was her, if not with her own hands, then at her express direction—had planted all of the flowers in as unorthodox a fashion as possible *specifically* to bother him.

Queen Esme, betrothed to him since the day of her birth, his wife for the past seven years—and for one reckless year across an ocean in a foreign city, his lover—was astoundingly good at bothering him. She had a talent for getting under his skin in a way no one else could. Or ever had.

A reality that he had never come to terms with, though he had learned how to control his reactions to her over the years of their marriage. Tadeo, in truth, did not wish to come to terms with the ways Esme got to him. None of that mattered now.

"It all ends today," he assured himself, his voice a dark spool of sound in the interior of the car.

He was glad he was alone.

Tadeo had driven himself, waving off his usual guards

Now it was Tadeo's duty to take up the mantle that his father had carried until the day of his death five months ago. It had taken him all of this time to feel comfortable in the role that he had been preparing for all his life. It had required all of his focus and commitment to make the transition from his father's reign to his own as seamless as possible. There had been the somber funeral, then the burial, then the typical period of mourning.

But spring was coming. The Kingdom of Bellaza was coming alive after its cold, hard winter.

Tadeo needed to divorce his wife and move on—though, to minimize scandal and disruption, the divorce would have to be civilized. He had already plotted out the messaging with his team, and he had come to do this unpleasant task in person because he felt that was appropriate and a husband owed a wife that much. He assumed that it would be an uncomfortable conversation, perhaps, but a brief one.

After all, he had made it perfectly clear during their widely publicized courtship that this was precisely what would happen once he became king. They would play the part of a royal couple so well-suited to each other that their subjects made up happy endings for them—though there would be precious few public displays as they went about their official duties. Tadeo's family was well known for its adherence to the strictest protocol. They would let the public make whatever meal it liked from perfectly polite and expected touches.

Tadeo had been told there was fan fiction about their private life all over the internet. He chose not to know what that was.

But this marriage would end. They would never see each other again once they navigated their way through a divorce so amicable it would be applauded. He'd already spent time

CHAPTER ONE

His Majesty Xavier Tadeo Santiago did not have to make it all the way up the drive to the remote manor house in the farthest reaches of the royal estate to know that it was far past time to divorce his queen.

The drive itself was a pageant of early spring flowers flung in all directions like a discordant quilt. They were clumped here and festooned there, their bright colors clashing with each other and running all over the place, making a dramatic visual cacophony on both sides of the drive.

He found them offensive at once.

Tadeo was well acquainted with the work of the groundskeeper and his staff. They kept the rest of the royal estate in pristine and orderly condition, as was right and proper, since the royal family served its subjects and was called to present—always—their best foot forward. These grounds belonged to the kingdom. As did the palace, its contents, and indeed, the royal family itself.

Even the king himself was no more or less than the property of the kingdom, or so Tadeo's father had always taught him.

It meant more with the ghost of Tadeo's mother hanging always between them. The spectacle she'd made of herself. The shame and scandal she'd rained down upon the palace and the kingdom. His father had done his best to remain stalwart in the face of her behavior—always an uphill battle.

Keep reading for an excerpt from Caitlin Crews's most recent title, King's Heir of Hate!

Did you fall in love with To Have & To Hate*?*
Then you're sure to enjoy these other
sensational stories by Caitlin Crews!

Kidnapped for His Revenge
Her Accidental Spanish Heir
Forbidden Greek Mistress
An Heir for Christmas
Sicilian Devil's Prisoner

Available now!

girls who also looked like their father, though some of them had her blue eyes.

They also adopted some of the orphans who stole Ivy's heart, to the point that some of their detractors in the papers made snide comments about their *home for wayward youths*.

But they wouldn't have it any other way.

Having been raised in that cold, isolating castle, no amount of family was too much. And love never ran out, like a tap. It only grew and grew.

Their life was loud. Hectic. But any time they began to feel too far away from each other, they found each other again. In their bed at night. And in that villa on Capri. They loved each other wildly, brightly, ferociously.

Time did not dim it. Age only made it glow.

They always held hands. They very rarely went to bed angry. They spent precious few nights apart.

And over the years, Ivy found herself profoundly grateful for her mother's legacy. For a heart so big that it could hold all of the people that Ivy was lucky enough to love. But she couldn't think of that legacy without a pang of sorrow, too. Because she knew that her mother had not always had the love that she'd given returned to her as she deserved.

Not the way Ivy did. Fierce and hot and deeper every day, because forever wasn't nearly long enough for Giaco and his little saint to love each other as much as they wanted. As much as they needed.

Though they gave it their very best shot.

* * * * *

parazzi, who clearly missed his exploits. "Then it is easy to find great beauty in the life you lead without having to attempt to amuse yourself with quantity rather than quality."

Ivy laughed when she read that quote in the paper.

"You really do love to torture all of your acolytes," she said. "You know they conduct grieving rituals on a daily basis, praying for my downfall."

"If their prayers worked, I would have found them more interesting in the first place," he replied.

And then demonstrated what he meant by *great beauty* right there on the floor of their library in Rome.

Ivy never returned to Umberto's castle. She didn't miss it, either. She certainly didn't miss *him*. Though she did take Leontina up on her offer to be the family she was missing. It turned out that the relationship they should have had when they were girls was easy now that they were grown women.

Suggesting that it had been all the external forces in that castle that kept them apart back then.

It was five years after their wedding, on her thirtieth birthday, when Ivy discovered that she was pregnant. And Giaco loved a celebration. He threw her a birthday party, then whisked her off to the villa in Capri, the place they still thought of as *theirs*.

And so she told him there, where the fact that they were in love had been impossible to deny any longer, that they were going to be a family all their own.

He grinned at her, holding her against him in that dreamy pool and running his hands down her sleek, naked back.

"Fantastic," he said. "I can't wait to taste you when you're ripe."

It turned out that he quite liked that taste. So much so that she spent most of her thirties having his babies. Four wild boys who looked just like their father and two little

CHAPTER TWELVE

Ivy never knew how Giaco convinced Umberto to release her inheritance, only that he managed it. And it only took a year or two.

She gifted most of it to her original charity in London. And with the rest, she sought out other charities that she could bolster, too.

"Not because I'm a saint," she told her husband when he teased her. "Because I'm not. Definitely not." Given what they had just done to each other in the marital bed, there was no denying that was true. "But I see this as dispensing my mother's love as far as it can go."

"She would love that," Giaco said, and kissed her.

Ivy knew she would. She could feel Alana's love inside her, bright like a guiding light.

It took longer than the originally agreed-upon three years for the world to begin to accept not only that they were going to stay married, but that Giaco Tavian really had calmed down. That he really had taken himself off the market, turned a new leaf, and become not just a better man but the perfect husband.

There was much mourning across the land, gnashing and wailing, but there were far more people who watched the two of them and saw something beautiful.

"All it takes is the right person," he liked to tell the pa-

a low voice. "That's it, and I acknowledge that most would laugh at the idea. But I swear to you, Ivy—I swear that I will do everything in my power to be worthy of that trust."

She blew out a breath. He thought he saw her shiver. Then she was moving closer herself, and putting her hands on him, too.

"I love you more fiercely than you could possibly imagine and I have no intention of letting go," she told him, with notes of that ferocity in her voice. He could feel it in him, too. More of that joy, and far better because none of it was tainted with the years of revenge. This was all his. And she wasn't finished. "I want our children to be happier than we ever were, Giaco. I want to raise them to know, always, that joy is an option worth fighting for. But most of all, I just want you."

"You're in luck," he told her, allowing his smile to take him over, and all of it was real. Because this was real, and true, and theirs. "You already have me. We're already married. And the only thing we have left to do is make sure that everything that comes after is steeped in joy."

That was exactly what they did, tucked up in his bed, with the future all around them like moonlight, making them glow on into forever.

"I want that love, Ivy," he said, leaning in close to cut her off, "because that is how I love you. That is how I will continue to love you for the rest of our lives. I just spent over a decade convincing the world that I'm useless so that I could take revenge on a man who could not, for the life of him, love my mother enough to make her want to live." He moved closer still. "I don't want any part of that kind of love. I want *you*. I want *us*. I want everything we had in Capri, every day, always."

He reached out with one hand and touched her, and everything was immediately better with her cheek in his hand. The heat of her seeping into his skin. "I don't want any half-assed, sacrificial martyr shit, my little saint. The only crosses I ever want to see you climb on in this marriage will be for fun, not self-flagellation. Do you understand me?"

"Giaco..." she whispered, and the tears were flowing from her eyes then. He could feel them on his hand. "You took revenge? This was all *revenge*?"

"You have never been anything to me but light," he told her urgently. "Even in the midst of darkness. I swear it."

"I don't think you understand," she replied, and then changed the whole world again with a smile. "Am I to assume that it worked?"

He took in her smile and found his own mouth curving in response. "It was a triumph in every regard."

"And here I thought I could not possibly love you more," she whispered, her eyes damp. Lest he forget that Umberto had not loved Ivy's mother, either. That they shared this very specific burden. That she, too, had every reason to celebrate this win.

It made him feel a whole lot more like celebrating than he had before.

"All you have to do is trust me," he promised her now, in

And also furious.

She pulled in a breath. "I've been thinking about it, and I don't think I would have agreed to this arrangement if it was anyone else but you. Don't you see? I'm already used to loving you even when it makes no sense."

"Who taught you this?" he asked, not sure he could speak until the words came out of his mouth.

She shook her head. "I don't know what you mean."

"I have no desire to be loved like that," he said—except it sounded as if he was shouting. Maybe he was. He wasn't sure he cared. He wasn't *acting* with her and that felt a lot like jumping off a very tall building. But he didn't want to stop. "I don't want someone to love me *even though* it hurts them. I don't want to be loved *despite* the fact I'm apparently so broken that I could betray the person I've made promises to without a second thought. I don't want to be loved *because* I am broken."

She frowned at him. "I don't understand. I think it could be beautiful."

He moved toward her then, coming so that he was on the bed too and leaning over her, his fists on either side of her folded legs. Directly in her lovely face.

"I want to be loved fiercely and possessively," he growled out at her. "I want to be loved with expectations. Of fidelity. Of trust. Of intimacy and honesty. I want to be loved so much that a single lifetime cannot contain it and anyone who happens to venture near it cannot help but bask in it, too. I want to be loved so hard that my own children admire it. That's the kind of love I want, Ivy. And I warn you, I won't settle for anything less."

"But..." She shook her head, and he could see that there were tears in her eyes. They made his heart hurt. "I can love you as best I can, but—"

the shower. Ivy reading her books and taking her calls and leaving that scent of hers everywhere. Always.

He was so hard it hurt.

He charged into the suite and threw open the bedroom door, and there she was.

At last, *there she was*.

That joy he'd been chasing flooded him then, vast and hot.

Ivy sat up quickly when he threw open that door, her blond hair cascading all around her and drawing his attention to the silken chemise she liked to sleep in—a detail that had plagued him this last two weeks—and then they were staring at each other.

He looked deep into all of that impossible blue, and now he had something to compare it to. The beautiful blue waters off Capri, turquoise and green, and still her eyes were more beautiful.

There was no contest.

"Ivy—" he began.

"I figured it all out," she said quickly. Ivy moved in the bed, kneeling up as if she wanted to run to him but didn't dare. He couldn't quite process that. "I don't think that Capri has to be a dream we had. I don't think things have to change."

"They absolutely have to change," he thundered at her. "You have no idea—"

"Here's the thing," she said in that same urgent way, and she sounded something like frantic. "I can love you enough for both of us. I don't need you to love me back. I can love you however you need to be loved. Wherever you go, whatever you do. I'm not saying it won't hurt, but I'll love you anyway, Giaco."

He stared back at her, something like awed and humbled at once.

"I believe I'll do that. Why don't you take the week off. Or the rest of the month."

"Is that a possibility?" Gabriele asked dryly. "Will your antics permit me to take a holiday of even the next quarter of an hour?"

"I suppose we'll find out," Giaco tossed back at him.

He started to walk past his assistant, but Gabriele stopped him. "Incidentally," the other man said, "the housekeeper wanted me to inform you that Saint Ivy has moved all of her things into your room. Herself."

The two men gazed at each other, and Giaco reminded himself that Pau was not his only friend. Gabriele was, too. And the approval in his friend's gaze meant more to him than he could express—particularly as Gabriele's blessing on anything at all was hard to come by.

But clearly his best and most trusted assistant—and friend—was delighted at Ivy's return, too. And Ivy herself, it seemed.

It wasn't that Giaco *needed* approval, but the truth was, he had lived a long time with only its opposite. Tonight he took it in and let it seem to fill him up, like a tuning fork deep inside.

He didn't say another word. He inclined his head at his friend, then he simply turned and headed for his bedroom.

For Ivy, at last.

He bounded up the stairs and took the long hallway that led to the suite of rooms that sprawled over the back of the house. The suite that he'd had built for himself, never imagining that he would share that space with anyone. Now he couldn't think of anything he'd like more.

There were already fantasies drip-feeding into his head. Ivy waking up with him every morning. Ivy coming out of

his dreams. He woke with her taste in his mouth and her scent in his nose and found himself alone in a hotel bed.

It was like leaving her all over again, every time.

But as he'd told those reporters months ago, instant gratification had always taken too long as far as Giaco was concerned.

He had never felt that so keenly as he did now.

"I must go," he told his friend abruptly. Then he left Pau staring after him as he stood up and left the office. He had already called for his plane before he got on the elevator. The flight was interminable, and his people were waiting on the ground.

It was not until he was being driven back into the Eternal City that it occurred to him to wonder if she would even be there. He had left her, after all. Given her no instruction or invitations to do anything. For all he knew she could be... anywhere.

The notion did not sit well with him.

He stormed into his house and glared at Gabriele, who always endeavored to meet him when he returned. And Gabriele, who was well used to Giaco's moods, stared right back.

"Where is my wife?" Giaco demanded.

"She's here, of course," Gabriele said, with exaggerated and rather pointed calmness. "She got back yesterday."

"Got back from where? Capri?" Something in him turned over uncomfortably at the thought of her on that island. *Their* island, as far as he was concerned, but by herself.

He didn't like that, either.

"My understanding is that she was in London and then sojourned a while in France," Gabriele said lazily. Then he lifted a brow. "But you will have to ask her yourself."

Giaco laughed, and clapped his assistant on the shoulder.

And then he settled back to enjoy the shouting—and the vast joy he expected would accompany it.

But that, too, didn't land the way he'd imagined it would. It took Giaco longer than he cared to admit to realize that where he'd expected to feel a fierce and overarching joy, he felt nothing.

Except empty.

Much later, after the magnitude of what Giaco and Pau had pulled off had been made abundantly clear to Umberto—rendering him little more than an old man frothing at the mouth, impotent and deeply aware of that fact—the two old friends were back in Pau's office. Pau poured them both the stiff drink they deserved and they clinked their tumblers together.

"And now you can be anyone," Pau said. "No longer must you play the dissolute reincarnation of Pan, wreaking carnal havoc wherever you go."

"The world is mine," Giaco agreed.

ABs he sat there, his own words came back to him. Words he'd said flippantly to a scrum of reporters within sight of the Spanish Steps. Words he'd used to paint a picture, to build a narrative.

Empty words, he would have said if anyone had asked.

But now, as he sat in Madrid with his best and only friend, having finally achieved what he'd expected to be the crowning achievement of his life, he realized that every word he'd said that day was true.

I never expected to fall in love, he had told a pack of mercenaries, in service to the story. Always the story. *But now that I have, I naturally wish to be with her. Always. I want forever, immediately.*

He had not slept much since leaving Capri. Ivy disrupted

knew him well enough to sense his deep pleasure. "Not only is Giaco a full partner in my business, *Signore* Tavian, but he's a majority shareholder in yours."

That sat there, in the center of the conference table, like so much lead.

"Some fathers teach their sons how to be men," Giaco murmured into the tense silence. "Good ones, even, or so I am told." He smiled at his father. "What you taught me was how to play shell games with money and, better yet, how to hide my true nature in plain sight."

And he could see it then. He could see the dawning awareness on his father's face that he had been outplayed. The contracts he'd signed when he'd come into this room repeatedly over the past week, filled with his usual gloating arrogance, had in fact signed away a significant portion of his fortune. If not most of it. The rest of it was tied up in real estate, but this partnership had been meant to ease Umberto's latter years. Then carry on his name forever.

Giaco watched his father play all the usual chess games in his head and then come up with the only possible answer.

"This is revenge," he gritted out. "But you would have had to set this up…"

"A very long time ago," Giaco agreed. He leaned forward, and made sure that his father was staring straight at him. He took a moment to enjoy the way that vein bulged on his father's forehead. It felt like a blessing. "I didn't like you very much to begin with, but after my mother died?" He shook his head. "I don't believe I have ever hated anyone more."

"Your mother was mentally ill." Umberto bit that out.

"I believe that," Giaco retorted. "Insofar as I believe that spending that much time with you would cause mental illness in anyone. As far as I'm concerned you might as well have shot her yourself."

ence room and let himself in, sauntering into the middle of a scrum of dark suits, all bespoke and understated.

Giaco, naturally, was in battered jeans.

For a moment, everyone inside the room fell silent at the sight of him. The *fact* of him, no doubt. What, after all, could Umberto's feckless tabloid-fodder son have to do with the serious business men like this trafficked in daily?

Giaco looked around, taking in the looks of incomprehension on so many dark-suited faces. He saw the gleam in his friend's gaze. Then, at last, taking his time so he could best savor what was to come and hold it close forevermore, he turned his attention to his father.

Umberto stared at him, his cold eyes without comprehension. "Have you gotten lost on the way to a whorehouse?" he asked starkly.

"Not exactly," Giaco murmured. He stood there a moment, making sure everyone was looking at him. Reliving his greatest tabloid scandals, no doubt. Only when he felt they were all sifting through his greatest hits did he take his time ambling around the table to take a seat next to Pau.

He let the awkwardness and confusion build as he lounged there, smiling faintly.

Pau waited even longer.

"I think that it is time I introduce you to my partner," Pau said, eventually, with his usual quiet menace. When Umberto barked out a laugh, Pau's dark eyes gleamed even more. "Giaco brings many things to this particular deal, I think you'll agree."

"Has he notified the paparazzi that he actually entered a building in which business is done?" Umberto asked, acidly. "I was unaware this fool possessed any other skills."

Pau gazed at the man who had been a nemesis to the both of them for too long to count. He did not smile, but Giaco

whole of the game? Umberto will almost certainly hold on to her inheritance out of spite."

Giaco frowned. He hadn't exactly *forgotten* Ivy's virtuous reasons for marrying him, but he'd set them aside. He had been working toward this day for so long that he'd developed a kind of tunnel vision. Nothing that didn't serve the end goal mattered.

The fact of the matter was, Ivy was the only thing he'd seen outside that tunnel in years.

"Let's handle one problem at a time," he said, and put his hand on Pau's shoulder for a moment. They looked at each other, a whole lifetime of working to get *right here* between them.

Pau nodded again, and then strode from the office to get it all started.

And for the next five minutes Giaco stood quietly in his friend's office, looking out at the city below him once again. But this time without seeing it.

Because strangely enough, none of this felt the way he'd expected that it would. He had dreamed about that call he'd received in Capri for long years before it had finally happened. That everything was in place. That it was done—all done and dusted, save the gloating. He had fantasized endlessly about the joy he would feel once he knew that triumph was right here, right within his grasp.

He'd been pretty focused on the gloating, too.

But instead, it all felt…hollow.

He twisted the wedding ring on his finger. Surely all he needed was this confrontation with his father. Once that happened, it would feel the way it should.

That was the missing piece, he was sure.

At the appointed time, he walked directly to the confer-

"Are you ready?" Pau asked, in his usual ruthless, formidable way.

"I've been ready since bloody university," Giaco replied.

Pau only nodded at this. It had been a long road, but they were at the end of it. All that was left was the big reveal that would turn Umberto's world upside down and keep it there. *The good part*, Giaco always said, *will be the look on his face.*

"Five minutes," his friend told him. "We will start with some niceties to make certain he is not prepared. This will hurt him more once all is revealed."

There was nothing else to say at this point. They had plotted this out, every moment of it, across years. Their plotting and planning put Giaco's dating-to-wedding itinerary to shame. Nothing had been left to chance. They had set a trap for Umberto and lured him in, and now all that remained was telling the man that what he thought was a win on his end was, in fact, a severed limb.

They'd distracted him with Pau's supposed purity tests and the clamor and commotion of Giaco's very public romantic life while they'd pulled the rug straight out from under Umberto's feet. They had always planned on a wedding that would seem like a surrender on Giaco's end, but the fact that Umberto had managed to manipulate Ivy Amis into it? Fate had clearly been on their side.

This day, this revenge, was nothing but sweet. Giaco had anticipated he would savor it forever.

His friend walked by and slapped him on the back, then nodded toward his wedding ring. The one he was forever fiddling with, and not because it bothered him the way he'd assumed it would.

"Will you tell her the whole truth?" Pau asked. "The

CHAPTER ELEVEN

GIACO HAD WAITED his whole life to walk into a conference room in a gleaming corporate office set high in a skyscraper—this one in the Area de Negocios de la Castellana in Madrid—and finally turn the tables on his father.

He and Pau Calixto had planned this since they'd met at university. They had lived on the same stair at Cambridge and had met because they were both predisposed to taking long walks in the middle of the night. By the time Giaco was inevitably sent down in disgrace, he and Pau had cemented a lifelong friendship.

His friend, no stranger to the issues of legacies and difficult fathers, had suggested a remedy years ago. The catch was, it would take a long time. It would require that Giaco show the world the worst parts of himself—his basest urges and lowest moments—and claim they were the sum total of who he was, so that Umberto would never think to suspect his son *capable* of plotting against him.

The shameful truth about that was that he hadn't minded being seen as the most disreputable man alive. Not at first.

But then again, a man never fully understood the contours of his prison cell until the door was locked tight behind him.

Today, his friend gathered up a few items from his desk and nodded toward Giaco, who stood by the window with Madrid far below his feet.

Not even if it was patently obvious that the man she loved was not worthy of her.

Standing there in the South of France where her mother had told her once that she'd been conceived in the deepest love imaginable, Ivy stopped thinking about what she *should* do. What she *ought* to do. What would be the *strong and powerful* thing to do, as some kind of response to Giaco's departure.

Instead of all of that, she listened to her poor, broken, wildly optimistic heart instead, because it still believed in magic.

She still believed in magic.

And then she went back home. To Rome.

Because she could love Giaco enough for both of them. She had her mother's heart, and lucky for her, she was more resilient than her mother had been.

And it was high time to prove it.

to anyone on the outside—the kind of chemistry Ivy could never have understood until now. But what Ivy knew for a fact about her mother was that Alana had never been mercenary. Alana had loved deeply or not at all. She had put her heart into everything she did and it had made her weak in a way, Ivy supposed. It had been her greatest strength and her greatest vulnerability. It had made her the luminous actress that she was and it was why her legend would continue long after Ivy was forgotten.

It was also the legacy that Alana had left her daughter.

The ability to love against all odds, in the face of adversity—and in many ways, Ivy thought, without hope.

There was nothing weak about that, Ivy understood now. It was a wild and terrible strength. And it was no wonder it was hard for Ivy to accept what was happening to her now, because she'd shut her own heart off on the day she'd watched them put her mother in the ground.

Looking back, she couldn't even have said what specific thing had happened at the funeral to set her off. All she'd known that day was that she was done. She couldn't stay in the place where her mother had died, married to a man who had treated the woman who loved him so much, against all reason, like an afterthought at best.

But the way that Umberto had behaved had nothing to do with the way Alana had loved.

Ivy understood that more in this moment than she ever had before. More than she would have been capable of understanding a few months ago. Maybe she'd needed all of this to happen with Giaco so that she could finally see her mother as she'd really, truly been.

Flawed, certainly. Insecure and needy, also true.

But when Alana Amis had loved, she had loved with every single part of herself and she'd never given up. Not ever.

Ivy was looking for her mother on the breeze or out there in the sunshine that dappled the blue waves, but she didn't find her. Not the way she wanted to. Not the way she had before.

Still she let herself wander, avoiding any hint of tabloid gossip or snarky papers. It was just her and the sea. Her and her memories. And as she sat on a bench near the water, in a place no one alive knew to look for her, she found something else instead.

Her poor heart.

Her optimistic, foolish heart that had hated Giaco Tavian for all the right reasons—and would love it if she could hate him again.

But she didn't hate him.

She couldn't hate him—and she'd tried.

When she understood that, she understood her own mother, too.

Baffling as Ivy had found it, Alana really had loved Umberto. Her memories told her that truth whether she wanted to face it or not. Maybe not as time went on, but at first, the man had made Alana feel safe. He'd vowed to cherish her, and had not revealed until much later that the way he cherished anything was to collect it and forget it. But long before that became clear, Umberto was the first man since Ivy's father who had made Alana seem...peaceful.

That was a realization Ivy didn't want any part of, but she couldn't escape it once it came to her. Once the inescapable truth of it settled into her bones and stayed there. She found herself staring out at sea where sailboats danced on the waves and the larger, overwrought yachts of the very rich slid by like planets orbiting the sun.

Umberto had made Alana feel safe, and even happy, for a time. Maybe they'd had a chemistry that was inexplicable

She really did hate him, Ivy decided. He wasn't even here—she had no idea where he was, as a matter of fact—and yet he'd still managed to ruin her safe space for her. It was unforgivable.

Ivy spent another restless night in Kensington, but even though the sun came out that following morning, she couldn't settle. She felt…inside out. More than that, it was like she was *marked*. She'd gone ahead and married the man and now she was linked with him. No one who knew her in London wouldn't also know of her change in circumstances because the entire world knew about her wedding, and she didn't think she could bear discussing it.

Because he could be anywhere. Doing anything. They had both promised Umberto discretion. Not abstinence.

And she hated herself for thinking that. If she hadn't gone ahead and foolishly fallen in love with him, what would she care what he was doing?

Yet the reality was that she cared entirely too much, and that was why she booked herself on the Eurostar and headed for France. She took the train under the Channel into Paris and the fast train down to Nice with glorious views as they approached the Côte d'Azur.

Once there, she didn't go to Cap Ferrat. She found herself a room in an old hotel in Nice the way her parents had one year, according to the stories her mother had told her. She tried to recreate those memories of hers that were not true memories of what happened, but memories of the tales Alana had shared with her. Of the nights she and her mother would cuddle in Alana's bed and Alana would talk of markets in the streets, of macarons in colorful lines in glass bakery cases, of echoey hillside villages, of lavender fields, and the gleaming coastal walk from Nice to Villefranche-sur Mer.

She walked to the charity's offices, picking up a proper coffee on the way, and decided that it perked her up considerably even if it wasn't quite the same as the *caffè shakerato* she'd become enamored with on Capri. Ivy felt much better almost at once, and told herself that in no time she would have her life back and running the way she liked it. Thoughts of Giaco would fade over time, or until she was presented with a new itinerary, and they would manage their marriage that way until they were done.

Ivy was caffeinated and *looking forward* to throwing herself into work so she could hasten this process along.

But once she arrived at the charity, she found that everything was running swimmingly without her. Exactly as she'd planned all along, having gone out of her way to hire the very best people to do this work that she continued to feel was so important.

The last time she'd needed to escape the Tavian family, she'd created the charity. It had taken all of her time and attention.

It hadn't really occurred to her that she wouldn't have that option this go-round.

"Did you really come here without that delicious husband of yours?" asked one of her directors, smiling wide. "We were sure we'd get an inside peak at all that marital bliss since we know you."

"I'm afraid not," Ivy had to respond, with a little laugh and a big smile, neither of which she felt. *There you go*, a voice inside whispered. *Apparently you're just as much a liar as he is.* "He couldn't accompany me this time."

And after planning to go and make herself useful for the whole day, she found herself leaving again after an hour and finding herself roaming around Central London, as damp and gloomy as the weather.

off somewhere, eating out of Giaco's hand. If she really fancied it, she could look him up online and see where he was, what he was doing, and who he was doing it with—

Yet surely that was a recipe for misery.

Because even though she knew how he choreographed his appearances, she also knew how convincing his act was. Why would she want to see it?

"Why do you *want* to see it?" she snapped at herself, and realized then that she was lurking on her road, talking to herself, and would likely scare the neighbors into calling the paparazzi themselves.

She let herself into her house and then stood there, leaning with her back against the door. It was quiet and dim inside and she told herself that she could breathe at last, but when her lungs didn't seem to respond to that the way she thought they should, she decided she was simply exhausted. Ugly tired, even. She went upstairs, wrinkling her nose because her house didn't smell right anymore. It didn't smell like *hers*. It smelled musty and shut up and very much like it belonged to a stranger.

Ivy decided that, too, had something to do with how deeply exhausted she was. She ran a bath, had a soak, and then put herself to bed.

But she dreamed of Giaco and woke restless and yearning time and time again throughout the night.

In the morning it wasn't bucketing it down outside, but it was still gray. She rummaged about for some kind of breakfast in her kitchen, but Giaco's people had cleared everything out when they'd swept her off all those months ago. She had to make do with a bit of instant coffee and some dry crackers.

Rather a comedown from the magically stocked villa, she had to admit.

of clothes, and didn't contact any of Umberto's or Giaco's people. Why bother, when she didn't intend to involve herself with Umberto or Giaco after this. She walked to the Piazzetta, a long and pretty amble down from the villa, and then took the funicular down to the bright and colorful marina. Once there, she got herself a coffee in her favorite café and considered her options.

She'd known all along that Giaco was like a drug and yet she'd imbibed freely. He'd been slightly more than the oversexed clown he played for the tabloids, just slightly more human, and she'd dropped her guard completely.

As if she hadn't grown up in that castle, subject to his little reigns of terror every time he'd come home and turned things inside out. Simply because he could.

"You're a mess," she muttered to herself.

How had she managed to forget that she hated that man?

She boarded the first ferry she could, but she had no plans to go on to Rome once she made it to Naples. Instead, Ivy did the exact same thing that she'd done five years ago. She figured if it cured her once, it would again. She bought herself a ticket in the airport and flew home.

Not the home that she'd been so sure, secretly, that she and Giaco were building together. But the one she'd made for herself, to save herself, once before.

Ivy landed at Heathrow on a grim, rainy sort of summer day and told herself it was a great comfort after the glare of all that Mediterranean sunshine. She slogged her way onto the Tube, and only remembered when she walked from the Tube station nearest to her road that there might very well be paparazzi hanging around when she got to her house. But when she drew closer, she allowed herself a deep breath because she didn't see anything that would suggest that.

After all, it had been a while. Paparazzi were no doubt

And he didn't.

Finally, a week after she'd woken up to find him gone, Ivy decided that she was done with this. She felt a similar surge of clarity to what she'd felt the night of her mother's funeral, when she'd looked around at the guests in the castle—and the family that had never been hers in any real sense—and had realized that the only thing that tethered her to these people was gone. She didn't need to stay and suffer with them.

She didn't need to do anything with any of them, ever again.

Five years ago, that had felt like freedom. She tried to tell herself that this did, too. Because the more she thought about it, the more she thought that she never should have demeaned herself like this. She never should have put herself in a position where Umberto could direct any part of her life.

Yes, she wanted her inheritance—for good reasons—but she wasn't sure that it was worth all *this*.

Because even if she could accept that she'd made a practical decision for all the right reasons, she certainly never should have fallen in love with the biggest manwhore of all time.

That was the part that was inexcusable.

The thing she really should have remembered, all throughout their time on Capri, was that Giaco was particularly talented in playing a role. *Of course* she thought he was falling in love the way she was. What was the man but a mirror? He showed everyone he encountered exactly what they wanted to see.

Once she accepted that unpleasant truth, clarity was simple.

And something like urgent.

She left the villa, taking nothing with her but a change

might or might not have happened on their honeymoon had no bearing on that.

Just because Ivy felt that they were in a completely different place now and would have sworn that he did too, that didn't change the fact that they were doing all of this for their own, very specific reasons.

That being a whole lot of money from a terrible, exploitative person they both despised.

She didn't think that finding herself alone on a gorgeous Italian island gave her the right to call Giaco up and demand that they change every aspect of the relationship they had both agreed on some time ago. Not just because it was her personal doom to be so deeply in love with him.

That wasn't the sort of magic that left when he did. It felt a lot more like a curse, and it had not exactly improved during their time on the island. Quite the opposite.

Ivy hadn't had the slightest idea that it was possible to love another person like this.

Heart. Mind. Soul.

And every last centimeter of her body.

A not inconsiderable part of her wanted to rage at him for doing this to her. For making her laugh. For teaching her all the things two bodies could do together, an ever-changing adventure through emotion and excitement. For making her understand that she was the best version of herself when he was a part of her, and how was she supposed to pretend she didn't know that now?

How was she supposed to pretend she was still the same person who'd seen him rise up out of that hot pool like a Roman god returned to earth to rule at will? She couldn't. Ivy wanted to share her feelings about that with him, too.

But he would have to come back for her to rage at him about anything.

An urgent matter to take care of, he'd written. *You know how to reach me.*

It was tempting to assume the worst. That he had lost interest overnight—something it seemed he'd done many times before, according to all available information about him. Ivy might have believed that she could read the intensity in him, that she could feel the way it matched her own—but he was *Giaco Tavian.*

Everyone who met him thought they knew him. What made her anything special?

Aside from the fact she was his wife, of course.

But the thing was, she knew that mattered to him. The way he always touched her rings. The way he called her *my wife* in that growly voice of his that never failed to make her heart skip a beat. If she stepped back from second-guessing herself because of his reputation and his past and thought about everything rationally, it made sense that he would simply take himself off to do whatever it was he did when he wasn't creating fantasies for the media to overdose on.

They had both agreed that this marriage would last three years, as required by the stern and upright Pau Calixto. It was what Umberto had promised the man and demanded of Ivy and Giaco. So whatever urgent matters Giaco had to attend to, the marriage would lurch along. Because it had to.

She assured herself that knowing such a thing was comforting. When the truth was, she did not feel the least bit comfortable, here in this magical place that felt more like exile without him.

It took her days to conclude that that *lurching* was all she really needed to focus on. The rules of their relationship had always been clearly outlined in the agreements they'd made with Umberto and, naturally, in the itinerary. What

CHAPTER TEN

Ivy DISCOVERED VERY quickly that Capri was not the magic.

Capri was lovely. Possibly one of the loveliest places she'd ever been, and she'd been lucky enough to see a great many spots on this planet that anyone with eyes would find stunning. But even so, it was just an island.

The magic, it turned out, was Giaco. And when he'd gone he'd taken it with him. All of it.

Leaving Ivy with...herself.

Her decidedly less magical self, who found that his absence meant she was suddenly called upon to figure out what, exactly, she planned to *do* with herself now that she was outside the tractor pull of this attraction she had to her husband.

When she'd spent most of her own life knowing precisely where she needed to go and what she needed to do.

It was a bit humbling to have spent no small part of her youth watching her mother lose herself in a man, and having assured herself that *she* would never allow herself to be at someone else's mercy like that. Only to discover that she was no stronger or better or more immune than anyone else. She had simply been lucky, before Giaco, never to encounter any man who could affect her like this.

Maybe it was more than simply a *bit* humbling, really.

His note had not exactly been illuminating.

Even when he was in the helicopter, flying high on his way back to the mainland, he was fully aware that he had left his heart behind.

Giaco would have sworn he didn't have one.

And now it didn't matter, because it was hers.

And little as he wanted to risk this now, he knew there was no choice.

He'd made this decision long ago.

It defined him.

Giaco rolled out of bed and he took his mobile outside, out onto one of the terraces that looked down at the sea that seemed to have become part of him now. Much like this island that didn't feel to him like a means to an end. Not any longer.

Nothing felt that way, and that was a problem, because the end was nigh.

He picked up the call and asked one question. "Is it ready?"

The voice on the other end of the call sounded as dark as Giaco felt. "It is."

Giaco rang off and stayed where he was, his hands braced on the rail before him.

He could see the hint of dawn, those bright summer colors streaking over the horizon, as if he was watching a painting in real time. Behind him, he knew that Ivy, his wife—*his wife*, and that mattered more than it should—was warm in their bed, that lush body of hers always willing, always ready, always somehow new.

But he had always known that this would end. He had always known that this day would come.

So he went back inside and he scribbled a note to her, then left it by the bed. When he was done he leaned over and smoothed her hair back from her face. She murmured something in her sleep, and then quieted when he kissed her on one flushed cheek.

Then he walked away, made a few terse phone calls to make arrangements, and drove away from the villa before the sun fully made it over the horizon.

Not in the storm of sex or the intensity of desire. Not that those things were absent in this moment. He knew they were never far.

But right now, in the sea air, it was as simple as the ringing of a bell tower calling out the hour.

It wasn't a feeling. It was a fact.

For the first time in his entire life, the most infamous despoiler of women in Europe was in love.

Head over heels, impossibly, and probably irreversibly in love.

That fact settled in him, and he let it.

When they finished their meal and headed back down the ancient streets toward his car, he took her hand and guided her into the moonlight, away from the shadows.

They were there another week before the call came.

Another week of shadowless, impossible joy.

Then his mobile buzzed early one morning. Giaco almost pretended he didn't hear it—and that told him things he wasn't sure he wanted to know about himself. How much these weeks had changed him. How much *she* had changed him.

But the only way out was through. He had always known that. Really, that had been the point. Giaco had never anticipated meeting someone who would make him regret all these choices he'd made and committed to, long ago.

Or, if not regret them, understand that once he went through with this thing that he had been working toward for so long, it would change them, too. He could not see how it could not. For one thing, it would fundamentally disrupt the agreement that he and Ivy had made. He hadn't considered that a factor when he'd agreed to their marriage. He hadn't expected to *care*.

Everything on the island of Capri was bright. The sun, the sea. The colors of the buildings, the smiles of all the people.

The two of them were, too.

Sometimes he was certain that Ivy knew as well as he did that they could only stay safe if they kept away from the shadows.

"I know exactly who I am," he told her, and that was true. He played with her hand in his, moving her rings on her finger. "You asked me for no masks and I'm not wearing one. Maybe I am pensive, little saint. Maybe this is who I am when no one's looking."

"I'm looking," she whispered.

"But you are like the moon over the sea," he told her, not sure where the words were coming from—only that they needed to be said. That he *had* to say them, like they were coming from a part of him Giaco barely knew. "Not a spotlight or flashbulb. And don't you know? Everyone looks better in the moonlight."

She shook her head at him, and then leaned across the table to kiss him. It was sweet. It was perfect. It was only a kiss, and they were in public, so there could be no deepening it.

Not that the public part mattered as much as the *kind* of public this was. A restaurant was not a hiking trail. It was not a grotto off the beaten path where it was worth the risk.

That was not the sort of press Giaco wished to make.

So she kissed him, and they held hands over the table, and it was so simple. It was so *easy* to be here, sipping Capri spritzes beneath the stars while gentle music played. They ate food fresh from the sea and simple, perfect Caprese salads and talked of absolutely nothing at all—yet hung on each other's words.

And that was when Giaco knew.

run through your hands like water and leave no trace behind."

She shrugged. "That's not my experience."

He blinked, not sure if he was taken aback by what she'd said or that brisk tone she'd used. As if it was so obvious that she wasn't sure why she was even saying it out loud.

"I mean it," she said when all he could manage to do was stare at her. "You tried, back at the castle. You did your best, but that version of you that everyone seems to know is not at all believable once a person spends time with you." She tilted her head slightly to one side then and he had the strangest urge to pull his hand away from hers. That he didn't felt heroic. "But it seems as if *you* believe it."

And there were so many things he couldn't tell her. Secrets he had agreed to keep—secrets that had never been any hardship to keep. This had all been too long coming. It had taken years.

He wanted to tell her, but he didn't. He couldn't. It wasn't that he didn't trust her—it was the simple truth that he didn't trust himself.

Giaco had kept his secret for so long that it had become a kind of superstition. He worried that if he shared it with anyone, for any reason, that would make certain that it all fell apart. That he would fail when he was so close to the end.

He didn't dare risk it.

He *couldn't* risk it.

But he also couldn't play his usual role with her any longer. Not after the weeks they'd spent on this island, wrapped up in each other. Not only would she not believe it, but for the first time in as long as he could recall, he *couldn't*. He didn't have it in him. Not now. Not when they'd learned so many truths about each other while they'd been here.

He had taken her around the island over these days that bled one into the next. They had explored the Roman ruins. They had driven through the rural splendor of Anacapri. They had climbed in the hills, lain out on the beaches, and found ways to have sex in a variety of public places like they were a pair of teenagers.

Though he couldn't recall having quite as much fun when he'd actually been one.

Normally, if someone accused him of something like *being pensive*, he would drawl something impertinent, change the subject, and have them wondering why they'd imagine him capable of such a thing.

But this was Ivy. "I don't feel pensive," he said. "Or not unduly so."

She leaned closer and propped her chin on her hand.

"Do you think it's Capri that has changed us?" she asked, with that directness and simplicity that killed him every time. "Or do you think we're not changed and this is simply a fun holiday, and when we go back we will simply... act as if this never happened?"

He found that his ribs hurt and he could not account for it. "I think that learning how to live in the moment, since it's the only thing we really have, is always wise," he told her.

Yet Ivy, rather than taking his sage counsel, rolled her eyes. "I love when you say things like that." Though her tone suggested that she did not, in fact, love it. "Because, of course, you like to make it seem as if you've lived only in the moment your whole life. But I know better."

"Ask anyone," he dared her, but not in his usual joking, careless tone. There was something else inside him tonight. It felt almost like a kind of grief. "I am reckless, untrustworthy, undependable, and impossible to pin down. I will

a kind of goodbye the night before their wedding and he had been, because he'd understood that their wedding was the start of a countdown that would end all of these games and schemes.

This was only a little bit of interstitial space as he waited for the phone call that would change everything. The phone call he'd been working toward his whole adult life.

This was a breath in between. It could never be anything else.

So perhaps it was unsurprising that it felt like more.

"You seem so pensive," Ivy said one night. They had ventured out again and if pictures of them had made it off the island, he wouldn't know, because he'd set his mobile to block every number save one. They sat at a restaurant that was right there on the pretty bay in the marina. They were both sun-kissed and bright, and he had spent the better part of an afternoon teaching her how to go down on him while he returned the favor on her.

This seems inefficient, she had complained.

It's an exercise in patience and restraint, he had replied.

An inefficient and tedious lesson, she'd retorted. *Did you know that you were this Catholic, Giaco?*

He had laughed, because she always made him laugh, and then made certain that she had better things to do with her mouth.

Now he reached over and took her hand across the small table, playing with the rings he'd put on her finger. It was an enduring shock to find how much he liked them there. The rings themselves and the very *idea* of this woman wearing his mark—this claim he'd put on her. He liked it more than he'd ever imagined he could like such a thing.

His mother had not raised him to think highly of the institution of marriage.

He could not seem to solve any of these mysteries. If anything, they only deepened the more time he spent with her.

So ten days in, they finally dressed. This took longer than it should have, because Giaco insisted on choosing her clothes and that led to him taking them off again, and so it was much later when they finally emerged from the villa and wandered their way down from the villa into the famous Piazzetta to take in the beating heart of Capri at last.

Giaco told himself that he needed to be on alert, making certain that they were seen. Reported upon. Made into myth and wonder for the consumption of the world.

But how could he remember something so tedious when Ivy walked with her arm around him, holding on to him as if she couldn't bear to let go? How could he concern himself with the grimy business of selling himself to the tabloids when every step they took felt so precious?

It took him another ten days to understand what was happening.

That she had worked some kind of magic on him, he could admit. That she had wrecked him when all along he'd been so certain he had the upper hand, he could grudgingly accept. That she had somehow turned him inside out and found her way beneath his skin when he least expected it—all of that he could come to terms with.

But there was only one word that really fit all the things he felt in her presence, and it was not a word he'd ever thought he'd have any sort of passing acquaintance with. Not about himself and his feelings.

Hell, Giaco had made it his life's work to pretend he'd never had a feeling at all.

He told himself that the reason this intensity did not fade away was simply because he knew it couldn't last. Because it wouldn't. It couldn't. She'd asked him if he was saying

ever as long as they were touching. As long as they were always, always touching.

They were insatiable.

Something about Ivy's wide-eyed wonder and heated delight made everything seem new to Giaco, too. Every time he touched her, it got harder and harder to recall if he'd ever touched another. He was creative, but she—

Well. She was a legend. And she was his wife.

In his experience, intensity depreciated at a rapid rate. Intensity required mystery, and once mysteries were solved, boredom set in. He had experienced this cycle more times than he—or anyone else—could count.

But there was nothing boring about Ivy.

Ten days into their honeymoon, they lay in their bed rumpled and panting. She shifted, then smiled down from where she lay stretched out on top of him. "There's a beautiful island out there," she said, pausing to kiss him. "I think we ought to explore it."

Giaco had the lowering thought that perhaps she was bored. That perhaps this wasn't about him at all.

He wasn't sure he knew what to do with that notion.

She smiled wickedly. "I want to see if we can take a walk like civilized people. Or if we really are the wild animals we seem to have turned into here."

And he laughed, because he laughed a great deal in her presence, it turned out. He wasn't sure he had ever laughed so much in all his life—not *real* laughter, anyway. It was one more reason why Ivy wasn't boring.

He tried, repeatedly, to demystify her. It never worked.

Giaco was fascinated by the way she *breathed*. The small noises she made while she slept. He was captivated by the difference in the way her collarbone tasted when compared with that sweet spot at her navel.

CHAPTER NINE

G‍IACO HARDLY KNEW HIMSELF.

They stayed in bed that first night. The villa had been stocked for their arrival and he knew that he could summon staff if he wished. But the idea of having people in the villa with them did not sit right with him.

Not when his most unexpected wife—his *wife*, a role he'd expected would be filled by some dullish sort of nun who he would have to work hard to pretend to fall in love with, but fate had given him Ivy instead—had shocked him with her innocence.

He felt…humbled. Altered in ways he was afraid to entirely examine.

Simultaneously unworthy to be in her presence, and yet certain that there was nowhere else he wished to go, nor would go.

A week into their honeymoon—that Giaco had decided to have in a place like Capri because it would lend itself to so many "accidental" photographs as they walked about the charming village and explored the island—they still hadn't left the house.

What they had done was explore—lazily, urgently—the menu that he had mentioned. They rose only to shower, or sit in the bath, or find their way out to the infinity pool, where it seemed as if they could float on the horizon for-

the one who got impatient as all of that heat grew inside her. She was the one who wrapped herself around him, crossing her ankles in the back and gripping him as tight as she could.

Until, eventually, he propped himself up on his hands so he could look down at her as he pistoned in and out of her body.

She loved it. She met every thrust. She lifted her hips to take more of him and it was like a wild flame, everywhere. Tightening. Tightening more.

Until, at last, he came down and gathered her close to him. Then he slid one hand between them and pressed down.

Hard.

And then there was nothing at all but stars. All of the cosmos, every constellation, and all of it somehow contained between them and in the two gold bands that marked them as married.

As husband, as wife.

As *one*, at last.

But when she went to put him in her mouth, he stopped her.

"Not today," he told her.

"But I want—"

"Don't worry," he said gruffly. "We have a vast menu to work our way through. But today I thought we'd keep it strictly traditional."

A breath seemed to escape of its own volition. "Traditional," she repeated. "There's not one single thing about you that's traditional."

"It's the missionary position that's traditional, little saint," he said, as he moved up her body and settled himself between her thighs. "But not usually the way I do it. Yet I haven't been married before, either. It feels rather ceremonial, doesn't it?"

And she could feel the head of his cock as he worked himself into all of her soft heat. It felt so good, just like that, that she was shivering already. Her body was filled with sensation, so bright and hot she hardly knew what to do with it, and before she could say anything at all, he simply thrust deep inside her.

There was a shock of pain. A hot, deep tear.

Giaco froze. She froze, too.

There was nothing save the thunder of her heart and that overly taut feeling deep inside her. The sense of him there, filling her. Changing her. Her body forced to shift to accommodate him, and it did.

That thought made it better. She experimented, moving her hips, and that was better still.

"Ivy," he said, thickly. With a kind of sorrow. "Ivy, it never occurred to me—"

"Giaco," she whispered fiercely. "*Do* something."

So he did.

He started slow, a slick, deep slide. So slow that she was

And then he showed her what he meant. First he shrugged out of his own clothes, and Ivy thought that having seen him naked before should have prepared her for the impact of it again, but it didn't. He took her breath away. Again.

Then again as once more, he knelt down before her and proceeded to worship her body as if he had never seen a woman before in his life.

There was no place his mouth didn't touch. No place his hands did not move, roaming all over her, making her glow with heat and longing.

When he slipped his fingers between her legs, he found her molten hot and wild. For him.

"Too pretty," he murmured. And then his fingers were thrusting inside her, making her breath hitch and her hips move to meet him, and it happened so fast. Giaco's fingers were a magic spell and her undoing at once, and she fell apart so quickly that it almost made her laugh. Maybe she was laughing. She couldn't quite tell.

Then he was pushing her back on the bed and crawling up the mattress with her until they were rolling all around. She wanted to put her mouth on him at last. She wanted him with a ferocity she couldn't explain.

Maybe it didn't need explaining. It was simply who they were, wrapped up in the heat of this. They were wearing nothing at all save the rings they'd exchanged and something about that made her feel…calamitous.

But the calamity felt like joy.

Ivy explored that chest of his, at last. She traced her way over all of those ridges and flat planes of muscle. She followed the sprinkling of dark hair all the way down to that giant cock that had been imprinted in her mind since she'd seen him come out of the water like something mythical.

And he was much bigger now.

He kissed her over and over and then he lifted her up in his arms and carried her through the sprawling, airy villa, stopping time and again to get his mouth on her. Until finally, everything spun around and they were both on a bed.

For a moment, they only stared at each other, and she knew that this was going to be different. That this time there would be no holding back. That everything had been building to this bright afternoon with the sun streaming in the windows and all that blue in the distance, but nothing but dark jade intensity here.

She felt her whole body shudder at that, while the heat of it all washed over her.

"You're my wife," he said, gritting out those words as if his life depended on them. "And you're wearing entirely too many clothes."

Wife, she thought. It sounded different when he said it like that. It sounded real, not like a charade at all.

It felt different when he pulled back, but only so he could pull her with him and stand her on her feet next to the bed. And she was absurdly grateful for every woman he'd ever touched, because it had taken a team to put her into this dress but Giaco had her out of it in a flash.

He stripped her down and stopped, gazing at the lingerie she'd put on in what seemed like a different life, back at the castle. It had been handed to her with the rest of the things she was meant to wear today and she tried to read the expression on his face as he stared at it.

"I assume you picked this out yourself," she managed to say, though her voice sounded insubstantial. Breathy. "A groom's gift you already knew you would like."

He took his time dragging his gaze back to hers. "There is not one thing I don't like about pretty, flimsy silken things on a woman's body, but I was not expecting…this. You."

his typically off-color remarks. He didn't slink toward her, brandishing his sexuality like a club.

He stared at her, and she noticed his hands flexing at his sides.

"On the other hand," she said quietly, "I happen to know a bit about masks myself. I don't think that if you chose to go without yours here it would be the end of the world."

He moved toward her then, but without all of that grace of his. He looked...jerky. Uncoordinated.

Something kicked deep in her belly, but she didn't move. It didn't occur to her to move. He kept coming until he was standing right there before her, staring down at her.

"There is not one true thing stitched into me," he told her. "I am a patchwork tapestry of lies, so many that I cannot keep track. I could not untangle them all, even if I wanted to."

She could hear a loud noise and only belatedly realized it was her own heart in her chest. Pounding out a rhythm all its own. Slamming into her ribs. The closer he came, the louder it got.

"You don't have to untangle them all," she whispered. And this, then, felt the way she thought their vows should have. "Tell me one true thing, Giaco. Just one."

He moved even closer then, a look of such powerful intensity on his face that it made her heart stutter in her chest. Then he reached out and slid his hands over her cheeks, to hold her hair. To touch her.

"This," he said, sounding gruff and unlike himself. Or possibly more like himself, at last. "The only true thing I know is this. You."

And when he kissed her it felt like all the vows they'd made, writ large. It was as if she could *feel* them, now.

It was as if the kiss made them real.

nity, its inhabitants could gaze at the sea. And more, down the hill at the village of Capri that clustered into the hillside.

Inside the main room, she turned her back on the view and stared at her husband. *Her husband*, something inside her whispered, as if that term had only now landed in her.

She folded her arms. "Do you know what I've been doing to pass the time today?"

His gaze seemed hot and dark at once. "I shudder to think."

"I've been counting up all the times I know you've lied to me, and it's quite a few. They keep coming and coming." Ivy considered him. "What I can't decide is if you're so busy wearing masks you can't tell the difference between a truth and a lie any longer. Or if you mean it. Every single lie you tell."

He stood there across the length of the room from her, and he didn't come any closer. "I don't know what you mean."

"I think that you do. And I think you might have miscalculated."

There was a flash of his smile. "Impossible. I never miscalculate."

"Everything we've done has been a group project," she pointed out. "Your house in Rome is filled with all of your people, all of the time. Your father's castle is even worse. We go on dates but we only pretend that they're private. We conduct ourselves in the glare of publicity at all times."

"That is because our affairs are publicity," he said, in that silken way of his.

"But now we are all alone. No staff. No intrusive family members. No paparazzi." She shook her head, almost as if she felt sorry for him. "You must be terrified. When your masks drop this time, you must know I'll see it."

To her shock, he didn't laugh. He didn't make one of

said, as if he was devastated it had ended. "Alas, I do believe our duty calls."

There were more pictures, because of course there were more pictures. Elaborately staged affairs to make the most of the opulent elegance on display here. No doubt fodder for another puff piece that would make it seem as if Umberto Tavian himself had personally put together his own son's wedding ceremony and reception out of the goodness of his loving heart.

No one who had ever met the man could possibly believe he had a heart. But then, rich men did not have to be kind. They only had to stay rich and no one would care what they were or to whom.

Ivy couldn't wait to read about her own wedding in a glossy magazine, with pictures of herself that would look like a stranger.

Happily, soon enough, a helicopter landed out in the field and the staff loaded it up with bags they'd packed on their own with no input from Ivy about what she might need on a honeymoon. She was getting used to that now. Once the helicopter was packed, she and Giaco were helped on board. Where they could wave out at the crowd as they flew away.

It felt a lot like an escape.

The flight wasn't long and after what felt like a short while they were circling into a landing on one of the prettiest islands in the Tyrrhenian Sea and touching down on a landing pad where a sleek convertible with a stretching cat ornament on its hood waited for them.

This time, the driver was Giaco. Thanks to the itinerary, Ivy knew that Giaco had a small estate here on the island of Capri. When they got to his villa, Ivy was charmed despite herself. Most of it was windows, so that at every opportu-

way he stiffened. "What you see is what you get when it comes to me."

"That's not even a good line. It was obvious to me the moment I saw you again."

"Though perhaps not from the very first moment," he replied, his voice a silken bit of darkness.

Ivy wasn't immune to the way that curled around her. How it sank deep into her and curled around and around until she was nothing but the heat he'd made.

But that wasn't the point.

"I actually wonder if that's why." She held his gaze. And even as he moved the two of them across the floor, with all of that elegant grace that seemed so effortless from such a powerful body, he looked very much as if he didn't see anything but her, either. "I saw all of you, and so it was impossible to see less."

"I hate to be indelicate on the day of our most blessed union," he said, his voice that dark blade that told her he was being deliberate. And likely provocative. "But seeing me naked is not exactly unique."

"I wonder," she replied. She tilted her head back and gazed at him. "You take such pride in showing yourself off but I'm beginning to think it's just a little bit of sleight of hand. If everyone is so busy looking at everything you show off and too busy concentrating on your antics, then they'll miss what you're really doing, won't they?"

She expected him to laugh at that, but there was something too sharp in his gaze. Then he twirled her around instead, which was no kind of reply. He twirled her out and then brought her in again, then dipped her low. And when he stood her up again, Ivy was dizzy and flushed and Giaco had that usual mocking curve in the corner of his mouth.

"What a fascinating line of interrogation that was," he

lie about the tedious corporate shills my father surrounds himself with," Giaco said, sounding deeply offended.

"As far as I can tell," she retorted, "you will lie about anything. Everything. Is that not so?"

But the stare he leveled on her was interrupted when they were beckoned out onto the dance floor. Ordered, more like.

"I danced with your mother at her wedding to Umberto," he told her, almost abruptly. His eyes darkened when hers widened. "She was beautiful, of course, but also unnecessarily kind to a feral young man who wanted badly to hate her when it was, in fact, his father he loathed."

"My mother was always kind," Ivy managed to say, though there was a lump in her throat. She remembered the wedding too, though Umberto had thankfully ignored her. She smiled at Giaco. "Never unnecessarily."

More beckoning from the dance floor interrupted the moment. Ivy's heart was tripping in her chest and she had to wonder if, perhaps, that was best.

Because this wasn't in the itinerary, this memory of Alana. This wasn't part of the show.

In a show of obedience, Giaco rose. He led her out into the middle of the floor, took her hand, and drew her into his arms. And Ivy knew she ought to have been listening to the music or paying attention to the steps they were meant to be doing as they danced, but she didn't care about any of that. She was too busy studying his face.

His beautiful, impossible face.

"I don't understand how it is that you fool so many people," she told him, because it was that or weep over the gift of a story about her mother that she'd never heard before.

"I don't fool anyone," he replied, though she was holding on to him and she could feel the almost imperceptible

fervent wish that she did not have to do this while being stared at by so many people who quite actively wished her ill.

But this, here in a moment that was only theirs, felt hushed.

She felt something chime deep inside her, like there was a power in the rings themselves. As if there was a magic here she hadn't understood.

Ivy could have sworn he felt it, too.

But they were still at this reception. Being watched on all sides. She swallowed, hard. "You don't like your father's business partner," she said, to change the subject.

Giaco looked at her sharply, and she thought she saw something like surprise cross his face.

"Whatever do you mean?" he asked. "I make it a point of personal pride to have no awareness whatsoever of my father's business affairs."

"He's right over there," Ivy said, and she searched the crowd until she found Pau Calixto once more, standing in the corner talking to... Well. That looked like Leontina, though she was certain she was mistaken. She'd never seen Leontina talk to anyone. She pointed him out anyway. "There, by the fountain."

"Yes, yes," Giaco murmured, with only a quick glance that way. "I don't know him. I don't like his type. Prudish. Forever on the verge of a lecture. Deeply and surpassingly boring, at a guess."

She turned to look at him, because none of that sounded like him. He almost sounded as if he was parroting himself. Ivy shook her head. "That's a lie."

Those jade green eyes widened, and he looked at her in astonishment. Astonishment laced through with arrogance, that was. "You cannot believe that I would lower myself to

they were adhering to all the rules of that kind of dress, but none of them shined bright the way Giaco did. If any of them had lost their tie or opened their collar or looked a bit as if they might have rolled around somewhere, they'd probably be so embarrassed that they would be going to the castle to change.

Giaco, by contrast, looked better than he had standing so properly at the altar. And he had looked pretty phenomenal up there, Ivy could admit. That was just a fact.

"This is not the crowd to hit up for donations to an orphans' charity," Ivy said with a shrug. "The women are feral and all want a taste of you. They are unlikely to support my endeavors. The men are too busy jostling for position around your father. They have no time to spare for the insignificant needs of the sorts of human beings I'm certain they find disposable."

"How astute," he replied in that low voice of his. "And you didn't even have to circle your way through the crowd to read them all so well."

She looked over at him, certain that she would see that mocking glint in his dark eyes, but felt a kind of shuddering inside her when there wasn't. He wasn't even looking back at her—he was looking down at her hand. Then he reached over and picked it up, playing with her finger that now sported two rings. That beautiful engagement ring he'd given her. And the platinum band beside it, its simplicity somehow as arresting as the stones.

He wore a platinum band on his finger, too. It was flatter and wider and equally absent any adornment.

Ivy hadn't felt much of anything up at that altar that the staff had made beautiful, beneath a pergola bright with summer flowers in bloom. It had all been rote recitation and a

enigmatically the way her mother always had, looking both unapproachable and at her ease.

Truly, she thought, one of the greatest gifts her mother had ever given her. All the guests continued to look at her but they didn't come near her and for the first time since she'd woken up this morning, she felt like she could breathe.

She watched Umberto fawn all over a much younger man who looked to be about Giaco's age and who, unlike everyone else at the castle today, seemed completely unmoved by the Tavian influence. If anything, he looked stern and forbidding, as if he was the one taking the measure of Umberto.

This could only mean that he was the famous Pau Calixto, the morally upright Spaniard billionaire who was the reason Ivy was in a wedding dress today. Even more interesting, to her mind, was the fact that Giaco seemed to dislike him. He was busy charming everyone else at the party, but when it came to Pau Calixto, he looked…as if his famous magnetism was unavailable to him.

And here Ivy had always thought that Giaco could make it look as if he was intimate with anyone and everyone. No matter who they were.

When Giaco finally came to find his bride at her solitary table, he had done two full circuits of every last guest at this reception.

"You really do know how to work a crowd," Ivy murmured. "It's really quite impressive."

"I would have thought you'd be doing the same thing," he said as he came to stand beside her, then bonelessly slid into the chair next to hers.

The moment he was sitting, he was lounging. And he already looked rumpled, the way he always did. It was something she thought only outrageously beautiful men could get away with. Everyone else here was in formalwear, and

who clearly felt that they ought to have been Giaco's bride. Not content to simply throw dirty looks at her from across the bit of field near the vineyards that had been turned into a luxurious, tented reception area, they liked to come up and introduce themselves. So she could see their talons up close.

Ivy smiled and greeted each and every one of them as if they were long-lost friends. She wondered if this would hurt her more if she and Giaco actually had true feelings for each other. Or, at least, if they'd started that way. If it hadn't been an ice-cold business arrangement from the start.

Though as Ivy nursed her drink, because somehow she didn't think a fuzzy head would help with anything, she had to question her own characterization of the start of this whole marriage thing. Her memories of that day were not *ice cold* at all.

It was all Giaco naked. Then Giaco lounging on that couch. And then the pictures that he'd taken, that she sometimes remembered as if they were the truth of what had really happened. As if the story they told was what had gone on between them when she knew it hadn't.

Or not then, anyway.

Her body clenched around the memory of his fingers. His mouth.

No, *ice cold* was not how she would describe this marriage at all. Nor was it all that *businesslike*—not according to any definition of that word she'd ever known.

This wedding, on the other hand, was both of those things.

After one too many rounds with the society women who went out of their way to let her know that they had sampled her husband—or wanted to, it was hard to tell the difference—Ivy retreated. She found a place to sit at one of the tables almost out of the tent entirely, where she could smile

that. Not when she had barely slept last night, too aware of the tender place between her legs that he'd claimed so intensely, so completely.

And because she'd understood, as she'd watched him walk away, that this wedding was no new beginning. Not for them. What she didn't know was *how* he planned to leave her when they'd agreed to the same terms.

But when Gabriele hissed at her to look lively, Ivy headed down the aisle—on her own—and surrendered herself to one of the most over-the-top weddings and receptions she'd ever experienced in her life.

The only way to make it bearable was to remind herself that it really wasn't about her at all. Because it wasn't.

There were those moments when she and Giaco said their vows. There was that odd light in his dark eyes, and the way he looked at her when he slid a ring on her finger—but that was overshadowed by the spectacle that Umberto was putting on all around them.

Even Giaco seemed different, lost too firmly behind his mask today.

Ivy told herself that all she had to do was smile, look pretty, and pretend this was all happening to somebody else.

The reception was a whirl. Gabriele collected Ivy's train and bustled her dress so she could walk around, though she didn't see the point to it. She didn't know anyone here. She didn't care to know them. They weren't even the sorts of people that she would normally reach out to for donations to her charity. These were powerbrokers on a different scale. They weren't here to talk about donations. They were trafficking in far higher stakes.

This meant that Ivy could excuse herself from having to do anything at all but observe.

She watched the vultures circle, particularly the women

So the fact that she had no father to walk her down an aisle and no mother to hug her fiercely and make her smile didn't matter, either.

She'd tried her best to believe it.

Because she could not quite accept that getting married to a man who she knew was only pretending to care about her—likely even when he touched her—made her feel some kind of orphaned all over again.

She told herself what mattered was what came when this particular circus show was finished. That was the only thing she should be thinking about.

But what she really felt as Gabriele ushered her down the steps of the castle, and outside toward the cleverly sophisticated altar that had been arranged in a beautiful spot overlooking the vineyards and the hills, was that she and Leontina had a lot of lost time to make up for. That really, that was something worth *feeling* about. And that when her sister-in-law got married—whether at Umberto's command or not—Ivy would be there.

Whether she was still playing charades with Giaco or not.

As she thought that, she saw Umberto sitting in the front row of the chairs that had been set up for this wedding, loudly holding court. And the enormity of what was happening here seemed to land on her with all its weight.

It was a charade, sure enough, but it was going to hurt.

Life in this castle had been every person for themselves. There had been no room for connection. Only survival. She had to assume that her marriage would be more of the same. Ivy already knew that when it ended, at the three-year mark she and Giaco had agreed to, her heart would be broken and she would have to find a way to live without the endless frustration and fascination that was Giaco.

She honestly didn't know how she was going to manage

getting married. And even if it had, said two people were putting on a show anyway.

But Leontina proved her wrong that easily, with her honest, earnest expression and the way she looked directly at Ivy. Ivy felt salt prickle the back of her eyes.

"I don't want to overstep," Leontina continued in the same quietly sincere manner. "But last night I found myself thinking that should I get married as my father insists I will, and at his command, what I'll miss the most is my mother. That made me wonder if you did, too. And she can't be here, I know. But I can."

The prickle behind Ivy's eyes became more of a threat. "That is the sweetest thing anyone could possibly have said to me today," she said. She reached out a hand to grab Leontina's, and it was like a new understanding bloomed between them. A new bond. She could feel it warm her, deep inside. Maybe this was what healing felt like. "*Thank you.*"

And after Leontina left, Ivy sat with that. The offer, the warmth. The notion that somehow, she and Leontina had become the friends they always should have been this morning. Even as Gabriele and his minions hurried her into her gown, and spent what she considered an unnecessary amount of time debating the fall of her excessively theatrical train, she kept coming back to that offer.

As if Leontina had figured out something that Ivy wasn't sure she'd known herself.

Or maybe she had, because she'd been telling herself all along that it didn't matter that she didn't have anyone at this wedding. It didn't matter because it wasn't a real wedding. It was just a game. A show.

A show she had to perform in, and beautifully, to finally have access to her money so she could pass it on to those in far greater need than she'd ever been.

Leontina said in her quiet voice, though even that seemed to hit different today. It sounded far more intense, and measured, than Ivy remembered. "My brother doesn't get married every day. I thought I ought to represent the family right, though obviously, normally, I prefer not to be noticed." Color dusted her cheeks and she looked away down. "I also wanted to make you an offer. One that you can refuse, of course."

"What kind of offer?" Ivy asked, intrigued.

If her former stepsister, soon to be sister-in-law, offered her a getaway car, she honestly didn't know what she would do.

Instead, Leontina sat down on the chair Ivy had waved her to. She blew out a breath. Ivy tried not to feel self-conscious. Her hair was done and her makeup perfect, but she wore only a robe as Gabriele and the rest of the stylist battalion were doing something with her dress in the other room. She hadn't asked what.

She also hadn't imagined that she'd be entertaining anyone in this state, but she was too intrigued to let the small matter of being underdressed get to her.

"I wanted to offer my services as a stand-in family member," Leontina said, smiling at Ivy with what looked like determination more than anything else. "I know you don't have any. And I'm not entirely sure that you *like* Giaco all that much, which, fair enough. He's a lot. But this is your wedding. So if you feel like you wish you had family of your own, well, I did used to be your stepsister. And I always wished that things were different here. What I mean is, I can be family for you, if you like. If that would help."

Ivy had thought that it was a long shot that she would shed even a single tear at this wedding. Given that it was such a circus and had nothing to do with the two people

she'd never sat in here. It was too exposed. There was no lock on the door. She'd always preferred to hide away in her bedroom, behind a lock and beneath the covers of her bed—but that was a long time ago.

Today she was halfway through her preparations for a wedding that had felt real last night, with Giaco's clever mouth between her legs. Yet today, the profound fakeness of what they were doing seemed to weigh upon her like blocks of concrete hung from her shoulders.

She could have done without all these contradictory emotions altogether.

Perhaps that was why it took her longer than it should have to register that Leontina did not look the way she normally did. On the contrary. She was wearing a dress, and not the usual sort of dress she wore, shapeless and deliberately unforgettable. This dress was a bright magenta color that clung to her body, so that all a person looking at her could really see was her endlessly long legs in the high shoes she was wearing. It also called attention to her dramatically lithe figure that would not have looked out of place on a runway model or a prima ballerina.

It made Ivy wonder all over again if it was, in fact, genetics that gave Giaco his outrageously beautiful form. But she focused on the woman still standing in front of her, noticing the other major difference. Leontina did not have her hair scraped back into her usual severe bun. Today it was flowing all around her, thick, dark waves that fell halfway down her back.

"My God," Ivy said, a smile taking over her mouth. "Look at you. You're absolutely stunning. I can't believe you hide all of this all the time."

Leontina smiled back, and that only drew attention to the dark jade eyes she shared with her brother. "Thank you,"

CHAPTER EIGHT

LEONTINA WALKED INTO Ivy's rooms in the castle the following morning without an invitation, but with a cautious sort of smile on her face. "I hope I'm not intruding," she said, softly.

Ivy wasn't sure that she and her former stepsister and soon-to-be sister-in-law had ever had a proper heart-to-heart. Back in the day, growing up here, everyone had kept their head down and handled their own trauma. It wasn't much of a bonding experience. And this time around, though Ivy had spent a good deal less time in the castle, she'd only seen Leontina when Umberto demanded that there be so-called family gatherings. She still had the impression that the other woman deliberately kept herself to the shadows.

That she'd sought out Ivy of her own volition seemed like a significant shift. That alone would have intrigued Ivy.

But it was also Ivy's wedding day. And she very much wanted to stop thinking about the implications of that. The same way she didn't want to think about what had happened last night, either. Much less how it had ended, with Giaco walking away.

It had seemed prophetic.

"Of course you're not intruding," Ivy said, and waved Leontina to a chair near hers in the sitting room that had always abutted the rooms considered hers here. As a girl,

looked at him, all heat and desire. Like then, he'd thought she had never been more glorious. Except this time he could taste her in his mouth.

They studied each other for what felt like an eternity.

"Tell me," she said, in a voice that was little more than a rasp after all that pleasure, while her blue gaze moved all over his face and made him feel as exposed as if she flayed him open, "why does this feel like a goodbye?"

Giaco made himself smile, though it sat on his face wrong. He could feel it. "I can't imagine," he said. This should have come easily to him. This was what he was good at. Blowing smoke. Flashing mirrors. "We marry in the morning. This is the very opposite of goodbye, Ivy."

But later, after he'd walked away and left her there—after he forced himself not to look back—he knew that they were both perfectly aware that he was lying.

Yet again.

He kissed her instead, because she tasted like wonder. Like hope.

She tasted clean, like truth.

And more than that, she had somehow managed to insinuate herself so deeply beneath his skin that some days he thought that he had nothing at all in his mind but her.

Ivy was dressed as if she was a bride already, in exquisite cream from head to toe, and he couldn't bear it. He turned her around and sat her down on the window ledge, then knelt down at her feet. He looked up the length of her lush, lithe body to see all that wild heat in her blue eyes.

Giaco slid his hands up her legs, pulling up the hem of her skirt as he went. He stroked his fingers beneath the panties she wore, pulling them to one side to find that glistening heat that he knew waited for him there.

And then he leaned in and buried his head between her legs.

She made the most beautiful noise he'd ever heard. Her hips jolted, and then rocked against him as he licked his way deep inside her, and then ate his fill.

He lost track of the number of times she shook against him. The way her fingers dug in hard to grip his hair, leaving pricks of pain that he hoped he would feel later.

He lost track of the screams she stopped bothering to muffle, and he half hoped the whole castle heard.

If he could have broadcast to the world that everything between them was real, just like this, he would have.

When he finished, he tucked her swollen, sweet center away again, covering her with the scrap of lace he tugged back into place. He smoothed her skirt back down her legs and when he sat back to look up at her, she looked…disheveled.

It reminded him of that night in the study when she'd

done with this, even though he felt the same way. There was something about her wanting to be done with this terrible castle, with his family, too.

With him, was what he meant.

He didn't like how very much she wanted to be done with *him*.

But, "I can't wait to find out," he replied as he followed her to the window.

When she looked up at him, he had a sudden, spectacular vision of who she could be for him, if this was real. What kind of partner and ally she would be, if things were different. If they were what they seemed. What a glorious thing indeed it could be to be married to this woman.

But reality came in on the heels of that vision, hard.

Because Giaco couldn't have that, could he?

Because she wasn't wrong about him. He was made of lies. He couldn't be honest with her or anyone else. Not after so many years of waiting for this very moment.

That was not a possibility. And it meant that no matter how much he wanted her—and he was beginning to realize that wanting her had become the cornerstone of his existence—he couldn't really have her.

Because this game they were playing was one thing. But the woman he'd come to know while they played it would not accept anything less than honesty from a man who was her *real* partner. He didn't have to ask. He knew.

And all of this sat in him like lead. It was a sour taste in his mouth.

He hated it.

Giaco didn't think. He kissed her, taking her mouth with a kind of urgency he couldn't fully explain to himself, because he didn't wish to know himself quite that well. Not when there was so little he could do to change.

Leontina as a last-ditch effort to fix her unfixable marriage, only she had not come out a boy—had not died on purpose.

He had made certain she'd never thought that. He'd gone out of his way to make sure she thought their mother hadn't had a choice about whether or not to leave her. It only seemed right.

"It doesn't matter what I believe," his little sister told him, her gaze grave. "It only matters what *he* believes. I don't think you've been paying attention."

And then she left the table, so that it was only Giaco and this woman he would marry the following day. This woman who he should never have turned around and seen through that window. This woman that he should never have touched.

She stared back at him for a moment that quickly became uncomfortable. Then she rose from her seat and made her way over to the windows. It was early summer in Tuscany now. The hills were covered in wildflowers. Everything was lush and green. Outside, the sun was still busying itself with setting and the sky was orange, melting into the dark hills and making them glow.

But he had long since ceased to find anything more beautiful than Ivy.

"Imagine when we'll be gone from this place again and that man won't matter anymore," she said quietly.

And that hit Giaco harder than it should have. Harder than expected, anyway. He would have said that there wasn't much that anyone could say about his family that would bother him any longer. None of it could be worse than the things he said himself. Certainly not when it came to his father.

There was something about this moment. This woman on this night.

Because there was something about *her* wanting to be

Giaco did was laugh at the old man. Which, predictably, drove the narcissistic asshole up a wall.

But despite the fact that everything in him *wanted* to do it, and he felt somehow misshapen because he was playing the part of the dutiful son he wasn't, the real truth was that he didn't seem to have it in him anymore.

Giaco stared across the table at Ivy, whose fault this was. He might not know what was happening to him, not really. He wanted to say that it had started that night in his library, but he knew better. It had started before that.

It had started the moment he'd looked up from that damned hot pool to find her watching him from the window.

The supreme unfairness of this happening now, when he could least afford a misstep, wasn't lost on him. He was just lucky that he'd intended this little show of meekness. That this wasn't throwing the whole plan into disarray.

"Well," Umberto said, glowering at the rest of them as he stood abruptly from his chair. "I don't know that I've ever had a meal more tedious. I expect all of you to be on exemplary behavior tomorrow. Or there will be consequences. *Dire* consequences."

Then he stormed from the room after all, no poking or prodding required.

Ivy blinked. "He does realize it's not his wedding, doesn't he?"

"It's all his," Leontina said then, looking up from her lap briefly. Her eyes widened as she looked from Ivy to Giaco. "You must have noticed already. It's his world. We live in it only because he allows us to."

"You don't actually believe that," Giaco said, frowning at his younger sister. His much younger sister who, as far as he knew, had always believed that their mother—who'd had

Giaco was old enough to do without her. Not after she'd decided that she no longer wished to worry about any pandering herself when what she could do instead was be done with it.

The trouble was that Giaco couldn't access that version of him any longer. He could picture that version of himself in his own mind. He could see the sorts of things that he would have said in a situation like this. It wasn't even hard. It was all right there, on the tip of his tongue.

Yet he also understood that it was what Umberto wanted. It was why he'd forced them all to sit down to this unpleasant dinner in the first place. He *wanted* reasons to shout, to be furious with his son. To have more reasons to threaten Giaco.

That Giaco was not giving it to him fit with Giaco's supposed acquiescence to his father's demands. It was all part of the plan. What had never occurred to Giaco, in all his plotting, was that *not* acting out, *not* indulging in a battle of wits with the father he found ill-equipped, would feel like amputating his own limbs.

Umberto probably wouldn't have minded if Leontina got mouthy instead. Or at least if she drew a bit of fire, as hard as that was to imagine. That would give Umberto an opportunity to berate her for the quiet, forever-hiding-in-plain-sight personality she'd cultivated to deal with him, because Umberto took pleasure in making the people around him feel small.

Giaco could see exactly how to start poking at everyone to make Umberto huff away again tonight, muttering threats at his only son as he went. He'd done it a thousand times before. He'd protected his sister this way. He'd even protected his mother, back in the day.

It was satisfying to draw fire from Umberto, because all

come through, as always. Ivy looked like a dream. Her blond hair was piled on top of her head and the moonstone and opal earrings she wore set off her ring beautifully. She was dressed in shades of cream, like a good bride-to-be.

Once again, he thought of the way she'd clenched around his finger and nearly embarrassed himself right there at the table.

The silence in the room marched on, unabated, as this was not a family who *chatted*. It was a dire, quiet meal, while everyone who wasn't Umberto waited for the inevitable explosion. Surely everyone else could feel it, pressing down on them like so much memory and too many ghosts.

It took Giaco all the way to the sullen dessert course to realize that normally, he would have provided the comic relief and/or the drama for the evening. He would have been outrageous from the moment he'd entered the room. He would have poked at everyone around the table, made withering remarks on the one hand and talked in overwrought innuendo on the other. He would have made everyone so uncomfortable and so furious that it was likely at least one person would have stormed off, and he would have laughed his way all through it.

That had been his primary role in this family for as long as he could remember. He poked. He prodded. Whatever thunderous, scathing thing his father might like to say or do, Giaco would ruin it in advance. He would steal all the thunder out of the room before it had a chance to start the faintest bit of rumbling.

And he knew why he did it, too.

But his mother would not thank him for continuing to pander to this man, even if it was only make-believed and peppered with a good deal of provocation, too. Not after she'd affected her own escape the moment she'd thought

tuous change of heart. The love of a good woman and all that shit. Buon lavoro, *and so on.*

Giaco had found himself having the entirely uncharacteristic urge to argue with his father. To tell him that, in fact, he would be lucky indeed if a woman like Ivy loved him. And he had been so appalled that the idea of saying such a thing to his father had even occurred to him that he was still recovering from it now.

His father had insisted that the family gather together. Giaco couldn't say he understood why. As far as he knew, Umberto was as disinterested in his children as he was, historically, in his wives.

His younger sister, Leontina, sat opposite Giaco, her posture perfect. She looked like a dancer, he thought. The sort of ballerina who had been caught in a music box, kept under a glass shell, never to see the light of day unless someone wound her up. In the castle, of course, no one ever did.

He had done his sister the very great favor of giving her his distance. He had taken the brunt of his father's temper as best he could, and he knew he was the child who most often drew Umberto's fire. He'd thought that was the best he could do for a younger sister he hardly knew.

Only tonight did it occur to him to wonder if perhaps he might have taken a different tack with her. Perhaps offered the family she hadn't otherwise had. After all, he was the one who had known their mother better. He'd had that gift.

Giaco did not share his musings with the group.

And not only because he didn't like how said musing made him feel about his actions as a brother all these years.

He turned his attention to his soon-to-be-bride instead, a surefire way to distract himself.

Ivy looked stunning, as always. Gabriele had thrown several epic fits about timeline readjustments and then had

"Whyever not? Isn't that why you're doing this?" He didn't wait for her to answer that. "We leave for the castle tomorrow. The wedding will be this weekend. It will seem the obvious conclusion to this glorious whirlwind we're caught up in. I can't wait to read all about it."

"Me neither," she said, that blue gaze of hers a little too intent on his. "After all, you can find the truth of things in the strangest places, can't you?"

He opted not to answer that, either.

Though being subjected to Ivy's entirely too all-seeing, all-knowing gaze seemed like a far better option than finding himself seated at an extremely awkward family dinner later that week.

It was the night before their hastily arranged wedding. Umberto had been complaining bitterly for days about the extremely powerful people whose schedules he'd had to ask them to rearrange in order to attend.

I suppose we'll find out how powerful you really are, Giaco had said with an excessively insolent shrug, lounging about bonelessly in his father's office. He'd been trying his best not to remember the last time he had been in his father's office, mesmerized by his former stepsister's shocking beauty. Proving to her that there was chemistry in the pictures he'd taken when he'd already known that there was chemistry. He'd felt it immediately.

It had taken an effort to concentrate on his father's sneering, profane response. He'd only shrugged again. *If you are as omnipresent as you believe, surely they will all drop everything to dance attendance upon you*, he'd said. *How clarifying it all will be.*

All you need to do, his father had growled at him, *is get married tomorrow and keep doing whatever it is you're doing to convince the world that you had a beautiful, vir-*

away in the corner of his house. Other times, there was a certain thumping from her room that made him think that she did the sort of workout videos he knew were available everywhere now. She spent much of her day taking calls and sending emails. And then in the evenings, she liked to walk. They didn't walk out into the city unless it was planned out in advanced, so she did it here.

He stood in one corner and watched her as she moved. And he knew that she saw him and had heard him, but she didn't say anything until she came back around. She stopped then, a few feet away from him. "Why?" she asked. She studied him. "I thought the itinerary was an immutable document, inerrant and inflexible."

"You object?"

"I have no feelings on it one way or the other," she said, and Giaco felt extremely virtuous that he did not call her out on her emotions. Or the fact that she was lying. He could see it written all over her, though he kept that to himself. Besides, she kept going. "Obviously the sooner we're in, the sooner we're out, and that works for me. But since this is an enterprise that we're both engaged in, I think you should probably update me on what's really happening."

"Love," he said, because it turned out he couldn't help himself. Not really. Especially when she frowned. "Everyone loves a love story, my little saint. I think it might be best to strike while the iron is hot. And while so many people remain this deeply interested in us."

"You haven't told me why you're really doing this," she said then, surprising him. He decoded that he already regretted this interaction. Her skin was glowing from her walk in the sultry evening heat and he didn't need further reminders that she was, by far, the most irresistible woman he'd ever encountered. "It can't only be money."

a look they were used to seeing from him, so the pack of them quieted down immediately.

"I never expected to fall in love," he said simply. "But now that I have, I naturally wish to be with her. Always. I want forever, immediately." He smiled. "I'm still the same man I ever was, my friends. Instant gratification has always taken too long for me."

So it was that Umberto, who no doubt would have ordered him to stick to the original itinerary if he'd suggested any changes to it, called Giaco the very next day and demanded that the wedding be held as soon as possible.

The old man was entirely too predictable.

Giaco and Ivy were both at home that night and he opted not to dwell too much on how using that word—*home*—to mean the place where both of them lived…got to him. Because he didn't think that it should have. It should not matter to him at all. After all, she had her own set of rooms and they barely saw each other.

He made certain of that, in fact. Ever since that night in his study—

But he tried not to think about that.

Which was to say, he woke in the night, broken out in a full sweat and his cock so hard it hurt, wondering why the hell he'd walked away from her.

"We decided to accelerate the wedding timeline," he told her, in as dry a voice as possible. As if they both worked on a factory line somewhere and he was discussing something as arid and unemotional as the mechanics of the machines they used.

He'd come upon her on one of the laps she took around the open-air gallery that looked down on the courtyard. He knew her routine by now. She woke in the morning and had a light breakfast. Sometimes she visited the gym tucked

CHAPTER SEVEN

THE ORIGINAL PLAN, thanks to a timeline handed down by Umberto, had been to carry on with the romance over the summer. To tease it out to the public, particularly now that they were engaged, and continue stoking the flames of all the public's interest until it was nothing short of an inferno.

But after that night in Giaco's favorite room in his house in Rome—his personal library that he doubted he would ever enter again without remembering the little noises that Ivy made in the back of her throat right before she came—Giaco decided that the timeline needed to be accelerated.

He could have discussed this with everyone involved. He could have called a meeting, solicited opinions, and taken notes, but he didn't.

Instead, he allowed himself to be captured by a group of reporters as he was enjoying an excessively priced espresso in a famous café that sat not far from the Spanish Steps. Not a place anyone went for privacy.

"Don't you think that you and your stepsister are moving too fast?" one of the reporters shouted at him as he left the café and presented himself on the busy Via dei Condotti, bustling with foot traffic and thick with tourists.

Giaco laughed. "I don't," he told them.

Then he shrugged and made sure he looked *rueful*. Not

Ivy had a deep certainty inside her, then. It wasn't something she would have wanted to defend, but she knew it was true all the same. She was pretty sure that Giaco had exposed himself tonight.

Because surely, if he was the cynical, emotionally detached fuck boy that he liked to pretend he was, he would have simply tossed her down on the couch behind her and been done with it. She had the strangest notion that what she'd seen tonight was his true face.

She had accused him of wearing a mask, and then he'd dropped it. If he hadn't, why would he have bothered to run away?

And later, when she stood in the shower in her suite, she was even more certain of two things. First, that she was never going to sleep again, not with all of this in her head now. And second, that the more she saw of him—the more real parts of him he showed her, whether against his will or not—the more she wanted him.

Not because they were playing their parts.

But because she was starting to think that Giaco Tavian really was the narcotic everyone claimed he was, after all.

Giaco muttered something she couldn't understand and then shifted her again, this time pushing a finger deep inside her.

Then it began all over again. The rocking. The heat. The inexhaustible build—

This time, when it hit her, she cried out.

And then stood there, bewildered, because he was suddenly...gone.

It took a terrible effort to come back into herself.

He wasn't *gone*, she realized. Giaco was standing a few feet away from her with a stark look on his face. She couldn't quite read him.

But she could see that enormous cock of his, pressed hard against the loose fabric of his trousers. She was still riding through her aftershocks and she couldn't imagine what she must look like to him, her mouth wet from his. Her whole body ravaged, and shaking. She wasn't even sure about the state of the shorts she was wearing, much less how far up her abdomen her tank top had rolled.

Yet Giaco looked at her as if she was a ghost.

Then he turned, abruptly, and left her there.

And it took her a long time to catch her breath. Ivy stood there, still gripping that sofa, until her heart settled down. Until her body calmed...

To some degree, anyway.

It was tempting to see what had happened as some kind of cruel rejection, but she didn't.

She thought about that kiss in the alleyway and how she'd been the one who'd had to break it. How she'd been the one who'd had to step back, and how she'd thought at the time that he'd looked a lot as if that wasn't something he'd been about to do at all.

And here, now, that *look* on his face.

so easily. They moved over her, stirring up a restless hunger everywhere he touched her. One moved over her hair, caught back in a loose, messy braid. Another moved down her back, then tested the curve of her butt.

It had been a warm day in Rome and she was wearing a loose pair of shorts that she sometimes slept in, too. And a tiny little tank top because she'd been sitting out in the courtyard, encouraging the sun to dust her skin something more than its usual pale white.

Now she wondered about her motivations for that, too.

But the thing about Giaco was that he didn't seem to wonder about anything.

He just did as he pleased.

His hands moved to the low waist of her shorts and then his fingers slid beneath the elastic band, and then it was happening.

It was so smooth, so inevitable, that she didn't have time to process it. It wasn't happening and then it was—his long, hard fingers curving into her heat, slipping beneath her panties she wore and finding her molten hot folds.

He stroked her there, he stirred her up, and she hardly knew what to do with herself. Her hands were fists in that shirt of his, and he moved—shifting her up so she was straddling one of those thick, muscled thighs of his.

And still he played with her core, his fingers working a magic she hadn't understood as possible until this moment. All the while he kept that thigh a hard pressure between her legs, and she couldn't seem to help herself. She rocked against him, and his fingers didn't stop, and there was a rocking and the pressure and the friction and—

She shattered, hard and wild. It came fast and hot, like a punch. Then she shook and shook against him, her head falling forward against his chest.

her way. A glance behind her told her she was standing at the back of the sofa that faced the currently unlit fireplace.

But if he noticed that he'd pinned her, he certainly didn't seem to care.

"Everybody lies," Giaco said in that same quietly dark way. "If you don't think that someone is putting on a performance for you, you're not looking closely enough. Let's talk about your performances, shall we? Lady Bountiful. Saint Ivy of the Orphans, casting her goodness all about her like palm fronds. Who are you when you're at home, I wonder?"

"I suppose we'll never know," she retorted, "as I was chased out of my home by the demon horde you have on speed dial."

"What I cannot understand is this act," he replied, as if she hadn't spoken at all. "You were raised in celebrity. It has touched every aspect of your life. Yet you act as if no one ever told you that it was a game, and I cannot account for that. You're damn right that *I* play it, and well."

"Do you play it?" she asked, leaning closer to him. "Or at this point, is it just playing you?"

Giaco leaned in, his hands gripping the back of the sofa on either side of her body, caging her there. "I don't care," he murmured.

And then his mouth was on hers again.

It was as if sheer exultation was a tap that he could turn on and off, because it flooded her. And it occurred to her only now, only with his mouth on hers, only when she could arch forward and wrap her arms around his neck and press her body to his, that this was exactly what she wanted.

That maybe all those feelings she couldn't quite name were this.

A deep yearning for *this*. For him.

For the way his hands seemed to know her body so well,

is you, but you don't live anywhere, do you? You merely… exist between photo ops. Isn't that right?"

It was possible that she was being too harsh. But this was some strange amalgamation of all of these unwieldy feelings that she'd been combating since the start of this. Maybe it was the ring. Maybe it was that damned kiss. Maybe it was the fact that she felt as if she'd been hunted out of her own home, like a hapless fox.

Maybe it was just that she didn't like feeling hapless *or* hunted.

Also, she thought it was true.

"How astute," he said, in that cutting way of his.

He set his heavy book aside. And then he was rising up with more of that impossible effortlessness of his. All of that athletic grace. It set her teeth on edge.

It did more than that. It made her remember the taste of him, and the way that perfect, cruel mouth of his had coaxed so much sensation out of her. Perhaps he'd even licked it *into* her. It was too much.

He was too much.

"You're putting on an act so no one can see who you really are," she managed to say, though his gaze was trained on her now and he was heading her way. "Aren't you?"

"Thank you," he drawled, drawing closer. "Without this incisive psychiatric breakdown of my innermost self, how could I possibly go on?"

"Obviously everybody plays certain roles as they go about their lives," she said, frowning up at him as he came upon her. "But not the way you do. You literally have a director on staff. You have an entire production team. Do you think that's normal?"

She didn't realize that he'd backed her up across the whole study until she had to stop because there was something in

And in private much of the time.

"I'm delighted that someone has finally noticed the great burden that I bear," he said without looking up. "It is amazing how few seem to care about my many travails. But I'm telling you, Ivy, long have I struggled with all of this beauty and wit. It is a curse."

"I meant your lack of privacy," she snapped at him.

"That is a feature, not a bug," Giaco told her, finally lifting his gaze from his book. "I determined long ago that it was not fair to the world to conceal the glory that is me from the public. They have so little, do you not agree?"

Ivy did not agree. She stood there, staring at him. She took in the state of him, lounging here in the privacy of his own home yet still dressed as if he expected a photographer to happen by at any moment. One of those buttoned-up shirts of his that he never managed to button to the top. Those loose trousers made her think of islands in the sea. He liked his feet bare in the house, she noticed, and she wondered at the contrast between the outrageously debonair figure he could cut when he chose to, all black-tie sophistication and urbane grace. This was a far more casual version of him.

"None of this is real, is it?" she heard herself ask.

Something changed. She watched it move over his face and then his gaze was different, too. Almost...cannier, perhaps.

"Are you talking about our relationship?" he asked quietly. "The one that has currently captured the attention of the entire planet? No, my little saint. It is not real. Have you become confused?"

"I'm not talking about that, I'm talking about you," she said. "When I first saw this house I thought that it seemed so authentic. A real home that someone lived in. That someone

She had to get a new mobile. Ivy had thought that she was used to a certain level of notoriety and celebrity, because she certainly traded off that in London. In all the circles she moved in, for that matter. Everybody knew who her parents had been.

This was something completely different. It was on a whole new level.

She understood in a brand-new way why Giaco lived the way he did. It only occurred to her now that he had chosen this house because it was built like a medieval fortress. The public could camp out at the outer entryway all they liked, but there was no access to the house itself. They couldn't peer in his windows or bang on his doors. Not to mention, she began to realize that half the staff that he employed here were, in fact, his security force.

Meaning he was not quite as lazy and feckless as he appeared.

She came upon him while she was still feeling out of sorts and glared when she found him lounging in one of his outrageously comfortable armchairs in what she was fairly certain was his library, though *he* called it a study. As if to distance himself from what it might say about him if he had an actual library.

Though the shelves upon shelves of books told a different story.

"Why didn't I know how difficult your life is?" she demanded.

Giaco did not look up from the book he was reading. She filed that away to come back to later. The fact that he was reading a book at all. The fact that the book he was reading looked big and thick and dense, and he appeared to be in the middle of it. Yet more evidence that he was not who he played in the press.

ment swung hard toward Giaco and Ivy almost immediately, with commenters across all platforms decrying the intrusion and the publication of what was surely meant to be a completely private moment.

And that was how, with very little discussion, in the course of a few days she found herself not only engaged to Giaco Tavian but completely moved into his house in Rome.

Not into his bedroom, of course. That would be taking things too far. That would be *real*, and whatever else happened, she knew *that* wasn't allowed. *Maybe you should ask yourself why you're thinking so much about his bed*, a small voice inside her kept asking.

She found herself sitting in his pretty, private courtyard one evening, still not certain she was adjusted at all to this new life. She couldn't go to work. She could conduct video calls with her charity, but she didn't feel it was the same. She thought that every call seemed to get caught up somehow in all the questions these people she'd worked with for years didn't dare ask her directly.

Ivy grew tired of the courtyard, for all that it was pretty and soothing. She grew tired of staring at a water feature, wondering what else in her life was going to change. Wondering why she hadn't anticipated any of this when everyone else clearly had.

She walked back into the house, wondering why it was Giaco had known that she would end up here. Probably from before their first date, or he wouldn't have installed her itinerary-friendly wardrobe in her suite. She was tempted to think he'd planned all this.

But even as she thought that, she didn't think that was entirely fair. *Planning* suggested a whole different level of machinations. What he'd been—and what she had not been, clearly—was prepared.

those words. What she felt was…too much. She wanted to cry. She wanted to run downstairs, fling open her door, and shout at everyone who was standing there, forming a scrum outside, possibly already rooting through her rubbish in the back. She wanted to rewind back to that meeting at Umberto's office, and tell him to go to hell.

She wanted to live forever in that kiss, which paradoxically enough still felt to her as if it was only theirs.

When it wasn't, of course. None of this was real. None of this was hers. None of this mattered outside of this production they were putting on.

The kiss that still haunted her had been published just like these pictures were. It was part of the body of work that they were giving the world so that everyone who wished could tear it apart. Dig into it. Make it theirs.

She would do well to remember that.

Just as she would do well to remember the orphans who were the reason she was subjecting herself to all this in the first place.

Ivy rubbed at her temples and then closed the screen of her laptop with a decisive click. She closed her eyes. "What do you suggest we do next?" she asked, and was proud of herself for sounding nothing at all but businesslike.

When she felt anything but.

His team descended upon her house within the hour, indicating to her that Giaco had anticipated this response. They cleared out the paparazzi and whisked Ivy away. She read the prepared statement from Giaco's representative—Gabriele, she assumed—who expressed horror and disgust at the violation of their privacy and the revolting response that had made his new fiancée feel as if she was under attack during what should have been a happy time in their lives.

It was a terrific statement, Ivy could see. Public senti-

"I take it you've seen the pictures," he said without preamble.

"I think the entirety of the British gutter press is kept out of my doorstep." She laughed, though it came out a bit... wild. "They clued me in."

"I thought that might happen." He sounded odd, she thought. Or perhaps he *didn't* sound lazy and mocking and unbothered by it all. "We'll issue a statement from here. But this is what I meant by things getting difficult. I don't think this is the kind of furor that's going to die down, Ivy. You're too exposed in London."

"I wouldn't call myself *exposed*," she argued, though she certainly *felt* exposed. She kept looking over at the window as if she expected the mob to levitate up from the street. "There are any number of people in this neighborhood who command more attention than me—"

"That was yesterday," Giaco said curtly. "Now you are engaged to one of the most famous men in the world. You no longer live in the same world you did when you went to sleep last night. And the level of interest in you, particularly this kind of tabloid interest, will no doubt make your high-profile neighbors nervous, which I'm certain they'll make clear to you soon enough."

She wanted to argue with him. But her doorbell kept ringing and ringing and ringing. So did her landline. Ivy was beginning to feel a headache developing in her temples. She had the strangest sensation that a barrier had been crossed here. A boundary, maybe.

That there would be no going back from this, no matter what happened.

And she wasn't sure how she'd ever imagined that she wouldn't end up here. Still, she found it *surprising. Upsetting.* Or maybe she didn't really mean to use either one of

to something near enough to stern. *You forget, Ivy. I did actually know your mother. And you.*

The photographer had kept snapping pictures from his perch on the roof that the public would confuse for a drone, and so she could see the exact moment she'd looked down at the ring, that intense look on her face. What it looked like to anyone who was seeing this photo now—and she assumed the world had seen it already—was that she'd been fighting back tears.

When what she'd actually been fighting back was a sense of disorientation. *No*, she had told him, the ring gleaming between them. *You don't know me. You certainly didn't know me back then.*

I know you like moonstones, Giaco had replied. A bit stiffly. As if she'd offended him.

She hadn't seen any reason to push at that assertion, even if she'd wanted to. Even if it had been like a burning thing in her throat, the need to correct him. Now, hidden in London these last few days in preparation for this photo drop, now with a baying mob outside her door, she huddled in her bed and stared at that ring on her hand.

The ring he'd put there when she'd stopped arguing about whether or not Giaco Tavian *knew her*.

It was, bar none, not only the most beautiful ring she'd ever seen, but it was also essentially what she would have designed for herself if she could have. And that made her feel...

Well. She didn't know what she felt. Not about the ring, anyway. Or maybe she didn't really *want* to know how she felt, because—

Her mobile rang again and she looked over out of habit, then picked up only because it was Giaco's number.

Are you ready to take the next step? he'd asked. *It's probably going to make things difficult.*

Ivy had laughed. *More difficult than they already are?*

I've been with lot of women, he'd told her, as if she might have forgotten. As if anyone could possibly have forgotten. *The scrutiny on you will increase a hundredfold.*

I'm aware of who you are, she'd replied, through a smile that had felt stiff on her mouth.

Then so be it, he'd said, rather darkly.

Not exactly love's young dream, Ivy thought now, but it certainly looked that way in the pictures. She looked down at her hand and felt that same jolting sort of reaction that she'd felt that night, too.

She'd had no doubt that Giaco would produce something beautiful. Every item of clothing that she'd been given to wear as part of her official wardrobe had been exquisite. She would be hard-pressed to think of a single objection she had to any of it. She even liked most of the pictures she'd seen of herself at these events. He'd staged romantic moments, took her to marvelous restaurants, and while their relationship might have been fake, the food was always divine. She'd assumed the *engagement upgrade*, as noted in the itinerary, would be the same sort of thing.

In terms of the ring Giaco would choose to sell their engagement to the world, she expected something extravagant, but elegant. Instead he'd gone sentimental, and she still didn't know how she felt about that. The ring was a collection of opals and moonstones, clustered around a diamond.

I love moonstones, she had whispered, out there in the soft breeze on a Mediterranean cliff top. *My mother loved opals.*

I know, Giaco had said, all dark jade and that mouth set

no matter how sincere he seemed, no matter how intense it felt to her, she always knew that he was acting.

He sold it. There was no denying it.

All of the dinner pictures showed him entranced. Enchanted. He held her hand as they ate. He leaned in, as if every word that dripped from her lips was some nectar he wanted to taste.

And then, after their breathtakingly romantic dinner, were the money shots. The point of the whole thing. Giaco Tavian getting down on one knee and gazing up at Ivy, clearly proposing, a small jeweler's box in his palm.

She had to hand it to Gabriele, Ivy thought now. She didn't know if he'd summoned that breeze with the force of his will, but it made the flowing dress that she'd worn that night even more beautiful. The breeze caught it and played with it, and her hair blew back too, and it looked so intimate, so achingly romantic, that she felt something like teary as she stared at the photo now. At the look on Giaco's face as he gazed up at her. At the look on her own face as she put her hands on him.

She couldn't help thinking this was a scene that should never have been photographed.

In her house in London, with the phone still ringing and the doorbell sounding and hammering at her door, she sat back and rubbed her eyes.

"It isn't real," she reminded herself. Sternly. "None of that is real. No one is intruding on anything, because it didn't really happen."

They were engaged. That part was real enough. He had actually proposed, after a fashion, though what he'd actually said while down there one knee had not been romantic in the least.

And there they were. Paparazzi on her front door. Packs of them.

Because she was the woman who had finally claimed the eternal bachelor. She was the only one who had managed to do the thing no other woman had. She had the ring on her hand to prove it—and now the papers had the evidence.

Her time as a relatively private citizen was up.

Ivy backed away from the door and heard the old landline she'd forgotten about ringing. She didn't answer it. Instead she found herself running up the stairs to her bedroom, her heart pounding as if she was under attack, only to find her mobile under the same assault. So many messages. So many calls. But she was afraid to pick it up in case she accidentally answered the wrong person. The very idea made her feel panicky

She pulled out her laptop, ignored her inbox, and typed in her name at the top of her browser. And there they were.

Gabriele had put them through their paces. He had taken care of everything. It had been a beautiful day and had become a lovely evening—likely because Gabriele had decreed the weather needed to be perfect and it, too, had obeyed.

Staring down at the photographs, Ivy tried to make her memories match what she was looking at on her screen. She remembered walking down the path toward the cliff-top gazebo, the way lit by lanterns. Giaco had been waiting there for her. The photographs showed the two of them smiling at each other, sitting down, and enjoying a beautiful dinner overlooking the sea. In the pictures, she saw a couple lit up with each other. Consumed with each other.

And the truth was, she had felt that way while it was happening. But that was the thing about spending time with Giaco. She could feel whatever she liked, and she did, but

Whatever it was that Giaco was hiding, it wasn't a love affair with Gabriele.

"What do you do when you're not plotting out these elaborate set pieces?" she asked now, her gaze on the sea in the distance.

"Haven't you heard?" Giaco asked her, and it took everything she had not to turn and look at him. Because she was certain that she could feel all of that wild, dark jade beating into her. "All the world's a stage, little saint. I decided long ago that if that was the case, I might as well play out my part to my own satisfaction."

She did turn then. She couldn't help herself. "Is that how you'd describe yourself, Giaco? Satisfied?"

It was moments like this when she thought she saw so much...*more* there. That glittering dark gaze of his. The ghosts she was sure she could see move through his eyes. The way his face changed, as if he really was wearing a mask.

"I will be," he told her in a voice that matched his simmering gaze. "I can promise you that."

When he walked away, she felt as if he took part of her with him, though she couldn't have said what. Or why she found herself pressing her palm to her chest, right over her heart, as if that might get it back.

And a few days later she was back in gray and drizzly London, tucked up in her little house in Kensington, when all the pictures hit the media.

She knew they hit because her doorbell started ringing, loudly and repeatedly. It shocked her so much that she almost threw the door open to see if a neighbor needed medical assistance or perhaps a fire had broken out—but some shred of self-preservation intruded at the last moment. She paused and looked through the peephole instead.

rolling fields and lush olive trees, she could hear Gabriele in the background. He was barking out his orders, making sure that everything matched *the vision*.

When she heard a particularly frenzied bit of carrying on, she found her way outside to one of the terraces that looked out over the rest of the small island, making it clear that there was no one here but them. She found Giaco out there, standing at the railing much the way he had in Cap Ferrat.

"I'm sorry," she said. "I don't mean to intrude."

"I find it better to let Gabriele do his thing," Giaco said, without turning to look at her. "He will anyway, so it's better that he has the space to bring his various ideas to life. Otherwise we'll pay."

"It sounds as if some people are already paying," Ivy murmured. She moved to stand next to him at the rail, but not *too* close. They were both so careful in these unscripted, uncoded, unplanned moments. If anything, it made her more aware of him, not less.

"He is invaluable," Giaco told. "I've never met another person who can so perfectly capture the public's imagination. Gabriele is always on point. He always knows exactly how the scenes he stages will be received. It's quite a talent."

Ivy opened her mouth to ask him a question, but thought better of it. There was no need to ask, was there? Gabriele had been here long before she was. For years, one of the other staff members had told her. Since university, another had said. They had been inseparable ever since.

If it weren't for the fact that Gabriele had been married to his husband for the bulk of this time, Ivy might have been tempted to assume that all of the staging was to disguise Gabriele's relationship with Giaco himself. Before the kiss, that was.

The kiss had been clarifying in a multitude of ways.

One night she made a great show of scrolling through her mobile in the car, until he asked her what she was doing.

"Oh," she said, brightly. "I couldn't decide whether or not to put on lip gloss, so I was checking the itinerary to see if there might be more kissing. I wouldn't want to get that stickiness all over you, you understand. So tacky."

It was worth it, she thought, because of the dark look he threw her way. Then and when she spent the rest of the evening theatrically reapplying that sticky lip gloss.

Reminding them both about that kiss.

As if she was likely to forget it.

But their whirlwind romance was picking up speed and better yet, according to the excitable Gabriele, *inevitability*. Soon enough it was time to head off to a private island in the Mediterranean that was owned by one of Giaco's old friends. Or possibly Giaco himself—he had been offhandedly opaque about its provenance.

Ivy supposed it didn't matter, really. They weren't going to interact with anyone. They were going to sell the big upgrade to their story—the impossible engagement of the world's most untamable lover to his personal saint—and deliver Umberto what he wanted. So that once they did, it would get them what *they* wanted. Win/win all around, or so she kept telling herself.

They took a private jet boat from Athens and were delivered to an unspoiled beach in the Ionian Sea. They were met there by staff who ushered them up steps carved into a rugged cliffside and into a gleaming villa that sat on top. A number of the staff members Ivy was used to from Rome came with them, and Gabriele was there too, because he would be directing this particular production.

While Ivy wandered around the villa, gazing out at the spectacular views of shining sea and white-sand beaches,

And she could admit—when she tried to turn off how she *felt* so that she could look at the pictures analytically, and with some kind of distance—that they were unquestionably romantic photographs. That must have been why they were getting attention even in places where she would have thought neither one of them was known enough to matter.

But it was hard to be analytical when she woke up on the nights she slept at all with her entire body on fire, his taste in her mouth, and the feel of his perfect, rock-hard chest beneath her hands.

Ivy just counted herself lucky that since no one believed that she and Giaco would last, she didn't have to worry about being hounded by packs of paparazzi the way he was. He and Gabriele had both assured her that wouldn't last.

She told herself to enjoy it while she could.

They continued to meet after the kiss, because that was what was in the bloody itinerary and the itinerary was the boss of them all. They attended a charity event in Luxembourg, a lovely opportunity to glitter and be seen while obviously head-over-heels. Intimacy code at six. They took a weekend away with each other, or so it seemed to the breathless public, in Venice to see an opera with much hand holding and *leaning*, intimacy still at six because it was public.

More pictures. More black-tie functions and society photographs. More indications that they were becoming a part of each other's worlds.

He didn't kiss her again. It wasn't on the itinerary.

And he only touched her when necessary, she thought. While dancing, for example. Or when ushering her with great solicitousness to a banquet table. Only in places where others could see them and marvel at the *taming* of Giaco Tavian.

Only when it benefited their little performance, that was.

They'd been too busy wandering around starry-eyed in the castle, whether because they were bowled over by Alana's magic or sent into quivering joy at the sight of Umberto's riches.

Ivy had never thought that she was worse off for it. When she talked about her childhood and her schooling, she called it *eclectic*. And because she was lucky enough to not have to try to find the sort of employment that cared deeply about things like schools, she got away with it. It was seen as charming. It was never held against her.

So she had to hold it against herself as she found herself drifting off in the middle of a board meeting, paying absolutely no attention to the details of her own charity because all she could think about was the way their hands had fit together. As if they'd been separated cruelly from each other at birth and had only found each other again now. As if their hands had been *made* to clasp each other like that.

The way he tugged her with him into that alley and backed her up against the wall, so that all she could see of Rome, of the world, was the serious dark jade of his gaze.

Even thinking about that, about his *eyes*, made her whole body shiver into awareness. A rich, wild heat that seemed to consume her from deep between her legs, only to roll out so that there were flames everywhere.

And that was before she even got to the carnal magic of his mouth on hers.

In case she thought she was imagining all that, there were the pictures to prove it. Did she love them? Did she hate them? She could never decide.

The truth was he wasn't only affecting her job. He was affecting her sleep. Her breath. He was with her everywhere.

Just as the pictures of that kiss were everywhere. All over the papers. Impossible to miss online.

A kiss that she couldn't help but think should have been only theirs—even though she knew that made no sense. There was no *only theirs*. There was only the performance they were putting on and the kiss was a major step forward with that—no matter how many snide reporters dismissed Ivy as but one more affair for a man who'd had legions of them before her.

No one believed they would last.

Ivy herself would not have believed it, except she knew exactly where they were headed and how long they'd stay there.

She had been surprised that he wanted to talk about her work with orphans at dinner that night. She had been even more surprised when he'd actually told her things about his mother. Much less what she was fairly certain was a huge secret, because she knew she'd never heard anything to suggest that the wife before Alana was anything but deeply unwell.

No one had ever indicated that her death was anything but a tragedy brought on by mental instability, and certainly not a clear-eyed, coolheaded, deliberate decision.

It had been weeks now and Ivy still found herself going over and over it in her head. The dinner. The way Giaco had actually *shared* with her. Then after. Back in London, she sat in the usual meetings and tried to look as if she was paying the kind of attention that she should have been. But she wasn't.

She kept going through that night. She felt like the silly sort of schoolgirl she'd never been, because she'd never had the experience of overwhelming crushes and packs of friends to giggle about those crushes with. Her mother had not liked to be left alone and so Ivy had been taught by a succession of tutors, none of whom had ever given her much of an education.

CHAPTER SIX

Ivy was haunted by that kiss.

However overwhelming she had found those pictures he'd taken of them and the scenes she'd imagined around them even though she knew none of that had occurred—well.

That was nothing next to the reality of the way he'd kissed her in that alleyway.

She'd been teasing him a little when she'd talked about his *romance writing*, because the truth was, she found the itinerary depressing. It wasn't that she didn't realize that a campaign like theirs had to be planned, it was the *extent* of the planning. It was dispiriting to have a script and to know at all times that they were following it. That those little glimpses that she got of him were probably not real. They were likely all part and parcel of the *intimacy code* that was on every entry in that itinerary on a scale from one to ten. The itinerary mapped out an emotional, intimate progression. Every time they were seen by the public, they should seem more connected, more into each other, more real.

And the more *real* they appeared, the more fake it all felt to Ivy.

Or it had, anyway. Until that kiss.

A kiss she had then seen hundreds of photographs of, splattered across every tabloid. A kiss that she'd relived again and again and again, every time she saw it.

Which is how he knew, in a rush of horror, that he'd forgotten himself in the first place.

He, Giaco Tavian, who had a preternatural ability to spot any possible hint of a camera from a mile away. He, who had set up this whole night and had literally written the script.

Giaco couldn't think of a single other time he had ever lost his head like that. He had never forgotten himself so completely. If she hadn't stopped him, he would have been deep inside her already—when he'd known going in that there was a paparazzo in this alley with them.

Because he'd called the man himself.

He pulled back and ran a hand down the side of her face, because he couldn't resist. Or he couldn't help himself. They were beginning to feel like the same thing.

There were no words, or possibly he couldn't speak. Instead, he took her hand again, led her out of the alley, and spent the rest of their walk home unsettled and something very much like thrown.

Because if he couldn't play this role of his in every possible circumstance, then the real truth was that Giaco didn't know who the hell he was.

And that had the power to ruin everything.

around the nape of her neck, which he had spent too long now feeling like another brand in the palm of his hand.

This didn't exactly help. He cradled her head and he moved her where he wanted her to go. Because where he wanted to go was even deeper. Even wilder.

Even hotter, if that was possible.

And he could feel his whole body shudder into that blast of heat. He could *feel* her, everywhere.

He could smell a hint of the scent in the crook of her neck. It was something complicated, like citrus and cloves. Because, of course, Ivy Amis would never wear bog standard vanilla or anything else that smelled like sugar.

Giaco wanted to eat her alive. He thought maybe that was what he was doing.

He dropped his other arm from its lazy position propped up over her head and then he had both hands on her face, kissing her and kissing her. Her body was pressed to his and he could feel all of her, at last. Those plump breasts, pressed into him. The sweet, searing heat of her body, warming him.

His fingers were moving into her hair, threatening the pins that held it all in place, and the only thing he could think about was how best he could get inside her—right here in this alley—because he thought that if he didn't he might die.

She pulled away then, though that made no sense. Then she looked up at him, her chest moving too fast. Her blue eyes wide, and much darker now.

"Giaco…" she whispered. "We can't."

For a moment he had absolutely no idea what she was talking about. He couldn't understand why she would end something so perfect. So wildly *necessary.*

Then, like a key in a lock, it clicked. And he remembered himself.

drawling little barbs that made people around him think he meant the opposite of whatever it was he said. He tried to make it over into the usual sort of verbal performance art that he was so well known for, but it didn't work this time.

He could see it was perfectly clear to her, here in the hush of this alley while Rome swirled in all its bright noise and motion almost within reach, that it was nothing short of the stark truth.

"Giaco," she began.

"Pucker up, little saint," he ordered her, in that same dark voice. "It's time to be romantic."

And then he leaned in and took her mouth with his.

He felt her stiffen beneath him for just a moment, and then she kissed him back.

Giaco shifted and caught a glimpse of the paparazzo he'd explicitly tipped off tonight, lurking farther back in the alley. He knew all the best angles to use to give the man the proper photos. He knew how to kiss so that both he and his partner looked their best in the inevitable two-page spread.

But when she surged toward him, flattening her hands against his chest and arching into him, the kiss got deeper. Harder.

Not entirely within his control, though that should have been impossible.

He felt seized with some kind of fever. Or possibly that damned wine he'd had with dinner had gone to his head, suddenly and irrevocably. He felt as if he was spinning, and yet somehow there was nothing sickening about it.

There was only her.

Only Ivy, her mouth a bright, hot counterpoint to his as if she was as swept away in this moment as he was. As he shouldn't have been.

His other hand found its way to her face, and wrapped

"Yes," she said, sounding something like formal. She tilted her head back a bit more, and smiled up at him—though now she was back to the practiced smile of hers. He could not pretend to like it. "I read it. Did he write all that?"

"He did," Giaco said. And he could have left it there, because he already knew how little the whole world thought of his intellect. Most assumed he had none worth mentioning. But for some reason, he couldn't let Ivy think that. "He typed it up quite neatly as I dictated it, in fact."

"Then it's you, then," she said, and she was still looking up at him like that. As if they were standing in a shadowy place only steps from the crowd, bantering the way lovers might. Meaning, he knew, that she had absolutely read the itinerary. When he only stared down at her blankly, and only partly because he didn't know what she meant, she laughed. "I had no idea that deep beneath your indolent and cynical exterior beats the heart of a romance writer."

"I beg your pardon?"

"Because it's all so tidy, isn't it?" Somehow, her blue eyes seemed to burn even brighter here in the dark. "It's a perfect love story, delivered directly to the masses. Tonight our first kiss. Each outing will advance us into hints of more and more intimacy. This will inevitably lead to the perfect engagement with photos leaked to the press against our will, as if what we really want is to fly under the radar. And then, of course, we'll perform a spectacular wedding that makes our happy-ever-after a foregone conclusion. A triumph of three-act structure, Giaco. I had no idea you were such a dedicated storyteller."

"I am one of the greatest storytellers you will ever meet," he told her, not sure why his voice sounded so dark. "The best story I tell is me."

And he tried to make that come out like one of his usual,

he closed that last bit of space between them and set his mouth to the crook of her neck, the curve of her lips—

Giaco couldn't count the number of times he'd had to take himself in hand since that day, hoping to dispel this hold she had on him—but it always seemed to make the memory more intense.

She made the memory more intense. She made everything intense, when he had always prided himself on keeping everything *easy*. Simple.

Now they walked down the streets in Rome, melting into the crowds in this busy part of the only city he had ever truly loved, and he was *on fire*.

When all she was doing was holding his hand.

He could not for the life of him understand why such a simple, prosaic touch should hum through him like a thousand hymns sung in Saint Peter's Basilica, like this was something sacred.

It was nothing of the kind, of course. It was business and could never be anything else.

Giaco kept telling himself that.

When he got to a certain bit of shadowed alley that snaked between a few buildings and was set back from the street, he pulled her into the mouth of it with him, then backed her up against one stone wall. He propped himself above her, one forearm above her head, and looked down at her.

Though it was difficult to focus when her mouth was *right there*.

"You got the itinerary, I assume." He said it matter-of-factly.

She swallowed, and he watched the motion of her slender throat. "As you are no doubt aware, your assistant is nothing if not thorough."

"That is one of Gabriele's many strengths," he agreed.

ested in this woman when he had only ever conceived of her as a means to his own ends.

And he couldn't lose sight of what was important now, no matter how she might *glow*.

Or how his forearm felt branded by her touch, well into the evening.

He lectured himself on these things all the way through dinner and then afterward, it all promptly went to hell when he took her hand as they exited the restaurant. "I thought we would walk back home," he told her, his voice gone gruff again.

And he could feel her immediate reaction to what he said. Not the walking part. *Home*.

Her reaction meant that he reacted, too. And it felt like a spark causing a flame and then a flame developing into fire in the space of a heartbeat. Or maybe it was simply that her fingers were in his, linked together, and he already knew that touching her was dangerous.

Giaco had always loved women. He was fully aware that his reputation suggested quite the opposite and he hadn't done much to fight that, but the truth was that he reveled in the female form. If he was an artist, it was in this. He delighted in the mysteries of a woman's body.

It would not have said he had a *type*. There was not any particular form or color hair or height that drew him in. He had been lucky enough to sample everything. And he had never regretted it.

But Ivy was something else altogether.

He spent significantly more time than he would ever wish to admit torturing himself with what else might have happened on that couch in his father's office, had he simply... followed the cues that he could read all over her body. Had

then, particularly in my father's house. I did not need to be spared though I do realize, in the fullness of time, that it was a gift she gave me." He shook his head. "I don't know why we're talking about this."

She smiled, though it was not a practiced thing. It was soft. Real, he thought.

"Orphans," she said quietly. "It inevitably leads to dead parents, I'm afraid." She reached over and put her hand on his forearm, if only briefly. "I'm sorry."

And he found he missed that touch when she took her hand back. Far more than was wise.

He sat back as their first course of food was delivered then, and he studied her as she interacted with the server. He marveled at how easily she had taken to this role she played now, when he knew it couldn't possibly be something she was comfortable with. She had never claimed to have her mother's ability to *inhabit* every space she occupied, simply by being *herself*.

Ivy was also glowing, which was a version of that, he supposed.

Having left nothing to chance, not for years now, Giaco had made certain that Ivy had every available stylist on call. Not to make her over, as she was beautiful without any help, but to carefully tailor her appearance so that over time, she looked as if she was on some kind of dimmer switch. Brighter and brighter in his presence, so that the papers would call it *love*.

Tonight she seemed brighter than should have been possible from a simple application of cosmetics, but something in him reacted a little too strongly to that notion. Maybe he wanted to believe—too much—that it was something else. Something more.

The trouble with all of this is that he was far too inter-

No matter that it meant leaving a teenager and a six-year-old behind.

"I'm sorry," Ivy said after a moment. "That can't have been easy."

"I don't view it as a weakness on her part," he found himself telling her, stiffly. This was something he believed, deeply. Though it had never changed the fact of being left behind, it was a kind of comfort in its own way. "I am aware that my father likes to go on about her mental illness, but I always saw it as an act of extreme clarity. She knew exactly what she was doing. She left all of her affairs in order. She made certain to do it where she would be found by strangers and while that cannot have been good for them, I believe she was attempting to spare…"

"You," Ivy finished softly, when he didn't. When it seemed he couldn't. "She wanted to spare *you*."

And something about the way she said that seemed to grab him by the throat. Or maybe it was simply because he didn't talk about this, not to anyone, because everybody thought they already knew what had happened. It had been a major news story in its time.

Though that was all it was, Giaco knew. A story.

And the story was simple, if sad. Umberto Tavian's high-strung wife, after a long struggle with an incapacitating yet never defined mental illness, had locked herself away in a Paris hotel room and taken entirely too many pills. Deliberately. She had been discovered several days later, when housekeeping had entered the room despite the do-not-disturb sign after she had missed a raft of calls.

That was the story, though Giaco preferred his take. That it had been an act of defiance from a woman who had felt she had no other cards to play or places to go.

"I was sixteen," Giaco told Ivy. "Enough of a man by

twenty years old at a fancy charity do and I related so much to an orphan girl half my age that I really did cry. It's disorienting enough to lose one parent." She shook her head. "But you must know this yourself."

She gazed back at him then and he realized she expected him to say something about his own mother. His fierce, beautiful, highly educated mother had been raised by parents who had escaped from their homeland and had raised her to consider the France she'd been born in a foreign country that could never truly accept her.

He understood how she had seen Umberto as an escape from too many wounds that could never close. But she'd made a terrible mistake. And she'd known it.

"My mother chose her exit," he told Ivy, gruffly.

Though he didn't realize that he was going to tell her that until it was out of his mouth. He didn't understand himself. He never told anyone that. It was a secret—sometimes he thought it was a secret only he knew, as he suspected that his father had done what he always did and wiped clean any memories that didn't serve him.

Giaco expected Ivy to flinch or gasp in shock or make some other huge sort of movement that he could focus on and use to change course, but all she did was gaze back at him. Her fathomless blue eyes filled with what looked like…empathy.

God help him.

He ordered himself to stop, but instead he found his mouth opening against his will. "If you knew her, this would not surprise you in the least. She had always vowed that she would be no prisoner and when she determined that she had somehow ended up held in a situation she couldn't escape, she did what she felt she had to do."

"I'm still very young by any reasonable measure," she replied, with a laugh. "I suspect you and I only feel old because every day in your father's presence is like a decade. A long, grim decade." She reached out and picked up her wineglass. "And, of course, you actually *are* old."

That was so surprising that he laughed. "Apparently even the most holy martyr among us has claws when she needs them. Who could have imagined it?"

He thought she looked rather pleased with herself when she kept going. "My father died in a car accident when I was quite young."

"I remember," Giaco said. And when she looked surprised at that, he moved his shoulder in a shrug that did not feel like his usual elaborate, affected fare. Neither did his voice as he continued. "I was a teenage boy. There were very few humans alive I admired more than Llewellyn Amis, the greatest action hero of all time."

The way Ivy smiled at him then made him almost feel as if he'd downed the entire bottle of wine himself. It was that bright, that warm. That dizzying.

"He always felt James Bond took up too much oxygen," she told him, leaning in closer to him, which did not help the dizziness any. "That's what my mother always told me. I don't remember much about him myself, I'm sorry to say. I knew my mother much better, and for longer. And I know all the stories she told about him. By heart."

She seemed to remember herself then, because she sat back. Or maybe, like Giaco, she was having trouble remembering the boundaries here, the lines between a good act and an actual conversation. Much less a real moment.

He had to swallow then, though his throat felt unduly rough.

Ivy cleared her throat. "In any case, there I was, all of

Even though it was unlikely that anyone could possibly overhear them, she always reacted. Though he could have used a far less socially acceptable word, he could still see splashes of color on her cheeks and the hint of it on her neck. Tonight he could see even more than usual because her hair was twisted up and out of her way, in another one of the seemingly casual yet elegant styles she wore now because they photographed so beautifully.

But her beauty wasn't the point here. What he could not understand was how Ivy had grown up in the same castle that he had and had somehow emerged capable of shame or embarrassment of any kind.

"I do take my charity work seriously," she said after a moment, her eyes a darker shade of blue. Clearly jumping right over the sex of it all, as usual. "When I moved back to London, I went with some friends to a charity event one evening and happened to hear a young orphan speak. She made me cry."

"You mean following your mother's funeral." Again, her blue eyes were on him. This time he felt certain that there was something like reproach in them. "You must have been very young."

Unbidden, the image of Ivy all in black, with only the searing blue of her gaze—shining bright with unshed tears as she'd stared down Umberto—came back to him.

Young, yes. But stunning all the same, though in his memory, it was now less because of the simple fact of her beauty and more about the deep fury she'd clearly been holding inside her.

It made the previous memory of her in the gallery doorway even hotter in retrospect, and if he recalled correctly, she'd been who he'd thought of anyway. His dirty little release.

about him again. A precious commodity, no doubt. Particularly when one was widely held to be missing a full set.

He had his people drop them at one of Rome's most exquisite and currently sought-after restaurants, currently vying for its second Michelin star. They were greeted at the door and then ushered to a table that was set away from the main dining room, as if—despite having managed a pap walk outside one of the hottest restaurants in the world just now—Giaco and Ivy were trying their best to stay private.

"You take your charity work very seriously," he said, realizing as he broke the silence between them that he sounded...awkward. When he was Giaco Tavian, who had never encountered an awkward moment his entire life.

This woman made him feel like some kind of untrained adolescent. The kind of adolescent he had never been, that was for certain.

Ivy looked at him, her blue eyes as fierce and piercing as ever. He always had the feeling she was as good as punching him straight to the chest. Every time she gazed in his direction. What he couldn't decide was whether she was doing something deliberately or if he was simply...*feeling* it like a blow.

When he had sworn off *feeling* long ago.

"Is this going to turn into one of your routines on my supposed canonization?" she asked coolly.

"Little saint," he found himself murmuring, "it's never *routine*. I am an endless font of new experiences."

"Not according to the tabloids," she retorted, a touch too quickly for his peace of mind. "They're quite certain you're up to your old tricks."

"The only old tricks they are ever referring to involve sex," he said, because he liked saying things like that in public places.

Of course, she said, still rolling her eyes. *The maestro himself, etcetera.*

Just so. He had gazed up at the statue before them, noting the exquisite lines and the emotion that seemed to be captured in hard stone, and could not have said why it felt to him like another impertinence. Maybe that was why he'd offered up something different. Something more than his usual playboy prattle. *I did paint once.*

Really? Ivy had shifted closer to him. Her head had canted slightly to the side as she'd studied his face. *Let me guess. You astonished everyone immediately with your innate and unstudied talent and could easily have been the next Picasso, had you managed to stop all the carrying on in the bedchambers of Europe? That sounds like you.*

I was appalling, he'd replied, and had then…actually found himself laughing. *Embarrassing, really. I would have been better off simply pouring the paints onto the canvas and spreading them about with my hands. I could have claimed that was modern art, at the least. Alas, it was a figure-drawing class and the goal was an adequate representation of said figure.*

He could still remember, pounding through the water in his cold pool, the way Ivy had laughed at that. As if he had surprised her. She had laughed so hard that she'd actually leaned against him, just for moment, as if his confession was some kind of connection.

The trouble with Ivy was that she made him feel like a regular man.

Giaco knew he couldn't have that. He couldn't allow it.

It would ruin everything.

He kept swimming until his arms felt numb, though it was a pity the rest of him refused to follow suit.

A few nights later, Giaco was convinced he had his wits

but his end goal and bonding with nothing but his own thirst for vengeance, he found that his fake girlfriend was actually fascinating.

I would love to be a sculptor, she had told him as they walked through the gardens at the Musée Rodin in Paris.

I didn't know you were artistic, he had replied.

It had been a great day, meaning it had been perfect for their purposes. They had walked about a selection of museums. They'd stayed next to each other, clearly together, and the pictures that had come from that day supported it. They'd looked lost in conversation, as if they might at any moment have reached out for each other, though it had been chilly.

I'm not at all artistic, Ivy had replied. *I know that there are those who believe that everyone has a certain amount of creativity lurking around inside of them, but I'm pretty sure that I missed that boat entirely. That's all right. In this life, I get to admire the creativity of others. And imagine what it must take to mold clay into such wonder with my hands, or find these perfect shapes in a block of stone.* She had smiled when she looked at him and only then had seemed to remember who they were. He'd found that he didn't much care for that, though he had opted not to ask himself why that was. *What about you? Do you have secret creative outlets?*

There's the obvious answer, he had said, almost by rote. She had actually rolled her eyes, which he'd found nothing short of astonishing. He couldn't remember the last time someone had dared. Whatever people might think of him, they had always taken him seriously in person. He'd assumed that was part of his so-called boundless charm. *And I assure you, of course, that my creativity in the bedroom knows no bounds.*

might be anything more between them than a hot, hard night in his sheets from time to time.

The less talking, the better. These particular women understood that when he called them, it was for a specific purpose.

But when he arrived home, he hadn't called anyone.

Later, when he and Gabriele had started discussing this particular media campaign, Giaco had decided that authenticity could only help push the narrative.

Besides, every paparazzo in Europe would go looking for proof that he hadn't reformed at all. They would dig into every connection he'd ever had—no matter how seemingly tenuous—looking for any indication that he was actually still the degenerate he'd always seemed to be.

And as discreet as he always was and as much as he had been able to trust his usual paramours for years, this was different. This was too important.

Giaco couldn't take the chance that any one of them might jump at the opportunity for a payday.

That was what he'd told himself. That was what he continued to tell himself as he grew hungrier by the day. And yet as he sliced through the water, all he could think about was Ivy. And not just that *appetite* inside him that he was determined to believe was simply because she was the woman nearest him—

But didn't. Not really. The craving was so intense. It didn't help matters that she was so intriguing.

He could not remember the last time he had been intrigued by anything or anyone. Giaco had always had a singular focus for the whole of his life, and everything else that came along was a casualty because of it.

But now, suddenly, there was Ivy.

And despite a lifetime of paying no attention to anything

Giaco Tavian did not do *personal*. He couldn't afford it. He hadn't come this far only to toss it all away on a pair of blue eyes.

No matter how they seemed to see deep into the heart he could have sworn he didn't have.

He found himself staring up in the direction of her room, like a lovesick fool, and he hated that. It told him things about himself he refused to take on board. He turned on his heel and stormed through the house until he reached the pool he'd had installed on the lowest level, far away from any windows or prying eyes. He didn't bother looking for a swimsuit, simply stripping off his usual robe and boxer briefs and diving into the water.

It was crisp. A deliberate slap. He kept it cold enough to clear his head, but just in case the water temperature didn't do the trick, he started banging out laps. Down one length of the pool and back, over and over.

He told himself it was simply because he hadn't found any kind of release in far too long. He hadn't been kidding when he'd told Ivy that he required a significantly high amount of sex per day. He hadn't intended to forgo that pleasure, either, no matter what image he was projecting to the outside world. Despite what everyone believed—what he had worked so intently to *make certain* they believed—he was perfectly capable of discretion if it suited him.

And yet he hadn't done it.

He'd left the castle as soon as possible, putting the necessary space between him and his loathsome father. Throughout the entire drive back to Rome he'd planned to call one of his trusted paramours as soon as he arrived. He had a very select few of them. They distinguished themselves by keeping their mouths shut and never imagining that there

cate it was all a deliberate stunt. This was one of Giaco's specialties.

A trip to Paris to take in the museums and stroll the boulevards, the way a pair of new lovers might. A dinner in Rome, hidden away in the back of a humble local trattoria, sitting close together and talking intensely, the way a new couple would do.

The two of them were caught exiting the car together outside a charity event in London, and then firsthand accounts about their behavior leaked out from within, with universal descriptions of Giaco's adoring behavior.

He had learned long ago that it was always better to create the story he wished the papers to run. And also that less was always more. The more it seemed that he attempted to keep his private life private, the more real people believed the things they saw were stenographers' renditions of his actual life.

Something he found he needed to remind himself of, lest he become too caught up in his own performance.

He pushed back from the table in his courtyard in Rome now and stood up, shoving his hair back out of his face. Ivy was still asleep in her guest suite upstairs—or he assumed she was still asleep, as she had not yet emerged—and the real trouble was that he was finding it increasingly impossible to ignore the fact that he was attracted to her.

At first he'd thought it was simply because she was beautiful. Who was he to swim against the tide of a beautiful woman? He'd never failed to appreciate beauty when he saw it before. There was no reason to start now.

But as the weeks passed, it had become terribly clear that this was something far more personal than a reasonable appreciation of feminine pulchritude.

The thing he had to keep reminding himself was that

CHAPTER FIVE

Giaco thought it was all going as well as could be expected. Better than that, even.

His relationship with Ivy Amis, who the papers were already calling *Saint Ivy* thanks to the excellence of his sales pitch and most tabloids' desire to stay in his favor, was splashed across every possible tabloid, in paper, online, on television, and on radio, too. The speculation was at a fever pitch and only grew as the days passed, staying forever at a boil.

He was excessively good at remaining at that same simmer, day in and day out.

Their first date in Cap Ferrat had caused an orgy of speculation. They'd appeared two other times that same weekend in various places along the coast, once the next morning on a stroll along the Plage du Midi in Cannes before disappearing into a café that did not allow paparazzi. The second, Sunday afternoon, while coming in from a yachting adventure.

That the virtuous daughter of the lost and widely lamented Alana Amis had spent the weekend with the Prince of Debauchery himself, her former stepbrother, had been talked about everywhere.

They had been seen in various places all over Europe since. There were always just enough pictures to suggest a narrative without any posed photo shoots that would indi-

For a few moments, it was as if everyone else on the terrace simply faded away. Ivy knew they were there but they were little more than shadows as she moved. It was the past that was brighter now. She heard her mother's laughter in her head, the most beautiful song imaginable and one she'd almost forgotten. She could see her father's smile, one of the few memories she had of him. She could smell roses and lavender in this charmed place, but the only thing she could really focus on was Giaco.

On all of that dark jade, taking her in as if he'd been waiting all of his life for her to walk toward him, just like this.

She knew he was playing a role. But still, she could feel that look all over her. She could feel *him*. It was shocking to realize how good he was at this. If she didn't know better, he could have convinced her—easily—that he really was a man who had accidentally fallen in love and now had no idea what to do with it. And that he was something like a mess as he watched the agent of his destruction draw near.

He *looked* like he was made entirely of agony and hope and something far hotter, and she didn't know how not to be affected by that.

When she reached him at the railing, he turned toward her, looking as if he meant to grab her hand—

But didn't.

And that affected her too, because she could *feel* that near-touch like heat between them.

It occurred to her then that this was going to be significantly harder than she'd anticipated. For a number of reasons she hadn't thought to prepare herself to face. It was clear to her now that this was very likely going to make a mess of her, too.

And that was before she saw the pictures splashed all over the world the next day.

Alana and Ivy had spent many a pleasant season right here, and yet Ivy had forgotten, somehow, that there was so much more to her mother's life than the way it had ended. And when she stopped looking for her mother, she looked out toward the gleaming sea instead and felt the truth of that lodge inside her too, like another benediction. There had been a whole, beautiful, sometimes heartbreaking life before Umberto. She'd been there for some of it.

I'm going to make more of an effort to remember you happy, Ivy promised her mother then, in her head and her heart. *I promise.*

When she finally focused on the man standing by the rail, watching her with that same intensity that she couldn't believe no one else seemed to notice in him, she found she was filled with emotion.

That probably didn't bode well for this date of theirs, but Ivy couldn't regret it.

She gathered herself and walked toward him, noting that when Gabriele had spoken of a vision, he'd meant it. Giaco was dressed all in black. It was a flowing sort of black, a button-down shirt with the sleeves rolled up and loose trousers appropriate to the South of France. And yet somehow he gave the impression that he was both breathtakingly formal and charmingly informal at once. The shirt was open at the neck, showing off that gold skin of his. His hair was slicked back, but not like it had been when he'd come up out of that pool in Italy. This version gave the impression that he'd been running his hands through his hair all day.

Or, this being Giaco, someone else had been.

Ivy had expected to feel foolish, dressed up in a costume and made to look like someone who was playing the role of Ivy Amis rather than simply being herself. But as she walked toward him, that…wasn't how she felt at all.

was five. This hotel had always been about glamour. Any and every kind of glamour imaginable, as people with all kinds of power, from every corner of every industry, were drawn here.

But to Ivy, this was her childhood. The one she'd lost when her mother had packed her off to Umberto's castle.

"Il Padrone waits for you on the terrace," she was told, so she got out of the car and walked toward the iconic entrance of the hotel, feeling as if she was walking back through time.

She could see her mother in a convertible, Alana's hair swept back beneath a bright silk scarf, laughing into the sun. She remembered the parties, none of which she had been old enough to attend. Ivy had stayed hidden away in her hotel room, peering out the windows at the gleaming lights on the water, and the sound of clinking glasses and gaiety from below.

As she walked through the lobby, she nodded at the staff. Who greeted her by name, she noted, because that was the kind of place this was.

She made her way out back and found her way into a bar that opened up over the pools and the sweeping view of the Mediterranean Sea in all directions. And realized as she looked around that she wasn't looking for Giaco.

There was some part of her that was looking for her mother.

But it didn't make her feel sad. It felt more like a blessing. Ivy had almost forgotten that Italy and Umberto weren't the sum total of her mother's last years. She'd been happy here in France. She had loved coming to this part of the world, especially when the film industry gathered here, too. She had adored it when she could be among the people who understood her best because they lived the same sort of nomadic life she did, forever moving from one film set to the next.

cise measurements. She didn't want to know how they'd managed that.

Or maybe it was more accurate to say she was afraid to ask.

Then, when it was all done, she got it. She stood before the mirror, hair and makeup and wardrobe done. She looked like herself, so there was that. But a different version of herself.

A very specific different version.

"I understand this now," she said, catching Gabriele's gaze as he stood behind her, texting furiously. "I might as well be Little Red Riding Hood setting off for the forest. And he'll be the Big Bad Wolf everyone already thinks he is, I suppose?"

"You understand this, *che delizioso*," Gabriele cried, and he even grinned. "That's good. It's going to be a team effort, Signorina Riding Hood. This I promise."

Then she was once again swept away. Into the car, back onto the streets of Rome, and then back once more into a plane. This time it was an even shorter flight and when she landed, she found that she was in France. The Côte d'Azur, no less, and it was impossible not to be enchanted.

She was driven on roads that overlooked the gleaming, dancing sea, bright and blue. They drove from the private terminal in Nice along the coast until they turned right to drive into Cap Ferrat, ripe with villas and hushed elegance, and kept going until they pulled up to the Grand Hotel that had stood at the foot of the peninsula for some hundred years.

Ivy swallowed, hard. She knew this place. She had stayed here with her mother, in fact. There were pictures of her with both of her parents here, though she had only small flashes of her father in her memory, as he had died she

"Everything about you is wrong," declared Gabriele in some mix of Italian and English, waving his hand in Ivy's direction. "*Meno male*, you're gorgeous!"

"Wait a minute," Ivy began, frowning at him. "There's nothing wrong—"

But Gabriele was already barking out orders to the stylists and Ivy couldn't help but be dragged along. Mostly because she suspected that if she didn't go along, she really would be dragged.

"There's a vision we are working toward," Gabriele told her as he hurried her out of the sitting room. "We have to highlight the contrast between you and il Padrone at this point. You understand."

"I don't," Ivy replied, which was hard to do when she was surrounded by what seemed like every stylist in Rome, all of them performing various beauty treatments on her. Whether she liked it or not.

There was a lot of waxing. Her nails were buffed, clipped, and polished—and her thoughts on color schemes were not solicited. She was hurried into the shower and then out. Her hair that she quite liked was subjected to a cut—*ever so little*, Gabriele assured her, *just to capture the shine*—and was then styled to look exactly the way it had before.

Except, she had to admit when she looked in the mirror, it was not *exactly* the same. There was something about it. The hint of a curl in her ponytail. The way it swooped, it somehow made her seem...

Something she couldn't put her finger on.

She didn't really get it until they dressed her in the outfit that had already been chosen for her for tonight. It was a pastel shift dress and a pair of darling shoes, everything not only her general size but seemingly created to her pre-

"Oh, I'm so sorry," the woman said then, with a laugh. "He does not wish you to *choose* an outfit, Signorina. He has already chosen them all. There will be a series of encounters, you see. The master is very exacting when it comes to appearances and has created a *stylistic journey*."

"A...stylistic journey?" Ivy echoed, sure she wasn't hearing any of this right.

The woman nodded enthusiastically. "You will start at this rack, and work your way through to the wedding attire."

Ivy decided she did not need to investigate *wedding attire* on this, the afternoon of their first, very fake date.

Her guide led Ivy over to the rack farthest to the left and pulled the first three items off. Ivy looked closer and she could see it was true. The racks were separated and color-coded, and this level of organization contradicted every single thing she had ever known about Giaco, to the point that she wasn't sure she could actually take it all on board. She cleared her throat.

"Forgive me," she said to the woman. "I can't believe that he actually put all this together."

"His assistant put it together," the woman said with another laugh. "Don't worry. You will meet Gabriele."

That wasn't a promise, Ivy discovered soon after. It was more of a threat.

Because when Gabriele swept in, he came with a cloud of stylists, barking out orders into one mobile while texting on another. He didn't knock. He simply stormed in and found Ivy in the sitting room, having succumbed to the lure of a meal since it was clear there was no avoiding the rabbit hole. She'd been answering emails, conducting her life as if she was back home and not tucked away in some ancient Roman town house, awaiting the pleasure of the man she had to pretend to marry.

aesthetic. If she had walked into this house with no knowledge of who might live here, she would have assumed that the owner was eccentric, had unlimited funds, cared deeply about comfort, and had a wicked sense of humor.

She wasn't sure which part of that shocked her more.

Her staff guide took her into a set of rooms that were clearly a guest suite. The woman looked askance at the small tote that was all Ivy had brought with her, but indicated that she should place it on one of the tables in the outer sitting room.

"The master has prepared a selection of items for you," she told Ivy. "The stylists will arrive at 3:00 p.m. But first, there are the looks, if you wish to take a peek."

She didn't wait for Ivy to respond, she simply walked into the next room, where Ivy found herself confronted by racks of clothing.

Ivy was no poor country mouse, overwhelmed by the sight of high fashion. By most standards, she lived a flash life. She went out of her way to appear to live even more bright and beautiful than she actually was. One thing she knew from her mother was that rich people loved nothing more than to give money to people who already had it. The more that Ivy presented herself as an *it girl* who happened to have a passion for charity, the more likely she was to get the donations she needed. Any hint of need or desperation and she'd get nothing.

She had a very nice wardrobe and she knew how to dress the part, but she was still surprised by everything that waited for her here. Outfits upon outfits, all of them extraordinarily beautiful—even the simplest pieces.

"This is much too much," she found herself saying, shaking her head. "I wouldn't even know where to begin to choose something."

somehow managed to make it seem as if they were not in a busy city at all.

She climbed out, not surprised to find a different set of staff waiting for her. Though she was slightly surprised to find them standing *just so*, as if posing with the blooming wisteria canopy overhead—

You are confusing his staff with him, she lectured herself. *Not everything is a photo opportunity.*

"*Bongiorno*, Signorina Amis," said one of the women waiting for her. She stepped aside, making it clear that the old, thick vine marked the entrance to the house. "If you will come with me."

Ivy nodded and followed, expecting to be led into yet another sterile museum of a house, created entirely for clout and having nothing to do with the way that anyone actually lived.

This house was nothing like that.

It turned out that the beautiful wisteria was a hint that Giaco did not treat his house the way his father did. This house of his was eclectic. Surprising and interesting. The rooms were bright and filled with a haphazard sort of collection of things, from whimsical rugs to art that was clearly not there as investments, but because its owner liked it.

Or perhaps that was what he wanted her to think, she corrected herself.

It was not until they'd walked up a flight of stairs and into an open gallery that looked over a different courtyard below, this one green and lush with a water feature in the center, that Ivy realized this was actually a *home. His* home.

It was obvious, once she accepted the possibility that a person like Giaco Tavian could actually *have* a home that he poured this kind of energy into. There was no connecting or overarching theme between rooms. There was no

What was he hiding, she wondered, that he would do it in such a blinding spotlight?

"You will not get your inheritance or help a single orphan if you focus on the mysteries of one of the richest and most spoiled men alive in the world," she muttered at herself and set her mobile aside again.

But since Giaco was so good at these games and clearly loved to play them at all times, Ivy decided that the better part of valor was to not respond to his text at all. Let *him* wonder about something for change.

Assuming he ever did something so pedestrian as *wonder*.

The next day, she presented herself at the same airfield outside London where she'd caught Umberto's plane two weeks before. And once again, she was greeted by exquisitely polite staff who ushered her on board. She refused the offers of food and drink and told herself it was because she was preparing herself for whatever battles awaited her.

It was more truthful, if silly, to admit that there was some part of her that worried if she ate and drank something Giaco provided for her—however indirectly—she would be dragged straight down the rabbit hole and actually turn into that girl she'd seen in the photos he'd taken.

That girl she still had trouble believing was her.

Once in bright, sunbaked Rome, a waiting car whisked her into the ancient city and brought her to what she at first thought was a hotel, then realized it was a private house in a tony neighborhood, not far from one of the most famous squares in Italy.

She supposed it stood to reason that Giaco would live in a place like this, an eternal disaster in the eternal city, surrounded by untold centuries of the remains of creatures who looked just like him. Perhaps he was his own pantheon here, she thought as the car slid into a private courtyard that

pictures and each one of them told its own story. In one, he was staring hungrily at her mouth while she looked utterly blissed out, her lips parted as if they had already kissed. In another, he was smiling at her—that twist in his lips—but this time there was no smirk in it. It was sex. It was *hunger*.

The final one was the worst. She didn't remember him moving back in to get closer to her, but it looked as if he was scant seconds away from pulling her onto his lap when she knew he hadn't been doing anything like that. Ivy-in-the-photograph looked as if she was on another planet, and he was its only sun, and she couldn't really parse how she felt about that. But Giaco…

Giaco looked *consumed* by her. His own lips were parted, as if he was breathing heavily, and it looked as if he was only inches away from taking her mouth with his.

She had deleted them all immediately.

But they had stayed in the recently deleted file, so since she was looking at them again—and not for the first time since she'd landed on British soil—she moved them back out. She told herself that it was forensic evidence, nothing more. It was a learning guide.

It was the way she was going to teach herself how to do what needed to be done.

Though it seemed that the answer was to simply let Giaco take the lead, no matter what it did to her nervous system. What these pictures taught her was that it didn't matter what she *felt*. It mattered how *he* made it *look*.

A thought that made her think about the discoveries she'd made in the castle that day. The ones that led her to be certain that his whole act was one big charade. Because if he could make things look anyway he wanted them to look, what did that say about all those splashy tabloid exposés that everyone took as the truth of him?

Ivy blew it out and ordered herself to *breathe*, for God's sake. I'm going to need more information than that.

And she realized that she expected him to flirt with her in text, or make some of his suggestive comments at the very least, when he didn't. Be at the airfield at 11 a.m. Don't worry about wardrobe.

She frowned down at that message for some time, trying to tease out all the variables. She wanted to ask him what he meant. Did *he* intend to dress her?

Ivy had to get very stern with herself when certain images flew at her then. She wasn't sure she wished to have a man sort out her wardrobe. Especially not when the entire conceit of what they were doing was that she was some everyday version of normal next to him.

Then again, she also knew that Giaco Tavian liked to play games.

Against her will, she swiped over to her photo app and pulled up the pictures he'd taken that day in the castle. She'd been so *unsettled*—that was definitely the right word, she assured herself—by what happened, by his fingers against her skin, that she hadn't even thought to look at them until she was on the plane and in the air on her way back to England.

Once she looked, she'd wished she hadn't. She'd felt as if her stomach dropped down out of her body and plummeted some 35,000 feet to slam itself into the Alps.

Because if she hadn't been fully present in the moments he'd captured on her camera as they were happening—if she hadn't literally been there herself—there was no way Ivy would ever have believed that the people involved weren't engaged in an affair.

An *extremely carnal* affair at that.

Ivy didn't understand how he'd done it. There were three

back to London, twenty years old with no skills and a sporadic education. Work was the lifeline she'd found to get her out of Umberto's castle of sick games and gaslighting that she'd been trapped in for too long. She'd found herself as she'd clung to it.

Why should this be any different?

Ivy thought the bracing British rain helped, too. Nothing like walking down London streets while it was bucketing down rain to make her forget all about *molten gold* or anything else remotely warming.

By the end of those two weeks, she'd decided that she'd embellished that morning in the castle. It had been nothing special. Just the Tavians up to their usual tricks, but she'd been in and out quickly and while she didn't have her inheritance yet, well. There was a path toward getting it. That mattered.

All the rest was just…the usual nonsense that could be chalked up to life in that family, in that place, in that desperate world that Umberto liked to marinate in.

She had better things to do than to focus on that kind of billionaire black-box theater.

When her phone buzzed one night as she was settling into bed after smiling so much during a fundraising event that her cheeks still hurt, she didn't react. She didn't even race to pick it up. She debated looking at her screen at all. And when she finally reached out for her mobile, she froze when she saw that the text was from him.

Tomorrow night, Giaco had texted. Rome.

She stared at that text for a good two minutes and while she did, she took stock of all the reactions she was having—none of which she liked. The elevated heart rate. The sudden flash of heat to accompany it. The fact that she was holding her breath. Again.

CHAPTER FOUR

Two weeks later, Ivy was back in London, happily immersed in the life she'd built, and convinced that she'd allowed the simple fact that she'd been back in that castle to mess with her perceptions. To make her imagine things that weren't there.

Because she didn't like any other explanation for what had happened with Giaco. What she had *felt* while it happened.

In the first couple of days after all that—fleeing Italy as soon as she could make herself get up from that couch and managing to get home the same afternoon she'd left—she had jumped every time her phone indicated there was a new message. But as the days passed, she thought her nervous system was actually settling back into place. The more time elapsed between that day and now, the better she was. The stronger she felt.

The less delusional she was about what was or wasn't lurking behind the mask Giaco Tavian clearly preferred to wear. The simple answer was that it didn't matter. Her job was to sell a story to the outside world to get her hands on what her mother had left her, not to start an excavation project into a man who exulted daily in his supposedly charming disinterest in anything but the pursuit of his own pleasure.

She could get her head around work. *Work* made sense. Work was what had saved her when she'd come stumbling

Then, while she was still more or less gaping at him, he rose from his lounging position—taking that hand of his with him—and wandered back out of his father's office without so much as a backward glance.

Leaving Ivy behind to try to find her breath again—and pick up the pieces of her she hadn't even known could break apart like that, into all of that *golden heat*.

Then try to piece them back together as well as she could now that she knew that Giaco Tavian wasn't a joke. He wasn't a tabloid construction. He was *exactly* as lethally sensual as he appeared in every story ever written about him.

And Ivy was going to have to figure out how to handle him if she wanted her inheritance, like it or not.

tance between herself and Giaco when there was precious little of it physically.

She should object. She should leap away. It wasn't as if he was holding her still. *She* was the one doing that.

But on the other hand, she felt as if she was wrapped up in that hand of his exactly the same way she'd imagined earlier. She couldn't breathe. His hand on her nape seemed to be directly connected to parts of her body she'd never spent any time thinking about too much, aside from their basic functions.

Ivy knew how to dress for her figure, but she couldn't think of the last time—or any time—that she'd ever felt the curves of her own breasts as if they were plugged in to some kind of wildfire current. She didn't understand how the faintest motion of his fingers against the tender skin beneath her ponytail could seem to flow down from that single point of contact to pool between her legs. Just as she didn't understand how she could feel golden and molten at once. Or how she could find herself captured completely by the look in his eyes.

Eyes that were much closer to her now. *All of him* was closer than he'd ever been to her before.

His gaze dropped to her mouth and seemed to hold there. And all of that molten gold inside her seemed to spin into something hotter, thicker—

But all Giaco did was sit back. Then he looked away, though he didn't move his hand, and she had to work not to give in to that trembling sensation she could feel deep inside her as he flipped through the photos that he'd taken. He looked back at her, and tossed the mobile onto the cushion between them.

"It looks like chemistry to me," he said. "Thank goodness. I hope you're ready for your tabloid debut, little saint."

Ivy already knew all she needed to about Giaco Tavian.

"Fantastic," she managed to say in place of any pointless questions. And she did feel that her throat was a little too dry for this moment of pure business and self-interest— on both sides, as far she could tell. Maybe it was that her tongue wasn't working the way it should. She did not care to examine why that was. "I'll text you my email. I'll look forward to your response."

But Giaco didn't hand her back her mobile. Instead, he swiped through to something else and when she frowned at him, he leaned in closer.

As he no doubt meant it to do, his suddenly being *right there* got her attention. Completely. Ivy almost flinched away from him, but that would be telling and she did not wish to *tell* him anything she didn't have to. It took everything she had to stay still as he came closer, and then closer still. He lifted his head from his hand and let that hand move in a dreamy sort of arc until he was…touching her.

Not a brush of hands this time. Giaco was actually *touching* her.

She froze the way she had at that window. And this time there was no pretending she couldn't feel that inside, she burned bright.

He traced the outer edge of her ear with a fingertip and then slid his hand to hold the nape of her neck in his palm. She felt her lips part of their own accord, which she was sure she would be horrified by later, but she couldn't seem to do anything about it now.

Giaco leaned closer still. And then she heard the shutter sound of the camera on her mobile, a sound she often wondered if the youths these days even recognized. Since it had no relation to any machine they were familiar with.

But a random thought like that was her trying to put dis-

as long as he did what was necessary. For a moment, she wasn't sure that he would—

But after a pause, Giaco took the phone from her. And he also let their fingers brush as he did it. Maybe they simply brushed against each other because they were close. She wasn't sure she should ascribe that much intention to the things he did, no matter what she thought she saw when she was this close to him.

Either way, she felt the spark of that touch race through her body. It was alarming.

It felt a great deal like the way she'd had narcotics explained to her. A wild burst of euphoria followed by heat.

It took everything she had not to jerk back as if she'd received an electric shock. When she was pretty certain she had.

He poked in a number, then hit the call button, and they both sat there as if waiting for another mobile to ring. But there was no sound.

Ivy felt as if she was holding her breath. That was likely because she was, in fact, holding it.

"I think we both know that I don't have any pockets," Giaco said after his factory-set voicemail message could be heard in the tinny distance of her mobile. He waved lazily at his bare torso and his boxers, and Ivy did her best not to stare at the ridges in that absurdly perfect abdomen of his, golden and gorgeous. "But as we can both hear, it certainly rang somewhere in this castle. Assuming I left the ringer on."

She had the strangest urge to ask him about his phone habits, and why he left his mobile lying about when surely he must have acolytes forever trailing around behind him in search of intimacies, but that all seemed...like the sort of conversation a person would have with someone they actually wanted to get to know.

geous and fit and lovely anyway. Or were chemically made that way because they could afford to fix whatever they broke. And there were certain physiques that could come as a natural result of partying, or as a result of cleaning up after said partying, but his wasn't one of them.

Those muscles of his required *work*.

Which meant that all of this was a charade. A long-term, very deliberate game.

Ivy was going to have to think about what that meant.

But not now, because she needed all her wits about her to deal with the *fact* of him sitting there entirely too close to her, regarding her with those dark jade eyes that should not have been as affecting as they were. From afar, they were arresting. The tragedy was, up close, they were even more mesmerizing. They were shot through with hints of gold, but it was a dark gold. As if a treasure reserved only for those who truly saw him.

She couldn't believe she'd actually had that thought. But the good news was, it was so inappropriate and off the chain it was galvanizing.

"Right," she said briskly, sitting much too straight on the cushion next to his. "I could do with less *gazing*, if you don't mind. It's not really productive."

That curve in his mouth deepened, a lot like he was *tasting* this moment—another unnecessary thought. "I have certainly never been accused of being productive."

She pulled out her phone, opened the screen, and handed it over to him when she pulled up the phone pad. "Call yourself," she ordered him.

Brusquely.

"I live to serve," he replied merrily, though she could hear that sardonic undertone.

She decided she didn't care about his undertones. Just

separate sofa cushion from the man was too close. She could *smell* him. And it was an outrageously pleasant scent. She told herself it must be some kind of aftershave, though if so, she had never smelled anything like it. He just smelled... good. The way sunshine would smell if it had a scent.

It made her think of the few blissful holidays she'd taken in her time, her face tipped up to the sun, all of that heat and ease—

Somehow, she schooled her expression to something impassive and gazed back at him, ordering herself to stop with all the *sunshine*.

Giaco watched her closely, and Ivy wondered how it was that he'd convinced the entire world that he was nothing but a pageant of indolence. When she could see that he was studying her intently, like he was taking the pieces of her and examining them.

Almost like some kind of bird of prey. As if he could see every single thought that scrolled across her mind. In flashing neon lights.

This took significantly more attention to detail than a professional playboy like Giaco Tavian had ever been imagined to possess. It was also the last thing she wanted.

He shifted in his seat, his outstretched arm curling in so he could prop up his head with his own hand. As if the mere act of talking with her was exhausting. Ivy had never beheld such a lazy creature in all her life—except that, too, didn't make any sense.

She had inspected his naked body earlier, against her will and frozen into place. And while it was possible that genetics played a role in his physique, no one could maintain *all that* without effort. She knew that people liked to believe that it was possible. That some humans simply wafted around, treated their bodies horrendously, and were naturally gor-

"We're about to become famous lovers, Ivy. The very least we ought to do is exchange mobile numbers. Not to mention that email address I'll need to contact you as you have demanded. I do so enjoy obedience, as I mentioned."

"When it benefits you," she replied, parroting what he'd told her.

His dark eyes gleamed. "Indeed."

She felt as if she was something small and fluttery, caught in a trap. Or possibly between his hands.

And the thought of that, of being held between his palms, didn't actually do anything to steady her breathing. Much less sort out whatever was going on with her heartbeat.

All she could see when she looked at him was danger.

But if they were really going to do what Umberto wanted them to do, Ivy didn't see that she had any choice when it came to dealing with him. And since she didn't have a choice, it made sense to treat him the way she intended to go on.

Meaning she couldn't let him set the tone. She couldn't let him control everything.

She *really* couldn't let him think that she was intimidated by him. She was fully aware that he wanted her to be. That he *expected* her to be.

Maybe he remembered her scuttling off from that gallery, too.

Ivy made herself walk back across the room and sit down next to him on that couch, even though every iota of self-preservation she had within her was telling her to run in the opposite direction. Like the little mouse he made her feel like she was.

She might *feel* like one, Ivy counseled herself, but he didn't need to know that.

It was just an unfortunate fact of life that even sitting on a

Ivy realized that she could continue to stand there, fighting her own body's bizarre response to him, or she could act as if this was all settled. Because it should have been settled. She chose the latter, so she nodded at him and then started for the door.

"Now, now, little saint," Giaco said, sounding…decadent and lush, somehow. "Don't be in such a rush. We have so many things left to discuss."

"I'm happy to have a discussion." She stopped walking and looked back over her shoulder at him. "All you seem to want to do is muddle around in all your innuendo. It's boring. If we're not going to have a practical conversation about the way this is going to work, I don't see the point of it. You can go ahead and email me your thoughts, or whatever schedule you come up with, hopefully without all the smirking and the sighing and this endless performance you like to put on."

She didn't really mean to say that the way that she did, so forcefully. But she wasn't sorry she'd done it that way when she saw his reaction. Oh, it was small. Almost unnoticeable. But something about that perfect face of his changed. Just for a moment.

But Ivy saw it.

Unless she was very much mistaken, she had landed a significant blow.

The trouble was, she just couldn't imagine *how*.

"I had no idea you were so stern and dominating," he murmured in that idle, yet richly tenored way of his. "How delicious." He crooked a finger at her, watching her intently. When Ivy made no move toward him, he sighed a little—yet not with the histrionics from before, so she supposed she ought to have been grateful for small mercies. He patted the sofa seat beside him, and she felt…less grateful.

"I will be doing absolutely nothing of the kind," Ivy told him, and she was aware that she sounded more prim and proper than she'd ever felt a day in her life. But for some reason it seemed like a defense. Yet he only gazed back at her, too much dark jade and that curve to his impossible mouth. She huffed out a breath. "I don't need to prove anything to you. In fact, the more I think about it, the more I think it makes sense that my reactions to you should be organic. After all, if this ridiculous performance is to be believed, it would make sense that you would have to do more convincing than me. No sane, reasonable woman, virtuous or not, would ever wish to be seen in your presence. Much less imagine that she could *date* and then *marry* you."

It was so absurd that she laughed.

But Giaco only inclined his head as if she'd complimented him. "It is true that I am a movable feast, indeed. Hemingway would be so proud."

Ivy did not want to think too much about how or why *this* man of all men was making literary references. It was one more thing that made no sense. "You still haven't told me how this is all going to work," she said instead, briskly. "Do you just wave a magic wand? And lo, fawning members of the press appear before you?"

He looked amused, and not in that sharp, painful way he often did. "More or less. Sometimes I simply step outside."

"You should text them, then." It sounded like she was giving him orders, and she could tell he wasn't used to that in the way his dark brows rose. Ivy decided to take that as a sign she was on the right path. "Once you sort it out, you can tell me where to meet you and what sort of date it is so I can turn myself out appropriately, and we'll get this moving."

"Stop," he murmured. "This is so scandalous. You're making me blush."

Ivy's mother and more because they thought Alana's death meant they were in with a chance with Umberto.

Ivy had been all of twenty years old, more sheltered than she would have admitted at the time, and yet had still been perfectly aware that had she come a few moments later, that woman would likely have been kneeling between Giaco's legs as he lounged back on one of the viewing benches.

She had already been hovering there, knees bent, as if in mid-kneel.

Giaco had looked over lazily. He'd seen Ivy standing there and had only shrugged. Clearly not caring if she stayed or went.

She had, obviously, turned right around and gotten out of there.

Yet for some reason, it had taken her longer than it should have to forget about that moment. She supposed the trauma of her mother's actual funeral hadn't helped, because what she remembered now were all the times she'd had flashes of that expression on his face afterward. For far too long after she'd escaped this place and made her way back to London.

Happily, it had gone away. And she really didn't know why she was remembering it again now.

Or why she could feel something deep within her kindle into an odd little flame as she stood there, as if she too felt that same voracious *need* she'd watched in another woman years ago. To kneel before him. To place herself between those carelessly outspread legs. To gaze up at him, tilt her face toward him, and—

Good God, she thought. The man was like a drug. The sort that came with dire warnings and distressing media campaigns.

And now he wanted to make her believe that *her* virtue had redeemed *him*?

CHAPTER THREE

THE WILDEST PART was that Ivy actually wanted to do it. Or if she didn't *want* it, necessarily, there was something inside her that was urging her on. A kind of *tugging* she'd never felt before in her life. Like there was a band of *need* wrapped tight around the very center of her, pulling her toward him.

She didn't understand it at all.

Logically, it made no sense. She knew exactly who Giaco was, for her sins. She knew what he did. How he did it, even. She'd spent years witnessing the chaos and carnage he left in his wake every time he visited his family, usually in the form of Umberto's temper tantrums after his departure that the old man doled out indiscriminately and with a certain relish, to Ivy's mind. And in case she'd been predisposed to think that was a family issue, the unavoidable tabloid coverage of Giaco made it more than clear that such upheaval was his raison d'être wherever he happened to find himself.

Ivy'd had something of a run-in with him five years ago in the run-up to her mother's funeral, those hazy, heavy days while the arrangements were being made by the very people who hadn't cared about Alana while she'd been alive. Ivy had been…raw. And she'd stumbled across Giaco in one of the castle galleries, flirting outrageously with a woman Ivy hadn't recognized. Maybe she'd been one of the mourners who had been there less because they cared at all about

attended? That sounds like a work camp. Were you perhaps incarcerated without your realizing it?"

Giaco shrugged. "That is entirely possible."

"In any case, it has nothing to do with me," she continued. "You're completely unbelievable as a romantic lead. No one who has ever heard of you—and sadly, everyone has heard of you, against their will—would ever believe that you would date only one person, much less propose to her. And it absolutely beggars belief that you would ever marry."

"A stinging indictment indeed," he murmured. Then lifted a shoulder. "But you forget that the camera loves me. It will show the world precisely what I wish it to, never you fear."

"But I do fear," Ivy said. "I don't believe it's possible."

"Well," he replied, with a theatrical sort of sigh. "If you insist, I'll be happy to give a demonstration."

She only stared back at him, and he sighed again. So put upon. So beleaguered, as he lounged about half-undressed in the company of a beautiful woman that he was going to marry, and likely soon.

Giaco lifted a hand and beckoned her to him with two fingers. "Come on, then. Come here, little saint. Let's see if I can make you believe that your virtue has redeemed me."

games you like to play?" She shook her head, her gaze cool. "I don't want any part of that. I find the way that you slink about as if you might spontaneously burst into an orgasm repulsive in the extreme."

He threw back his head and laughed at that, too. Then sobered as he watched her look down the length of him, then up, then flush again. "I don't think that you do."

"I fear that says more about your powers of observation than anything else."

"This puts us in a bind," he said, heaving a sigh and making it sound sorrowful. Vaguely. "Because if you and I cannot work up some believable chemistry, I'm afraid you'll have to go back, hair shirt and penitent cross in hand as I assume one so holy does, to apologize to your poor orphans for failing them."

She looked...mutinous. Possibly enraged, though he doubted she would unbend enough to be *truly* angry. Certainly not in public.

She folded her arms and glared at him. "I don't think chemistry is the issue."

"Chemistry is almost always the issue," he assured her. "But indulge me. What do *you* think the issue is?"

"You," she replied flatly. "No one will ever believe that any woman could possibly settle you down."

"You need to believe in yourself more," he suggested. "I think there are meditation retreats for that. A whole lot of heaving about, concerned with breathing and unattractive yogic poses. At the end you'll come back a new woman. All you have to do is pay an obscene amount of money to sleep on the floor and eat plain, uninspiring food and perhaps scrub a few floors and windows, all in the company of bored socialites just like you."

She blinked. "What sort of meditation retreats have you

he thought. He knew one when he saw it. "I don't pretend to know you. That's never been of the slightest interest to me, or to you, I'm sure. Yet I can't help thinking that you have ulterior motives here."

"But surely that is impossible," he drawled. "I'm empty-headed. Merely a dissipated, pleasure-seeking fool, forever at the mercy of my constantly changing passions. An ulterior motive sounds like work."

"And yet I need to be assured that if I start down this road with you, it won't blow up in my face." She eyed him with a little too much of that practicality and efficiency then. "I don't care what you do with your life, Giaco. What I do care about is mine."

He waved a hand. "Did you run out of your money already? It happens to the best of us."

"I have plenty of money," she retorted. "But the orphan's charity that I run does not."

He threw his head back at that and her prim, outraged expression, and laughed. "I didn't realize I was in the presence of an *actual* saint. I do not typically run into such virtue, you understand. To me it merely looks like self-flagellation."

"Charity seems like self-flagellation?" She let out her own laugh at that, though hers was more brittle. "That doesn't even make sense."

"I don't believe in charity," he said, mostly so that he could see her bristle. "Unless you mean in a sexual sense."

She blinked. "I…absolutely do not mean it in that sense. I don't think I want to know what that means to you. Really."

"I would be happy to tell you, Ivy. *Stepsister.* You need only ask."

"What I'd like you to tell me, person with no relationship to me at all, is how you intend to make this thing work to your father's satisfaction. All the rest of it? All of these

each other, sometimes they pull off all of their clothes and roll around together—"

Her blue gaze was withering. "Your father seems to think that you can mount a publicity campaign with a snap of your fingers. Is that true?"

"It is less a snap of my fingers and more a few well-placed texts," he acknowledged. "But it is true that the papers and I have a kind of symbiotic relationship."

"Right." She looked at him, as if studying his face for flaws. He knew that there were none. Yet, oddly enough, he found himself sitting just the slightest bit straighter all the same. He watched her as she clearly came to a decision. "I'll go along with this because I think the ends justify the means. I'm still not clear why you would do the same, though. As far as I know, you've never done a single thing your father ever asked of you."

"I have dedicated myself to disappointing him, it is true," Giaco agreed with a sigh. "But into every man's life a shadow must fall. I'm afraid that I have no option but to obey him in this."

She did not look convinced. Giaco took that as something of a compliment.

"Obey?" she asked after a moment. "This is something you do?"

He smiled. "Only if it benefits me."

Giaco stretched out one arm over the back of the sofa and lounged there, fully aware—almost too aware, to his mind—of the way her gaze kept lowering to his bare torso. She would look down, then her gaze would flick up again. More than once. And all the while, the color on her cheeks intensified.

Interesting.

"Forgive me," she said with a smile. A practiced smile,

have been one thing if he had actually had malicious intent toward her. But I don't think he did, and that's worse."

"The only things my father cares about are money and power," Giaco said. "He's like a dragon with a horde."

Ivy nodded. "I always called him the Lizard King. Sadly not to his face."

He laughed at that, surprising himself. "Just so."

Ivy stood up from her chair and he watched, fascinated, as she…paced across the stone floor. She even fidgeted, using her thumb and forefinger to pull at her bottom lip—quite absently, he was sure. He could tell.

Giaco had a sudden, perfectly formed image in his head—almost as if it was a memory, when it wasn't, of course it wasn't—of nipping the place her fingers touched as he lifted her up and then lowered her onto his cock—

Settle down, he told himself sharply. This was business.

"How does this work?" she asked abruptly, frowning at him as if he was a clerk who was holding on to information he required. Or a secretary of some kind. All efficient practicality.

It was true that this was business, but Giaco was not used to beautiful women behaving this way in his presence. They tended to…flutter. Melt. There was a lot of helpless giggling, melting gazes, sultry smiles.

A lot like the way she'd looked when she'd seen him by the pool.

But then, he was quite certain she hadn't realized it was him at first.

That would be a lowering thought, but it was difficult for Giaco to achieve a lower place than the one he inhabited. So he shrugged it off.

"It's very simple," he told her. "Though perhaps less so for the officiously virtuous. When a man and a woman like

little bit, hide it, and then release a breath when she saw that he was covered after all.

Most people did not pay enough attention to Giaco. Oh, they paid attention to the stories. To the spotlight that followed him wherever he went. To all the smoke and mirrors and the outrageousness he threw about like so much confetti.

But if there was tension between how he behaved and how he was *thought* to behave, or any question of aesthetics or intentions or anything else that didn't match—well, that wasn't the sort of thing people thought about when it came to him. No one thought Umberto's useless son was bright enough to know what he was doing.

He counted on that.

"And have you studied my aesthetic at great length, then?" he asked Ivy. "I am fascinating, it is true. There are many who have engaged in a doctoral level of research into the topic. Is that why you came back?"

"You know why I came back." She blew out a breath. "Or maybe you don't. My mother left me money. It's my money. A normal person would have given it me according to her wishes five years ago, but, of course, we're talking about your father."

"Your first impulse was the better one," he told her, making sure to sound idle and bored. His specialty. Even though he meant it. Maybe especially because he meant it. "Nothing good ever comes of succumbing to my father's wishes."

Ivy laughed. "Who do you think you're telling? I watched him catch my mother in his nasty little net, pull off her wings, and pin her down. She was never the same. He took everything that was good and sure about her and destroyed it. Because he could." She shook her head, her mouth firming. "That's the part that I keep coming back to. It would

that when I look at you I feel nothing but adoration. Instead of the more natural revulsion."

"Revulsion?" Giaco smirked at her. "Are we certain that's what it is?"

And he was more pleased than he probably should have been to see the hint of color on her cheeks.

His father stood in a rush then, likely because this was no longer about him.

"I want to read about the two of you in the papers as soon as possible and I don't care how you do it." Umberto glared at his only son and heir. "I know perfectly well that you have contacts among the paparazzi. Sell the story I want to read, Giaco. Your total redemption at the hands of the sort of saintly female you would normally take such pleasure in befouling, etcetera, etcetera. Or you will wish you had."

"Dearest Papà, I have never experienced a moment of regret in my life," Giaco murmured. "I wouldn't recognize it if I did."

His father sneered. "You will recognize it, Giaco. This I promise you."

And then Umberto stormed on out of the room, no doubt off to smite down some enemies and ruin more lives. It was his favorite pastime. And possibly his only pastime.

Giaco did not move. He did not allow himself to think too deeply about what was actually happening here, beneath the surface, because there was no point in it at this stage. He watched Ivy instead.

"I'm surprised that you allow him to threaten you," she said after a moment. "It doesn't really seem to go with your whole..." She waved a hand. "Aesthetic."

That interested him against his will. He actually sat up and let the robe fall open as he did. He watched her jolt a

if she'd ever taken a Pilates class in her life, but he knew where she'd gotten that inherent elegance she wore so easily.

Here in his father's office, which had all the aesthetic appeal of a prison, she looked cool. Unruffled. She wore slim-fitting jeans, flats, and a simple sweater, but the cut of each of those items was exquisite. There was the hint of diamond sparkle in her ears and single pearl drop around her neck.

Giaco knew battle armor when he saw it.

More telling, to his mind, was that she had said absolutely nothing since his father's announcement.

"You seem undone," he pointed out, pillowing his head on his folded arms. He shifted his legs, entertained by the way his father huffed and looked away and Ivy dropped her gaze. Both of them expecting to see him, cock out, on the sofa.

He did not intend to let them realize that he was wearing boxer briefs. What fun would that be?

Ivy still didn't answer, so he lifted his brow. "Is it the acting job for such a wide audience that you find unappealing? Or is it the daily fucking that, it has to be said, a great many people do insist is excessive. I'm afraid I run at a higher intensity than some."

"You will stop using that word," his father growled.

"I know this is distressing, father," Giaco said, so pleasantly he should have been smiling ear to ear. He wasn't. "But I am, despite all protestations to the contrary, a fully grown adult. And will use whatever vocabulary I please."

"I'm going to take this opportunity to make it clear that I don't care who or what you fuck," Ivy announced in that British accent of hers that made her vowels gleam like polished glass. "That has nothing to do with me. If this is the only way that I can receive my inheritance, I suppose I will have to find a way to channel my mother's gifts and pretend

And Giaco could not remember the last time that he been even remotely surprised. By anything.

He scoured his memory for hints of her when she was younger, but all he could pull up were vague impressions of the adolescent version of her—the odd glimpse of blond hair and a sullen expression.

That had changed when he'd seen her at her mother's funeral. And also before it, if he recalled correctly, when he'd allowed an overeager acolyte to pleasure him and had looked up from the bench he'd been lounging on—just before the woman in question was about to busy herself with him—and had seen Ivy loitering about in the doorway.

There had been a look on her face, however briefly, that had…made the situation far hotter than a desultory bit of oral usually was.

Today Ivy did not have grief in her eyes. She looked polished to a gleam. She was still blond, though today all of that blond hair was pulled back into a sleek sort of ponytail that looked effortless and had therefore likely taken hours to perfect. She had impossibly, distractingly blue eyes. A different sort of man might have been tempted to compare them to summer skies or the deep blue sea. Giaco was more interested in the way they appeared to be clear, yet were unreadable.

Not what she seemed, then, was Ivy. That was intriguing.

Her mother had been a great, rare beauty. Giaco could see Alana Amis's famous influence in the exquisite bone structure of Ivy's face. In her aquiline nose and wide, offhandedly sensual mouth. She looked like one of those women who heaved about on those recovery machines and called it a workout, then attributed their lithe forms to the practice when it was clearly just genetics.

In Ivy's case it was *excellent* genetics. He had no idea

Especially because Ivy hadn't been anything like *this* attractive when she'd lived here. He'd barely noticed her, appropriately, as she was a good ten years younger than him. He had been in his early twenties and had only returned to the castle for his monthly sessions with his father, wherein Umberto had made him perform for his monthly stipend. Luckily, Giaco had discovered long before that all he really needed to do was disgust the old man with tales of his exploits. The monthly meetings had been discontinued at some point in his twenties.

These days Giaco preferred that his father read about his exploits in various papers or hear about them from his business associates. He dedicated himself to this task for many reasons, one of them being that Umberto thrived in the murkiest of shadows. Umberto was the sort who liked to hide behind a throne because kings came and went, but men like Umberto always remained.

Giaco liked to think of himself as a bright bit of sun—a spotlight, if you would—that shone upon Umberto wherever he went. Umberto had usually sent him off again in a fury, stipend dispensed, just to get Giaco out of his sight.

If Giaco had seen Ivy over the course of those years, she had made no impression on him.

That had changed in that last year, when her mother was ill. He had noticed her then. She had grown into her angular face, he could remember thinking. And she had looked far too pretty next to her mother's coffin, an observation even he had known to keep to himself.

But he couldn't say he'd thought much of her or about her since.

The Ivy who had turned up today and who had watched him like he was her favorite dirty movie, on the other hand, was a surprise.

CHAPTER TWO

Giaco Tavian had long ago made his life into performance art, the more outrageous and inaccessible to the observer, the better.

Also, he did indeed enjoy a good daily fuck.

But never had he enjoyed himself more than he did right now. He had assumed that his objectively hideous father was cooking up some or other unfortunate plan—because Umberto was always so busy with all his plotting that Giaco assumed it was what kept him alive—when the old man had summoned him home to the family castle. Particularly when he'd insisted rather darkly that it was Giaco's turn to *pay the piper*.

He had been tempted to ask his father what, if any, experience Umberto himself had with pipers of any description. Because Giaco knew that the old man was the sort who believed that he could buy himself out of any situation. And frequently did. No pipers requiring payment. None to lead blind mice. It was a piper-free existence for a man so corrupt he made the crime families all over Italy seem virtuous in comparison.

But Giaco was nothing if not committed to the role he played. To finding a new low in everything he did.

Though he had to admit that looking up from a morning dip to find his former stepsister ogling him was really more of a high.

him? She was not an actress. She was only related to a late, legendary one and had not inherited the faintest shred of Alana's talent. How would any of this work?

She found herself drawn to look at him again, telling herself it was the horror of this that was making her seek him out for some kind of confirmation that he was hearing the same things she was.

But all she saw was that too-dark jade, so mocking, and currently filled with what looked like some kind of glee.

"For you, Father, anything—if it affects my bank accounts. I'm sure that sweet, virtuous, stepsister Ivy and I can work it out," Giaco said, though that gaze of his was fastened to Ivy, and there was nothing about it that suggested he saw her as *sweet* or virtuous in any way. "As long as you're aware, my soon-to-be beloved and bride, that I require a not inconsiderable amount of fucking. Daily. Can you handle that?"

you have never exhibited the slightest inclination toward anything else."

Giaco shrugged, lying there on his back on the sofa as if about to drop off into a nap at any moment. "Fair point."

"There will be an engagement. The world will go wild. It will seem inevitable—fated, even—that the only woman capable of civilizing such a beast is the one who grew up in this house and thus learned the secrets of Giaco's benighted soul, whatever they might be. Again, the press will be encouraged to pursue the *virtue*. The *romance*. There will be no scandal. There will be no *dark intimations* about what you got up to with her when she was an adolescent."

"Father," Giaco said then, in mock astonishment. "I had no idea that you cared what anyone got up to, as an adolescent or otherwise. Or that such a romantic has lurked within you all this time."

Ivy found this significantly less amusing than Giaco seemed to. Yet she still couldn't bring herself to speak.

"And then, the coup de grâce," Umberto said, with deep satisfaction and what looked a lot like actual malice, to Ivy's eye. "You will marry. It goes without saying that during the period of this whirlwind romance and into your marriage, which will last for at least three years, there will be absolutely nothing but squeaky-clean behavior. More virtue. So much virtue that canonization will seem inevitable. Your transformation, Giaco, will be a thing of epic beauty or you will pay for it. Meanwhile, my deal *will* go through and it *will* survive its probationary period. Then I will wash my hands of the both of you and happily pay to never think of either one of you again."

Ivy couldn't breathe. She didn't know where to look. It was bad enough that she'd seen *all* of Giaco today. Now she was supposed to... Date him? Pretend to fall in love with

time sauntering over to the couch that stretched between her chair and Umberto's and flung himself down upon it. With no particular attention paid to whether or not his robe would cover him.

That it did was a miracle.

But even as Ivy thought that, she found him watching her, the dark jade of gaze mocking. Because he knew—somehow he *knew*—that she was thinking of exactly what he had beneath the fabric of his robe. He probably knew that she had committed it all to memory, damn him.

She felt herself *heat* and hated him. Hard. Then tried to focus on his loathsome father instead.

Umberto threw back the remains of his drink. "In order to close this deal, and I am determined to close it, I am afraid that the tawdry legend of Giaco Tavian, heralded cocksman, must come to an ignominious end."

"Must it?" Giaco asked, sounding bored. "But I am so popular and beloved as is. Ask anyone."

"This is what will happen," Umberto said curtly. "The two of you will engage upon a relationship. It will be widely photographed. A worldwide love affair, focusing on Ivy's rather impressive virtue and not the fact that she was once a stepsister. Finally, they all will declare, a woman who tames the savage beast—and whatever other maudlin story the papers choose to tell. You will see to it."

Ivy could not comprehend anything the demented old man was saying. She could not make any of those words make sense, much less *together*.

Giaco sighed, sounding even more bored and now amused besides. "And why would I do that?"

"Because if you do not, I will cut you off entirely," Umberto told him. "And I doubt very much that you have any skills outside your preferred bedsport, Giaco. Given that

tude, whatever the hell that was, qualified? She would climb to the top of his castle and fling herself off it first.

Instead, Umberto reached over and rang the bell beside him, then nodded when one of his servants opened the door. "Bring him in," he said, a crisp order.

And moments later, Giaco himself ambled in. He was not dressed. He had covered himself with a silk robe, but that was his only nod to civility.

Ivy could not bear to look at him any more than she already had today, especially not when his gaze found hers as he entered and lit up at once with that unholy amusement of his. Instead, she watched Umberto and found herself nothing short of delighted to see that Giaco got to him, too. The old man was fairly bristling.

She had always enjoyed how easily riled he was. This man who fancied himself the king above all kings could not tolerate the faintest poke in his direction, and Ivy dearly wished that she was in a place where she could deliver a few such pokes.

It was almost better, however, that it was Giaco. Since his existence, for all intents and purposes, was the greatest and most effective poke at Umberto possible.

"Is there some reason you are not dressed?" Umberto growled at his son and heir.

"I prefer not to dress at all," Giaco replied, in that lazy drawl of his. No matter what language he was speaking, he always sounded as if vocabulary itself made him sleepy. As if he needed to taste every word as it came out of his mouth, and that required all his energy. "I'm happy to remove this robe, father. Would you like that?"

Umberto made a growling sound. If Ivy didn't dislike Giaco so much herself, she might have applauded.

Then it was impossible not to watch as Giaco took his

I realized that there was a simple, elegant solution. I've watched what you've done with yourself over the years, Ivy. It's hard to imagine that such a spoiled, petulant girl could turn into the toast of London, but you've managed it."

The Lizard King never blinked when he was busy handing out insults, and this was no exception. He watched her, clearly expecting her to react to his characterization of her adolescent behavior while trapped in his clutches.

Instead, she smiled and said, "I've been lucky enough to make great friends in London. I suppose we all have the places where we truly shine, don't we?"

Umberto made a scoffing noise. "I don't know about *shining*," he said. "But most people in your situation, considered celebrities thanks to having been adjacent to the fame of others, follow a different trajectory. Yet you, by all accounts, are a living saint. Lady Bountiful herself, friend to orphan children, bestowing her kindness as best she can. Truly, a heartwarming tale to inspire the most cynical heart."

He neither looked nor sounded the slightest bit inspired.

"I found myself orphaned five years ago, when I was twenty, and it was shockingly disorienting," Ivy began calmly, as this was a story she had told many times before. "It made me wonder how much worse it must be for those who do not have my advantages, or my—"

"I've heard these little speeches," Umberto interrupted her, sounding bored. "It's why I brought you here. No one is more astonished than me, given the path I expected you would take when you left here, but you have made yourself a reputation for moral fortitude. And as it happens, I need it."

For a moment, the way he looked at her, Ivy had a creeping, *horrifying* notion take her over. Umberto was forever marrying trophies. Surely he didn't think her *moral forti-*

larly exciting deal. I won't bore you with the details. Pretty girls have much better things to think about, I'm sure."

Ivy gritted her teeth, kept her smile on her face, and wondered—not for the first time—what it was like to be poor Leontina, Umberto's usually wholly ignored daughter. She remembered her former stepsister as little more than a shadow in the corner, which had always struck her as odd when the two of them weren't far apart in age. But then, she supposed that was an answer in and of itself.

"But in order for this deal to go through, I'm afraid there is a challenge that I must overcome," Umberto continued. "There's a moral stipulation, you understand."

Ivy did not understand. She also didn't care. So she nodded, trying to look as if she was actively listening to this.

Umberto smiled. Always chilling. "As you are no doubt aware, *moral* is not a word that has ever been applied to my son."

That got her attention. Or rather, the sight of Giaco rising from the steaming water came back to her like a punch to the gut. She coughed into her fist, cleared her throat, and nodded. "I can't say I've kept up with him in all these years," she lied.

Well. It wasn't really a lie, was it? She hadn't kept up with him in the sense that she hadn't privately considered him at all. But he was inescapable. The legend of Giaco Tavian was an international preoccupation. His collections of lovers. Their breathless tales of his prowess. The not-so-subtle hints of his sexual deviance, his penchant for bedroom games, his wholly indiscriminate selection processes, and the high-octane, jet-setting, partying lifestyle that went along with all of that.

Umberto didn't seem to care if she was prepared to admit the omnipresence of his son's sins or not. "When you called

who'd learned a big word. "I will help you with this, my dear."

Ivy had to fight not to vomit. *My dear.* What a vile man he was. He knew she hated him. Got off on it, if she had to guess.

But, "Thank you," was all she said, as if she thought he was sincere.

Because what else was there to say? Her mother had made Umberto the executor of Ivy's inheritance. Ivy had some theories about how that had come to pass, most of them having to do with Umberto's controlling tendencies, but that didn't change the fact that she could not access that money without him signing off on it.

She had decided years ago that she would rather turn her back on her inheritance than subject herself to the kind of performative obeisance with too many strings to count that she knew Umberto would demand.

But times had changed. More importantly, her needs had changed. If this had been just about her, she never would have come back here. She would rather prostitute herself on the streets of London than demean herself for this man's amusement. It had been clear from the moment he'd accepted her call that Umberto would make her jump through hoops once she'd come crawling back and that she would hate every moment of it.

Lucky, then, that this wasn't about how she *felt*.

"I'm an old man," Umberto told her, with a smug look on his face, because men like him didn't really believe they were old. Not the way other men were old. Men like Umberto didn't believe that being old made *them* weak the way it did others. They were so sure their wealth and consequence made them *better*. "My only joys in this life come from my business dealings and I have on the table a particu-

phans didn't care how she got that money. They only benefited when she had it. It was her job to make sure she had as much as possible at all times.

"Yes, yes," Umberto was saying. He swirled his drink in its tumbler. "You are here for your little fortune, I know."

One of the interesting things about the way she'd spent the last five years of life was that Ivy knew a whole lot more people now. Many of them from entirely different walks of life than the one she'd grown up in. Her *little fortune*, as Umberto called it, was easily millions of pounds. Part of it was the money that her mother had inherited upon Ivy's father's death. He too had been an actor—but before that, he'd been born into the English aristocracy. Add to that the numerous fortunes her mother had made as a screen legend and no reasonable person would call her inheritance *a little fortune*.

But of course, to a man like this, it was nothing.

Ivy swallowed back her fury, the rest of the emotions this place and this awful man stirred up in her, and everything else she felt but did not wish to feel while she was subjecting herself to this game of his. Even the walls themselves were unsafe in Umberto's private castle. No doubt plastered over a hundred times with the indifference this man had shown every person he'd ever brought here. Her mother included.

Her mother was the reason she was here. Her mother and what her help from beyond the grave could do for innumerable children in need.

"The funds my mother left me, yes," she agreed, still with a polite smile. She had practiced and practiced, knowing that it would be difficult not to snarl at this man. It turned out it was even harder than anticipated.

Umberto nodded as if she was a small, precocious child

ago, having just buried her mother and vowing never to return, would have told him where he could shove that. With malice and pleasure.

But she'd gotten smarter, these past years. More strategic. There were things that mattered a whole lot more to her than attempting to land a blow on a man like Umberto when she knew perfectly well that he felt nothing. She supposed he was amply insulated not only by the rich food he preferred and the indulgent, debaucherous lifestyle he exulted in, but by all the money he'd extracted from every business enterprise he'd ever touched.

He called himself a *financier*.

But she knew that he preferred to play kingmaker. Regime toppler, if given the chance, because he liked a show. He had his thick, fleshy fingers in every possible pot and sat here in his castle like a big, round spider, casting his webs far and wide.

Young Ivy had felt smothered and claustrophobic and had dealt with that by lashing out, which had garnered her precisely nothing. But she'd learned from that.

Today she simply walked in, kept smiling at him no matter what he said or what tone he used, and took a seat in the chair opposite his.

"I don't want to take up too much of your time," she said, politely. She'd learned that, too. The clever art of conversation with unpleasant people. She'd spent years figuring out how to use her status as a well-known nepo baby to get done the kinds of things that needed doing, in her view. She'd spent years learning how to shine brightly for men like this, because that was the only way to get them to part with their money.

And Ivy loved nothing more than a man who could be flattered into giving large donations to her charity. The or-

Ivy thought of her own mother then. The world-renowned Alana Amis, who had been so beautiful that men had fallen over in the street at the sight of her, yet had carried around an insecurity that far outstripped her looks or her accomplishments or the simple, joyful person she could be when no one was looking. Her lovely and wildly talented mother, who was so luminous on-screen that a single tear from her could make audiences sob for days and who, despite all her fame and her enduring legend, had wanted only the simplest of things in the end.

To be loved. To be taken care of. To matter to someone.

Ivy would never forgive her stepfather for failing Alana on each and every point.

The door opened. Her eyes snapped open, her heart kicked at her again, and she was certain that she was about to see even more of Giaco Tavian. But instead, it was another member of the staff. He beckoned for her to follow him and then led her farther into the castle, to deliver her to what she knew was Umberto's private office.

She walked inside and found the stepfather she had never intended to see again looking as if he was relaxing—a sure sign that this was going to be a bit of blood sport on his end. Nothing about Umberto Tavian was leisurely, and yet today he was sitting in a chair in one of the seating areas that dotted the large room with a drink in his hand and his usual heavy-lidded, contemptuous look in his eyes.

"What a marvelous surprise," he said, speaking English as if he thought Ivy was perhaps not fluent in it. Or, more likely, as if he assumed she was simply dimwitted. See: the silly, foolish, idiotic girl he thought she was. "You were so certain that you would never return to the fold, Ivy. And yet here you are. Just as I knew you would be, one day."

The Ivy she'd been when she'd left this place five years

always loathed Giaco. His smoldering about. His utter disregard for the feelings of absolutely everything and everyone he encountered. His obvious pleasure in making as many people around him as uncomfortable as possible. He made alley cats seem like monks. He was pathologically boneless, confronting, and deeply comfortable with the outrage that followed him around like his baying packs of adoring would-be lovers.

He was a very particular kind of fantasy made flesh, there was no denying it. Yet how he could possibly have emerged from the loins of his father, who Ivy had always thought of—without a shred of affection—as the Lizard King, she could not imagine.

It was likely a gift from his Persian mother, another renowned beauty who had been lost too soon—no doubt to the same neglect that had destroyed Ivy's mother. Because one thing about Umberto was that he did like to collect beautiful women and then destroy them. If he had a leisure activity, it was that.

Ivy blew out a breath, happy to feel that her heart was slowing down a bit. That she was getting back to normal. She needed the reminder she wasn't here for…whatever that was that had just happened. Giaco was nothing if not a distraction. She was fairly certain that was his entire purpose in life. But his nonsense had nothing to do with her.

She made her breath even and tried to make herself relax. She hadn't expected to see her former stepbrother today. She certainly hadn't expected to see *so much* of him. But the more she thought about it, the more she decided it was like diving straight off the high dive into deep water, and probably good for her.

It could only benefit her to remember who she was dealing with and why.

Once her stepbrother. Always the bane of her existence.

But he was a whole lot more than that, sadly. It was impossible to walk past a single tabloid magazine without seeing his shockingly beautiful face. Not to mention most of that internationally renowned body of his, particularly since he did enjoy spending as much time as possible parading it about. Some years it seemed as if all the yachts in the Mediterranean would sink as one if he were not personally there to keep them afloat with his exploits.

There were a lot of words to describe a man like Giaco. *Lothario. Romeo. Casanova.*

The more modern and less poetic *fuck boy*.

If he was a woman, they simply would have called him a whore.

From a distractingly young age, Giaco Tavian had distinguished himself by being faithless and immoral in every possible respect. His father's only son, and therefore the heir to Umberto's vast empire because Umberto thought his younger daughter was good only for potential gains via marriage, Giaco had used his wealth, privilege, and astonishing good looks to make himself the very embodiment of sin.

In some countries they called him the devil. But that only increased the general appetite for him.

To this day, Giaco remained possibly the most debaucherous creature who had ever swanned his way in and out of the bedrooms of Europe, which he did with such regularity that some theorized—without hyperbole—that he might possibly have *actually* slept with *everybody*. He was a scandal in a distractingly beautiful male form that she had now experienced personally.

Even though she had previously been gloriously immune.

Ivy didn't understand how this was possible, and no matter that she could still feel her own body's betrayal. She had

depth and incapable of understanding what was happening all around her—especially if he was involved.

He stared at her and brought back memories of her embarrassing adolescence that she'd thought long-banished to the dustbin of recollections that were no longer welcome now that she was older.

He stared and when she didn't respond, he lifted one dark brow.

Daring her.

Ivy couldn't even have said what it was he was challenging her to do. Not if her life depended on it—and she was dismayed to discover it felt as if it did.

But somehow she managed to wrench herself away, turning back around and retreating from those glass doors as quickly as she could without giving him the satisfaction of seeing her run.

Once she was all the way on the other side of the room, she found that her knees were weak. She had no choice but to lower herself down onto the nearest overtly fussy chair and then had to take a deeply embarrassing inventory of all the ways she was trembling. Shaking. *Goose-bumping* all over. Her heart was pounding so hard it made her feel slightly sick.

And she was slick and hot between her legs, a humiliation from which she was not certain she would ever recover.

She was wrecked, in other words, and she could not understand how any of this was possible.

Because that man was no Roman god. There was nothing the slightest bit holy about him and if there had been at some point he had systematically removed it thanks to his lifelong pursuit of the deepest, darkest depths of any and every vice available.

He was Giaco Tavian. *The* Giaco Tavian.

her and Ivy could move then. Suddenly. She found her hand was shaking, but she wiped the fog away.

To find him staring directly at her.

Everything in her froze again. Then seemed to blare back into light and sound and *sensation* with a punch that made her feel as if she had been knocked back across the room. It was a disorienting shock to realize she hadn't moved, but the bigger shock was staring straight at her through the glass.

Ivy knew that face. She knew those dark jade eyes, lit as ever with amusement and mockery. That perfect nose of his that would not look out of place on precious old coins and that cruel mouth that was so often—like now—curled to one side. Derision a certainty.

He stared back at her and she could only imagine what she looked like from his perspective. Panting up a windowed door, clinging to the glass as if it was the only thing keeping her upright.

Oh yes, she knew that face. She knew *him*, for her sins.

She also knew that something terrible had happened in the years since she'd last seen him in the flesh. Because Ivy had known this man since he'd been younger, more obviously feral, all of him somehow *sharper*. His face had been more of a hatchet when he was twenty-two, a deadly object if wielded correctly but more a tool than any weapon.

Now, though he was no less of a blade, that face of his was *honed*. Not the careless sharpness of his youth, but the refinement of his years. Lethal, in other words.

He did absolutely nothing to cover himself, of course. Instead, all he did was stare right back at her as if *she* was the one parading around nude on a bright and sunny April morning in a place where there could be no possible expectation of privacy. He stared at her as if she was the foolish girl she'd been when she'd lived here, always out of her

Still he rose, some kind of ancient god brought to life, as if the old Roman deities had never really disappeared at all. As if he had been here all along, Neptune himself, carved from wonder and sex, water and desire.

He stood at the top of the ladder now and she watched as he speared a powerful hand into his dark hair, currently slicked to shape his skull. A normal, everyday movement that this man—if he was a man and not a figment of her imagination—made into poetry.

Ivy was still frozen solid as if her bones had locked her in place while inside, everything that could soften, melted. And ran hot. She felt as if she was boiling, as if her body couldn't handle this, because what mortal could?

He turned and she saw the rest of him, like the slow dawning of the sun. The wide shoulders, the chest a hagiography of male musculature, more golden skin dusted with dark hair, and all of it arrowing to a narrow waist. And below, a large and heavy cock that did not appear to be reacting to what she imagined were the cooler temperatures outside that hot tub.

Or then again, more worryingly, perhaps this *was* his reaction. Maybe that enormous appendage was, in fact, his shrinkage.

The idea made her entire body break out into goose bumps.

Yet she kept looking. His thighs were powerful, suggesting levels of performance and dedication that she found staggering. But not as staggering as the clear evidence that he did not have a single hint of a tan line. Anywhere.

It was as if he had been created out of Roman gold, dancing sunshine, and pure lust.

Her own breath fogged up the glass window in front of

ers, each competing to be brighter and more riotous than the next.

Instead, she stopped dead.

Because this particular room did not face the vineyards or the fields or the gardens, as expected. This one looked out over a half-shaded terrace that boasted a set of pools. If memory served, each one was set to a different temperature and they were all arranged so that a person could float in any one of them and look out at the landscape as if they were part of it.

Though what she was looking at right this particular moment was not a part of the landscape, for all that it was... primeval.

A man was rising up out of the hot pool, the vapor rising up from the water's surface with him and making it seem as if he, himself, was generating the kind of heat that steamed up a spring morning.

Ivy felt herself freeze. As if her muscles themselves betrayed her, unable to make sense of what she was seeing.

But she couldn't look away.

He rose slowly, climbing up the ladder at the side of the pool with a kind of careless athletic grace that made her head go light. She was half convinced that she'd lapsed off into sleep on one of the self-referential settees inside, suffering from heretofore unknown effects of jet lag from a simple ninety-minute flight from London down into Italy. Because otherwise, she couldn't account for this.

His back was toward her. And yet her mouth went dry as she found her gaze moving over the impossible, powerful shifts of lean muscle beneath golden skin as he lifted himself from the water. He moved up another step and she blinked, because she could suddenly see what had to be the most perfect, bare-naked ass not currently cast in marble and tucked away in a museum that she'd ever beheld.

here somewhere. Actual cells, not simply all the mind games that were played here the way some families played a bit of cribbage of an evening.

"You may wait here," a serene-faced woman told Ivy as she led her into a room on the ground floor of the castle, away from the far grander reception rooms and a ballroom as famous for who wasn't invited inside as who was—Umberto did love to make a Hunger Game all his own whenever possible. The woman even bowed her head as she retreated.

None of the staff had looked familiar to Ivy, which didn't surprise her. It wasn't easy to have a personal relationship with an angry, despotic old man who thought he was smarter than anyone he'd ever encountered simply because he was richer. Having to *work* for him had to be nothing short of torturous.

Ivy looked around the room they'd left her in. It was one of the castle's numerous salon-type places because, apparently, outrageously wealthy people got too easily bored with only *one* place to sit. She drifted farther into the room, noting in an almost clinical fashion the pedigreed art on the walls. The sort of antiques that would make a Christie's auctioneer weep. Carefully arranged objects were stacked here and tossed there—because the *suggestion* that the occupants might really come and read all of these books, or might have collected these pieces on some sentimental journey instead of simply buying them because they were sought after by others, was the real truth about what was considered fashionable in houses like this.

But staring at yet another example of Umberto's collection of things quickly lost its appeal.

She drifted over to a series of glass doors that took the place of any outside wall in this room and looked out, expecting to see more bucolic fields brimming with flow-

lition. This time, Ivy had decided that she would play Umberto's game and beat him.

Assuming that was possible given Umberto had been running his power plays since long before Ivy was born.

The Range Rover purred its way up the drive and then stopped at the imposing front door of the ancient castle that was habitually featured in architectural magazines. The sort of publications that liked to fawn over each and every one of Umberto's choices and suggesting his *discernment* in financial matters made him *keenly situated* in the *lexicon* of style. As if a corporate titan like Umberto—who had never polluted his business bona fides with an actual day of leisure in all the time Ivy had been forced to live with him—actually sat about poring over the incidental details of the many investment properties he owned. Much less the details of this castle that had been called the *quiet bedrock of the Tavian brand*, because, yes, the man considered his family a marketing tool and used them that way, too.

Obviously, he had his staff hire more staff to handle all such details and yet more staff to disseminate the myth of his greatness in all things to the wider world in the form of the odd puff piece.

The actual bedrock of the Tavian brand was Umberto's bottomless greed.

Once the car was parked, the usual phalanx of indistinguishable staff members poured out to greet Ivy. They took the small bag she'd brought with her and ushered her inside, pretending to ask after her needs and desires when any guest to this place must know that what really mattered was the way Umberto had decreed they ought to be treated.

Ivy was slightly shocked that she wasn't marched off to the dungeons.

She'd always been convinced that there were dungeons

She'd nearly told him where he could go right then. It had hurt her jaw to keep it clenched so tight.

But she told herself to shake it off and shape up, sitting there in the back seat of one of Umberto's fleet of shiny, obnoxious Range Rovers. He had insisted that he send his plane to come pick her up. That she not lift a single finger to get herself to Tuscany—something that a person who didn't know Umberto might consider a kindness.

Ivy, sadly, knew her former stepfather—the man who had made her lovely mother so desperately miserable—entirely too well.

There wasn't a single thing the creepy old man did that wasn't about control.

Especially the things he dressed up in solicitous disguises.

She looked out the window and reminded herself that she was no longer the awkward girl she'd been when she'd first been dragged here against her will, forced to leave her home behind to follow this whim of her mother's. On the contrary. These days Ivy was what this place had made her. There was a strength in that.

Besides, she was here for a purpose.

This wasn't her starry-eyed mother making up fairy tales in her head. This wasn't the notably romantic screen legend Alana Amis allowing a powerful and mysterious Italian to sweep her off her feet—and then sweeping up her daughter along with her because Alana had been lovely in so many ways but had never been one for boundaries.

Ivy smiled, remembering what her mother had said on that topic. *Darling, I am* an *actor. My life is about expanding past boundaries, not collapsing into them.* Something Alana had taken seriously.

This time Ivy had decided to come here of her own vo-

CHAPTER ONE

Ivy Amis had once declared—after having to put up with entirely too many self-congratulatory speeches from those who should have chosen respectful silence on the occasion of her mother's funeral—that returning to her former stepfather's ostentatious Italian castle would occur only if she first crawled the length of England on hands and knees. Over broken glass. Twice.

In fairness, that was how it felt now that she was actually doing it five years later.

Even the ancient rolling hills of Tuscany, with so many cypress trees dressed in pockets of mist in formation along the edges of old, lush vineyards, failed to mask the sensation of too many sharp edges pressing into her flesh.

Her typical reaction to anything having to do with the Tavian family.

Made worse now that she was actually back in their vicinity.

It had taken exactly one phone call to be thrown back into the worst memories of her teenage years. Umberto's oily, patronizing voice. That knowing chuckle, as if he'd expected this call all along—which he probably had. As if all the work she'd done to turn her back on this place and these people had been nothing but an exercise in futility.

A silly girl's attempt to escape reality.

TO HAVE & TO HATE

CAITLIN CREWS

MILLS & BOON

Were you blown away by the drama in
Her Enemy's Secret Son?
*Then why not explore these other passionate stories
by Julia James!*

**The Heir She Kept from the Billionaire
Greek's Temporary Cinderella
Vows of Revenge
Accidental One-Night Baby
Marriage Made in Hate**

Available now!

ing. Telling Laurel that now that she knew for herself what a truly happy and fulfilled marriage was, she would only wish the same for her. Just how the suggestion had arisen that Olympia should be Laurel's matron of honour he still could not fathom. Laurel had said she'd need one—every wedding needed two witnesses to be legal—and Olympia and his father would serve that purpose.

"And she says she wants to see you marry the right woman this time, not the wrong one," Laurel had said to him. "She'll only stay for the ceremony itself, then she and her husband are heading straight off to Italy to visit his family and show off their baby."

Xander's eyes glanced to Olympia now, the woman he had made the mistake of marrying. She looked…happier. He gave her the slightest wry nod of acknowledgement, received the faintest trace of a smile in return.

Then his eyes went back to Laurel. Olympia vanished. No other woman but Laurel existed. Nor ever would or could. The only woman in all the universe. The music gave one final swell, and died away. Xander lifted the hand he was holding and raised it to his lips. In homage and in love. Her eyes twined with his, love-light radiant.

Then they both turned to the celebrant.

"Time to get married," said Dan happily.

And it was.

So they did.

* * * * *

dining privately at the hotel, Dan staying up with them, and spending their wedding night here, with Dan safely tucked into an adjoining bedroom, just like at the jamboree.

Xander's expression flickered. That night he had been flying blind, but now...

Now I know exactly where I am going—into a future happiness that will be as golden as the sun!

He heard the softly playing background music change, swelling in anticipation. The celebrant cast a smile at him. At Xander's side his father got to his feet.

An excited voice sounded beside him. "She's coming, Dad!"

He turned, unable to resist. Approaching him along the sunlit path was Laurel. His breath caught. The wedding dress she'd chosen, and which he now saw for the first time, was in palest pink-blush white, with a ballerina skirt and sweetheart neckline. A delicate wreath of pink roses adorned her hair, caught back in a low full chignon, and her wedding posy was also of pink roses and a tracery of ferns.

He could not take his eyes from her.

"I told you," whispered Dan. "And don't worry, I've got the rings." He patted the breast pocket of his tuxedo, a miniature version of Xander's.

"Good man," Xander murmured now, as Laurel gained the folly.

Beauty lit her like the sun, and his eyes melted with love for her as he reached out a hand.

Across from his father Laurel's matron of honour was taking her seat.

Olympia.

Xander still couldn't get over it. She had written to Laurel, wanting, she'd said, to make her peace with her. Wishing her every future happiness with the man she was marry-

EPILOGUE

XANDER STOOD, RAMROD STRAIGHT, in front of the celebrant. Beside him his best man Dan spoke in a reassuring way.

"It's all right, Dad. She'll show up. I made her promise, and she said she definitely would," he told his father confidently.

A low chuckle sounded from the seat nearest Xander. His father, who had become a firm and instant favourite with his grandson, and Dan the immediate adored apple of his doting grandfather's eye, spoiling him shamelessly and devotedly, sat there, waiting like Xander and Dan, for Laurel to make her entrance.

They were in a Palladian folly set in the grounds of the country house hotel where Xander used to stay, where his father was now staying. The stone folly, licensed as an open-air wedding venue, was in the style of a miniature Greek temple, which seemed an appropriate way, Xander thought, of paying tribute to his own heritage, as this was to be a civil wedding only. And a very small one. The big celebrations—which his father was insisting on, and which Xander knew was for Laurel and Dan's sake, to give them an official welcome to the Xenakis family and friends—would take place when they went out to Greece in the summer.

For now, over Dan's brief half term school break, they were staying in England. Tonight, though, they would be

She took another breath, spoke in a different voice, easing her hands free from both of them. "Now, I must go and fetch Dan from school. You two stay here," she said. "And make your peace."

She headed back into the kitchen, reaching for her handbag on the hook by the back door. She felt wrung out emotionally, yet walking on air.

As she slid her bag over her shoulder, she was whirled around. Xander was enveloping her in a bear hug, so close, so tight, it melded her body to his.

"Thank you," he said into her hair. "Thank you!"

He drew back a fraction, and Laurel could see his eyes were wet as well. It started her off again too. She touched his cheek with her fingers.

"Oh, my darling," she said. "Our own happiness reaches to the stars. We will not shut your father out. He will be part of our life—and of Dan's."

Xander's eyes burned into hers. "I don't deserve you," he said, and such emotion was in his voice that it made her melt.

She patted his cheek, her eyes soft and tender, and so very loving. "No, you don't, but you've got me all the same."

She smiled, a smile that wrapped them both in the love that after seven long years of anger and distrust, of unjust condemnation and separation, now finally united them.

And always would.

of his own choosing. To know you ensured he knew nothing of his own son and that you caused him—and yourself—to lose precious years with him. I don't," she said, and took a breath, holding his eyes, that one tear still wet on his cheek, "want you to miss any more." She swallowed. "My father died when Dan was three, so Dan has no other grandfather, and both his grandmothers are dead too. So you see—" she could feel her throat closing now, tears welling in her own eyes "—I don't want Dan to lose another grandparent, the only one he has now."

Her eyes went to Xander now, standing behind his father. "If I can forgive your father," she said, her voice low, "as I have forgiven you, so can you. So can we both."

She swallowed again. Spoke to them both, father and son. Grandfather and father of her most precious son. "Things went wrong seven years ago. Now—" she drew breath again "—we are putting them right."

She felt her hand taken, clasped tight, by the man who had parted her from his son, and lost his own grandson thereby.

Emotion filled his voice. "Thank you! From my heart, I thank you, whom I wronged so deeply!"

Her own tears were spilling now, and she could see, through the mist, that Xander's father's eyes were filling too. She blinked hers away, clearing her vision. Then with her free hand she took Xander's, drawing him fully back into the room. She lifted her mouth to his cheek.

"It's the right thing to do, Xander. You know in your heart it is."

She led them both forward. "To a happy future," she said. "For all of us."

She kissed Xander's cheek again, and then, softly, his father's tear-stained cheek. She felt her hand that he was holding so tightly wrung more fiercely.

But behind him a voice spoke.

"No, wait!" said Laurel.

She propelled herself to her feet. They were unsteady, but she hurried to the sitting room door.

"Wait!" she cried again. Urgency in her voice and more.

Paulos Xenakis turned. And in his face she saw what she had just caught sight of as he'd turned away. A single tear coursing down his wrinkled cheek.

She caught his arm. "Wait," she said a third time.

She drew him back, and with her other hand seized Xander's.

"We can't end like this! We can't!" she said, the same urgency in her voice, the same emotion that was filling her.

She let go of Xander's arm, turned to his father. Looked at the man who had done her so much harm, whose son was now banishing him from his life as punishment, denying him the grandson he'd been longing for through all the barren years of Xander's marriage to the woman he'd been manipulated into marrying.

Emotion filled her. She herself had denied Xander his son, clinging to her hatred of him. But Xander's father had also been denied him, too, through his own heinous act.

"You have already had your punishment for what you did," she said quietly. "You saw your son's marriage—which he never wanted to make, I know that now and so does he—end disastrously. Without the children you'd longed for. When all along—" her voice filled with emotion "—you had a grandson here in England who would have been legitimate, the son of a woman your son would have married—a happy, fruitful marriage, unlike the one he did make!—had it not been for you." She paused. "That is your punishment. To know you prevented your son making a happy marriage

"I would like you to leave," he said now. "You are not welcome here." He spoke English so Laurel would understand.

He walked to the sitting room door, held it pointedly open. Slowly, heavily, his father got to his feet. But he did not leave immediately.

He turned to Laurel first. "I am sorry," he said. "But I did not want you delaying my son from marrying. I did not personally wish you any harm."

The dam inside Xander broke. "You say that? *Thee mou*, you expose a woman who was entirely innocent to accusations of theft and lying! A woman I then threw from me in anger and disgust! A woman—" his voice choked on the storm of emotion inside him "—who left carrying my child! A child she raised on her own in endless financial struggle, bereft of support from the one person who should have been there to support her, marry her, be a father to the son your shameful act deprived him of! For seven years—seven years—I've condemned her because of you and have been deprived of my son because his mother could not bring herself to admit me into my son's life because of that unfair, unjust, unforgiveable condemnation!"

His face iced. "Leave," he said. "I don't want you in my life. Nor—" he took an arctic breath "—in my son's life."

For one endless moment he felt his father's eyes on him. He would not meet them.

His father walked towards the opened door. His shoulders hunched, head bowed. He turned, looking back at Laurel, still sitting immobile on the sofa, her face blank with shock.

"My punishment," he said to her, "for what I did." His voice low and heavy. "And it is only just. So I shall bear it."

He walked past Xander, not looking at him. Xander made to precede him down the hall, yank open the front door, thrust out the man who had done so much damage to so many.

Numbly, Xander sank down again. Shock, disbelief and incredulity overwhelmed him. That his own father—

"I instructed Andreas to take the bracelet and hide it incriminatingly for the following reason," he said. "A very simple one." He paused. "To end, unequivocally and finally, the affair you were having." There was no expression in his voice, nothing. Nor in his face.

A snarl formed on Xander's face. "How *dare* you do such a thing!"

"I dared," said his father, "because it was necessary." He took a breath, and Xander saw tension across his father's shoulders. Well, it should be there, after such a confession.

Emotions were bucking through him like an untamed horse, and he strove to master them.

"Necessary," his father said, "because I needed you to end your affair—which you had no business having and was going on far too long!—and propose to Olympia, who was impatient for all to be settled between you. As impatient as I was. So I arranged with her that you should collect her from her house party and convey her to Athens so that I could then finish your affair, as I did, most effectively."

"Did Olympia know what you were scheming?" It was all Xander could bring himself to say.

His father shook his head. "No, she would not have agreed to it. She herself was too honest. She would never have colluded with me. She believed—" his voice twisted suddenly "—what you believed." His eyes went to Laurel. "That you were a thief," he said.

"And all along," Xander said slowly, the words coming from somewhere very deep inside him, "you were the thief. And so much worse." Cold was filling him. He got to his feet, looked down at his father. The father who had done what he had shamelessly. Shamefully.

cented English. "I am here," he said, "because my son has told me about you. How he had an affair with you before he married. Telling me that he ended it when he discovered you had stolen a valuable bracelet from the woman who became his wife. That you have always denied taking it, despite his condemnation of you. You returned to England and unknown to him bore him a son, a son you never told him about."

His voice was heavy, as if, Laurel thought, he was a prosecuting judge setting out the brute facts of the case.

"I no longer believe—" Xander made to interrupt, but his father's raised hand silenced him.

The dark eyes, so like his son's, returned to Laurel, resting heavily upon her. "My son believed only you could have taken the bracelet, that Olympia was innocent, nor could any of the crew, all security vetted, have taken it."

He paused a moment. Looked now at Xander. The same heavy unreadable expression on his face.

"In that," Paulos Xenakis said to him, "you were wrong. A member of the crew, your chief steward, Andreas, took it. Placed it in the suitcase of the woman you were having an affair with."

Laurel heard a rasp from Xander, but his father had held up his hand again. His eyes encompassed them both.

"At my instruction," said Paulos Xenakis.

Xander surged to his feet. Fury—incomprehension—filled his face. But at his side Laurel had gasped. Breathless and disbelieving. He turned to her, consternation—so much more—taking over. He realised his father was speaking again, not done yet.

"Sit down, my son," he said. "I must tell you all."

he was. But she was also, Xander could see at a glance, tensely apprehensive.

His father's eyes went to him. They were completely unreadable. "I need to speak to you," he said to Xander in Greek. Then he changed to English, and his unreadable eyes glanced at Laurel. "To both of you."

Xander tensed as visibly as Laurel. "You'd better come in," he said slowly.

He and Laurel stood aside, and Paulos Xenakis walked in. Behind him, Xander could see the taxi move off. Laurel went into the sitting room, and Xander ushered his father there as well.

In the sitting room Laurel turned to the older man. "Won't you sit down?" she said politely.

Paulos nodded. "Thank you," he said, unsmiling. He lowered himself to one of the sofas. Xander drew Laurel down beside him on the facing sofa. She sat, back straight, hands folded in her lap. Xander cast her a brief flickering smile, his hand patting hers, as if for reassurance.

But it was hard to feel any reassurance. Nothing about his father's appearance like this, his manner now, his unreadable expression, boded well.

Xander steeled himself.

This would not be good.

Laurel sat uneasily, hands gripping each other. She knew Xander had told his father about her and Dan.

He won't welcome it—an illegitimate grandson with a thief for a mother, she thought bleakly.

His expression now confirmed it. It was like stone. She felt Paulos Xenakis's assessing eyes on her, felt her tension mount, and Xander's too, sitting beside her.

Then he spoke, addressing her directly, speaking in ac-

"We can't be late picking Dan up from school," she warned him. "We should shower and get dressed."

Xander's eyes glinted gold once more. "Good idea," he said with enthusiasm.

"Separately," said Laurel.

The glint in Xander's eyes came again. "So, you remember our showers on the yacht, do you?" he remarked wickedly.

"We showered together to save water," Laurel answered primly, and disappeared into the en suite to the mocking echo of Xander's laughter. Saving water had not been the only benefit of those shared showers.

She emerged shortly, despatching Xander in her place, trying not to be distracted—too much—by the sight of him strolling past her in all his masculine glory and nothing else as she got herself dressed. After remaking the tumbled bed, she headed downstairs. As she did, the doorbell sounded, and she went to open it.

A man in late middle age stood there, with greying hair and something about him that made her stare. A taxi hovered at the kerb beyond the garden fence.

"Can I help you?" she asked politely.

The man's eyes were on her. She could not read their expression. But there was something about him definitely.

"I am Paulos Xenakis," the man said. "Is my son here?"

Xander froze at the sound of the voice. He stepped out of Laurel's bedroom, fully dressed now, and stared down the stairs. What the hell?

"*Babas?*" he exclaimed. *Dad?*

He vaulted down the stairs, disbelief filling him.

Laurel stood aside. She was obviously as bewildered as

He cast her another look. A different one this time.

"Talking of while Dan's at school," he trailed, "I can think of an excellent use of our suddenly free time."

Laurel cast him a look back. "Oh, yes?" she said limpidly. "And what might that be?"

He flicked another glance at her. A wicked one now. "You'll find out soon, my adored bride-to-be, you'll find out."

She did, and being swept upstairs by her husband-to-be and made passionate love to in the middle of the morning was a heady experience.

"We've seven missing years to make up for," Xander said, his voice husking as his mouth came down on hers. "And I intend to make them up very—" he kissed her "—very—" he kissed her again "—very thoroughly indeed."

His gaze held hers, and Laurel felt her heart catch with the love melting in his eyes. In hers.

"Sounds good to me," she smiled, as she slid her arms around him to kiss him back and to give herself to the bliss that awaited her.

Xander had not exaggerated that he was going to make up for those seven missing years. Hunger filled them both, and then hunger of a different kind. But lunch was a sketchy affair, and then Xander was sweeping her back upstairs.

"You're insatiable!" she laughed as they collapsed down upon the waiting bed yet again.

His dark eyes glinted gold in their depths. "Always," he promised her.

But satiety came in the end—for now, at least. As they lay there, limbs tangled and entwined, Laurel propped herself up on her elbow.

He helped her back into the car, headed home. It was a good word—*home*. It would be their main base, for Dan's sake, though they would probably move to a larger house in the autumn. He and Laurel were already scouting local properties. He'd need somewhere with a dedicated study, not just working out of the dining room as he was currently doing. He would also, he acknowledged, need to make regular trips back to Greece on Xenakis business. His expression clouded a moment. It would be a balancing act, and not just in respect of business affairs, but family as well. His father had gone very quiet since Xander had told him about Dan.

Will he accept what happened?

He just did not know. He became aware that Laurel's expression had also clouded.

"I feel bad about Dan's old school, Xan. They do their best under huge pressures. Now that Dan has the privilege of going to private school, I'd like—" she looked at him uncertainly "—to make a donation to his old state school in some way, provide some much-needed equipment, something like that."

"I've no objection," Xander said. "I think it's a good idea—the same with your plans for your house."

Her expression lightened. "I'm glad! Keeping it, but letting it at an affordable rent to a single-parent family. Using the rent to pay my fees for my master's." She smiled. "I'm so excited to be able to pick up my studies again! And I would like to keep going with online tutoring too, and maybe do something voluntary, like museum work or stately home guiding or some such!"

Xander cast her a look. "Leave some time for Dan and me," he laughed.

She pressed his arm. "I'll only work, and do my studies, when you work and when Dan's at school," she promised.

boree, whether I was going to be your mum's boyfriend again? Well, how about—" he took a breath "—I go one better? How about," he said, "if your mum and I got married? You," he said, "could be my best man at the wedding."

Dan's face lit up. "When?" he said excitedly.

"Well, as soon as we can fix it," Xander promised.

Relief filled him. Dan had no objections to make. But he double-checked all the same.

"Is that okay with you?" he asked carefully. "Me marrying your mum?"

Dan looked at him sapiently. "Well, you are my dad," he pointed out.

Xander laughed a carefree laugh this time. Out of the mouths of babes…

"I am indeed," he said. "And now we'll be Mum, Dad and Dan. A proper family. Living together."

"Here?" asked Dan.

"If we like," Xander said. "Or we could be somewhere nearby, but bigger maybe. We'll all spend time in Greece too, in the holidays. Let's talk it over with your mum."

They had, and it was agreed that for the time being, they'd keep the cottage. They had the wedding to book, Dan's place at the new school to confirm, with term starting imminently, and his uniform to buy.

Now it was his very first day. They'd both taken him to see the school. It met strongly with Dan's approbation, as Xander had been sure it would, and they'd met the headmaster and his future form teacher.

They drove him over now to start the new term. The other boys were streaming in, but Dan's form teacher was waiting for him. She would take him in, introduce him to his classmates. Dan went off with her happily.

"He'll be fine," Xander said, reassuring Laurel.

CHAPTER THIRTEEN

"Oh, darling, you look so smart!"

Xander could hear the catch in Laurel's voice as she beheld their son dressed in his new school uniform. He did look smart, and Xander confirmed Laurel's proud exclamation.

It was the first day of term, and Xander had just returned from Greece. He'd made it back there just in time for the Orthodox celebrations and was glad that he had. The conversation with his father he needed to have was overdue. He'd left it till just before setting off again for London. It hadn't been an easy conversation, and Xander had kept it as simple and as short as possible. His father had said nothing, but his expression had been troubled. Xander could understand why. He would need time to come to some kind of terms with it—deeply shocking though the news must have been to him.

For himself, though, now there was nothing to think about. He and Laurel had agreed on everything—and so had Dan.

Especially about getting married.

Xander had taken Dan aside right after the pancake breakfast and talked to him while Laurel went back upstairs in her dressing gown to shower.

"Dan, remember when you asked me, the day of the jam-

self down on the bed, right in the middle, holding Mr. Teds. He didn't seem fussed by his father's presence, and Laurel was glad. Glad for so much. For so very much.

"Are you here for breakfast?" Dan was asking Xander.

"Definitely," Xander replied. "In fact, I'll tell you what. How about you and I going down and making us all a special breakfast. What would you like?"

"Pancakes!" Dan said immediately.

"Excellent," said Xander. He paused. "You'll have to show me how to make them. We'll leave your mum to come down when they're ready."

"Okay," said Dan, then slithered off the bed and ran out of the room to put Mr. Teds back on his own bed.

Xander dropped a kiss on Laurel's head. "See you downstairs," he said.

Then he vaulted out of bed. Laurel saw the moment when he realised he was not only stark naked, but there was no handy robe to head downstairs in. She laughed.

"You'll just have to wear yesterday's clothes," she told him.

"For one day only," he promised, reaching for his boxers. "Today we sort everything. The rest of our lives."

She smiled. A smile as warm as the brightness of the day—the shining, brand new, golden and wondrous very first day of the rest of their lives.

"Sounds very good," she said.

"It does indeed," he said, crossing back to the bed to drop a kiss upon her, and in his answering smile she saw all the love his heart held for her and always would.

And how could she possibly, possibly argue with that?

"No." She loosed her hand, cupped his cheek. "They are tears of joy, only of joy."

She loosed her other hand as well, folding both now around his back, as he did of hers. He held her to him, his cheek against hers.

"And joy is all," he whispered now, "that I will bring you."

"We will bring it to each other," she said. And held him close against her heart.

And she to his.

Forever now.

"Mum?"

Dan's voice was puzzled. Laurel knew why. Usually when he woke in the mornings he trotted into her bedroom, clutching Mr. Teds, to snuggle in with her before they both got up. It was a precious time for them both.

Now it was even more precious. At the hotel she'd panicked, terrified that Dan would find her in Xander's bed, where she'd had no business being.

But now...

"I'm in here, darling. The big bedroom."

The door was pushed open, and Dan appeared. Enquiry was on his face. Beside her, Laurel felt Xander stir, not used to being woken by a child. He sat up, yawning.

"Dad?" Dan's voice was even more puzzled.

"The very same," Xander confirmed. He held his arms out as Laurel sat up as well, keeping the bedclothes pulled over her torso.

"Why are you here?" Dan asked curiously, clambering up the bed.

"Your mum's bed is too small for us both," Xander said.

The explanation seemed to satisfy Dan. He settled him-

"It's really ours," he said. "And I shall show you."

Slowly, tenderly, he touched his mouth to hers. Slowly, tenderly she kissed him back.

Then as slowly and as tenderly he started to make love to her, and she to him.

It was as sweet as honey, their bodies exploring each other's, finding themselves again with all the time in the world, a lifetime ahead of them. In the darkness of the night he kissed her breasts in homage, as the tips of her fingers made a journey across the strong wall of his chest, her lips teasing and caressing, until he caught her hands, lifted his mouth to hers, and drew her across him.

"Make love to me," he said, his voice low and husked, his eyes dark in the dim light, glinting with the faintest gold. "Make love to me, so that I know I am forgiven."

Her answering smile was slow, and glowed in her eyes. She kissed his mouth gently and then eased him into her so that he filled her very being. His hands held hers still.

"If you move," he said, and the glint in his eye made his meaning clear, "it will be a very swift forgiveness."

She smiled again, her loosened hair a veil around them. "Be forgiven," she said.

And moved.

She felt his release, like a slow wave breaking within her, felt her own body begin to pulse around him, find its own release. It was a slow wave like his, spreading through her, its intensity filling her. Their arms were outstretched on either side, fingers meshed together, her head bowed over him.

Long after, as her body returned to her, she gently lowered her torso to his, brushing his lips with hers. They lay like that, still in their union, and she felt tears fill her eyes, fall on to him. She felt alarm go through him.

caused you so much pain, Laurel, so much hurt. Seven years of hurting. And I will spend seven times seven years—seventy times seven!—healing that hurt, telling you—" his voice softened, melted around her heart "—how very much I love you." His eyes clung to hers, never to let her go.

He kissed her then, a healing kiss indeed. A kiss of love so long denied, all but destroyed, and now, at last, claimed for them both. And around her battered heart she felt flow the balm of peace, and trust, and quiet and certain love.

He led her upstairs, treading quietly. At the top he turned to her. "Your room is too close to Dan's—"

She nodded, and they went into the master bedroom beyond the bathroom, closing the door so that it was only just ajar. Not turning on the bedside light, she drew back the counterpane. The bed was made up already.

"It's waiting for us," Xander smiled.

This time, as they shed their clothes, there was no hurry, no rush, no urgency. This time, as they went into each other's arms, there was no madness or insanity.

For this was love.

The wonder of it washed through her.

This could have been ours seven years ago.

If they had just kept sailing on into sunset and let love grow between them from passion and desire to what they now possessed.

But now we do possess it. Now it is ours forever!

Gratitude filled her. She lifted her arms and looped them around Xander's neck, drawing them both down upon the bed.

"Is this really happening? Is this really ours?"

His smile was warm, and his heart was in his smile. She could see it with every fibre of her being.

so, touched his mouth with hers and settled down her feet again. All in a single movement, fluid and free.

"Too late for me," she said, and the softness in her voice, her smile, fulfilled her words. "Because I already have," she said. "Our night together showed me."

Seven years ago, his cruel condemnation, his harsh denunciation that had thrust her from him, his marriage to Olympia, had made her cling to thinking what they'd had was just a holiday romance, that she'd had no expectations of it, denying that she had been falling in love with him.

And she had denied it still even after their night together now.

"When you said that we should marry it was a torment to me! You desired me, but you still thought me a thief." Her face shadowed, and she pulled her hands free. Her eyes met his, full-on, unflinching. "Do you still think me one?"

For a moment he did not speak, did not answer her. Then he took her hands again, took a breath, a razored one. His eyes held hers. "Laurel, I believed you a thief because I needed to believe you one. Now," he said, "I no longer need to. I am finally free of that. So whatever the explanation, Olympia lying to me after all, some under-vetted crew member panicking in the search and hiding the bracelet in your suitcase? I don't know. And I don't care! Because all I know and care about is this." His eyes were pouring into hers now, telling her all she had longed to hear for so, so long. "That the woman I love, with all my heart, after so painful a journey for us both—that woman is not a thief."

She closed her eyes, she could feel the tears on her lashes. Feel his mouth softly kiss them away. Her hands clung to his.

He drew back again, but never relinquished her hands. Remorse filled his voice. "Accept my love, I beg of you. As I accept, with all my heart, the wondrous gift of yours. I've

sadness etching the beauty that had captivated him. That he had thrown away because he'd lacked the courage to claim her, to win her love, to make his life, his future, with her. He'd taken the easy way out instead. Done what had been expected of him.

Failed catastrophically.

Wasted seven long pointless years.

And yet, all along, those years had not been wasted.

His thoughts went to the room above them, where his son slept.

Our son—the gift that I have been given by the woman I should never have thrown away.

That now he wanted only to reclaim.

Without realising what he was doing, he reached for Laurel's hands, which lay inertly in her lap, and drew her to her feet. She came unresistingly, did not pull free. Emotion was full in him. So much emotion—seven long years of it.

He looked down into her eyes, which were lifted to his but still veiled.

"Is it too late?" he asked. "For us to fall in love again?"

She did not move, but he felt her hands tighten. "Yes," she said.

A single word. Yet it was a knife thrust with killing force into his heart.

She heard the echo of her own single word. Saw its impact on him.

Pity flooded into her. And much more. She felt her eyes mist with it. Emotion was filling her, a swelling tide, welling up in her. Her heart had stopped hammering, for now there was no confusion, no incomprehension, no misunderstanding.

She reached up with her face, standing on tiptoes to do

"I needed you to believe it too. I needed you to believe me guilty."

He frowned, looked at her strangely, as if her words could make no sense. Slowly, she spoke again. "It was the only way to hate you, because of your accusations and condemnation. And I needed to hate you, Xander, because if I didn't hate you, then—"

She broke off. She could not say more. Confess no more. Her heart was still thudding inside her. Deafening her. But not so she could not hear him speak now.

"And if I hadn't clung on to your guilt…" He left it unspoken. "Making myself hate you for it…"

He broke off. Something was changing in his face, his eyes. Something that melted through her.

"Shall I say it for both of us?" he asked softly. "Say what would have happened if there had not been such cause for anger and hatred between us? Say," he said, his eyes, filled now with so, so much, never leaving hers, "what would have happened? Should have happened?"

Xander's voice was low and slow, and saying what had been impossible to say until now.

"We nearly fell in love, you and I, Laurel, seven years ago. Out there in the sun-filled Aegean days and in the moonlit nights." He paused, his voice changing. "But I never let it happen. Instead, I threw you away, banished you from my life, because I didn't have the courage to face what was happening between us, that it meant I must not marry Olympia, despite all the expectations that we should do so. When I saw her bracelet in your suitcase I knew I had found the means to go on being gutless." Self-accusation lacerated him, but he deserved it.

He looked down at her now. Her face was still drawn,

CHAPTER TWELVE

Laurel's heart started to thud. Heavy, bruising strokes. Xander was looking away again, and an expression she could see filled his eyes. Sadness—and guilt.

"Though I married Olympia, making everyone happy, it seemed, it was always doomed to failure. Because you, Laurel, destroyed my marriage."

Her eyes flashed, repudiation in them. "Don't you dare blame me!"

He gave a negating shake of his head, his gaze coming back to her. "I don't blame you. I blame myself."

He took another breath. "All through my marriage I could not forget you, however hard I tried. However much I excoriated you as a liar and a thief to try and crush your memory, obliterate it. Trying, so fruitlessly, to make my marriage work. The marriage," he said, "I should never have made. Because of you."

For a moment Laurel was silent. What he had said churned within her. That he'd needed to believe her guilty. The tightness in her chest was like a vice. Yet it was a vice that was forcing her to speak, to answer him. The words, when they came, were low and painful. Hard to speak. They were new to her. Until this moment she had never known them. Now she spoke them. Making herself look at him. Say what she must admit—confess.

"When her bracelet went missing and was found in your suitcase, I found my weapon too. One I desperately needed."

She frowned. His words made no sense. "I... I don't understand."

He gave a rasp in his throat. "No more than I. Until now." His eyes rested on her, like weights she could not bear. "I condemned you for stealing Olympia's bracelet, Laurel, because I needed to believe you were a thief."

She didn't understand. Nor did she understand the sudden constriction in her lungs.

"I needed to believe it, Laurel, because it was the only way to get rid of you. And make myself marry Olympia."

"I don't understand," Laurel said again, her voice faint.

But then he hadn't understood, either, not for for seven long, tormented, wasted years. Not until he'd stood in his father's garden did he realise why he'd needed to believe in Laurel's guilt.

She was looking at him with an uncomprehending expression that did not hide from him another emotion in her face, that self-protective withdrawal from him. It hurt him to see it—guarding herself from him from what he'd done. Done to her so that he could make the choice he never should have made.

"No more than I," he said again. "But now I do. Now I know that I needed to accuse you, condemn you." He took a breath that came from the bottom of his lungs, said what he had just flown two thousand miles to tell her. "Or I could not have let you go."

to you. So we sailed away, you and I, and had our affair. Happy and carefree. And it was incredibly good," he said, "like I'd never known before."

He stopped, did not look around.

"I never wanted it to end."

Still he did not look around. "But it had to end so that I could do what everyone was waiting for me to do. Marry Olympia. She even—" his voice twisted again "—turned up on board to remind me of that."

"She made that clear to me," Laurel said, her voice as dry as sand, "that my time was up. So there we were, two women, hackles raised, scrapping over you, and you, moody as hell, wishing us both to perdition."

"No," he looked at her now. "Only one of you."

She tried not to flinch, not wanting it to show. Yes, Xander had wished her to perdition all right, and she had gone. There was a heaviness forming inside her, hard and painful. Jerkily she reach for her wine, but it did not go down easily, or have any bolstering effect on her. She set down her glass. She didn't want to look at him. So she didn't. She stared down at her half-eaten pasta instead. It blurred beneath her gaze. She realised he was talking still.

"Laurel," Xander's voice was sombre, "you need to understand what happened when Olympia joined the yacht. Reminding me, just by her presence, what I was supposed to be doing. Proposing to her without further delay. Which meant you had to go. But she knew your fantastic looks totally outshone hers, so she was waspish and condescending towards you, fighting you with what weapons she had." His voice changed. "And so did I."

She looked up him then. Not understanding. He was looking at her, his expression shuttered. His voice heavy.

He took a breath, began his sorry story.

He did not figure well in it.

"A lot of people, Laurel, wanted me to marry Olympia. Her parents wanted it. I was a good catch, well-matched for their daughter, comfortably wealthy, and our families were friends. My father wanted it too for reasons I can make… allowances…for. After my mother died my father pressed me increasingly to marry. He wanted me to find the happiness he'd found with my mother. He did not want me to delay. He longed for grandchildren now that his wife was gone. And as my mother had always liked Olympia, been fond of her, she seemed therefore, to my father, the ideal match for me."

He paused. "Olympia thought so too. So—" he took a breath "—there I was, four people all wanting me to marry Olympia. And why should I not? She was intelligent, attractive, of good character, perfectly compatible, with the same social and financial background as myself. The ideal match indeed."

He let his gaze rest on Laurel. "All I had to do was propose and name the date."

He took a breath, a difficult one. "Instead—" He broke off.

Abruptly, he pushed back his chair, scraping on the stone floor tiles. He turned towards the window, dark against the night outside. His hands gripped the windowsill. Then he began to speak, his voice low and rapid.

"Laurel, when I set eyes on you for the very first time in that café on the beach, I wanted you. I was ripe for an affair, I admit that freely. Though just why that should be, when I was all set to propose to Olympia—" his voice twisted "—I did not wish to consider. I only knew that I wanted you and that you—well, you made it obvious the idea also appealed

that I would ever stoop to marrying a man who treated me as you did? Who thinks me a thief?

But it was his voice that spoke out loud.

"Everything," he said. His voice changed. "Starting with this meal." He reached for the parmesan, started to grate it over his pasta. "You should eat, Laurel. You're strung out like wire. And me, pretty much the same." He offered her the parmesan, and she took it automatically, mechanically shredding it over her spaghetti, then setting it down again. She reached for her wine glass, taking a mouthful, needing it.

Xander was already stuck into his pasta, and she did likewise, though she could taste nothing. Tension was, indeed, racking through her. Was he going to say again what he'd said before, wanting a different answer from her? She had none to give.

"This is good," Xander said, indicating the pasta, twisting another forkful of spaghetti. "Thank you."

She gave a half shrug. "It was easy enough. The sauce is out of a jar."

"Lunch on the plane was a long time ago," he said, "so this is much appreciated."

He finished off his bowl, pushed it aside. Reached for his wine. Took a breath as he replaced the glass. Looked right across at Laurel. Something was in his eyes, but she didn't know what. Only that she had not seen it before. She was wary and tense, guarding herself from whatever he might say.

But what he said was nothing that she'd expected.

"I want to tell you, Laurel, about my marriage."

My marriage.

The words tolled in Xander's brain. His disastrous failure of a marriage, which Olympia had finally cut and run from to find her own belated happiness. He wished her well.

* * *

Laurel set down the two dishes of spaghetti, into which she'd stirred pasta sauce out of a jar, together with a block of parmesan and a grater, putting it all down on the kitchen table. Xander was already sitting there and had poured them each a glass of red wine. He waited till she took her place, then lifted his glass. Looked across at her. He was way too close, the kitchen table way too small. And Xander dominated it and the entire kitchen, the house, her consciousness. Awareness of him vibrated through her, but like an electric current on alternating frequency. Generating completely opposing emotions. One wished Xander a thousand miles away, the other—

She felt her heart rate quicken, felt the urge, almost overwhelming, to let herself sink into returning his gaze for the sheer pleasure of it, just as she'd done that evening of insanity that had brought them to this impossible impasse that could never be resolved, divided as they were now every bit as much as they had been seven angry years ago. She drank in his familiar features, all the enticing details, the way his dark hair feathered his forehead, the length of his lashes, the strong line of his jaw, the sensual contours of his mouth.

With a start she jerked her gaze away, fumbled for her glass. Xander was speaking, his voice low, intent, but with something in it she couldn't recognise. He tilted his glass towards her.

"To getting this right, Laurel," he said.

Her eyes flew back to his. "To getting what right?" she said. She could hear a trace of breathlessness in her voice and hated herself for it. This had been a bad idea, to let Xander demand dinner of her, to sit himself down at her table, create this exchange with her. There was nothing else to be said between them. How could there be?

Her own voice echoed back to her: *Do you really think*

"We can talk over dinner," he said, cutting her off.

"Dinner? Can't you eat at your hotel?" she protested.

He ignored her objection. "Something simple like pasta will be fine. I'll give you a hand. I bought a decent bottle of wine at the airport. I'll fetch it from the car. You get the pasta going." He made his tone of voice sound reasonable, hard for her to object to. He couldn't have her seeing that he was flying blind.

He'd done that once before, and it had brought him to this moment now.

So, am I crazy to think I can do it again?

But he had no choice. Too much depended on it.

The rest of my life.

And Laurel's too. And their son's.

All of us.

For a moment he saw her fulminate, then, whisk away and yank open the fridge to extract a packet of fresh spaghetti. Xander went to fetch the wine from his car, glancing up at the sky. The night was clear, and stars blazed, not as brightly as in Greece, the visible constellations different too, and the air was nowhere near as warm. No chorus of cicadas serenaded the night, but the lonely hoot of an owl from the woods sounded hauntingly. He felt his heart beat more heavily than indoors. Emotions passed through him that were strange but potent. He looked back towards the cottage, dim light showing through from behind the drawn curtains of the sitting room, the hall light outlined by the open doorway. Inside was the son he and Laurel had created seven long years ago. Precious beyond measure.

To us both.

He fetched the wine, went back inside. Still flying blind. But certain of his destination. Of Laurel's too.

If he could just get them both there.

All evening she'd barely spoken to him. Dan, blessedly, hadn't noticed; he'd just been delighted Xander was back, and Xander had focussed on Dan as well. They'd played football till the light went, then headed up to Dan's room, then been called down to tea. Laurel had only cooked for Dan—fish fingers and a microwaved baked potato with tomatoes and broccoli. Xander had made no comment about the obvious lack of food for Laurel and himself. After tea had come TV, an adventure serial Xander had shared with Dan, Laurel disappearing into the kitchen, doing God knows what. Avoiding him mainly, he supposed. He'd taken Dan up for his bath, and Laurel had still said nothing, so he'd let her be.

But now Dan was asleep.

At the foot of the stairs Laurel was hovering. Waiting to launch at him. "Why did you come back like this? There's no point, Xander."

"There's every point," he said.

He'd never said anything truer in his life, nor more crucial.

Laurel stared at him. She wanted him to go away right now. Back to his hotel. Back to Greece if possible. Him being here was impossible, unbearable.

He was taking her elbow. She wanted to pull away, but she felt nerveless, helpless. "Let's go into the kitchen. Our voices will travel less."

He guided her in, and the moment they were inside she stepped free of him.

"Xander, I don't know why you've come back so soon, but if you intend a replay of what you said to me on Easter Sunday I don't want to hear it—"

"No, I don't want to replay it." With effort Xander kept his tone even.

"So what do you—"

Xander dropped a kiss on his dark head. "I missed you too," he said.

Though it was not just his son he'd missed.

With Dan abed, the evening loomed ahead. The most important evening of his life. He eached across for Mr. Teds and tucked him in beside his son as he eased himself to his feet.

"Where's Mum?" Dan asked, still sleepy.

"I'll call her," Xander said. He crossed to the door, went out on to the landing. "Dan's ready for lights out," he called down, then went back into his son's bedroom. Dan was yawning, hunkering down in the bedclothes, Mr. Teds beside him, and Xander settled the duvet over them both. He turned the bedside lamp off and the night light on, throwing a dim glow over the room. Footsteps sounded on the stairs, and then Laurel was coming into the room.

"Night night, Mum," Dan said drowsily. Xander watched her come up to Dan's bed, lean down and kiss his cheek tenderly.

"Night night, darling," she said. Xander could hear the love in her voice. Emotion speared within him. He came up beside her. "Night night, son," he said. He laid the palm of his hand gently on Dan's head.

Dan's eyelids were shutting, his breath slowing.

Xander felt Laurel move slightly away from him. As Dan eased into sleep, Xander spoke, his voice low, intent.

"Our son needs us both, Laurel, needs us as family."

But it's up to me to show her how. Now that I finally understand.

He stepped away, waiting by the door. For a moment longer Laurel just went on standing there, looking down at their sleeping son in the dim light. Then she moved quietly away, walking past Xander. She made no answer, but he followed her downstairs.

Dan's voice made her open her eyes. He was holding his football but not looking at her. He was staring at the back of the garage, the pathway that led between it and the wall of the cottage beyond the patio, his expression alert. The sound of tires on gravel, the low note of an engine.

Then he was running, dropping the football, racing across the patio and onto the pathway.

"It's Dad! Mum, it's Dad! It's his car! It's Dad!"

Behind him, Laurel froze. No, it couldn't be Xander. He was in Greece, away till after the Orthodox Easter. Taking himself off early because she'd wanted him gone, because what he'd said to her, asked of her, was impossible.

I won't drink that poison. I won't. I dare not.

Beyond the garage she heard Dan's voice exclaim excitedly, "Dad!"

Xander's deep voice answering, Dan saying they were in the garden, the two of them appearing down the pathway, walking towards her, Dan clutching his father's hand, his little face beaming.

"Dad's home!" he cried, happiness radiating from him.

She went on standing there, frozen. But inside her a tumult.

Xander paused. His presence leaping at her, eyes going to her.

"You're supposed to be in Greece," she said. Her voice sounded hollow.

"I couldn't stay," he answered.

Xander shut the book he'd just finished reading to Dan and put it on his bedside table. He was propped on Dan's bed, one arm around him. It was so good to feel Dan's strong little body snuggled against him.

"I'm glad you're back, Dad," Dan said sleepily. "I missed you."

Laurel felt her throat tighten. "He has family in Greece as well. His father for a start. Probably lots of cousins. I... I don't really know."

It wasn't something Xander had ever talked about, way back on his yacht, except that he'd mentioned his father and that his mother had died when he was at university. It was something they had in common. Understanding each other's loss. A rare moment when reality had made its presence felt in their headlong, lotus-eating idyll.

Until reality had slammed in big time. Olympia coming on board, wanting a ride back to Athens. Making it very clear just who she was to Xander.

Unlike me.

She pulled her thoughts away. Her pointless, futile thoughts. In the four days since Xander had taken himself off at the end of Easter Sunday it had been impossible not to let those thoughts in. Playing and replaying what Xander had said to her that day.

He wants to marry me.

The "perfect solution," he'd called it.

The perfect poison.

Because that's what it would be, she knew. Marrying Xander. Poison that tasted so sweet yet killed all the same in the end...

Wearily, she shut her eyes. Had he really thought she would agree to drink that sweet poison, killing her slowly, day after day.

Night after night in his arms.

Wanting him so much, yet knowing that what had parted them seven years ago was still there between them.

Keeping them apart, dividing them still. That always would.

"Mum—"

in Greece. He'd asked no questions about what had been keeping him returning to England, and Xander suspected his father was hoping it was because he was dating again.

His mouth compressed as he accepted the martini being handed to him. He was going to have to tell his father the truth about why he was spending so much time in England. But how could he when his own mind was in such tumult? The words that had come to him out by the pool circled again, still making no sense.

It was the only weapon I had.

And then, as they circled, meaning came to him, explaining everything. Why he'd needed a weapon, and what he'd used it for.

My accusation of her was the only weapon I had so I could make the choice I made.

He stilled, feeling cold wash through him. Realisation.

The choice, he faced it now, expression drawn and sombre, forcing himself to face it, as he stood in his father's house, the father who had longed for him to marry—the choice that he should never have made.

That had ruined his life.

Laurel was out in the garden kicking a football around with Dan in the last of the daylight. But Dan was not enthusiastic, she could see.

"I'm not as good as your dad, I know," she said apologetically.

"It's okay, Mum," he said. He dribbled the ball past her and back again, then stopped and turned to her.

"When is Dad coming home?" he asked. "I miss him."

"Not till Greek Easter is over," she said. "He explained that to you. He's gone back to Greece to see his family."

Dan looked at her. "Aren't we his family?"

"It won't make you fat, Mum!" Dan had teased.

Xander's eyes had gone to her, sitting opposite him on her own sofa, while he sat on his. Remembering, with burning vividness, just how very perfect her body was, how wonderful making love to her had been.

He was remembering it again now. Remembering everything about that night and the day that came after. The day when he'd screwed up completely.

I thought I'd found the perfect way forward for us. Putting the bad part of the past aside, taking the good forward.

It still seemed so right.

It's the perfect solution, the perfect answer! Dan is part of my life forever, and why should Laurel not be too? Marriage solves everything, provides for everything!

But she'd said no.

Heavily, with face grim, he stared blankly over the gardens, the sun slipping lower and dusk gathering, the endless cicadas striking up, it seemed, even more loudly with their incessant chorus.

She said no because she would never marry me for what I did to her. Because I think her a thief.

His expression set. That accusation he'd first made seven long years ago, had gone on saying, lay between them like the blade of a sword. The blade that he'd used, seven long years ago, to sever her from him.

Because it was the only weapon I had.

He frowned. What did that mean? It hung there, making no sense. Why should he have needed a weapon? What for?

The sound of his name being called from the terrace made him turn. His father was beckoning him, and Xander made his way back indoors. He glanced at his father's face as his manservant poured their usual aperitifs. His father's mood was good. He was glad that Xander was back

CHAPTER ELEVEN

XANDER STOOD BY the edge of the pool at his father's house. If Dan were here he'd be straight into that water, splashing away happily. For an instant Xander could see him there. But Dan was two thousand miles away in England. A wave of missing him went through Xander. Video calls were just not the same.

Dan had said as much to him. Asking him when he was coming back. He'd sounded plaintive, and it had wrung Xander's heart. He wanted to get on to a plane and rush straight there. But how could he? He'd only arrived in Greece three days ago.

He'd left the UK the day after their Easter. He hadn't intended to leave that soon, wanting to spend the Easter Monday holiday with Dan.

And with Laurel.

With them both.

But Laurel had wanted him to leave. Made it clear she wanted him gone. Crystal clear.

She had refused, point blank, to say any more to him. She'd got up from the table, gone indoors into the sitting room and sat down on the sofa, taking her cooling tea with her. Xander had followed her with his equally cooling mug of coffee. Dan had beamed at them, offered them some of his Easter egg. Xander had taken some; Laurel had not.

strangely blank, he spoke. "If I give you my word of honour that never again will I call you liar or thief, can we finally put it behind us?"

She went on looking at him. "No," she said.

Seduction was in his voice, the poison sweeter still, his eyes washing over her now, his hand reaching for hers across the table, winding his fingers into hers.

He smiled, and the sweet deadly poison filling her veins flowed more deeply yet, reaching into her. Oh, dear God, that smile.

Memory, flooding in on the poison, burned in her. Not just of last night, of that hectic, urgent fusing of their heated bodies, but from so much longer ago. His smile—lazy, knowing, seductive, caressing—as they'd raised champagne glasses to each other on the deck of his yacht, as they'd lain beside each other, limbs entwined, on the hot sand of a secluded cove after a swim to shore, as they'd lounged negligently amidst the tangled sheets after he'd brought her to the ecstasy that had made her cry out in sobbing crescendo.

Dear God, that smile.

Through the haze of memory she heard him speak. That same seductive caressing voice, his fingers, warm and strong, capturing hers.

"Marry me, Laurel," he said. "Marry me so we can make a true family for Dan, a home for all of us and bliss for ourselves. Marry me."

His eyes were pouring into hers, that lethal smile playing about his sculpted mouth, willing her to yield to him... tempting her so, so much...

But slowly she drew back her hand. Looked across at him. Her face was expressionless, her voice the same. Saying what she must now say.

"Do you really think," she said, "that I would ever stoop to marrying a man who treated me as you did?" A razor was in her voice. "A man to whom I am, and always will be, a lying, despicable thief."

For a moment he said nothing. Then, in a voice that was

portant, vital thing for our son." He paused, never letting his eyes off her, his gaze boring into her. "We can give him a proper, united family. Once," he said, "we are married."

Laurel heard him speak, but the words made no sense. She heard herself echo the one that made least sense of all.

"Married?"

Xander's eyes were fixed on her still.

Eyes that had flashed with harsh accusation and scathing condemnation, accusing her of stealing that bracelet, stealing his son. Eyes that had been hard as iron and cold as ice as he'd thrown her off on the quayside at Piraeus, when he reeled off his demands of her in the car he'd hauled her into outside Dan's school, denouncing her for keeping Dan from him. Eyes filled with vicious vitriol as they'd raged at each other in earshot of their son.

"Yes," he was saying now, his eyes never leaving her. "Married."

He lifted a hand, as if to stay anything she might be about to say, but it was impossible for her to speak. Impossible to do anything except meet his gaze. He was speaking again, his voice insistent.

"It's the obvious thing to do! Last night proved that the flame between us still burns as fiercely as it ever did. How can you deny it?" His voice changed, and the look in his eyes too.

"And why should you want to deny it, Laurel, after last night?"

She heard the change in his voice. It licked at her like the sweetest poison.

"Taking you into my arms, making love to you, glorying in your incredible beauty, finding the ecstasy again for both of us, making you mine again, making me yours again…"

She cut right across him, her voice terse and tight. "I told you. It should never have happened! It was insanity."

"No," he said evenly, "it was the opposite of insanity." Certainty filled him. As strongly as it had when he'd realised the one thing above all: that he wanted was to make Laurel his again. To recapture what had been before Olympia arrived.

But now, after last night, a new certainty was filling him. One that went beyond mere recapturing. He leant forward, folding his hands around his coffee mug.

He let his eyes rest on her. Even back in her rubbish clothes, playing down her beauty as she stubbornly sought to do, he felt desire course through him. Last night had been... incandescent. It had shown him, indelibly, what he was now going to say to her. What was essential to say to her.

"Laurel, last night showed us the way forward, for us both. For us all. You, me and Dan. Don't you see? We've already achieved so much. Dan is taking to my presence in his life, is taking to the new life he can have if you agree to it. He's happy! And now, after last night, we can move on even further."

He paused a moment, trying to read her expression, but it was shuttered, her mouth pressed tight, so he took a breath, forged on with what he must say.

"You asked me, a while back, what my plans were when it came to Dan, how much would I be in his life. I said I didn't know yet, because too much still divided us. But now—" he took another breath "—I do know. And you know too, Laurel! You must! That after last night, what it showed us is the perfect, obvious answer!"

That overwhelming sense of certainty filled him, drove him forward now.

"Last night has shown that we can do the one most im-

sion that had been winding around her like steel wire ease fractionally.

She seized her cup of tea, gulping it down.

She dared not think, dared not remember, dared not anything at all. In her head, like a neon light flashing, mocking, were the words *Just for this evening.*

Oh, dear God, why had she gone along with it? She should never have done so. The unforgiveable folly of it.

Her eyes were bleak.

All I can do is blank it out—now and forever.

Consign it to oblivion.

Xander was biding his time. He had no other choice. Breakfast, swimming with Dan, driving them back to the cottage—all had to be got through. At last Dan was settled in front of the TV, sprawled on the floor, Easter egg beside him, happily watching a children's Easter special programme.

He waited for Laurel in the kitchen. It was a sunny day, breezy and fresh. Fine for sitting out in. Out of any possible earshot of Dan. He'd made tea for Laurel, coffee for himself. As she came back in he opened the door to the patio.

"Let's sit outside," he said.

Immediately her expression changed. "Why?" Her voice was filled with suspicion.

"So we can have the conversation we couldn't have this morning," he said. His voice was bland, but there was steel beneath. "Laurel," he said, "this has to happen."

Emotions were visible in her face, but he gestured her to go past him, taking their mugs with him as he joined her. She sat down at the ironwork table, stiff as a poker. He sat down opposite her. Took a breath.

"About last night," he started.

knotted, face free of make-up, and somehow it served as armour for her. Yet even so, Xander's eyes swept over her, making her heart pound. She focussed all her attention on Dan, who was well stuck into sausages, hash browns, and an excessive amount of ketchup.

"Dad says you loved last night!" he said to her. "He says you were the most beautiful lady there! He says you both ate yummy food and drank champagne, all fizzy, and there was music and songs and a band, and then you danced!" His eyes were bright, alight with pleasure that she had so enjoyed her Easter treat.

"It was a lovely evening, Dan," she said. Lied.

Lovely until I committed an act of unforgiveable insanity...

"It was indeed, Dan, a lovely evening together." Xander's deep voice echoed. He was putting away a full English. Laurel made do with sliced fruit and yogurt. All she could manage.

She looked brightly at Dan. Too brightly.

"When you've finished your breakfast, Dad can take you swimming. I'll just stay here, I think, and have another cup of tea."

"Dad said I could have my Easter egg after breakfast. Can I?" Dan asked.

"Just a little bit," Laurel answered. "Goodness knows how you've room for it after all those sausages! Don't get a tummy ache in the pool!"

She was glad to wave him off, relieved. Even if she was on the receiving end of a very old-fashioned look indeed from Xander. Knowing exactly, she was burningly aware, why she was shooing them both away. But only when they'd both gone, Dan hurrying off, could she start to feel the ten-

Xander's expression warmed. "Hi there," he said.

"Happy Easter!" Dan beamed. He advanced into the room. "I've got an Easter egg for you, but it's at home, as I couldn't tell Mum we'd be spending the night here after the Easter Jamboree." He looked expectantly at Xander.

Xander laughed, mood lifting. How could it not? He ruffled Dan's hair. Gave him the answer he was obviously hoping for.

"Yes, I've got yours here but you can't have it till after breakfast, okay, or it will spoil your appetite!"

"Okay," said Dan. "Is it time for breakfast now?" he asked.

"Why not?" Xander replied. "If your mum is ready?"

"She's having a bath. A very long one. It's full of bubbles. She said you and me should go down first."

"Did she now?" Xander's voice was dry.

He glanced at the time. "Okay, go back and tell her we're heading down, but give her only fifteen minutes max to join us!"

Dan nodded, and ran back through, and Xander heard him repeating his message to Laurel. He was back a moment later, taking Xander's hand in his. "Let's go," he said enthusiastically. "I'm starving!"

Hand in hand with his son, Xander headed off. His thoughts were full but very clear. Clearer than they had been since he had discovered his son's existence.

Now all that was necessary was to make them clear to Laurel as well. Resolution filled him, because this time she would hear him out. So very much depended on it.

Somehow, Laurel got through breakfast. Dan and Xander were already halfway through when she joined them. She was back in her shabby clothes from the previous day, hair

She lurched back again. "No! I can't hear it—won't hear it! Last night should never have happened!"

She took a ragged breath that she had to force into her lungs, made herself look straight at him. He was standing there, almost naked, his superb body illuminated in the morning sun, every muscle, every sinew, every honed contour. The body she had once known so intimately and now knew again.

A wave of desire washed through her, weakening her limbs, setting that disastrous fatal flame running through her again. Looking him in the face was no better. His darkening expression sculpting the planes of his face, narrowing his lidded eyes.

"Laurel, *listen* to me."

But she would not. Could not. Dared not. Could only plunge away from him, heart still pounding frantically, towards the communicating door, getting through it.

Locking it against him.

Against the disaster she had let happen, falling into Xander's arms. His bed.

Xander watched her go, frustration filling him. His eyes went to the bed, the tangled bedclothes. Memory flooded. Last night had been unforgettable indeed.

But more indeed, than just the past returning.

He felt emotion move within him, inchoate, powerful. Urging him to drag Laurel back.

But now was not the time. Dan would wake soon, and his day would begin. With an indrawn breath he headed to the en suite. His mouth twisted again. Maybe a cold shower would be good.

As he emerged again, freshly shaved, he started to get himself dressed, heard the communicating door open and glanced round. It was Dan.

"Don't wake him!" she hissed urgently.

He stepped back, and she rushed past him, desperately looking about for where her own discarded clothes were. The splash of vermilion over the back of a chair made her target it immediately, scrabbling around for her underclothes dropped on the carpet.

In my rush to get naked.

She grabbed her clothes and pressed them against her.

"I've got to get out of here!" Panic was in her voice.

In Xander's amusement, as he said, "Dan's fast asleep. Leave him be." His expression changed, she saw it happen. Heard the husk in his voice as he spoke again. "Come back to bed."

Clutching her evening gown and underwear like a shield, she lurched away again.

"Xander, no! What happened last night was impossible!"

His mouth, his beautiful mouth, which had kissed her body all over so devastatingly, quirked.

"What happened last night, Laurel, was unforgettable," he said.

"But we must forget it!" The cry, the plea, came from deep within. A desperate place.

The amusement left his face. "That is what is impossible! Forgetting it." He stepped towards her again. "Laurel, there is no need for this panic! Last night has been waiting to happen ever since I came back into your life! I told you, the flame that burned so fiercely seven years ago is still alight. Last night proved it. How could it not?" Something changed in his face, something she had never seen before. "But now, Laurel, there is more. More than what there was then. Shall I spell it out to you?"

He held out a hand to her. "Listen, Laurel, to what I have to say."

CHAPTER TEN

Light stirred Laurel awake. Or something did. Then, dimly, she realised it was not just the daylight filling the room that had awoken her. It was a sleepy, questioning voice, from beyond the connecting door, still slightly ajar.

"Mum?"

She straightened instantly, shock and dismay seizing her. In a few heart-pounding seconds, she had leapt from the bed, panic taking over.

Oh, dear God, he mustn't find me here.

She snatched up the towelling robe provided in the en suite and pulled it on, hurrying through the doorway. But to her abject relief, Dan seemed to have gone back to sleep again. She went quietly up to him, small in the double bed, looking down at his dark hair just showing. A wave of love went through her, but more than that. Confusion, dismay intensifying and one dominant, overwhelming emotion. An emotion she knew the name of—knew it bitterly in the clear, brutal, pitiless light of day. *Regret* was far, far too weak a word for it. *Insanity* was the only one that fit. Total, unbelievable insanity.

"Laurel?"

The voice from the communicating doorway made her whip round. Xander was standing there wearing nothing but a towel snaked around his hips. She surged towards him, panic uppermost again, pushing him back.

and over again. For a second, the merest second, it seemed to him he held himself in check.

Then he joined her in her ecstasy. Their bodies one, their passion one, fused and fusing, going on and on and on.

And then, all there was was her shaking body, trembling, stricken, as he felt the tumult ebbing from her, from himself.

Sweet heaven, but where had that come from? The intensity, the urgency, the hunger.

The sating.

She was still trembling, still shaking, and he could feel her heart pounding beneath her skin. Skin that was cooling, shivering in the aftermath of what consumed them both.

He slipped from her, turning her into his arms, smoothing her hair, her face buried in his shoulder as her body slowly calmed, her pounding heart eased and her breath quietened, until she lay very still, hands splayed against his chest, legs still tangled with his. He soothed her with murmurings in Greek that he had once spoken to her so long ago, cradling her against him after the storm of their passion.

And now he spoke to her again, making her his own once more.

As their heartbeats eased against each other, and the sleep of passion spent embraced them both.

* * *

He advanced upon her, and all she could do was stand there. Her heart was pounding, blood surging. The voice in her head frantically telling her that she must stop was silenced in the pounding. She would not listen, would only reach for him, wanting him so much, a hunger for him she could not stop. A maelstrom was in her head, and she caught at him, crushing her half-naked body against his, feeling the glory of her breasts pressed against the hard wall of his chest. She bent her head so that her cheek pressed against it too, and her arms snaked around him, fingers indenting into the strong planes of his back.

"Oh, God, Xander, I want you so much." It was a broken cry against him across seven long cruel years…

His arms were around her, enveloping her. "And you shall have me."

In a single fluid movement, he had loosed the gown from her, and the glorious silk pooled in a vermilion splash on the carpet. She did not care, hectically kicking off her shoes.

He laid her down upon the waiting bed, coming down beside her. Waiting only to strip the last impeding barrier from her, the matching lacy wisp around her hips, he moved across her.

She opened to him. She could not wait—not one minute more. Desperation fuelled her to possess him again, to be possessed.

He reared above her, and her hands looped around his neck, pulling him down on her. All of him.

In a single, powerful thrust he entered her.

And she convulsed around him in a burning blaze.

She throbbed beneath him, crying out, a sobbing cry, head thrashing, her long hair whipping, calling out his name over

opening to his. He delved within, twining with her, hungry for her, sating himself on her. But it was not enough. His hands slid to her shoulders, down the satin columns of her bare arms to come to rest on her waist, draw her against him. Instinctively his stance changed so that he could settle her against his hips. He felt, in her throat, as their kisses deepened, the little gasp she gave as the full strength of his desire for her was manifest.

Urgency possessed him, urgency to possess her. For a moment longer his mouth held hers. But his hunger craved much more. His mouth slid from hers, down her throat, the hectic, beating pulse at the base and further still between the enticing valley of her breasts. He felt them engorge beneath his lips, their peaks unfurling, and his hunger rose. His hands lifted from her waist to the narrow straps of her dress, peeling away the vermilion silk, the lacy wisp beneath.

He heard her give another gasp, and her head went back, lifting her revealed and straining breasts to the ministrations of his mouth, as he laved them each in turn. Her hands had come around his waist, clutching and unclutching as moans escaped her. Her own stance had widened, pressing his thrusting hips into her eager cradle.

Greek burst from his lips, urgent and low. He stepped away from her, starting the essential process of stripping his clothes—his tie, so useless an object, his jacket the next to go, ripping loose the studs of his dress shirt, impatiently freeing his cuffs, shrugging it off.

She stood watching him, lips parted, eyes distended, not taking them from him, her luscious, ripened breasts exposed to him. Frustration leapt in him and he shed the rest of his clothes in an agony of haste.

Then it was Laurel's turn.

Desire, arousal, an intoxication of all her sensual being, all possessing her.

They reached his room, and Xander was sliding his key card through the lock, then pushing open the door, leading her inside. It was his room, she realised, in the daze that was taking her over.

"Dan," she said faintly.

Xander slipped his hand from hers. "Wait," he said. He was striding to the connecting door, opening it quietly, going through. Laurel, through the drumming in her head, heard dim voices, then Xander was stepping back through, leaving the connecting door open only a fraction.

"Babysitter gone," he said, keeping his voice low, "and Dan fast asleep—"

He came towards her. Purpose in his stride. His face. His eyes locked to hers.

Through the storm inside, she made one last, frail, hopeless attempt to seize back sanity. "Xander, no. We can't."

It was all she said, all he let her say, for he had cradled her face in his hands, his long strong fingers cupping her head, tilting it up. She saw his eyes burning with all that she had once, so long ago and now saw again. Her breath caught.

"Too late," he said. "Far, far too late."

And as he said them, low and husked and final, she heard them echo inside her.

Then his mouth lowered to hers, and she was lost.

All that she could hear echoing inside her head were the words that had brought her to this point.

Just for this evening.

And now, *Just for this night.*

She was all that he remembered. The seven long years melted away. Her mouth was velvet, as sweet as honey,

obvious. She'd given the tiniest flutter of shock, and then, just as he had, she had yielded to it.

His voice as he spoke now was a murmur below the level of the lilting music. "How can I deny what my body is honest enough to crave?" He drew back a little from her, a fraction only, so he could look into her eyes. His speaking, eloquent eyes.

"We used to dance like this on the deck, beneath the stars, and then I'd lead you down into my state room and kiss your mouth, your throat, the swell of your sweet breasts, and peel your dress from you, and take you to my bed."

His voice was low and husked, and with an instinct as old as time, his mouth reached to brush hers so very lightly.

He saw her eyes flutter shut, felt her lips tremble a moment beneath his, and then he'd lifted his mouth away.

His eyes poured down into hers. His speaking, eloquent eyes.

"Come," he said.

This was madness, insanity. Laurel said the words to herself over and over and over again as Xander led her off the dance floor, across the lofty hall and up the grand sweeping staircase to the upper floor, along the wide, thickly carpeted corridor. Madness and insanity, insanity and madness.

She should halt him, pull her hand from his. Dig her heels into the soft pile of the carpet and say, *Xander, no! Too much divides us! We can't go back—we mustn't!*

But it was impossible to do anything but what she was doing—letting him glide her forward, not daring to speak, feeling her heart hammering inside her chest, her breathing ragged, and through her veins, her treacherous champagne-and-wine-laden veins, a river was coursing in full flood, unstoppable, pouring through her, possessing her.

held out an inviting hand towards her. For a moment she hesitated, wine glass still in her hand, eyes still locked to his. Then, heartbeat hectic, she took his outstretched hand.

She knew that she should not let Xander's strong, warm fingers close over hers, draw her to her feet, set down her glass for her, lead her forward, take her into his arms. Yet she did...

Just for this evening.

The words echoed in her head as her body folded into his embrace.

She was silky and slender and so, so close. He could breathe her scent as his arm came around her waist, her hand lifting to his shoulder. He heard her give a little sigh as she did, as in surrender.

They moved to the music instinctively, and just as instinctively he drew her closer against him, feeling the slender column of her body moulding against his. How good it felt, how right that after seven long years, Laurel was in his arms again.

Where he wanted her to be.

Certainty flowed through him. This was what he wanted. Desired. Holding her close, hand folded around hers, his cheek against hers.

He felt her fold against him, from breasts to hips, and he took her weight, treasured it, and let it have its effect on him that he made no effort to deny. For why should he? He had been struck by her beauty the very first time he'd laid eyes on her and desired her ever since. Nothing could quench that desire—not his marriage, not his wrenching her from his life, not her hiding his son from him, not the years apart from her.

That she knew what was happening between them was

She shook her head, sitting back, and reaching for her glass of sweet dessert wine. "Best not," she said. "It's a good life lesson. Don't ask for too much. Don't get greedy."

As she spoke, taking a sip of her wine, feeling it flow into her, as if directly into her already wine-laden veins, she felt the words echo. Had she been greedy once, wanted too much? She heard her own assertion made earlier to Xander replay. That she had never had any expectations of their time together in Greece.

It was a classic holiday romance.

She clung to those words now. Yes, it had come to grief, but that did not change that it had been a holiday romance, nothing more.

A romance that could not be rekindled, for it had ended badly and had been so long ago.

Yet her eyes went to him, to Xander in his tuxedo, just like he'd been seven years ago, as if those seven years of separation could not possibly exist. She could not help herself. Emotion washed through her. A weakness she should deplore, resist. But could not. Not any longer, not this evening.

Just for this evening.

That's what she had given herself to, to this evening here with Xander. It washed through her again. Dear God, but just how gorgeous he was. No man ever had come anywhere close to Xander.

He met her eyes. Held them. Locked on to them. Breath left her, and she felt weakness washing through her, possessing her, roaring in her heart.

"Shall we dance?" he asked.

The band had struck up again, the vocalist launching into a husky-voiced familiar romantic number, and couples were moving towards the dance floor.

He didn't wait for an answer, only got to his feet and

Was that it? In Greece, for all their idyll, he'd known that in the wings, Olympia had been waiting for him. Had that shadowed his time with Laurel? Even before that calamitous ending?

But Olympia is gone now, finding her own happiness, her own future, without me in it. Freeing me.

And if Olympia was freeing him for Laurel, something else was binding her to him, uniting her to him.

Our son.

His eyes rested on her. The mother of his son. The woman he desired. Both in the same person. He felt emotion rise in him.

The song ended. Their waiter was whisking away their wine glasses, setting down dessert wine, their dessert plates and disappearing off again.

Laurel turned back to him, smiling. "I do love that song," she said nostalgically. Her eyes went to her dessert. Gleamed appreciatively. "And this looks delicious!"

She lifted her spoon, dipped it into the rich confection and gave a happy sigh.

Xander smiled indulgently, took a mouthful of his sweet but delicate Sauterne, and made a start on his own dessert.

It was a peaceable moment to be savoured and enjoyed.

Like all that this evening was bringing them.

Laurel gave a sigh of repletion. "That," she said, "was heavenly!"

She pushed back the silvered dish that had just held the most delicate and delicious *bavarois framboise*.

Xander gave a low laugh. It sent a tremor through her, but she did her best to ignore it, despite the champagne and wine coursing in her veins.

"Shall I order another for you?" he asked.

not until the disastrous ending—but because he wanted, overwhelmingly, to focus on the present, not the past.

The present that he had here and now. That they both had.

He was going very softly, very gently. Letting her see how he appreciated her, how wonderful her newly revealed and adorned beauty was to him, but not pressing her with it. Holding back.

He didn't want to scare her off, make her wary again, go back into denial, withdrawal.

So he made it easy to be with him, talk with him, enjoy the evening with him. And when their mains were cleared away, their wine glasses refilled with the rich ruby red he'd chosen for them both, they sipped it peaceably while the small band gathered beside the grand piano, the promised cabaret starting up.

The performers were good, highly professional, and the numbers they chose were a mix of old and new, the singers giving lively or haunting interpretations as the songs required. As the desserts circulated, applause was warm and appreciative.

Xander's eyes went to Laurel. She was sitting back, relaxed, finishing the last of her wine, her lips moving in echoes of the current number, a lilting familiar one from a musical, her eyes alight. He felt it go through him again, that wash of delight in her beauty, his desire of it.

Something moved within him. It was more than just what had made him want to conspire with Dan to get her here, achieve this evening with her, see her again as beautiful as he knew her to be. Something was happening to him that had never been there before, not in Greece. Back then, desire had flamed with the heat of youth, the carefree, avid indulgence of their private idyll. Now it was...

More. Somehow, there is more now. Something...free.

They drank more of their champagne, and then their waiter was there depositing their starter plates, refilling their flutes, gliding away again. All around was the sound of the other diners settling into their gourmet meals, the murmur of conversation, and on the far side of the dining room, where a second set of double doors opened widely out into the hall beyond, was a pianist sitting down at a large grand to gently waft soft music over the room.

The food was delicious, and Xander acknowledged it, Laurel agreeing. It gave them something to talk about, something entirely neutral. Several times Xander found himself nearly referencing back to Greece, but pulled away in time. He wanted nothing to upset her, nothing to allow anything in tonight that might drag in difficulties.

This is about now, about this evening. Nothing else.

He kept it light and easy and undemanding, and he felt Laurel be glad for it too. They talked about the hotel, when it had been a private home, the history of it—again, a carefully neutral subject. They talked about the music that was playing, identifying the melodies, capping each other. He felt her relax, give herself to what was happening, this evening of easy enjoyment, of gourmet dining and gracious surroundings. They talked about Dan, how he'd enjoyed all their outings and adventures, and more that could come another time.

And all the while, Xander could not take his eyes from her her incandescent beauty revealed to him again.

And she was returning it. No longer fighting it. Not denying it or dismissing it. Not hiding it.

It was like a cocoon around them, a silvered mesh gathering them together.

Was it like how it had been in Greece? He didn't want to think about it, not because there were any bad memories—

Let's just have this evening.

And suddenly they were her words too. She would have this evening, She would have it for herself.

For the pleasure of Xander at his best, for putting aside, just for this evening, everything tormented and tormenting that lies between us.

Just for this evening.

Slowly, very slowly, she nodded.

"Just for this evening," she said.

She felt the weariness of fighting him, of all that she must resist about him, fall away like a heavy cloak. Around her shoulders her loosened hair felt like the silk of her gown softly draping her body. To look good again…beautiful… was suddenly a release, a pleasure. If Xander was as gorgeous as only he could be, then she, too, she knew, was at her best as well.

Even in Greece she had never looked this glamorous, worn so beautiful a gown. Dan had chosen well.

A little smile lifted her lips as she thought it, meeting the smile in Xander's eyes—his dark gold-glinting eyes that had always made her breath catch when they rested on her.

As they were now. His lashes sweeping down, making her breathless all over again.

He lifted his champagne glass to her.

"Thank you," he said softly.

And the wash of his eyes was a caress.

Xander felt the last of his tension ebb from him. The very last of it. Before his eyes, holding hers, he'd seen her let fall the final hesitation. His smile on her was warm, embracing. Now he could give himself to the evening ahead.

Because now she is giving herself too.

Just as he was.

CHAPTER NINE

LAUREL SWALLOWED HER CHAMPAGNE, the delicate mousse beading in her throat. Xander's last words echoed in her mind. *Let's just have this evening.*

Her eyes were resting on him, and she felt something turn over inside her—familiar but from so long ago...

How gorgeous he is, how I revel in gazing at him. How I always did. And still do.

That was the truth she could not deny. Could only accept.

His words came again. *Let's just have this evening.* A wave of weariness went through her. Opposing Xander, fighting his condemnation of her, whether it was for the bracelet or keeping Dan from him, fighting his high-handed intention to uproot their lives, hers and Dan's, sweeping all before him in his imperious will, fighting—above all now—her punishing, unpardonable susceptibility to him. Fighting, fighting, fighting.

She was tired of it all. So tired.

Her eyes still rested on him as she set back her champagne flute. His eyes were resting on her in return, but there was in them an expression she had not seen before. Not challenging, not expectant, but waiting.

But not impatiently, not making assumptions, not doing anything at all except letting her choose to accept what he'd said. If she herself wanted to...

Working its magic again.

He took it in, her perfect features, her deep-set luminous eyes, her sculpted cheekbones, her lushly curving mouth, the way her golden hair swept around her shoulder, the soft folds of her silken gown.

There is no woman more beautiful than she who has this effect on me.

He felt it, knew it. Gave himself to it.

try and dream up...mitigating factors, if that's what you're doing. But they don't apply."

For a moment he said nothing. Then, "I don't want to think of you as a thief, Laurel."

His voice was low. The truth of what he'd just said filling it.

Because I don't want her to be a thief! I don't want it to be true!

"I want you to be the woman I knew seven years ago in Greece, the one I sailed away with." His voice cleared. "The one I want so very much—" his eyes were holding hers again now, willing her to hear what he was saying "—to be here again with me this evening."

He lifted his flute again, never letting go her eyes, holding them still as he gently touched his flute to hers as it rested in her hand.

"To this evening, Laurel. Just you and me, enjoying the treat our son was so eager for you to have." He paused, wanting her to accept what he was saying. "Let's just have this evening."

He raised his glass to his lips, eyes never leaving hers.

Slowly, carefully, she raised her own glass. Saying nothing. But her silence, as she took a sip of her champagne to match his, surely was acquiescence.

He felt the tension that had mounted in him ease away. The bracelet, Olympia, his failed marriage—all were unimportant. Only having Laurel here again, like this, was important, was all that mattered to him, here, this evening.

His smile on her, as they lowered their glasses, was warm again, embracing.

He let his eyes rest on her, deliberately, lingeringly. *This* was what he'd wanted the evening to be about. Seeing her beauty celebrated, revealed again, displayed again.

"But you know—" he looked at Laurel, wanting her to understand "—it was difficult for Olympia, too, discovering you on-board. I know she…sniped…at you, taunted you that she expected to be my bride, telling you on purpose that I'd given her that bracelet, making you jealous of her, perhaps, upset by her. So perhaps," he spoke carefully, "perhaps that might…explain…why you were so tempted to take her bracelet."

She was looking at him, and he could not read her expression. But he'd seen it before.

Guarded.

She spoke, her voice low, intentional.

"Xander, I never had any expectations about our time together for Olympia to puncture. It was a classic holiday romance, that was all. You bowled me over. How could you not? Gorgeous looks, private yacht, practised seduction, the whole glittering package! Lethal and loaded! Ideal, perfect, for a holiday romance!" Her expression changed, veiled suddenly. "Even without Olympia—or her wretched bracelet!—even though our time together might have lasted a little longer, it would have ended, just not so acrimoniously." Her eyes held his. "We come from different worlds, Xander. Nothing could come of it but what did."

She dropped her gaze. Reached, jerkily, for her champagne flute, took a mouthful, set it back down again, lifted her gaze to him again.

"Xander, I didn't steal Olympia's bracelet because she upset me by treating me like a good-time floozy. I didn't steal it because I was jealous you'd given it to her. I didn't steal it because I resented that she was going to be your wife. Because," she said, "I didn't steal it."

Something moved in her eyes. "It's…kind…of you to

"To this evening," he said. "To your beauty, Laurel." He paused. "I've missed it so much—"

He let his eyes rest on her, saw her expression waver. "And to our son. Our wonderful son!"

Her expression softened, and he went on, saying now what he wanted to be said. "And to us, Laurel." He held her eyes, saw her expression change again, saw her withdraw.

"Us?" There was a twist in her voice. He heard it clearly. "There can't be an 'us,' Xander."

He set down his flute again. "There already is, Laurel." His eyes never left her. "We can't deny it, and I don't want to. What caught fire between us seven years ago is still alight. Don't try and say otherwise, because I won't believe you."

Her expression was troubled. "What difference does it make, whether I do or don't? That bracelet—"

He made a sudden gesture, as if banishing that benighted bracelet to oblivion. "Laurel, we agreed that evening, after we lashed out at each other, that we had to put what happened in Greece aside. We did it then for Dan's sake. Now—" he drew a breath "—we must do it for ours."

She looked at him. If there was any expression in her face, it was sadness, he realised.

"How can we? You think me a liar and a thief." There was more than sadness in her voice. There was what he'd seen at the farm park, a kind of weary defeat.

Carefully, he chose his words. "Laurel, I don't know what made you do what you did, but—" he took a breath "—I do realise Olympia's arrival was...difficult...for you."

It had been difficult for him, too—a clash between two realities. The private idyll with Laurel, their hedonistic, carefree cruising from island to island, oblivious to everything else. Then Olympia's unwelcome arrival, puncturing that world.

"The scallops in saffron, I think," she said now, in answer to his enquiry. "With the carpaccio to start."

"I'm going for the lamb quenelles," Xander said. "Terrine to start."

He looked across at her. "What wine would you like with your fish? I'm thinking a red, but a white would be better for scallops."

She shook her head. "I'll have whatever you have. I'm not fussy. And it's bound to be ferociously expensive! I dread to think what this evening is costing you."

She spoke lightly, but it jarred a memory. When he'd first whisked her away on his yacht, though she'd been wide-eyed, she'd never mentioned money or cost, even when they ate ashore. She'd just accepted everything.

Then helped herself to Olympia's bracelet.

He slammed down on his errant thoughts. They were unwelcome. Not here, not now. Banned for this evening. He wanted nothing to spoil it.

"I can afford it, Laurel," was all he said, his voice dry.

"Even so..." she started.

"Even so nothing," he stopped her, closing the subject down. "Laurel, like I said, this is your treat. Dan and I both want you to enjoy it, and that's all there is to it. And I'll be enjoying it too," he reminded her.

Oh, I will indeed, purred the inner feline, pleased with itself. His gaze rested on her again, not wanting to tear his eyes away. Wanting to make the most of what he'd achieved, getting Laurel here—with Dan's essential help—and looking so breathtakingly, heart-stoppingly beautiful.

A waiter came by, presented them with gently fizzing champagne flutes and took their dinner orders. As he glided off, Xander lifted his champagne and tilted it to Laurel. His gaze on her was warm.

sake. She could hear his little voice in her head, exclaiming in wonder and delight, calling her a princess.

He'll ask me about it in the morning, want to know everything about it.

So she had to go along with it tonight, didn't she?

Was that reason enough?

As she walked down the corridor, heels sinking into the soft carpet, burningly aware of her hand on Xander's sleeve, her arm crooked in his, the trace of his aftershave, the closeness of him, she didn't know the answer.

Knew only that her heart was beating faster, way, way faster than it should.

"Made your choice?"

Xander's enquiry was polite. He was being uber polite all round. On his very best behaviour. Treading lightly as a cat and just as pleased with himself, his inner purring almost audible. He was here, dining with Laurel, and her beauty—finally revealed to him again in that show-stopping gown his son had chosen so sapiently—was taking his breath away.

She was going along with what was happening, and he was glad and grateful and appreciative. He said as much.

Her expression flickered as he spoke. "I'm doing it for Dan," she said. "I don't want to disappoint him."

But she seemed to have accepted being here like this, and that was good enough for him, for now at least.

She glanced again at the ornate, gilded menu lying on the damask table in the elegantly appointed dining room, which was filled to capacity, everyone in black tie and evening dress. Laurel surpassed all the women present effortlessly.

She always will, wherever she goes.

His gaze rested on her, drinking her in. Happy just to do that.

Exactly as he was doing now. Shamelessly.

"And why shouldn't you too? Why shouldn't you enjoy dressing up and being wined and dined, and making a night of it? I'm perfectly happy to run to Easter treats for you, as well as for our son. And I won't, I promise you," he said, holding her eyes, something there she hadn't seen before that caught at her, "consider it even a millimetre to hang you with! Because this is for me, as well as you." He took a breath. Eyes resting on her. "So, why don't we just go along with it? We'll have a gourmet dinner, enjoy the cabaret. Where's the harm in that?"

Her eyes met his. They were unreadable. In hers, she knew, was all that she was feeling.

Or wanted to be feeling: anger and outrage at being so shamelessly manipulated and manoeuvred into this.

That's all I should be feeling!

He was releasing her hands, then repossessed one to place it on his sleeve, hooking it through his crooked arm.

"Come on, Laurel," he said placatingly, but with clear intention too. "Let's just relax and enjoy the evening. Why not?"

He started to walk along the corridor, drawing her forward again.

Why not? His nonchalant words echoed in her head. She could have given a hundred reasons.

But she never said them.

Out of nowhere, she felt the fight go out of her. She didn't know why and didn't want to ask. Perhaps, she thought weakly, as Xander started to draw her forward along the corridor, and she went with him docilely, acquiescently, inexplicably, because it made no sense at all to go along with this, to give in to him like this. Maybe it was just for Dan's

feelings about what Xander had done now that Dan was out of earshot.

Xander merely raised his eyebrows. "It's just as Dan said, this is your Easter treat," he answered unconcernedly.

Laurel's eyes flashed again. "Why?" she demanded. "You put Dan up to this!"

"So?" Xander's retort was still supremely unconcerned at her accusation.

"It's despicable! Using him to...to..."

An eyebrow rose again. "To what, Laurel?"

To stitch me up! To manipulate me and...and...

Words failed her. She knew what she meant though, and she seethed with it. Her eyes flashed with fury yet again. Suddenly, her hands were taken, both of them, held in his. She tried to tug them free but couldn't. Xander had stepped up close to her. She caught the trace of his aftershave. He was too close. Far too close. And totally unapologetic.

He looked down into her agitated face, his expression quizzical. "Laurel, what is it that you're objecting to? That Dan and I plotted together? Of course I involved him! He's revelling in it, you saw that! And why shouldn't he? He wants you to have a lovely time, wear a beautiful dress, and have a wonderful time tonight. An Easter treat." He paused minutely, and something changed in his eyes. Something that suddenly made her try and tug her hands free again. "And so do I, Laurel," he said softly.

Far, far too softly.

Then the expression was gone, and the too-soft voice. Replaced by humour. Cajoling humour. Humour she remembered from long, long ago, when he'd wanted to win her round, get his own way.

Like the time he'd kissed her nice again after chucking her in the water on that memorable occasion.

the babysitter, one of the housekeepers, a sensible-seeming middle-aged woman who was now ensconced in the room's armchair with a low light beside her and her knitting, tray of coffee and a magazine. Dan had been kissed goodnight by Laurel with a heartfelt "Thank you, darling one, thank you for my lovely, lovely Easter treat!" to which Xander had added a fond "Sleep well, my treasured son!" in Greek, and was already asleep.

As he shut the door quietly behind him, Xander's eyes went to Laurel. His breath caught again. He wanted to punch the air with triumph.

Yes!

She had surpassed every hope, every expectation. She looked incredible, fantastic, unbelievable. Total vindication filled him, not just for Dan's brilliant choice of gown, which he fully endorsed, but for her entire appearance.

Glorious, that was the word to describe her.

His eyes swept over her, from her lush golden tresses, finally loosened from the restricting confines she'd wretchedly always pinned them back with, now flowing like a waterfall down her back, swept around one bare shoulder, his rapt gaze going all the way down her slender, perfectly proportioned figure, graced by that silken gown in its vivid colour, right down to her feet, arched and elegant in her evening sandals.

He could not take his eyes from her.

He was still gazing at her, triumphant and vindicated and so much more, when she turned to him.

Turned on him.

"What the hell," Laurel ground out, "do you think you're playing at?"

Her eyes flashed furiously. She didn't have to hide her

self up as Dan so gleefully wanted her to do, to style her hair and adorn her face with the conveniently provided make-up, to slip that fabulous silk vermilion evening gown over her head and feel it slither over the wispy bra and panties that had been discreetly included in a separate up-market carrier bag, and then ease her feet into the elegant satin shoes. Nursed it with a set expression on her face as she'd gazed at her own finished reflection, bearing undeniable witness to what Dan had just said.

But I've done it for Dan, for my adored son! So I wouldn't disappoint him.

She dropped down, which was tricky in her strappy heeled evening sandals and flowing skirts, and lifted her hands to his arms. "Thank you, darling," she said, her smile radiant, planting a kiss on his forehead and standing up again. Feeling resolute now, not fuming at what Xander had done so outrageously.

It was Dan she'd done this for, because he'd been so excited, so gleeful, only for him. Yet for all that she knew, with a tightening inside her, that despite that assertion, she could not bring herself to look anywhere near Xander right now.

Emotion churned in her. Heightening her colour. Then Xander was there, standing beside their son, his hand on Dan's shoulder, drawing her eyes to him again. "Beautiful indeed. A princess truly."

His voice was a murmur, and his eyes alight with a look that was as familiar as it was distant in time. With the same effect now as then. Somehow, her heartbeat seemed to have ceased.

Xander opened the door of Laurel's bedroom and ushered her out into the corridor beyond. Dan had been settled with

difficult dinner on board his yacht with Olympia playing gooseberry, but doing her damnedest to make Laurel feel she was the gooseberry.

Overstaying my time—the final-fling floozy who should clear off now.

Conversation had been stilted, and Laurel had known that she was trying too hard, emphasising her newly acquired history degree, deliberately asking erudite questions about Greek history to show she wasn't the bimbo Olympia clearly wanted to think her.

Xander, it had been obvious, was in a bad mood, and had been since Olympia had been dumped on them, but his moodiness had only, Laurel vividly recalled, made him even more darkly attractive. He always looked a knockout whatever he was wearing—or not wearing, because stripped down he was breath-stopping—but in his tux he was at peak Xander.

She blinked now. That Xander was right here, again, in front of her.

Whatever it was about a tuxedo, from the superb tailoring to the set of the sable shoulders to the old-world pizazz of the wing collar to the perfection of the bow-tie and the discrete but oh-so-classy gold studs at his cuffs and on his shirt front, whatever it was, whatever it did, took her breath away.

Dan had stopped gawping at her open-mouthed and thrilled, and had run up to her. "Oh, Mum, you look beautiful," he said, his little face upturned to her with open delight and wonder.

Her heart melted. Oh, she'd been royally stitched up, and Xander had used Dan shamelessly to achieve his ends, but in the instant of hearing Dan say what he had all her spleen vanished. She had nursed it all the way through the lengthy process of showering, washing her hair, then glamming her-

Flying blind—

The buzz of the house phone on the bedside table came to his rescue. He snatched it up.

After he hung up a moment later, he announced, "That's the babysitter on the way up." He nodded at Dan. "We'd better go and see how your mother is doing."

Dan sprang up eagerly and ran to the communicating door, not bothering with a knock, but opening it and running through.

Xander followed more slowly.

His son's innocently spoken words rang in his head.

Are you going to be Mum's boyfriend again?

He'd given the only possible answer.

But as he stepped through the doorway in Laurel's bedroom, and his eyes went to her, he knew, with a searing through his body like a hot brand, that tonight was going to be exactly what he wanted.

Starting right now.

Laurel jerked around at the sound of the communicating door opening. She was standing in front of the full-length mirror inset into the door of the mahogany wardrobe on which the silk vermilion evening gown had been hanging. Which she was now wearing.

Dan was running into the room, then he stopped dead. A gasp broke from him. His face alight. "You're a princess!" he exclaim rapturously. He turned his head back, calling out. "Dad, Dad! Come and see! It worked! Mum's a princess!"

Laurel's eyes went past Dan to the tall figure walking slowly into the room. She felt her breath catch. Memory burned instantly. Overpoweringly.

It had been seven years since she'd seen Xander in a tuxedo. She remembered it vividly. It had been that awkward,

Xander stilled even more. Babes and innocents...more forensic than a cross-examining barrister.

"It was," he said, "a holiday romance."

Because what else was it?

His own question hung there. He'd never had to answer it because of that ruby-and-diamond bracelet.

Condemning Laurel.

And yet now—

He got to his feet. How could he be planning the evening ahead with a woman he thought a thief? How could he just set that aside, ignore it? When it came to Dan, to sharing parenthood with her, he had no choice but to set it aside.

But for what I want now?

He didn't want to answer it. Didn't even want to ask it. Didn't want to think about it. Not now. Not here.

He looked down at Dan, who was still looking up at him with his dark eyes, so like his own.

"I'd better get dressed, Dan," he told him. "The babysitter will be here soon."

He fetched his tuxedo out of the wardrobe. He always travelled with one. The last time he'd worn it in England had been to take Fabia out for the evening. It seemed a million years ago. Another lifetime.

Dan watched with interest as Xander busied himself with his dress tie, always a tricky business. "It takes practice," he told his son.

Dan nodded wisely. Then a question was in his face. But it had nothing to do with dress ties. "So, are you going to be Mum's boyfriend again?"

Xander stilled again. Heard the continuing cross-examination of a barrister putting him to the question again.

"I don't know," he said slowly.

Tonight is as far as I can think.

bed, while Xander sorted out a children's TV channel for him, then left him to it, together with a bottle of fruit juice from the room bar to get his own ablutions done. Knowing how long it took women to glitz themselves up he took a leisurely shower and shave, then emerged from the en suite in the courtesy towelling robe to share in the ending of the adventure film with Dan.

"Can we go and see Mum yet?" Dan asked hopefully, as the film ended.

Xander cast his son a worldly-wise look. "Ladies don't like being hustled, Dan, when they're getting themselves ready. Boyfriends are strictly banned till they've done their hair and face. It takes them forever," he added, from long experience.

Dan nodded in an equally worldly-wise fashion. Then he looked at Xander quizzically.

"Are you Mum's boyfriend?" he asked. "Because you're my dad?"

Xander froze. Talk about out of the mouths of babes and innocents...

He picked his words carefully now.

"I was when your mum and I were in Greece," he said, keeping his voice nonchalant. The word *boyfriend* didn't really cover what had been the state of things in Greece, but he knew it was the only one that would make any kind of sense to Dan at his age.

Dan was still looking at him. Expecting more. Xander went on, even more carefully.

"Then she came back here, to England."

Dan's eyes, dark like his own, stayed on him.

"Were you in *lurve*?" He said "lurve" exaggeratedly, as if he'd heard it in a film, which he probably had.

heels, in matching vermilion, then dropped them back on the bed.

"You've got to have a shower now, Mum," he instructed, "and wash your hair. Dad's got you some make-up too, because he said that since tonight is a surprise you wouldn't have your own with you. I'm going to have my bath in Dad's bathroom, and he's bought me new jim-jams, and then he'll get ready for your posh dinner too, and I can watch TV in his room while he does, and then the babysitter will be here, and I'll come back in here and go to bed, and you and Dad go off to your posh dinner! It's all sorted, Mum! Me and Dad sorted it!"

He ran across to Xander. "Go on, Mum!" he instructed her, turning back. "You have your shower, and I'll have my bath! See you!"

He grabbed his father's hand and started tugging him back through the communicating door.

Laurel stood motionless.

Xander looked at her. "See you," he echoed softly. Far too softly. Mockery open in his voice. Knowing exactly just how royally she'd been stitched up. By a master tactician.

Laurel walked over to the dress. Emotion rose in her, but just what it was, she had no idea. Except that it was filling her totally...

Xander's mood was buoyant. Almost as buoyant as Dan's. Finally, he was getting his own way with Laurel. Getting her out of those damn rags she insisted on wearing. And to ensure the success of his cunning plan, he'd got the absolutely essential help of his son. Dan was as cock-a-hoop as he himself was. He had his bath—lavishly filled with bubbles from the complimentary toiletries provided—in record time, and was in his pyjamas and snuggled up on Xander's

CHAPTER EIGHT

"Do you like it?"

Laurel's head whipped round. Xander was standing in an open doorway at the side of the room. A linking door. He strolled in, nodding to what had caught her eye the moment she and Dan had walked in.

It was a dress hanging on the outside of the wardrobe. An evening dress. A beautiful vermilion silk evening dress.

Dan went running up to it. "Do you like it, Mum? Do you?" There was eagerness in his voice and glee. "I chose it! Dad showed me the pictures on his tablet and asked me which one you would like, and I said this one because it's red, so he bought it!"

Dismay was coursing through Laurel. Dismay and a whole lot more.

"It's your surprise Easter present!" Dan was still exclaiming gleefully, his face alight. "Dad and me planned it all! You're going to wear it tonight, and you're going to look like a princess in a fairy story! You can be Cinderella," he went on happily, "but not with glass slippers because we got you red ones to go with your dress."

Dan scooped up a cardboard shoebox on the floor by the wardrobe, and Laurel, still in shock, saw the very expensive fashion name on it. He put it on the bed and opened it.

"See?" he said. He held up a pair of elegant evening

of the hotel's baby sitters for Dan while we're at dinner." His voice changed. "Now, your mum said you could have an ice cream before we go in," he said to Dan. "What flavour would you like?"

"Chocolate, please!" enthused Dan.

Laurel watched the two of them head off to the ice cream van parked near the barbecue station. Inside she was fuming. What the hell was Xander playing at? Springing this on her?

Plotting with Dan! Making him a party to it! Just so he can—

She stopped dead in her tracks.

Can what?

She didn't know. Knew only that she'd been stitched up. But for what purpose?

It was only when she and Dan, ice cream consumed, went into the room that Xander had, without even the courtesy to consult her, reserved for them, that she realised the full extent of Xander's unholy scheming...

She expected to hear a groan from Dan, but instead he giggled, and cast a conspiratorial look at Xander.

"We're not going home," Dan told her. "We're staying here. At the hotel. All night!"

Laurel looked at him and then at Xander. "You and Dan?" she asked, puzzled, and not happy at having this sprung on her without running it past her. And how was she going to get home? A taxi she supposed.

"All of us, Mum!" Dan said gleefully.

She frowned, confused.

"It's your Easter treat, Mum!" Dan told her. "Dad's fixed it!"

"Yes," Xander corroborated. "This afternoon was Dan's Easter treat, tonight is yours."

Laurel stared. What on earth?

Dan was obviously bursting to tell her. "It's like a party for you, Mum! A posh dinner for you here, you and Dad, and then there's a show!"

"What?"

"Well, it's a cabaret," Xander said smoothly. Too smoothly.

Laurel eyed him. "Is it?" she said. Her voice was dry. Very dry.

"Yes," Xander said. Still too smoothly. "Over dinner. It's all booked."

Dan's face was alight with glee. "It's been our secret, Dad's and mine! He told me and told me not to tell you! It's your treat! We're all staying here, all night, and tomorrow morning after breakfast I can go swimming again with Dad and then have my Easter egg!"

"Well, you seem to have got it all sorted, haven't you?" Laurel's voice was tight.

"I think so," Xander said blandly. "I've taken an extra room," he went on, his voice blander still, "and booked one

Suddenly, his eyes gleamed. The jamboree he'd booked Dan in for was not the only Easter event the hotel had on offer. There was another one in the evening. A grand black-tie dinner and cabaret with dancing. His gleam intensified. Yes, that was it. It would work, perfectly. The ideal opportunity. She'd already be here at the hotel, doubtless looking like her usual dog's breakfast, making no effort at all as usual.

The gleam in his eye intensified, seeing the perfect solution to that problem.

But there's someone she will make an effort for—the only person.

Someone who would, he knew, be a gleeful co-conspirator with him. Yes, that was perfect too. Setting aside his beer he picked up the house phone, rang down to Reception. Bought two tickets.

Then he sat back, reaching for his beer again, relaxing back against the propped up pillows. This bed really was very comfortable. With easily room for two...

The satisfied gleam came again. And now he knew exactly how to get Laurel here to share the bed with him.

The Easter Jamboree had lived up to its name. Dan had enjoyed it hugely. From the Easter egg hunt, the egg painting, the races, the magician, the puppet theatre, the pony rides, the miniature carousel, the lucky dip, the tombola and the coconut shy, he'd enjoyed the lot. Now, Laurel knew he was completely enjoyed out. The jamboree had ended with a barbecue, and Dan, replete with a hamburger and two grilled hot dogs, was finishing off a length of corn on the cob. The light was fading, and though the day had stayed blessedly dry, it was starting to get chilly now that the sun had set.

"Time to make a move," Laurel suggested. "You can have an ice cream for pud, and then we'd better head off home."

I know what I want. Whether I should want it or not, I don't care. I didn't care seven years ago, nor do I care now. It took only a single glance at Laurel back then to make me want her. Desire her. It's taken longer now, but it's still there.

Desire—naked and potent. Making him want to reach for her, take her slender, beautiful body into his arms, fold it against his own aroused body, draw her down with him, sink into her, feel the hot flames lick them both, mounting, kiss by kiss, caress by caress, thrust by thrust, into an inferno.

Memory, arousing and enticing, washed through him. Making him want to make it far more than mere memory.

What we had then, we can have again—for the both of us.

Somehow, he had to convince her to accept what was happening again between them, to deny it no longer, dismiss it no longer. Fight it no longer. To accept that between them was more than the past, more than the son they shared, more even—and he gave it an impatient dismissal—than that damn bracelet.

After all, they'd set it aside for Dan's sake, hadn't they?

Now we can set it aside for ours. So it's no longer a barrier between us. Between what we both want.

All he had to do—restlessness filled him now, seeing his goal in sight—was get her to see it his way, to yield to what he knew she was denying.

I just have to convince her to stop fighting it, stop resisting me.

Memory sifted in him. How he'd told Dan how mad Laurel had been for chucking her into the sea, and he'd had to swim after her, kiss her nice again. He'd had to go on being nice to her all evening, wooing her back to him.

So, what can I do this this time around? To woo her back to me.

herself she was relieved Xander was going to be going back to Athens after Easter. But was she?

Yes, it would mean she could lower her constant guard against him, her continual awareness of his oh-so-disturbing effect on her, which had no place, none, in her life. But for all that, there was something else too. Something she ought to deny just as strongly.

Her eyes went to the sofa where he'd sat that dreadful evening when their vicious, toxic vitriol at each other had so devastated Dan, where they'd patched up some kind of peace, some kind of truce between them. Since then she'd got used to Xander sitting there, an arm around Dan's shoulders, watching TV together before Dan's bath-time.

He wasn't there now, and after Easter he wasn't going to be there until he was back again from Athens after his own Easter.

The strange thought came again. Illogical, incomprehensible, given all the discord between them, but there all the same.

I'm going to miss him.

Xander threw himself down on his bed at his hotel after pouring a beer from the fridge, his mind still filled with the certainty that had struck him earlier. Silencing everything else. He was flying blind, he knew, ignoring everything the instruments should be telling him.

Just like I did first time around.

I knew Olympia was waiting for me to propose, that everyone was expecting it, but I swept off with Laurel all the same. Blanking everything else—

Now it was happening again, that same overpowering impulse, and for the same reason. Yes, it was complicated, it was conflicted, but his sense of certainty overrode it.

opposite. Let it run. A sense of new certainty was filling him, born, he knew, out of his new understanding about just why she was being so obstinate about sticking to her dowdy, dreary appearance. After all the hostility, all the eggshelling, all the determinedly careful politeness to each other, something else was happening between them. Growing inexorably.

And he welcomed it completely.

Having showered after his pool session, and eaten his fill at the lavish late-afternoon tea, Dan needed no bath that evening, or supper other than a milky drink and fruit while he watched some TV before Laurel got him up to bed. Xander hadn't stayed, and she was relieved. This endless disturbing awareness of him was getting worse. Thank goodness there was only Easter to get through, then she'd have a reprieve from it.

The jamboree sounded good, she had to admit, and Dan was definitely keen, murmuring his anticipation as he fell asleep. Laurel kissed his cheek and headed downstairs. She made herself a cup of tea and went into the sitting room, settled herself down on a sofa. Since her father's death she had become very used to spending the evenings alone, Dan asleep upstairs. She'd used the time to do her online tutoring when it was term time. But with the school holidays and Xander's tumultuous eruption into her life, she had let it drop for the time being.

So there wasn't anything really for her to do right now, other than read or watch TV. She sat sipping her tea. The house was very quiet.

Out of nowhere, a thought struck her. Such a strange one. Contrary to everything she habitually thought. She'd told

And as for himself—

More truth slammed into him.

I am just the same. Just as susceptible.

Except for one crucial difference.

I acknowledge it. She denies it.

He resumed walking towards them, the words echoing in his head. He'd pay attention to them later. Decide what to do about them. Right now, though, he had something to tell Dan.

"The hotel," he announced, "is having a Grand Jamboree on Easter Saturday, and I've booked us in." He looked down at Dan. "There'll be an Easter egg hunt, organised games, pony rides, a carousel, a puppet theatre, a magician, sideshows, barbecue, the lot!"

"Wow!" said Dan, eyes widening.

"Wow, indeed," agreed Xander. He glanced at Laurel, hoping she would think so too.

She did. "It sounds great fun," she said. "Thank you." Her eyes went briefly to Xander. Very briefly. Self-consciously.

But now he knew why.

And as he guided them out to his car to drive them home, he knew something else. Something that was making itself felt that he couldn't—wouldn't—shoot down.

He wasn't going to fight it any longer. This constant awareness of her, the repeated kicks he got when his eyes went to her, however little she deliberately—as he now realised—made of herself.

Because there was no point fighting it.

It's there, it exists—as powerfully as it did from the very first.

And it wouldn't be repressed or ignored or denied. Or defeated.

So he was going to stop trying. Do, instead, the very

He frowned inwardly. Laurel had looked her worst yet as she sat poolside. She'd thrown at him that she wouldn't let him buy her better clothes because she'd said he'd only hold it against her. But even in cheap clothes she could have looked better, could have bothered to do her hair, put on some make-up. In Greece she'd always dressed with style and flair, even on her student budget, always looked her best with face and hair.

But now she makes no effort. None!

Why?

He stopped dead, realisation suddenly dawning. The truth hitting him.

Because she does not want to look good for me. She actively wants to look her worst!

Was that just because of her hostility towards him, or…?

Another truth hit him square on.

Or because I did not hide that I could not tear my eyes from her in that swimsuit she looked so fantastic in?

And if that were so…

Inexorable logic bore him forward.

There could be only two reasons she didn't want him making clear to her how her beauty wowed him still, didn't want his attention on her in that way.

Either I repulse her in that way now, or it's the very opposite.

His gaze rested on her now forensically. Everything falling into place like a perfect explanation, an irrefutable Aristotelian syllogism of the kind he'd learnt in school.

She is susceptible to me still. And she knows it. But is trying to hide it.

That was it, he was sure of it. Laurel was deliberately playing down her looks because she knew she was still drawn to him, the way she'd been in Greece from the very first.

shapeless. Deliberately, she reknotted her hair, exposing her neck to keep it cooler, knowing tufts of hair were sticking out in an unlovely fashion. She *wanted* to look unlovely.

It must have worked, because Xander's glance, as she settled down on a lounger, rolling up her trouser legs in a similarly unlovely fashion, was the opposite of the way he'd looked her over in her turquoise one-piece. His dark brows were drawn together as he frowned.

Her lips compressed, glad he didn't like what he was seeing.

As for him buying her new clothes—

Yeah, as if I'd give him any more rope! she echoed to herself grimly. She'd been right to spell it out for Xander as she had. "Mum! I'm going to swim a width! Watch, Mum, watch!"

Laurel's expression softened, relieved to have her thoughts, which she should not have, diverted.

"Go for it!" she called out. "And back again!"

Beside Dan, Xander stood waist-deep in the water, his perfect, smooth, leanly muscled torso on full view, ready to catch Dan if he floundered, which he didn't. But Laurel only had eyes for her son.

It was all that was safe for her to look at.

And she hated that it was.

I have to defeat this. I have to! Because if I don't—

No, she would not answer that. Must not.

Doggedly, her gaze stayed only on Dan.

Xander sauntered back from the reception desk in the hotel's foyer, once the grand hall of the country house when it had been a private residence. Dan and Laurel were waiting for him near the front door, ready to leave after another superb afternoon tea following their swim.

holding out a pair of dark blue swim-shorts with pale blue dolphins on it. With a start, Xander came back to the present.

"Great," he enthused. "Shall we find a couple of T-shirts to go with them, for the summer?"

He started going down the racks, Dan joining in enthusiastically. Laurel was standing a little way away now, an abstracted expression on her face. As if she, too, were far away in the past.

The past that brought us together, then ripped us apart.

His own expression flickered. But they were back together again now, sharing in Dan.

Is that all we have to share?

Or could there be more?

And do I want there to be?

The question hung motionless in the space between them.

Now the proud owner of new swim-shorts, Dan was keen to get them wet. So they headed back to Xander's hotel for another pool session. Much against her will, Laurel had succumbed to Dan's pleas to watch him swim this time and so had come poolside.

"I can only watch, Dan," she told him. "I haven't got my cossie with me." She fully intended never to have her swimming costume with her. She wanted no repeat of that first time, when Xander's eyes had so fatally gone to her figure. For the same reason she tried now not to let her eyes go to Xander. But it was hard. Far harder than she wanted. Anger at her own self lashed at her. She didn't want to be like this, didn't want it at all. She was fighting it as hard as she could.

And the last thing she wanted was to encourage it in Xander. As she stripped off her jumper in the heat of the pool area, she was glad that the T-shirt underneath was one of her worst. The neckline had gone, and it had been washed

frustration uppermost, that she was being so obdurate. Damn it, he wasn't trying to give her any more rope to hang her with.

I just want her to have some new clothes, show off her beauty. The way I remember it.

The way he wanted to see her again.

Is that such a crime?

No, it was not. Not in his book.

He frowned, thinking about what she'd said, that she'd enjoyed the lifestyle she'd had with him in Greece that summer. Yes, she had, but now that he thought about it, she hadn't expected him to buy things for her when they went out and about. She'd bought some extra outfits for herself—a particularly fetching ankle-length dress in fine white cotton splashed with embroidered blue flowers, he recalled, remembering how good she'd looked in it—and how he'd enjoyed slipping it from her when they retired that night—but only from tourist shops, and always paying herself. He'd bought her a silk shawl once, in an up-market boutique on a marina, and then she'd promptly bought him a baseball cap with the name of the island on it, which he'd solemnly worn all day just to please her, because she'd said she couldn't run to spending as much as the shawl had cost him, not that he'd wanted her to spend her money on him, the reverse if anything, because he'd have been happy to buy her things...

Including jewellery if she'd asked for it. But she never had.

So, why steal that bracelet? Was it more to get back at Olympia for looking down at her? Or was she jealous because it was a gift from me? Or both?

Did it make it less worse, her crime? Or not...?

"Dad, do you like these? Mum says she does." Dan was

happened, Laurel? Being with me opened your eyes to luxury, so when Olympia turned up, and you knew your time was up, you decided to take a piece of it home with you. A ruby-and-diamond piece."

The queue had moved on, and it was his turn to pay. As he put his credit card away, took the carrier bag, he turned to look at Laurel. Her face was half averted, and she seemed to be blinking, gaze unfocussed.

His gaze moved down slightly, and he frowned. She was wearing, as she always did, the same old cheap clothes she clung to. It annoyed him, annoyed the hell out of him. It was such a waste of her beauty.

"Look," he said now, decisiveness in his voice, "while we're here, I really want to get you some decent clothes!"

She looked round. "No." It was all she said. It annoyed him even more. Her mouth compressed. "Your money is for your son, not for me. How many more times do I have to say it?"

Xander felt his annoyance rise. "It's ridiculous!" he snapped.

Something flashed in her eyes. "Not to me," she bit back. "Yes, I admit that I enjoyed the lifestyle I had when I was with you. It was so very easy to enjoy! And because I did I got called a thief—then and now. So, no, I am not going to let you buy me clothes! I am not, Xander, giving you any more rope to hang me with! Not a single damn centimetre!"

She walked off, heading for the children's wear section. She'd walked away from him like that at Piraeus, never looking back, head held high. Past and present seemed to meld, two images merging in his memory—and in his present vision.

Collecting Dan, handing him the carrier bag with his toys, Xander walked after her. His emotions were mixed,

CHAPTER SEVEN

"Dan definitely needs a larger pair of swim-shorts," Xander declared, brooking no argument. He was driving them over to the retail park by the motorway. "And he can have some new summer togs while we're at it." He turned towards Dan in the back in his booster seat. "We'll check out adding another couple of cars for your garage too."

"He's already got four," Laurel said tightly.

Her interjection irritated him. "You can't have too many cars," he said. "Can you, Dan?"

"No," Dan agreed.

Laurel gave no more objection and Xander was glad. All the same, as they queued to pay for the extra cars Dan had chosen, he murmured sibilantly, "I am *not* spoiling him, so stop looking like you're chewing a lemon!" He glanced towards Dan, but he was examining a tabletop display of Easter bunnies, just out of earshot. "Do you begrudge me giving him things?" he asked. He could hear the slightest edge in his voice but didn't care.

She shook her head quickly. "Of course not! But I fear—" he saw her hesitate "—I fear that he will start taking the lifestyle you can afford for granted. It's—" she hesitated again "—very easy to do." She paused. "I should know."

His eyes held hers. He heard himself speak, put the question to her that her comment had invited. "So, is that what

And it was the last thing she wanted to do either. Or its corollary. Having his eyes wash over her.

A sense of danger plucked at her, disquieting and disturbing.

I should be getting immune to him, spending time with him like this. He shouldn't be able to affect me.

She had to try harder, because otherwise—

But there was no otherwise. There couldn't be. It was impossible that there should be.

And I must never, never allow it! However hard that would be. However strong his impact on me still. I have to deny it and defy it.

Seven long bitter, hate-filled years separated them. And nothing had changed about the reason for it. His marriage might be over, but what difference did that make? To Xander she was still a liar and a thief.

Dividing them forever.

other, she could never relax when Xander was around. She was continually wary—aware of him—and it was getting worse.

That constant flickering of her own reaction to him, which ought to be dying away—surely it should?—wasn't diminishing in the slightest. Nor did it seem to be doing so in Xander either. She could sense his eyes going to her, resting on her, disturbing her. Making her want to meet his eyes, respond to him…

Doggedly, she made to focus on their time with Dan. Giving him a good time and time with Xander. Whether that was Xander getting stuck in to Dan's enthusiasms, from his construction toys and, most lately, a train set addition, to taking Dan off to the playground by the green, feeding the extremely well-fed ducks on the pond, playing football in the garden, rambling in the woods behind. Or Xander piling them all into his SUV and venturing further afield to yet more sources of entertainment for a six-year-old, from some exciting caves hollowed out of the chalk hills to a fiendish maze at a grand stately home, which also had a miniature railway to entrance Dan.

They went swimming again, too, at Xander's hotel, though this time Laurel declined to join them.

"You two have fun," she said. "I'll just have a coffee at the café."

Her announcement drew a look from Xander. "Shame," he murmured. His eyes rested on her a moment, and she looked away quickly.

Protest rose in her. He must realise perfectly well why she was avoiding the pool, avoiding stripping down to a swimsuit, avoiding seeing him stripped down too.

For God's sake, the last thing he would want is me drooling over him!

through him when Dan raced up to him as he'd arrived and that bear hug he'd swept him up in had been the best feeling.

Yet a kick of a different kind had gone through him when he'd set eyes on Laurel. A kick whose cause he could not deny.

His mouth twisted self-mockingly. He'd told her that they had to set aside the enmity between them, but he should set more aside as well—that reaction he got every time he looked at her. Seven years separated them—his failed marriage and a stolen bracelet. All that drew them together was Dan. Nothing else.

He gazed unseeingly over the darkened gardens.

Except that that's not true—

There was more than Dan drawing them together. There was what had drawn them to each other from the very first. It had been extinguished, forcibly, in the moment he'd seen the glitter of rubies and diamonds in her suitcase. It had been even more forcibly extinguished in the years of his marriage.

But now it was making itself felt again.

Refusing to stay extinguished.

Abruptly, he turned away from the window, pulling the curtains across again. Seven years ago it had taken only a single glance at her sitting at that café reading her history book for him to desire her.

And it was happening again, just as swiftly and every bit as powerfully.

Carrying him along with it.

Laurel was counting the days towards Easter. Because when it had been and gone, Xander would be as well. Taking himself off to Greece for the Orthodox Easter celebrations. Dan would miss him, but she wouldn't. She'd be relieved. Even with their new agenda of civility and politeness to each

Laurel felt her heart squeeze.

The week she'd just spent with Dan but without Xander had, she knew—and it troubled her to know it—shown her even more just how very easy it would to be to accept this new life that Xander—courtesy of the Xenakis family's wealth—could provide for Dan. They could live in this lovely house in this affluent area with no more money worries. Dan could go to that nearby school with all its facilities, its excellent rating. She'd looked it up online and could not but be impressed by its vaunted ethos of character-building and team-playing. Dan could have a very good life here. She could feel herself weakening to accept what Xander wanted her to accept.

Can I really deprive Dan of this?

He had settled in so well, and they'd driven around, exploring the area, and all the while she'd wondered whether to tell Dan they could live here always, if he wanted. But he would say yes, wouldn't he? And then...

Then there'll be no going back.

The words were troubling. They troubled her again now as her eyes went to Xander, who was chatting away with Dan. She felt that little jump in her heart rate again, the one she must not allow to happen. Just because Xander had walked back into her life again—

There was no going back from that either.

And somehow, whatever way she could, she was going to have to accept that. Deal with it. Somehow.

Xander stared moodily out over the moonlit gardens from his bedroom window at his hotel. The night air was cooler here in England, but fresh with the fragrance of spring. He was glad to be back. More than glad.

A kick such as he'd never known in his life had gone

the cooked pasta, then set it to crisp under the grill while she fixed a green salad to go with it. She'd ventured out, cautiously, several times during the week with Dan in the car—a smart, brand new automatic hatchback Xander had ordered for her—and restocked on groceries.

Xander asked how it had gone as they all sat down to mac and cheese.

"I've had to get used to driving again," she admitted.

"She's getting better at it, Dad," Dan said reassuringly, man to man.

Xander's mouth tugged in a half smile. "Let's put her through her paces tomorrow, shall we? See if she crashes us!"

Dan chortled, and Laurel said with humorous tartness, "No, thank you!"

For a second, her eyes met Xander's, then she pulled them away. "So, what are your plans now you're back?" she asked instead, civilly and politely.

"It's Easter here the weekend after this," Xander replied. He looked at Dan. "In Greece, Easter is celebrated later, and I'll be going back for it, so we'll make sure we celebrate your Easter here first."

Dan's eyes brightened. "Easter eggs!" he announced happily.

"Yes, indeed," Xander said dryly, and yet again, his eyes met Laurel's for a moment.

"Mum gives me a small one before Easter, but then after it's over we go and buy one of the leftover ones because they're cheaper then, so we can have a bigger one," Dan explained artlessly.

Laurel saw Xander's face tighten. "Well, now you can have a big one before Easter," he said. "From me."

Dan's face lit up. "Can I really, Dad?" he asked disbelievingly.

* * *

Laurel forced herself to look at Dan, but it was too late. One glance at Xander had done it, one single glance. All day, with him expected back from Greece, she had been schooling herself. She must not react to him; she must only be composed, neutral, keeping to their carefully agreed cessation of hostilities.

But as her eyes went to him as he strolled towards the open front door, his arm around Dan's shoulders, she felt her resolve vanish. For seven days she hadn't seen Xander. Now he was here again. Right in front of her.

Lean, and lithe, and lethal.

She fought for composure, silencing the reaction to seeing him again. The stupid, pointless, totally unwelcome and unwanted reaction to him. How could it be otherwise? Given everything that had parted them.

Yet for all her arguments, all her intentions, she could feel her pulse quicken as she stood aside in the narrow hallway. He greeted her civilly, and she returned in kind, then Dan was tugging at him to come upstairs.

"I've built more of my garage!" Dan was exclaiming now. "Come and see!"

Laurel watched them head upstairs, then went back into the kitchen. Dan had asked for mac and cheese again for tea, so she set about making the cheese sauce, getting the pasta cooking. Telling herself what she needed to do, to be.

I need to be calm, composed. Civil and polite, nothing else. No ridiculous gazing at him, letting my heart rate jump. Because there's nothing left between us, and even if there were, there shouldn't be. Mustn't be.

Brave words, but keeping to them was going to be a challenge.

She gave a sigh, grated cheese into the sauce, mixed in

* * *

Xander pressed the accelerator, moving into the fast lane of the motorway. It felt odd to be driving on the wrong side of the road again, but it felt good—more than good—to be back in the UK. He'd ripped through his business affairs. As his father got older, he himself was now taking on more and more of the running, and he'd been relieved that his father had been away, visiting friends in Thessaloniki and wouldn't return till the Orthodox Easter. Xander did not want any awkward questions asked about what was drawing him to the UK yet again. At some point he would have to tell his father why, but not yet.

And just what he would tell him and how, he had no idea.

He wants a replacement for Olympia for me, not—

Not what, precisely? The complicated, tortuous existence of Laurel and Dan?

He shied his mind away. Right now he had only one focus: seeing his son again. Within the hour he was parked at the cottage, vaulting out of the car. He'd scarcely shut the driver's door before Dan came hurtling out of the house.

"Dad! Dad!" he called, face alight.

He ran up to Xander, and Xander caught him up. Bear-hugged him, emotion pouring through him. It was a good feeling. A very good feeling.

He set Dan back, keeping an arm around his shoulder as they walked up to the front door. Laurel was standing there. She was wearing jeans and a baggy sweater, her hair knotted, and she wore not a scrap of make-up. Her usual nothing look.

But something kicked through Xander. Something that shouldn't be there. Something he had killed off seven years ago.

But which now, as his eyes went to her, was there again. However much he might wish to God it wasn't.

swept them both away. Desire that had crashed and burned to bitter ashes...

And even without that wretched bracelet business, there would have been nothing left but the cold embers of a dead affair. He'd still have finished with her and married Olympia.

I was just a bit of summer fun. I knew it then, and it was just as well I did. Nothing could have come of it. So, what did it matter if it ended as viciously as it did?

Except for the long black shadow it cast for seven years. Was still casting.

Because he'll never believe my innocence. Never. He's made that clear now, just as he did back then. Guilty forever.

She felt that sense of depression, defeat, creep back in. But what was the use of it? None. All they could do was keep going as they were now, trying, as they had agreed, to put the past aside at least. Not let it flare and bite, and so harm and damage their son.

She seized up a pair of oven gloves, opened the eye-level door and extracted the tray with the salmon on it.

"Watch out! Hot! Coming through!" She set it down on the large mat in the centre of the table. She went to fetch the second tray of baked potatoes, then drained the beans and put them on the table too.

Xander and Dan were sitting there expectantly. Looking so alike...

Emotion rose in her. Father and son.

How much she loved the one and not the other.

And it's the same for Xander when he sees Dan and me.

And that could never change. The sense of depression and defeat crept over her again...

There was nothing to be done but accept it.

Judging by the noise—of splashing and laughter and the occasional yell from Xander, Laurel guessed that bath-time that evening was more about fun than washing, though when they both reappeared, Dan looked scrubbed in his pyjamas, and Xander's polo shirt was noticeably damp in patches.

Tea was ready for them. Baked potatoes and salmon and tomatoes with green beans. It was a treat to have salmon. On her own budget it was a rare occurrence. As she'd cooked it, her thoughts had been difficult. How easy, how very, very easy, it would be to get used to this kind of affluence, this up-market cottage, all superbly equipped and beautifully furnished.

How very, very easy, too, to get used to Xander being civil, behaving with politeness and consideration as he was doing now. After that exchange at the farm park, which had threatened to turn so ugly again, he had, she could see, made a visible effort to be nicer towards her. As if—she frowned—he was conscious of having upset her by what he'd said. And cared that he had.

That surely, though, was just an illusion. His solicitude, continuing now, was only for Dan's sake, never hers. The woman he would never think of as anything but a thief.

But whatever the reason, it was pleasanter to experience than his more familiar harshness. He was helping with tea, extracting cutlery from drawers, handing it to Dan to set their places, rustling up some place mats out of another drawer, getting drinking glasses out the cupboard.

As if he lived here, as if this were just part of everyday family life, a family supper together.

But they weren't a family. They were two people divided irreconcilably who just happened to share an innocent child between them. Two people who'd met on holiday, between whom desire had once flared with an intensity that had

more. Why should I? Nothing will make you think differently."

She walked off, going up to Dan, lightly resting her hands on his shoulders as they gazed at the tiny yellow fluffballs milling around, avidly pecking at the feed scattered into their pen.

Xander looked after her. The angry, bitter emotions had ebbed, but something else had taken their place. But he didn't know what. Only that he didn't want to feel that bitter anger.

Not any longer.

Laurel stepped up into the SUV and settled herself beside Dan on the back seat as Xander gunned the engine. The rest of the visit to the farm park had gone okay. She and Xander had kept scrupulously to completely innocuous subjects. But she still felt that sense of depression, of defeat, press her down. But why should it? Why should she care what Xander thought of her? It was hardly new. He'd thought it for seven years, and she'd known he did for seven years.

"Did you enjoy today, Dan?" Xander was asking, probably unnecessarily, as Dan had been regaling them both about the pleasures he'd experienced.

"The tractor ride was the best," he said enthusiastically. "And the lambs. And the hay-barn was good too!"

"You're bringing some of it home," Laurel said, putting aside dark thoughts. She was tired, so tired, of feeling them. She picked off a strand of straw attached to Dan's jacket. "An early bath, I think. You can have supper in your jim-jams. Dad can give you your bath tonight. A special treat for him."

"Great!" said Dan.

"Definitely great," echoed Xander.

stay her. She whipped it free instantly. He felt annoyance at her immediate repudiation. But let it pass.

"Laurel, we mustn't let this happen. Flaring up again as we just did. It's got to stop."

She looked at him, mouth tight. "How can it? When you think what you think of me?" Something moved in her eyes. "Xander, why, *why* do you refuse even the possibility that it was Olympia framing me? Why believe her, not me."

He drew a breath. "I'd known her for years, Laurel. Her parents were—are—friends of mine. She would never have stooped to such a thing."

He saw her eyes harden. "But I would, is that it? You knew that about me, did you?"

"I didn't *not* know it about you. We'd been together three weeks, that's all."

Even as he spoke, though, he felt protest rise. Yes, he'd only known Laurel a handful of weeks, but nothing about her in that time had given him to suppose she might stoop to taking Olympia's valuable bracelet. He had made to search Laurel's suitcase only because he'd felt that to exclude her from scrutiny would be unfair to the crew, whose quarters had been searched by his steward. When he'd seen the glitter of the bracelet in the folds of Laurel's clothes, it had been like a savage punch to the solar plexus.

I never expected it, never.

Shock—so much more than shock—had cut through him. Black rage had followed after, which he had loosed on her, hard, icy and condemning. Refusing to believe her protestations of innocence. As he still did…

Before his eyes, he saw her expression change. There was something new in it, something he hadn't seen before.

Defeat.

"Have it your way," she said tiredly. "I don't care any

that I was de trop. That she was your intended bride and I was just your last bit of bachelor fun and games, and now my time was up. Helped on the way by her planting her bracelet on me, then running to you that it was missing. And—bingo!—the next thing, I was being personally chucked off your yacht, and cursed by you to kingdom come! And you still are cursing me—" She broke off.

Two flags of colour were flaring across her cheeks, but there was more than familiar anger in her face. She was biting her lip, turning aside. Xander stared after her, emotions scything. Hell and damnation, could they really not get through a conversation without everything kicking off again?

Belatedly—and gratefully—he realised that the group around the lambs was on the move. Dan was coming up to them.

"Those lambs are just mega, mega cute!" he exclaimed. "When they're drinking the milk, their tails go round and round!"

"They do, don't they?" Laurel smiled down at him. The flags of colour in her cheeks were fading, her expression easing.

"We're seeing the baby chicks next," said Dan. "Come on!" He caught her hand, pulling her after the knot of children and other parents following the farm staff towards a barn entrance. Xander followed as well. He was calming down, but emotion was still slicing through him. He'd said they must set all the ugliness between them aside, yet here it was again.

As they went into the barn and up to the pen where the baby chickens were, irradiated with warm red light, and Dan loosed Laurel's hand to go up and look with the other children, Xander's hand caught at hers instead, simply to

"I don't know," she said. "That house has been my home all my life."

"But it doesn't have to be Dan's!" Xander said acerbically. Then, to soften the point, he added, "But there's no need to lose it. Keep it if you want. Why not?" It wouldn't bother him if she did. It was Dan he was concerned about, not her.

"Yes, I would want to do that. I couldn't risk—" She broke off.

"Risk what, Laurel?" There was an edge in his voice, he could hear it.

She looked at him straightly. "Risk being entirely in your power."

His eyes narrowed. "That's a loaded comment."

Her expression tightened. "I've been on the receiving end of your anger. I still would be if you didn't want to not upset Dan! So, no, I never want to be in your power, Xander. You hung me out to dry seven years ago."

"With good reason!" Xander shot back.

Her eyes flashed, he could see it. "With no good reason! You made it clear to me, Xander, that none of the crew could be to blame, because they were all security vetted and totally loyal to the Xenakis family, and anyway, why would they put a bracelet they'd stolen into my suitcase? And you made it crystal clear that the saintly Olympia couldn't possibly have been trying to frame me."

"What reason would she have had to do that?" Xander demanded.

Where the hell had this come from? One moment he was telling her he had to put in time in Athens, and the next they were rehashing the tired old tale of her innocence in the face of irrefutable evidence to the contrary.

"To get rid of me, of course!" She was keeping her voice low, and drawing away from him. "She made it clear to me

"Yes, I'm sure he would, but..."

"But?"

"If he sees round the school, and likes it, then, well, I'm committed. Committed to his going there, committed to living here."

He looked at her. "Would that be such an ordeal?" he asked. He strove not to make his question sound sarcastic.

She looked at him. "It's a big thing, uprooting my life—Dan's life. There'd be no going back." She took a breath. "Xander, we agreed we needed time—both of us."

"The trouble is, when it comes to school, time is finite. The summer term will start soon after Easter." He tried not to sound short.

"I know," she said heavily. "And I know the school is holding a place for him. But, look, one possibility is that we compromise. If you really are willing to pay the extortionate rental on the cottage here—"

"For my son, of course I am!" Xander said tersely. He was exerting himself to patience, but her hesitation was frustrating. He was not used to not getting his way.

"—then I could home-school Dan for the summer term, while the school reserved a place for autumn to keep that option open. That would give plenty of time to come to terms with, well, what's happening to us because of you."

Xander was silent a moment as they both watched the lambs avidly guzzling on their bottles, the children around them asking questions, Dan gazing transfixed.

"Do you really want to go back to living in London, keeping Dan in his current school—limited resources, large classes, no playing fields? And living in that cramped house with barely a garden?" Xander kept his tone resolutely temperate, but again it took effort. Could she really prefer that for their son?

CHAPTER SIX

"I'M GOING TO have to get back to Athens in a couple of days."

Xander made his announcement to Laurel the next day. He'd arrived to take them all out to lunch—the pizza parlour in the market town this time—and now they were visiting a nearby farm park that he thought Dan would enjoy. The website promised tractors, a huge hay barn and any number of farm animals from donkeys to chickens. Currently, bottle-feeding newborn lambs was the big attraction, and Xander and Laurel were standing a little way off from where Dan was clustered with other children and two members of staff, watching the feeding and having a go as well.

"How long for?" Laurel asked.

"About a week. I have some business matters that need attending to, which can't be done remotely, as I've been doing from the hotel in the mornings before I arrive. I'm having a car for you to drive delivered before I leave so that you can get about. Also—" he picked his words carefully "—why don't you use the time to visit the school I think Dan would like to go to? See what you both make of it. The headmaster, who understands the position—that you are only just moving to the area—assured me you could visit during the holidays. It might be a good opportunity." He paused. "It's a good school, Laurel. Dan would thrive there, I'm sure."

better go and join Dan and his father out in the hotel gardens. Better, surely, than remaining here, staring into the fire and brooding on her own shameful susceptibility to Xander Xenakis, to whom she was nothing but a thief, a liar and the woman who had deliberately kept his son from him.

Never to be exonerated for any of those crimes.

if she and Xander kept to what they'd agreed last night, to hide their enmity to each other from Dan, to mute and silence it, to behave better in front of Dan, better, even, towards each other, however strained that was, surely she could not wish that otherwise either?

She reached for a macaroon, the last one, and nibbled it absently, thoughts drifting around. There were far fewer people in the drawing room now, and it was quiet, voices only a murmur at the far end, logs crackling in the hearth. Her mood was strange. She could not make sense of it.

It was better, yes, that Xander and she sheathe their vicious anger at each other, for Dan's sake, but with that anger set aside...

It's allowing other things in.

Things that were dangerous to allow.

Seeing Xander at the pool stripped down to swim-shorts had opened dangerous floodgates. Seeing his reaction to her in the swimsuit he remembered. Trailing his forefinger along her bare skin. Bringing back so, so many memories...

Memories that should have withered and died...

It was seven years ago! she thought desperately. *Surely to God I've moved on since then? How can he still have such an effect on me?*

Yet he did, and she could not deny it. Fully clothed or stripped down, Xander still had the ability to make her eyes go to him, cling to him.

She felt her breath tighten. She mustn't allow this, she just mustn't. It was far, far too dangerous. Far too shameful.

That even after the hideous way it ended in Greece, even what he threw at me so vilely last night, that after all that, he can still make my heart beat faster, a flush of heat go through me.

Setting down her empty cup, she got to her feet. She had

So it proved, and Dan, too, finished off everything on his cake stand. Their attentive waiter kindly replenished it with another cream bun and miniature chocolate cake. Laurel, equally attentive, but for a different reason, fetched some moistened wipes out of her handbag and got to work once Dan had demolished the final cake, removing chocolate smears from his mouth and fingers, lest they transfer to the tablecloth or chintz upholstery.

Dan sat back replete. "Best tea ever."

Xander laughed. "I'm glad you approve." He looked across at Laurel. "What about you?"

"Memorable," she said.

For just a second, their eyes met. For just a second, their gaze locked. Then, abruptly, Xander got to his feet, looking at Dan now.

"What say we leave your mother to finish her tea while we explore the gardens?" His glance went to Laurel. "All right by you?" he said, as if remembering to ask her.

She nodded, because why should she object? And they headed off, Dan chattering away happily. A pang went through her. Dan was accepting his father into his life without question. So obviously pleased to have him in his life.

I denied him that, kept his father away from him.

Her expression was troubled as she poured herself another cup of tea, sipping it slowly.

She would justify her decision, would always justify it. When Dan was born, Xander had been a married man, a man who condemned her as a liar and a thief. She had been right to keep him away from Dan.

But now?

Should she be glad, for Dan's sake, that Xander knew about him, with Dan so clearly thrilled by having his father in his life? Surely she could not now wish it otherwise. And

coin-sized passion-fruit pavlovas—it went on and on. The cutlery was silvered, the napkins fine linen, the cups and plates porcelain, the individual teapots likewise, the champagne served in crystal flutes. A somewhat larger, more robust looking flute arrived with raspberry fizz for Dan.

Xander tapped his champagne-filled flute against Dan's, and then at Laurel's. "Are we having a good day?" he asked genially.

"Yes!" affirmed Dan.

Xander glanced at Laurel. "Are we?"

"Thank you, yes," she said. It would be ungracious not to. Dan had loved the pool session and was clearly eager to get stuck into his tea.

And that's why we're here—for Dan. No other reason.

That's what she had to remember.

I would never have seen Xander again for the rest of my life otherwise.

A shadow seemed to pass over her, and she reached for the champagne flute. How often had she drunk champagne with Xander that long-ago summer, cruising the islands, their own private odyssey, their hedonistic idyll?

How happy I was, how totally happy. Until—

"Mum, can I start?" Dan's plaintive voice brought her back.

"*May* I," she corrected automatically, setting down her flute on the pristine tablecloth. "Yes, of course. Sandwiches first, mind!"

Dan didn't mind her and tucked in vigorously. Laurel had taken the precaution of spreading his linen napkin widely across his lap and now shook out her own as well. Carefully, she poured her tea, then made a selection of savouries and sandwiches. Xander had got stuck in already, and she suspected he would put away a good deal more than her.

as they'd strolled in and knew why. He'd turned hers from the very first moment…

No, she must not let herself remember. The Xander she remembered from then was not the man he was now. So there was no point remembering how she had once wanted to do nothing but gaze and gaze and gaze at him, taking in all his irresistible masculine glory.

Even if he still possessed it in spades.

As she had witnessed when he'd walked into the pool area, displaying a body that hadn't gathered an ounce of flab, still perfectly honed, as it had been seven years ago. Her eyes had gone to him immediately. How could they not have? She'd been helpless to look away. Reacting just the way she always had. Compounded, disastrously, when his eyes had gone to her in her swimsuit, seeing his very familiar reaction.

Memory had ripped through her. Those endless days on Xander's yacht, swimming in the azure sea, basking in the sun. Retiring to his state room to shower, freshen up, cool down. Make passionate love—

No. She mustn't go there! Dear God she must not go there.

The arrival of their tea was timely. A towering multi-tiered cake stand was placed on the table, and a slightly smaller one for Dan, loaded with tiny sandwiches cut into geometric shapes, jammy strawberry biscuits, caramel wafers, a gingerbread man and woman, multi-coloured iced buns and three miniature chocolate cakes. Hers and Xander's was more adult-oriented, but no less laden. Delicate smoked salmon and cucumber sandwiches cut perilously thin, bite-size savoury tartlets, a variety of puff pastry amuse-bouches, and any number of pastel macaroons, slivers of multi-layered frosted sponge cakes, exquisitely decorated tiny profiteroles, feather-light crisp almond tuiles and

Knowing he should not watch her, but unable to look away. *How beautiful she still is. How very, very beautiful.*

He should banish the words from his head. They were irrelevant. Quite, quite irrelevant.

Yet they lingered, like his gaze.

Laurel looked about her as they walked into the hotel's elegant drawing room where afternoon tea was served. Plush, chintz-covered armchairs were grouped around multiple little tables covered with pristine white linen tablecloths, each adorned with a tasteful flower arrangement. A log fire burned in the fireplace with an ornate marble mantel, and the carpet was soft pile, the curtains draped velvet. They were shown to their table, gilt-edged menus presented. Dan had his very own kiddy menu, Xander's and her own more sophisticated, including a glass of champagne each. She said nothing, but it was clear that afternoon tea here would cost Xander a mint. She'd also been right to think she'd look underdressed, but there was nothing she could do about it. Anyway, she didn't care. Her wardrobe these days was cheap and practical. And there was no one she had to look smart for, let alone attractive for.

Least of all Xander.

Her face set. Once she had looked her best every day she spent with him. Now she didn't give a damn what he thought of her appearance. Her expression softened, though, as her eyes went to Dan. He was wearing the smart new clothes Xander had bought him yesterday, clearly enjoying them. As for Xander…

Unconsciously her glance went to him from Dan. He had gone back to his room to change after they'd left the pool and was now wearing a white shirt, though not a tie, and with the top button undone. She'd seen female heads turn

islands—she was sitting on the sun deck reading a book in that swimsuit, saying she wanted to finish the chapter first, but I wanted to go swimming straight away, so—" he made a face "—I scooped her up, dumped the book and chucked her off the boat right into the sea!"

Dan gasped.

Xander looked across at Laurel. "Do you remember?"

"Distinctly," she said. There was an edge in her voice. But there was something else as well.

Xander went for broke again. Turned back to Dan. "She was so mad at me she swam straight to the beach. We were anchored in a little cove. And she wouldn't speak to me. I had to kiss her nice again."

He looked across at Laurel again. "Remember that too?" he said.

He saw the flush come again, felt that wash of satisfaction go through him. Even though he knew it shouldn't. "As I recall, though—" he cast a sideways glance at Laurel "—you pushed me off the dive platform the next day to get your own back!" Then, belatedly realising his anecdote wasn't setting his son a laudable example, he said hastily, "But throwing anyone into the water isn't good, Dan."

"I won't," Dan promised, nodding. Then his attention went back to Laurel. "Mum, come on in!" he called to her pleadingly.

"Okay, okay," she conceded, getting to her feet.

Xander watched her walk to the edge of the pool, a distinct air of self-consciousness about her. She might be seven years older now, she might have borne a child, but her beauty was only enhanced, matured. Full-breasted, with a slender waist, rounded hips, long legs. As she waded down the shallow steps, water lapping at her body, her breasts, Xander could not take his eyes from her.

couraging him to doggy-paddle—with much splashing—he could not resist looking back to her.

She'd sat herself down on one of the loungers, one long leg extended, the other bent at the knee, looking effortlessly graceful, watching Dan.

But not just Dan...

Xander felt another wash of satisfaction go through him. Totally misplaced, totally superfluous, but most definitely there.

I always knew when she was looking at me, liking what she saw.

And he knew now too. She was trying not to make it obvious, but he could feel her gaze on him as tangibly as he had wanted her to feel his on her. His eyes glinted. It was a two-way street. It always had been.

"Dad, can I swim a width, do you think?" Dan's interruption was timely.

"Give it a try," he said, returning his attention to where it should be. His son—only his son. "I'll walk beside you. Take it steadily."

It took two attempts, but Dan managed it in the end and was triumphant.

"I did it!" he gasped as he reached the far side.

"You did," said Xander. "Well done!" He glanced back at Laurel.

"Well done, Dan!" she echoed praisingly.

Xander's expression changed minutely. "You should come in," he told her. "That swimsuit of yours shouldn't stay dry. I can remember—" He cut himself short.

Dan looked at him. "Remember what?" he asked.

Xander went for broke. "I remember once, in Greece, when your mother was on holiday with me there, and we were cruising around the islands—Greece has hundreds of

It was madness to do so. He was not here for Laurel, the woman whose beauty had beguiled him, who had had eyes only for him, had made passionate love to him—and then stolen from him and lied to him.

So it would be madness to be beguiled by her beauty again.

He felt a hand tugging at his and realised it was Dan's.

"Dad, can we go in?" he was pleading.

With a start, Xander put the dangerous past behind him. It was over and done with.

And it's got to stay that way. Because otherwise...

But he would not let his thoughts go there. Would not let himself do anything but pay attention to his son, for whose sake he was here, for whose sake alone he was in Laurel's company.

She is nothing to me but the mother of my son.

He had to remember that.

"You need your armbands, Dan," he heard her say now.

Xander cut across her. "There's a shallow entrance, and I'll be with him. He'll be fine."

Again she seemed to hesitate, then nodded.

Xander looked down at Dan. "Let's get you swimming, shall we? So you won't need armbands any more."

He led him off to the pool. It felt good to hold his son's hand, good to be about to teach him to swim. Good just to be with him.

Determinedly, he did not look back towards his son's mother. She might still look fantastic in a bathing suit, but that was nothing to him now. Not after seven years and a stolen bracelet she would not admit to. However polite they were now being to each other for Dan's sake.

Yet even so, as he stood with Dan at the shallow end, en-

over her breasts, hugging her figure like a second skin, and he remembered it as if it were yesterday.

Poised to dive off the swim deck, golden hair flowing down her back, looking so, so beautiful.

Slowly he walked towards her.

"I remember that suit," he heard himself say. "You always wore it when you wanted to do decent swimming, not just splashing around in a bikini."

For a moment, just a moment, he thought he saw her colour change. Her cheeks flush. Then she simply said, with a half shrug, "It still fits me."

Xander's eyes washed over her. All the way down, all the way back up. A visible caress.

"Oh, it most certainly does that," he said softly. "In all the right places."

Without thinking he had reached his hand towards her, letting his forefinger run a leisurely curve along her décolletage. Lingering.

He used to do that in Greece, he recalled. Before slipping the straps from her shoulders and drawing the clinging material downwards to expose her lovely coral-tipped breasts, cupping them in his hands lightly, seductively, his eyes never leaving her, scissoring her nipples as they peaked beneath his ministrations, her breasts engorging beneath his palms as his mouth lowered to hers.

She stepped back, but the vivid flush in her cheeks now showed him that she was remembering as vividly as he. Satisfaction went through him. A satisfaction he should not feel, because the Laurel of that time had nothing to do with the Laurel now. But he felt it all the same...

"Your figure is definitely still a total knockout," he said. Appreciation was in his voice. Deep appreciation. He let his gaze rest on her, drinking her in.

No, he wasn't going to go down that bitter path again. He drew back from it. Realised she was speaking again.

"Oh well," she was saying, "they can always take me for Dan's nanny, I guess!"

She said it lightly, without animosity, and in the same spirit Xander forbore from pointing out that even a nanny would look better dressed than she did.

They reached the former stable-yard, now the spa entrance.

"I can see the pool!" Dan exclaimed as they went in.

Xander smiled down at him, took his hand. "Let's get changed," he said. "See you poolside." He glanced at Laurel.

Did she hesitate a fraction, as if she didn't want Dan changing with him? Maybe, but then she handed Dan his swim bag.

"Okay, see you poolside."

It took Xander more time than he realised it would to get Dan ready to swim, his excitement rising by the minute. But with their clothes consigned to a locker, Dan's goggles and inflatable armbands remembered, courtesy towels collected, and Dan hopping from one foot to another throughout, plus getting himself changed as well, Xander finally guided him through to the pool. On this quiet weekday afternoon they had the place to themselves. He cast his eyes about for Laurel.

For a second he didn't see her. Then he did.

And he stopped dead.

She was putting her towel on one of a pair of loungers, and as Dan ran excitedly up to her, she straightened. Xander remained motionless, not taking his eyes from her. Not being able to.

She was in a one-piece, turquoise, cut high in the leg, low

Xander turned to Laurel. "I've taken the liberty," he said, "of booking us in for afternoon tea here at the hotel after our swim. Would you object?"

He was asking politely, because *politeness* was now his watchword towards her. She was matching it in turn. They were walking over eggshells around each other, but that was what they'd agreed to, hadn't they? In the aftermath of that hideous meltdown yesterday.

"Would it be suitable for a child Dan's age?" she asked, but her tone of voice was only enquiring, not combative.

"I did check, and was assured well-behaved youngsters are welcome. And Dan is very well behaved," Xander acknowledged, because to do otherwise would be unjust. "He'll do fine, I'm sure. They do a children's menu, so I'm sure he'll enjoy it."

"I'm sure he will," Laurel replied, her voice warming now. "The only thing is—" she paused, and Xander glanced at her "—I'm not exactly dressed for afternoon tea at a posh hotel."

Xander's gaze took in her chain-store skirt and top. It was little better than what she'd worn the previous day. Memory plucked at him. Even on her limited budget Laurel had always dressed with flair in Greece, always looking good. Now, though nothing could dim her inherent beauty, she did nothing to pay tribute to it. Glorious hair pulled back into a tight knot and not a scrap of make-up.

His own words to her the previous evening came back to him: *You're too beautiful not to have beautiful clothes.*

Her answer came back to him as well, that she would not let him spend his money on her.

For a moment frustration bit, and a sense of caustic irony too. Her scruples hadn't stopped her taking Olympia's bracelet...

said, making her voice carefully light, "Why not have a bit of a kick around in the garden while I clear up and get some lunch going?"

Xander hadn't said anything about eating out, so she'd make cheese and ham toasties in the smart new sandwich maker she'd found in a cupboard in the formidably well-equipped kitchen. Cheese on toast was one of Dan's favourites, and it was economical and filling. It struck her that now, with Xander bankrolling them, she no longer had to think economically. It would certainly make life easier.

But Xander's money would only be spent on Dan, she thought fiercely. That comment Xander had made last night, that she should buy new clothes on his credit card...

A flash of resistance flared in her. Xander already thought her a thief; she would not compound that accusation by letting him think she was happy to get her sticky fingers into his bank balance.

Forcibly, she made the flash subside. They were supposed to be making an effort to subdue their hostility. Had Xander seen that flash? Following Dan, who'd dashed off eagerly into the garden, Xander turned, his eyes going to Laurel, meeting hers.

"We can do this," he said, his voice low, his gaze intent. "We can both do it."

She nodded. Her lungs felt tight, but she acknowledged what he was saying. "Yes," she said, "we can."

Because we must, for Dan.

Xander parked the car outside his hotel on the gravelled sweep.

"The spa is in the old stable block," he said. He guided them towards it.

Dan was excited and ran ahead.

He settled himself down at the table, Dan doing likewise, picking up his reading book.

"He's doing very well," Laurel said encouragingly. With her worries about Dan's London school, she had always done a good amount of home-schooling as well, especially with reading practice. Of course, if Dan did go to this new school Xander was so keen on...

It would mean accepting that the move here is permanent, not just for a holiday.

Could it be? Could she—should she—really make their life here?

She let the question hang. It was far too complicated, too challenging, for her to answer.

As the coffee machine filled Xander's mug and she took it over to him, her eyes went to him. Against her will she felt her gaze rest on him, taking him in, sitting there, as powerfully physically real as he had once been to her seven years ago.

Having the same effect on her.

She put his coffee down, not interrupting Dan's careful reading out loud to him, and Xander glanced up at her. For a second, a fraction of a second, their eyes met.

"Thanks," he said, acknowledging the coffee. His attention went back to Dan.

Laurel moved away, conscious that her heart was beating just that much faster.

But there was reason enough for that. Today they had to put into practice what they had agreed to last night, to treat each other differently, without that glowering hostility constantly bristling between them. To achieve some kind of neutrality. She must make the effort to do so consciously, conscientiously.

As Dan finished his reading and Xander his coffee, she

them. Hell, that was four people out of five, so that was a majority vote, wasn't it? So he'd gone ahead. Married her.

He pulled his thoughts away from the way his marriage had turned out. At least there was one thing to be grateful for, and not just because Olympia had finally cut and run, finding her own alternative happy ever after, but for the timing of it. Freeing him to focus entirely on the son he'd never known he had.

And whatever it takes to ensure his happiness, his security, his well-being, that's what I'll do.

He depressed the accelerator, speeding up, eager to see his son. It would mean seeing Laurel again, but she and Dan came as a package. And that was something he just had to deal with.

Without any more destructive, dangerous, damaging-to-Dan anger…

"So, is the plan for the day to go swimming? Are you still okay with it?"

Xander was looking across at Laurel in the kitchen as she fitted a pod into the coffee machine. He'd just arrived, and Laurel had seen Dan leap from the table where he'd been doing his daily reading practice with her, together with some drawing and colouring.

"Yes please!" he said eagerly, but Xander was keeping his eyes on Laurel. Was he actually asking her if she was happy to go along with it?

"Fine by me," she managed to say, her voice equable. She got Xander's coffee going.

"I've been doing reading, Dad," Dan announced. "I'm on the next book now. Can I read to you?"

"Sure," Xander said.

CHAPTER FIVE

XANDER HEADED DOWN the gravelled driveway of his hotel out onto the road. Fields and woodlands stretched around, bright in midday sunshine. He was heading to the house he'd rented so his son could have the kind of life he deserved, a life way better than he'd had so far, but he was burningly aware that now he was going to have to tread carefully.

I can't allow my feelings towards Laurel to make me lash out like that again. They don't matter. Only my son's feelings matter.

And his son had been terrified by the anger he'd witnessed Xander unleash and the anger Laurel had hurled back at him.

That must never happen again, never!

From now on, his expression was sombre, obdurate—like it or not—and he didn't. It choked him. He had to set aside what he felt about his son's mother.

I can do it, because I must.

His mouth twisted. That's what he'd told himself when he'd married Olympia. Or rather, a variation on it: *I can do this because I might as well go along with what everyone expects of me, so I should just get on with it.*

Olympia wanted it, her parents wanted it, his father wanted it. All dead keen on it. Thinking it ideal for both of

sive, unable to believe that he could believe so instantly in her guilt.

Her expression changed. He still did believe it; he'd admitted as much even as he'd declared they had to find a better way forward for dealing with each other, for Dan's sake. Could she live with that, cope with that, knowing he still thought her a liar and a thief? Heaviness pressed on her, then, with a breath, she pushed it away. She would have to live with it, cope with it. As he had said, and with which she could not possibly disagree. The only person who was important was Dan.

For Dan's sake I can cope with still being thought a liar and a thief.

Xander had said they should put it aside. What other way was there for them now?

The question hung, finding no other answer.

It will have to do.

She gave a sigh, still feeling drained and exhausted, but perhaps, too, something else, though she still did not know what. Instead, she reached for the TV remote, flicked it on, wanting something, anything, to divert her thoughts.

Tomorrow would bring Xander back again, and she and he, she supposed, would take it from there.

What else could they do? Upstairs, their son slept, peaceful now after the trauma of the evening.

For Dan I can do this. For him.

And Xander must too.

She found a news channel and leant back, reaching for her unfinished wine. She let the news wash over her, let the fire die down, let her mind go numb.

he could see Dan's door slightly ajar. For a moment he just stood there as emotion filled him. Protective. Guilty.

How close they'd come, he and Laurel, indulging in their own rage, to devastating their own son...

But we'll do better now.

He felt resolve filling him—relief. Thankfulness.

With a lighter step, resolute, he let himself out of the house and headed for his car.

Behind him, Laurel heard the front door close, and then the sound of Xander reversing the car out of the driveway. Her eyes went to where he had been sitting on the sofa, the cushions still indented, the empty glass and pasta bowl on the side table. For a moment her gaze lingered, then she pulled it away.

She felt drained, exhausted. But something more as well, though she didn't know what. Perhaps it was best to let it be.

Fragments of what he'd said flickered in the firelight. She'd been wary—so very wary—instinctively guarding herself from what he might say to her, yet all he had said, in the end, was what she was glad of, if *gladness* were even a term to associate with him.

One thing, though, she could feel he was being different towards her. He'd asked her to agree, not told her. Not ordered her. It was not conciliatory, but it was at least not that constant knifing hostility he'd treated her with from the moment he'd hauled her into his car outside Dan's school.

From the moment he found that bracelet in my suitcase...

The change from the man she'd known, had come to know, those blindly blissful weeks together in their carefree cruising of the Aegean had shocked her to the core. She'd retaliated. How could she not have? But it had been defen-

a liar and a thief, who had deliberately, knowingly, kept his son from him, but it needed to be said.

It's part of the way forward we have to find—

"In the car, outside his school that morning," he said now, never letting go her eyes, her head turned to his, her expression impossible to read, except that he knew he did not want that guarded look in it, "when I confronted you that I now knew about Dan, you asked for time. I ask for it too. We both need it, Laurel. So…so let's just give ourselves time—take things…slowly. Find that way forward."

He paused again, took another breath. "We've made a start—this evening—here, and now, like this, haven't we? And it's a better place for us to be than the place we were before." He stopped. Letting what he'd said rest between them.

Slowly she nodded. She didn't speak, but something had changed in her expression. The guarded look had gone again.

As if she'd been protecting herself.

"Then that's good, isn't it?" he said. "We can…go on… from here. Go forward."

For a moment longer their eyes met and held. A veil of some kind was still over hers, but different now.

"Yes," she said.

He nodded. Some kind of resolution had been reached… achieved. For now it was enough. Draining the last of his wine, he glanced at his watch, got to his feet.

"I'll leave you now," he said. "I'll be here again at lunchtime." He paused a moment. "If that suits you?"

She nodded again, making to get to her feet too. Xander stayed her. "No, don't disturb yourself. I'll see myself out."

He paused yet again, standing there, then nodded, as if bidding her goodnight, then walked out into the hallway, glancing up the staircase. The landing light was on, and

over, all the anger and fury he'd felt at Laurel as he'd stared down at Olympia's bracelet in Laurel's suitcase.

He took another mouthful of his wine, wanting to let that weariness wash from him. Letting the quietness of the room, the warmth, the crackling of the logs, lap around him, his eyes still resting on Laurel as she went on sipping her wine, looking into the flames.

"Laurel?" He had said her name before he realised he'd said it.

She turned her head to look at him. Her expression was strange. That guarded look in her eyes again. He didn't want it there. Did not know why he did not, only knew that he didn't.

"We'll make this work," he said. His voice was low, his eyes holding hers. "We'll make it work, for Dan." He paused, his eyes not letting hers go. "He needs us both. I won't…rebuke you any more for keeping him from me, but that time is gone. He has us both now, and we must be, as best we can, the best parents we can be to him."

He paused again, took one more mouthful of his nearly finished wine.

"You asked, this evening, how much time I would spend with him. It will be as much as I can, but there are, yes, complications. Not Olympia. She's now gone, and I am glad of that for many reasons, but most of all because of Dan. Laurel, he won't—" his voice was intent, he wanted, needed, her to understand this "—be my 'secret son,' as you called him, but you must accept—" he caught himself, moderated his words "—please accept that I am feeling my way here. I will not promise what I cannot perform, but what that is I don't yet know."

He took a breath, said what was difficult to say. It did not come easily to him to say it to the woman who had proved

disastrously over with their vicious attack on each other, hurling such vitriol.

Had it lanced a festering wound, their raging at each other? He didn't know, but if it had, maybe that was, as he had said, to the good.

He set aside his empty bowl, sat back, and let his eyes go to her. Her gaze was resting on the play of flames behind the glass of the wood burner. What he had said just now was true. Her beauty was undimmed.

He let himself watch her, his eyes half closed, her face reposed, it seemed to him.

As beautiful as I remembered her.

A sense of regret filled him.

It ended so badly.

But what if it hadn't?

In the wood burner the logs crackled. The warmth of the room embraced him, created an atmosphere around them. It was very quiet. Laurel had left the door to the hallway slightly ajar, presumably to hear if Dan should call out. It was strange, sitting here like this. With his son upstairs, the mother of his son opposite him.

Like we were a family.

The thought was in his head—disturbing, mocking. For their son's sake they were now trying not to be at each other's throats, but that was for Dan, not each other. Whatever had been between them, whatever it was, had ended seven years ago. Ended with the glint of diamonds and rubies in her suitcase. How could it have done otherwise?

A great wash of weariness went through him. He wanted to let it go, that weight he'd carried for seven long years, that he'd had to pick up again as Dan had come into his life. The son he'd never known he had, who had been deliberately hidden from him, thereby compounding, a thousand times

She was back sitting on the opposite sofa, but leaning back now, propped by cushions, wine glass cupped in her hands. She took a sip every now and then. Her expression was still veiled. She shook her head.

He glanced at her again. "It won't make you fat, you know," he said dryly. "Your figure's just as knock out as it was seven years ago. Even in those rubbish clothes—"

He saw her expression change. Wished he hadn't mentioned her figure or her clothes. But it was too late now, so he waded in more. What was there to lose after what had happened this evening?

"Buy some new ones, please, Laurel," he said. "On me. Use your new credit card. You're too beautiful not to have beautiful clothes—"

Her expression changed again. "I won't have you spend your money on me, Xander," she said. She spoke quietly, but there was no anger in her repudiation. Only calm resolve.

He held up his free hand. "I thought we'd agreed we weren't going to argue again?" He kept his voice light, eyebrow quirking. It felt strange to be talking to her like that, without any jab of hostility. He hadn't spoken to her like that since before the moment he'd thrown open her suitcase in his cabin.

"Then we must stick to subjects that aren't controversial," she replied, again without any edge to her voice, only that calm composure.

Xander backed off. He wouldn't risk the cautious, careful rapprochement they seemed to have achieved.

"I daresay we'll find some," he answered dryly. He drank some more of his wine, finishing his mac and cheese. Both wine and pasta were having an effect, a good one, distancing him—and her?—from the precipice they'd plunged so

"This may sound crass, but I could do with a drink," he said. "Maybe you could too."

He didn't wait for her answer, only frowned slightly. "I think I included a bottle of wine with that grocery delivery," he said. "Where did you put it? I'll go and fetch it."

"It's okay, I'll get it." Laurel stood up. He had the impression she was glad to escape. She walked swiftly but stiffly and returned shortly, handing him the bottle, depositing two glasses and a corkscrew on a side table by the sofa he was sitting on.

Xander opened the wine and poured generous measures into each glass, holding one out to her. She took it carefully, clearly avoiding any chance of contact, resuming her place on the sofa opposite him. Her expression was still drawn, eyes veiled, face pale.

Xander lifted his glass. "*Yammas!*" he said. An automatic murmur.

Something flickered across her face. He didn't know what it was, but it was gone as soon as it was there. He took a mouthful of the wine. It hit the spot, and right now he needed that. He took another large mouthful, replacing the glass, suddenly hungry. The mac and cheese for Dan's tea seemed a long time ago.

"Is there any of that mac and cheese left?" he asked. "It was very good."

"There's a bit," said Laurel.

She set aside her wine and got up before he could do, and disappeared into the kitchen again. Xander heard the microwave ping, then she was coming back with a bowl of the leftover portion, handing it to him. He got stuck in. It hit the spot too. Washed down nicely with the red.

"You're not having any?" he queried.

He took another breath, kept his eyes on her face. Said what he needed to say now, what she needed to hear. What he did too.

His gaze on her was steady as he spoke. She met it full on, yet not defiantly, not hostilely. Nor guarded either. Just… hearing him out. He made himself continue, hard though it was. Made his eyes stay on her. His voice was sombre.

"What happened—seven years ago—we're not going to agree on. I can't make you confess, and you, you can't make me back off. So—" he inhaled heavily, eyes holding hers "—we'll just have to set it to one side. Try and…make progress…despite it."

His mouth compressed. "If we disagree about the past, at least we can agree on one thing. We both know that. Both accept it. That the only person who is important right now is Dan. He is all that matters."

He saw her swallow, saw her hands tighten their grip on each other. She said nothing, so he said it for her.

"We have to make this work, Laurel. We both wish the other one to hell, but we cannot take Dan there with us. For his sake—" he took another breath "—we have to find a way forward. Put the past aside."

He looked at her, held her eyes. "Do you agree?" he said.

She swallowed again, but her hands loosened their grip on each other. "Yes," she said.

He felt the tension leach out of him. Some kind of barrier had been dissolved. Some kind of way marker passed. A sense of relief—was that what it was?—went through him, and he leant back, flexing shoulders he hadn't realised had been so tensed. His mouth twisted, and he took a deep breath, as if he needed it. He looked across at her, his expression changing.

She dropped her eyes, but nodded. "Yes," she said.

He waited a moment to see if she would say anything else, but her expression was closed in on itself. He tried to think back to how that vicious row in the kitchen had escalated so hideously. Which of them was to blame?

He let the question go. It didn't matter how it started—only that it must never, never happen again. He let his gaze rest on her again, her eyes still downcast, staring at her hands folded in her lap. As if, he thought suddenly, she were guarding herself.

Against him—

Emotion flickered in him, but he didn't know what it was. Instead, looking at her, he spoke again. His voice as sombre as hers, and for the same reason. Making himself speak, saying what had to be said now. "Whatever way we find, perhaps—" he took a breath, realising it was ragged at the edges, knowing why "—this evening served a purpose. Not just showing us we cannot ever let that happen again, for Dan's sake, but maybe—" He broke off.

Her eyes had lifted to rest on him impassively. But they were veiled as well. Still guarding herself—

Yet there was something new about the way she was looking at him. Since discovering Dan's existence she had never looked at him like that.

As if, for the very first time, she isn't resisting me in some way. Resisting everything about me. Resisting my presence in her life—the reason for it.

"Maybe it did some good too. Got the worst out," he said.

"Lanced a festering wound?" There was no sarcasm in her voice, but there was something, definitely. Yet it was not directed at him.

At herself—

He nodded slowly. "Maybe," he said again.

"He's asleep," she said. "No bath, just straight to bed." He could hear the careful neutrality in her voice.

He nodded, making his way back towards the sofa, sitting down, leaning forward slightly. "We need to talk," he said.

He waited as she crossed to the sofa facing him. While she'd been upstairs, getting a suddenly exhausted and out-of-it Dan to bed, he'd lit the wood burner, and a cheerful flame burned behind the glass door, throwing warmth into the room. He'd set the central heating on as well, keeping it relatively low. There'd been heat enough expended, destructive and dangerous.

To Dan—

Laurel sat herself down, that same contained pose of knees and legs neatly parallel, hands in her lap. Tension was visible in her, her face still pale, but she was calm at least. The calm after the storm.

The storm that must never happen again.

For Dan's sake.

She had begun to speak, her voice low, expression sombre. Her words echoed what was in his own head. "What happened this evening must never, never happen again." Her words fell into a heavy silence.

Then he said, "No." His gaze rested on her. It was hard to do so, but he must. "Somehow—" he paused, then went on, picking his words through the impossibility of what he was now saying "—we have to find a…a different way…forward."

He studied her expression. It was still sombre, still netted with tension, but had that tension diminished, even if only very slightly, by what he'd just said? He spoke again. "I don't know—" he paused again, then made himself go on "—just how we're going to do that, but we must." His gaze rested on her. "For Dan's sake."

it, holding out the mug. "Here you go, Dan," he said. "Just what the doctor ordered."

Dan took it, and started to drink from it, the familiarity soothing him. He didn't say anything, but Xander did. He lifted his hand to close it gently around Dan's shoulder, his other arm stretched out along the back of the sofa.

"I'm sorry we scared you, Dan," he said. "We didn't mean to, your mother and I. We were just…arguing." His voice was low and quiet. Dan's eyes were half shut, the soothing repetition of drinking his warm strawberry-flavoured milk calming him, his little body warm against her side. She could feel him relaxing now, coming down the other side of the tumult in him.

"Mums and dads argue sometimes," Xander said in that low, quiet voice. "We didn't mean to upset you." He paused a moment. "We won't argue again like that." His eyes had been on Dan's face, but now they lifted to hers. "Will we?" he said.

There was a wealth of meaning in his words. Of intent. She could feel the will emanating from him like a force field. Telling her. Warning her.

But she did not need warning. She knew what they had done. What harm, what damage. What they must never, ever do again.

She swallowed. It felt like there was a rock in her throat, in her lungs. "No," she said. "We won't. I promise you, darling, we won't."

Xander stood by the patio doors. Night had fallen, but he did not draw the curtains. He stared out into the unseen garden, his thoughts heavy. At the slight sound behind him he turned. Laurel had come back into the room.

her arms around him, snuggling him up against her. She could still feel slight tremors going through him. Guilt still consumed her. Excoriated her.

She realised Xander was standing in the doorway.

"What can I do?" he asked. His voice was low. She heard guilt in it too.

Both of us—we both did this. We did it to our son—our own son.

She took a breath. "If you look in the top cupboard by the cooker you'll see a carton with strawberry-flavoured powder in it. Make it up with milk from the fridge, and warm it in the microwave. You'll find a sippy beaker in the cupboard for the mugs. I use it when he's not feeling well because it's easier to drink from."

She'd brought both with her, never dreaming she'd need them because she'd reduced her son to sobbing terror. Knives stabbed her, guilt and remorse...

She saw Xander give a brief nod and disappear. She went on nestling Dan against her, holding him close.

"Dad's making you your strawberry milk, pet," she said. She dropped a kiss on his head, arm tightening around her. He wasn't capable of speech yet, and she could still feel his little body trembling. She didn't try and say any more, just smoothed his hair again, holding him against her. She just wanted him calmer and restored, and not terrified any longer.

Terrified of me, of Xander and I yelling at each other. Filling the air with our rage. Our vile, destructive rage—

Through the open doorway she heard the microwave ping, and a few moments later Xander was there, coming up to the sofa holding Dan's old sippy mug that had been his since infancy. A safe, familiar friend.

The sofa dipped as Xander lowered himself down on

Then, suddenly, there was someone else there. Someone else hunkering down. Another voice added to hers. "It's okay, Dan. I promise you, it's okay."

Xander put his hand on Dan's back, his fingers spreading out, reassuring and comforting him. "It's okay," he said again. "We were shouting, yes, but it's okay. We won't do it again. It's all right now. I'm sorry we scared you."

His eyes met Laurel's. For a moment both were silent. Then she realised Dan's anguished sobs were subsiding, slowly turning into hiccuping gasps. His trembling was easing too, and Laurel slackened her arms around him but kept them there all the same. With one hand she reached to smooth his hair. As she did her fingers brushed the back of Xander's hand, which was still resting on Dan's back, but she didn't care. She didn't care about anything except that she'd reduced her own son to terrified shaking and sobbing...

"It's okay," Xander was saying again, his hand rubbing Dan's back now, calming him more, his words, his voice soothing him, reassuring him.

It took a while longer, but at last Dan had seen it through. Slowly, Laurel got to her feet but took hold of Dan's hand. Xander took the other one.

"Are you okay now?" he asked. His voice was low, concerned.

Dan gulped, not speaking, but half nodding, lifting his eyes, tear-stained and reddened, to Xander, and then to Laurel.

"Mum..." he said faintly.

She squeezed his hand, realising he couldn't say more. Shock and fear were still only just below the fragile surface. She led him back into the sitting room, drew him down beside her on the sofa, absently clicking off the TV. She put

CHAPTER FOUR

For one hideous second, the tableau held. Then, appalled, Laurel rushed to her son. As she swept him to her, terrified sobs broke from him. Tearing her to pieces. Remorse and horror ripped through her. Dan was shaking uncontrollably, sobbing, gasping.

"You were…sh..shouting," he said stammeringly, "shouting and shouting…" terror clear in his trembling voice, clinging to her desperately.

Knives stabbed into Laurel. "Oh, darling, it's all right! It's all right!" she said urgently, kneeling to his level so that she could hug him completely, arms snaking around him as his little body racked.

Oh God! What have I done?

Guilt crucified her. To have let rip like that as she had, allowing her fury to boil over, her rage and anger exploding, thinking of nothing but herself, her own fury, shouting as she had, hatred and rage naked, vicious in her voice.

"It's all right, darling!" she said again, in an agony of remorse, hugging him closer and closer still as his anguished, terrified sobs went on.

"I was scared!" He could hardly get the words out. "You were angry and I was scared!" he said, his voice choking.

"Oh, darling!" she said again, helpless and guilt-stricken, arms tightening around him.

throw all that garbage at me again! So just shut up! Do you hear me? Just shut the hell up!"

"Oh, you'd like that, wouldn't you?" The snarl came again, louder now, to override her, dominate her, allow her no voice, no defence.

Like he did last time—seven years ago! Going on and on at me! Trying to force a confession from me.

Sickness rose in her throat and such anger, such black, black anger. He was still denouncing her, that hateful, condemning refusal to believe her. His raised fury-laden voice slamming into her.

"Well, no dice!" His mouth twisted, ugly and thinned, knives in his eyes, narrowed and vicious, fury naked in them, black rage. "I know you for what you are! And, my God, if I could have chosen any other woman on earth as a mother to my son, I would! Do you think I want trash like you anywhere near him?" His face enraged, darkening and condemning, his voice louder yet, shutting her down, silencing her. He lifted one hand, brought it slamming down on the countertop. Voice rising even louder in his vehement rage. "You stole that bracelet. No one else did! You! So don't stand there and try and sleaze your way out of it! Don't even think you can—"

He broke off. Froze.

Expression changing. Eyes going past her. To the door into the sitting room.

Slowly, like in a nightmare, Laurel turned. And the nightmare became real.

Dan was standing there stark and motionless in the now fully open doorway, abject terror in his face.

Laurel's hands slammed down on the metal draining board by the sink, so the cutlery on it jumped noisily.

"I did not steal her bracelet! I did not steal it!"

Her voice had risen, fury in it. The same fury she had felt seven years ago when he'd made his accusation, his denunciation.

Contempt sheared across his face. "You stole it! Denying it, trying to blame Olympia, won't work now any more than it worked seven years ago! So stop lying to me!"

Laurel's hand fisted in frustration. Anger was boiling up in her, she couldn't stop it. It was happening again, a nightmare replay of his accusation seven years ago. Refusing to believe her, refusing to listen, refusing everything except to condemn her.

"It's the truth!" she spat.

He leant across the breakfast bar at her. His face was black, his eyes like knives. "It's a lie now, just as it was then! You're still nothing but a lying little thief!"

Fury boiled over in her. Burst out of her. Eyes blazing. Heart hammering inside chest, pounding in her veins. "Don't you dare speak to me like that! Never. Do you understand me? My God, I had to put up with your foul accusations seven years ago! But not any longer! Never, ever again!" she spat, loud and angry, fury contorting her face.

His was contorted too. Voice rising, overriding hers. Shouting her down. "I'll speak to you any damn way I choose! You don't get to dictate to me! You're a thief and a liar who couldn't even find the honesty to damn well admit it when the evidence of it was in front of my eyes! You just went on and on and damn well denied it!"

She reared back. "Because I didn't do it, that's why!" She was shouting too now and didn't care. Black fury was possessing her, boiling over in her. "And I will not have you

riage. Our divorce," he went on, his voice expressionless, "was rushed through just in time for her to marry and ensure a legitimate baby."

Thoughts rushed through Laurel's brain, messy and confused. Then distilled into one single realization. "You're not married," she said.

A curious light glinted in Xander's eyes. "No," he said. His eyes rested on her. There was something in them she didn't like. Didn't like even more than the way he looked at her when he was busy ignoring her.

"Does it make a difference, Laurel, that I'm not married any more? Does it...change things...for you?" She could hear a taunt in his voice. She didn't know what it was for.

"It...it makes things simpler," she said. Because it did, she had to acknowledge that. Didn't she prefer Dan's father not to be married to another woman...let alone with other children by that marriage?

He was still looking at her, and that expression in his eyes was making her even more uneasy.

"How simple would you like them to be, Laurel? You never approached me for child maintenance when you thought I was married, but maybe now that you know I'm not you see another opportunity. A better one. Maybe one you'd have liked seven years ago, had Olympia not spiked your guns."

Laurel's eyes flashed. "By hiding her own bracelet in my suitcase so she could call me out as a thief and get you to throw me off your yacht?" she bit out viciously.

An answering flash came from his eyes—darker, more vicious. "Don't try and badmouth Olympia again! You did it once before and I called you out on it! *She* didn't hide her bracelet in your suitcase—*you* did, then tried to blame her when I found it!"

tionally "—after you dumped me at Piraeus. Well, weeks after, at any rate..." Her voice trailed off.

He was still looking at her. Was she not supposed to know about Olympia, how he'd married her in some huge Greek socialite wedding costing a bomb, splashing photos in the press? Well tough, because she did—

Irritation bit at her. "Oh, for God's sake, did you think I didn't know? And whatever I think of her, I can see that discovering you have a son tucked away in the UK is not exactly going to be fun for her!"

His voice cut across hers. "Olympia," he said, "will not give a damn."

Laurel stared. "That's callous, even for you. Any wife at all would care whether her husband had a secret son somewhere! Let alone—" bitterness entered her voice "—that the mother turned out to be me!"

She saw Xander's hands fold around the edge of the breakfast bar. "Any wife might," he said heavily. "But Olympia is not my wife. So she will not, as I say, give a damn about Dan's existence. The only child's existence she cares about is her own."

Laurel paled. "Dan has a sibling?" Her voice was hollow. She should have expected this, should have seen it coming. After all, it had been seven years since Xander had married Olympia. Of course there would have been children in that time...

"One might, at a stretch," Xander said now, "call Olympia's baby a step-sibling."

"Step? You mean half—"

"No. Step." She heard Xander's sharp intake of breath. "Olympia walked out on me over a year ago, left me for another man and promptly got pregnant. Something—" his voice edged "—that had never happened in six years of mar-

He watched her with a sardonic expression on his face. "I need to understand," she started, eyeballing him, "just how much time you intend to spend with Dan. You'll be coming and going, back and forth from Greece, I get that, and I understand, right now, over the holidays, you'll want to see a lot of him, but what happens afterwards? I have to manage his expectations. How often will he get to see you?"

Xander could see tension in her face. It irritated him, yet he could also see why she was asking. Managing Dan's expectations was, indeed, crucial. But it was impossible to give her a definitive answer just now.

He said as much.

"There are complications," he said. "There's a lot I still have to work out." His voice was brusque, and he knew it, but he didn't want her pressuring him.

She's in no position to do so! I'm the injured party here. I'm the one she's kept Dan from!

And he, not she, would be calling the shots from now on.

He saw her expression change, tighten even more.

"Including, of course," she said, and it was her voice that was caustic now, "the big complication of your wife…"

Xander was staring at her as if she'd said something in an alien language.

"My wife?" he echoed.

Laurel's eyes flashed. "Yes, your wife! Remember her? Olympia."

"Olympia," he echoed.

Laurel swallowed. It was like swallowing a razor. "Yes, the saintly Olympia! Your intended fiancée, as she made very clear to me. I know you married her. I saw it on the internet. It was in a Greek newspaper, and I hit Translate. You married her straight…straight—" her voice wobbled frac-

Xander, teeth gritting, ignored her, focussed only on Dan. "We can go and check out the school sometime, see whether you like it. I think you will. Anyway," he said, not wanting a debate starting that he could do without, "tomorrow, the hotel pool. Shall we go for it?"

"Yes, please!" said Dan.

"Great," said Xander.

He didn't bother to wait for any comment from Laurel and got to his feet. "Shall we watch the rest of that film from yesterday?" he asked Dan.

"Yes, please!" said Dan to that too, and stood up, shooting into the sitting room. As Xander followed him, Laurel's voice stayed him.

"Tonight, before you leave this evening, I need to talk to you." Her voice sounded stiff, and he turned.

"What about?" he asked curtly.

"I'll tell you when I talk to you."

He gave an irritated sigh, wanting whatever she had to say over and done with. He wasn't interested anyway. If she had any more objections to raise, he'd cut them down. "Let me fix the film for Dan first."

He did so, with a tinge of guilt that Dan would enjoy it more than he would. Laurel's dry warning from the night before replayed in his head. He was back moments later, leaving Dan cross-legged and fully engaged with all the multifarious cartoon characters again. He pulled the door half shut, wondering what Laurel wanted. Not caring overmuch.

Back in the kitchen she was starting to wash up at the sink.

"There *is* a dishwasher," he said caustically.

"Not worth it for so little," she replied. She drew a breath, abandoning the dishes. She seemed to be steeling herself.

"In fact—" he broke off, about to say that her figure was still a knockout.

No, no personal comments. He hauled his thoughts away—memories. Dangerous memories. Irrelevant memories. Totally irrelevant.

He turned his attention back to Dan. The only reason he was within six feet of Laurel at all.

"What would you like to do tomorrow?" he asked him. "Because," he said, "I've got an idea."

Dan looked immediately interested.

"The hotel I'm staying at has a pool," Xander told him. "Would you like to try it out?"

Dan's face lit up. "Can we?" He turned to his mother.

"Why not?" she said lightly. She was using that light voice, Xander had become aware, whenever she got dragged in to the conversation. But he could hear suppressed emotion in it. He didn't give a damn. Her feelings were of no relevance to him. He just wanted her compliance with his plans for his son. Nothing else.

At least she wasn't coming up with some asinine objection to going swimming. Unlike the fuss she made over his buying clothes and toys for his son. *Six missed birthdays*, he thought bitterly. All to make up for—

That she took from her own son—

She'd not just deprived him of his own son; she'd deprived his son of his father. Anger bit in him again. But that anger must never be visible to Dan.

"It will give you practice for the pool at your new school," he said.

He'd been glad too soon about her not objecting to his plans.

"*If* he goes there!" Laurel interjected sharply. "It's not decided—not in the least!"

* * *

Laurel had no idea whether Xander intended to stay for tea but put extra pasta on to boil anyway. She would make mac and cheese, one of Dan's favourites. Whether Xander liked it or not, she didn't give a damn. It hadn't featured in Greece seven years ago.

She hauled her mind away. She would not, must not, let memory go back there, however hard it was to stop it, now that Xander was a physical presence in her life again, stirring up wayward, treacherous memories. If she remembered anything about that time it must only be the way it ended. Thrown off his yacht, denounced as a thief. Tears stinging her eyes that she should never, never have shed, because he hadn't been worth a single, single tear...

Deliberately, she whipped up her old, familiar sense of outrage, fury. That was all Xander was worth. All he would ever be worth...

And whether he was her beloved son's father, or whether he still had the same power to draw her eye as he had from the very, very first, did not change that an iota. Not a single iota.

The mac and cheese was good. Simple but tasty and filling. Xander cleared his plate.

"I'm for seconds, what about you, Dan?" he asked.

"Yes please!" Dan said enthusiastically.

Xander helped them both from the covered serving dish, then, out of politeness in front of his son, no consideration of her personally, glancing at Laurel. "You?" he said.

She shook her head.

"Mum says too much pasta makes her fat," Dan commented.

"Your mother isn't fat," Xander said without thinking.

Laurel had remembered his tastes it seemed. Without volition, his glance went to her. She was perched on the edge of the other sofa, elbows resting neatly on her knees, sipping at her tea. She looked very...demure.

That hadn't been a word he'd associated with her during their time together—

Ardent...blazing...passionate...

No! He slammed his mind down hard. That was dangerous—far, far too dangerous. Deliberately he hardened his expression, hardened his thoughts. Whatever had happened seven years ago between them had ended. Now it was enough simply to bring himself to be even superficially civil to her, and that was only for his son's sake. His gaze dropped to Dan, and the hardness vanished. He set aside his empty coffee mug.

"Let's get all this upstairs," he said, starting to gather up the unused pieces and putting them back in the box with the instructions.

Between himself and Dan they got everything up to his bedroom. There, half-completed garage safely in a corner, Xander looked around.

"You were reading this morning," he said. "Will you read to me a bit? Show me what you can do?"

Dan nodded, fetching his early reading book. Xander settled himself down on the bed, inviting Dan to sit beside him, putting his arm around his shoulder. It felt good, very good, to have Dan snuggled against him. As he started to read out aloud, Xander felt an icy fury shaft through him.

I should have been able to hold him from the moment he was born! All through his babyhood, his infancy. She took that from me! Stole those precious years from me—

Bitterness filled him for the years he had lost with his own son.

Black anger against her.

nies all his young life, and he'd never complained or asked for what she could not afford. She busied herself putting on the kettle for a cup of tea, poured a diluted apple juice for Dan, then braved the fearsome-looking coffee machine that came with the house. A packet of expensive coffee pods also came with it. Xander would not welcome cheap instant coffee.

When she went back into the sitting room, drinks on a tray, Xander and Dan were hunkered down on the floor, getting stuck into the construction, their two dark heads close together. Laurel's throat felt tight suddenly.

The construction kit was huge—a garage with a car lift, ramp, several floors, plus outbuildings, and came with four cars. Xander was closely examining the instructions. Laurel reckoned it would not be built in one go. Dan was passing pieces to Xander, discussing with him what went where. Silently, she handed Dan his juice, which he gulped down thirstily, then went back to his construction kit. Xander didn't look up as she put his coffee down on a table near him. She took her cup of tea to the sofa, watching them. Those two dark heads together…

Father and son…

Her throat felt tight again.

Xander sat back. "I think this is a good place to stop," he said. "We've made good progress, but we can't build it all in one go. Let's save the next bit for tomorrow, what do you say?"

Dan straightened. "Okay," he agreed amenably. "It's good, isn't it?" he said admiringly at their joint handiwork.

"Very good," Xander confirmed. He reached for his coffee, still hot. Black and unsweetened. The way he always drank it.

The way I did when she was with me—

smaller items. But now Xander was lifting down the largest box, and disbelieving delight was on Dan's face, his eyes widening like saucers.

"It's huge!" he exclaimed. "It's like a giant, giant birthday present!"

Laurel watched Xander hunker down to Dan's level. "Let's call it that," he said. "I wasn't here for your birthday, so this is a bit late."

"Oh, wow!" said Dan breathlessly.

Xander limbered to his feet. "Okay, what else?"

Laurel stepped forward. "This is great for now," she said firmly. "Save something else for next time."

Another killing glance came her way. "I have six birthdays to catch up on," Xander said in a harsh voice.

She took a breath. "But not all at once," she said. She took Dan's hand. "Let's look at the books while we're here." She knew the latest in a fantasy series that Dan loved had just been published, but affordable second-hand copies had not yet started to circulate. A rush of extravagance filled her. She'd buy the full-price new one and be damned.

"This is on me," she said determinedly, as Dan spotted the book and seized it happily.

Xander said nothing, only threw her a caustic glance as she made her purchase before getting out his gold-plated credit card to pay for the massive construction kit.

As soon as they got got back to the cottage, Dan turned to her. "Can I open it now, Mum? Can I?" he asked with eager excitement.

"Of course," she said.

She left him and Xander to it, and went into the kitchen, hearing a cry of glee as Xander got the box open and the contents displayed. Her heart squeezed. How could she resent Dan having such a lavish present? They'd pinched pen-

* * *

Laurel was keeping her temper. It was hard, but she was doing it, stifling the anger flaring at how Xander was ignoring her existence. Dan must have no idea of the enmity between his parents, each of them wishing the other to hell.

She'd managed to get through lunch—Xander had taken them to a family-friendly up-market country pub a few miles away, where conversation had focussed on Dan, and Laurel had mostly left them to it—and now Xander had driven them to a small retail park beside the motorway, which included an out-of-town branch of a national department store he evidently considered an acceptable place to purchase clothes for his son. It was clear he wanted to lavish an entire new wardrobe on Dan, but Laurel was standing her ground.

"Just three things," she'd insisted. "As he grows he can get more then."

Xander threw her a killing look, but she didn't care. Dan was quite excited enough at getting a jacket sporting his favourite adventure film character, a new sweater with another, and a pair of sturdy trousers. To defy her, Xander threw in a baseball cap and a pair of colourful socks. Dan beamed happily, and Laurel sighed inwardly. She didn't want to be a killjoy, but she didn't want Dan becoming spoilt. Whatever his father might want. It was all too easy to get used to luxe living...

Something twisted inside her painfully. That's what Xander had accused her of, that hideous day when he'd condemned her for taking that bracelet...

With a start she realised Xander was already heading off with Dan, making his way across the floor towards the toy section. She hurried after them. They were looking along the shelves holding boxed construction kits. They were Dan's favourites, but her budget had only run to the

erately timed his arrival for lunchtime so that Dan could have the morning to getting used to being in the cottage. For himself he'd put in some time working from his hotel room and made use of the hotel's gym facilities. The hotel was a large old country house, five stars and well suited to this affluent corner of the Home Counties. It also had a spa, and a pool, along with the gym. An idea came to him, but he would save it for now.

"Me!" Dan was answering him about his readiness for lunch.

"Great!" Xander smiled. "Let's get going." His glance went to Laurel. She had not stood up and was carefully closing Dan's reading book. Her expression was just as closed. He didn't give a damn. "No need for you to come," he told her.

She got to her feet, chair scraping on the tiled floor. "No, I'll come," she said.

He shrugged indifferently, focussing instead on Dan. That was why he was here. The only reason.

He waited while Laurel fetched a jacket for Dan, and Xander frowned. It looked shabby and distinctly second hand. None of his clothes were anything other than cheap chain store brands.

"After we've eaten we'll go clothes shopping," he announced. "Get Dan some decent clothes."

His eyes flicked dismissively across to Laurel as well. She, too, could do with some decent clothes. What she was wearing, some cheaply made baggy top over shapeless trousers, did nothing for her.

He didn't bother to wait for Laurel's reply. Her opinions, her thoughts, her views were all totally irrelevant. So was she herself. Her sole purpose was to be there for Dan.

My son—

The precious words still rang in his head as they set off.

CHAPTER THREE

XANDER PULLED UP on the driveway. He was organising a car for Laurel to be delivered; she would need to be able to get around on her own. Go shopping, take Dan to school next term. As for himself, well, it was going to be complicated. He'd spend as much time as he could now with Dan. That was essential, his overriding priority, but he would have to put some time in back home, and Easter—Greek Easter—was looming too. He would need to be there for that; his father would be expecting him. And then, far more complicated yet, was going to be telling his father about Dan…

He shut his eyes a moment, only wanting to block that out. It would be difficult for his father to hear about Dan, but he had to know sometime. How he would react, Xander had no idea.

He snapped his eyes back open. First things first. Right now, he would see his son again. Spend time with him.

He swung out of the car, headed for the front door, letting himself in, striding down to the kitchen, where he could hear voices. As he walked in, Laurel's head whipped around. She was sitting at the kitchen table, focussing on Dan sitting beside her as he read to her from a children's early reading book. As he saw Xander, Dan broke off, leapt to his feet, face alight.

"Dad!" he exclaimed, and Xander's heart caught.

"Who's hungry for lunch?" he announced. He'd delib-

and bedside read. She'd kissed him goodnight, faithful Mr. Teds, battered but much loved, snuggled beside him.

I like this holiday, Mum had been his last, sleepy words. *With you and my dad.*

They had wrung her heart.

Now, as she lay in her own bed, sleep would not come. Only thoughts she should not have. Pointless thoughts. But they came all the same.

What if that damn bracelet had never gone missing? Xander wouldn't hate me then. Nor I him.

But that would be all though. Xander was a married man. Missing bracelet or no missing bracelet, Dan could only ever be his secret son or, at best, his unintended love child, or whatever the coy term was. Not that *love* had ever come into it. Seven years ago she and Xander had had a heady, passionate fling—that was all. Olympia's arrival at the end had simply confirmed that, with all her snide insinuations that she was lined up to be Xander's fiancée any time soon.

I never expected anything more than what we had, Xander and I, even before Olympia turned up and her bracelet went missing. I knew it and faced it.

She shifted restlessly, pulled the duvet over her head, and turned onto her side.

So, what did it matter if Xander still thought of her as a thief and she was still bitter at his accusation? All that was important was making herself cope with the bombshell that Xander's reappearance into her life had caused.

Take it day at a time. It's all you can do.

The mantra was still running through her head as she finally sank into a heavy, uneasy sleep.

Why the hell did I do that? Dragging back the past. Remembering a time I had to consign to oblivion.

He was flooded with anger at himself. Then he realised she was speaking.

"Dan's pretty tired tonight," she was saying. "So it's best if I put him to bed. But tomorrow—" she seemed to be making a visible effort, an obviously stiffly unwilling concession "—you can lend a hand if you want." She paused, then went on, her voice awkward. "Where…where are you staying? You didn't say."

For a moment, just a moment, Xander found himself wanting to say that there were three bedrooms to the cottage and he'd take the master…

But that was the last thing he wanted. Once Dan was in bed he had no use for Laurel's company. No wish or desire for it. Why would he?

"I'm booked into a nearby hotel," he said. "I'll head off now."

He lifted his hand to ruffle Dan's hair lightly. "See you tomorrow. Today's been good, hasn't it?"

Dan nodded, another yawn escaping. "Yes," he said.

Xander headed downstairs, giving Dan a last wave, not bothering to say anything more to Laurel. She was irrelevant to him, superfluous in her existence for any purpose but for the good of the son she'd kept from him for seven long years.

Anger bit at him again, familiar and acidic, eating into him as he let himself out of the house. Cold, unforgiving anger.

Laurel lay in bed. Though her window was open there was scarcely a sound in the night, only the occasional haunting hoot of an owl. Dan had gone out like a light after his bath

the TV. Dan had requested it, and Xander had gone along with it, even though it seemed to be about a lot of fantastical cartoon creatures having improbable adventures that went on and on.

"You can see the rest of it tomorrow," Laurel said from the doorway. "Besides, you know it inside out!"

"But Dad doesn't," said Dan.

"I'm sure he can wait till tomorrow too," she said dryly.

Xander turned his head to her.

"This is one of Dan's current favourites," she told him. "He can watch it endlessly."

Her expression was limpid. For a second, just a second, Xander almost…almost…smiled at the implication.

Then her attention went back to Dan. "Five minutes," she reminded him. "I'm going up to run your bath."

She disappeared.

"Five minutes," Xander confirmed. Dan had already smothered a yawn. It had been a long day for him.

Five minutes coincided with a break in the story line, and Dan stood up, Xander limbering to his feet as well, turning off the TV. They headed upstairs to the sound of water running in the bathroom. Laurel emerged.

"Well done." She smiled.

It was a smile for Dan, but Xander stilled. From the moment he'd hauled her into his car to confront her over his stolen son, her expression had only been stony-faced. Or tense and drawn. Or filled with a false brightness.

Now, something caught at him.

I'd forgotten how she smiled. How it lit her face. Took my breath away.

For a moment, just a moment, memory pierced him. Just as it had when he'd reminded her about eating pizza in Greece.

A weakness she had felt every time Xander had looked at her like that...

"Mum, can I have ham and pineapple?" Dan's piping voice brought her back.

"Of course!" she said brightly.

"And dough balls?" he added hopefully.

"If you share them with your dad," she said.

She said it deliberately—"dad." Forced herself to.

He's Dan's father. On one of those nights—those passion-filled, incredible nights that I can hardly believe now ever happened—Dan was conceived. And he's here now, with the both of us, and I have to—have to!—accept that even if I don't want to.

"Order complete." Xander shut down his tablet, put it aside. "Delivery in twenty minutes. They're coming over from the market town." He got to his feet, went over to the huge TV in the corner. "Okay, Dan, let's see if we can get this going." He hunkered down, and Dan went over to him.

Laurel went into the kitchen, set the table there. Pizza didn't warrant the dining room. Outside the dusk was gathering fast. She stared out into it. Heart full.

But with what she did not know. Could not tell.

Only that it was powerful and disturbing.

And that she could not deal with it. But must.

"Dan, bath-time in five, okay?" Laurel's voice came from the door to the kitchen beside the patio door.

Xander ignored it, but Dan did not.

"But the film isn't finished," he protested.

Tea finished, pizzas polished off, he was sitting on the floor, cross-legged, and Xander had sat down beside him to keep him company, leaning back against the sofa, long legs extended while they watched a downloaded kid's film on

mesan, had been in the lavish delivery. That was always a favourite for Dan. But as she went into the sitting room, where Xander was resting on one of the two sofas, tablet on his knee, Dan exclaimed, "Dad says we're having pizzas! Come and choose yours!"

A blade slid into Laurel. Dan had called Xander "Dad."

Xander's eyes lifted, going to hers. As if he could read her reaction.

She swallowed. "That's nice," she managed to say.

"So, what kind of pizza do you want?" Xander said to her, his voice indifferent.

"Oh, margherita is fine," she answered.

His dark eyes rested on her a moment. "Once, you liked fully loaded, as I recall," he said. "That night we ate at a pizzeria—"

Laurel paled. She remembered the evening. Remembered every evening she'd spent with Xander. Every blissful evening. That particular night they'd docked at a popular tourist spot, and she'd insisted on treating him to dinner for a change. She couldn't run to the kind of gourmet restaurants he chose when they ate out, but she could run to pizzas. So they had, eating them outdoors at the little pizzeria catering exclusively for tourists, their table covered with a paper cloth, the wine homegrown and served in earthenware carafes, the pizzas on wooden plates. Hers had definitely been fully loaded—mushrooms, anchovies, olives, extra mozzarella, peppers and chorizo.

"You had red onion and goats' cheese," she heard herself say.

"So I did," he acknowledged.

For a moment, just a fraction of a moment, their eyes held. For a moment, a fraction of a second, Laurel felt weakness wash through her…

precious son. Who would never, never be parted from him again…

His eyes went to the house. Through the kitchen windows he could see Laurel moving, unpacking the grocery delivery.

Emotion swept through him again, but it was not a kindly one…

Not kindly at all.

While Dan and Xander kicked a ball around, Laurel sorted the grocery delivery, stashing things away in the huge fridge and freezer and the ample cupboard space, making herself a cup of tea as she did so. Then she went upstairs to unpack. She'd bought a selection of Dan's favourite toys and some books, too, as well as clothes to wear. Her thoughts were troubled, how could they not be? She'd tacitly agreed to spend the Easter holidays here, but then what?

The sense of unease she'd felt earlier filled her again. Uncertainty, confusion—consternation.

Am I really prepared to do what Xander wants? Move here, make Dan's life here?

She just didn't know.

She drew a breath, closing the drawer she'd placed Dan's T-shirts in. No, she didn't know, and she couldn't, not yet.

I just have to take it day at a time. It's all I can do.

She went into the bedroom next to Dan's that she'd chosen for her own. It wasn't the master, that was on the other side of the landing, but she wanted to be close to Dan. For his sake. For hers. She unpacked her own things, trying to pretend this was just a hotel room, nothing more than that. She couldn't see the garden from her room. It looked towards the village green, but she heard Dan calling from downstairs.

"Mum, I'm hungry! What's for tea?"

She headed down. Fresh pasta, as well as sauces and par-

on him. Oh dear God, was it possible that she should still, *still*, after all he'd done to her, *still* react this way to him? Still feel it like a blow to her solar plexus, taking in his tall lean strength, that sable hair, those planed features she had known so, so well...

Those dark, gold-glinting eyes resting on her...

Desiring her...

He slid the door back and turned towards them. And in his eyes, lancing at her, was not desire, but the same look she'd last seen in them, seven long years ago as he'd thrown her off his yacht.

A cold to chill her bones.

Xander flicked his eyes away, dropped them down to Dan. "Let's take a look at the garden," he said. As they went out, Dan running eagerly, Xander said over his shoulder to Laurel, "I've had a grocery delivery. You can pack it away."

He didn't bother to wait for an answer, just headed after Dan, who was purposefully targeting the summer house.

"Can I have this as my den?" Dan asked hopefully.

"Of course," Xander said. He stepped up beside him on the little wooden veranda and went inside. It was prettily set up, with garden furniture, a tiny kitchenette and colourful bunting decorating the wooden walls. There was a chest in one corner, and opening it revealed a football, a croquet set and badminton rackets and shuttlecocks.

"Cool!" exclaimed Dan, seizing the football.

Moments later they were out on the level lawn, having a kick about. Emotion swept through Xander.

Playing football—with my son—

He felt his heart clench with it...

"Goal!" shouted Dan, as the ball shot past Xander. He gave a laugh, retrieved it, and kicked it back. His precious,

school that would obviously be such a cut above the one in London, both in terms of facilities—all those playing fields and swimming pool and goodness knew what else—and of educational standard. She wouldn't have to worry about him falling behind. And that wouldn't be the only thing she'd not have to worry about. No more bills to pay either, no more money worries...

Yes, putting herself into Xander's hands would have its advantages.

Except that it came with Xander himself. Who condemned her as a thief...

"Mum! Look! There, at the back of the garden!" Dan exclaimed excitedly, interrupting her troubled thoughts.

She went across to him to see what he was seeing. At the far end of the garden, beyond the lawn which was easily big enough to kick a ball around in, was a wooden summer house. It would make a great den...

Just like this house would make a great home...

She turned away. "Shall we go out into the garden and take a look?" she suggested, her voice bright. But it was an effort to make it so. Unease was lapping at her. Xander was making it clear he was changing his son's life, and hers would change with it.

How can I cope with any of it? Come to terms with it?

And it was not—she felt that sense of unease grip more tightly—the mere physical circumstances that Xander was changing that she was going to have to cope with.

It's Xander—Xander himself! After everything that happened, I've spent seven years putting behind me!

And now he was back. Back in her life...

She could sense a hollow form inside her as she walked downstairs with Dan. Xander was in the sitting room, opening the patio doors. She felt her breath catch, eyes fastening

* * *

Laurel looked around her. Fernwood Cottage was more of a house than a cottage, and it was very swish indeed. The rent—she'd seen online—was sky high. But Xander Xenakis could afford it. She explored it with Dan, starting with the beautifully furnished sitting room with its log burner in the fireplace, and patio doors to the garden beyond, glancing in at the formal dining room on the other side of the entrance hall, and then the kitchen, a sunny extension with large windows and a partial glass roof, top-of-the-range units, a breakfast bar and a separate kitchen table. It was all very, very nice, she had to concede. Consternation filled her. Of course it would be lovely to live here. How could it not be? It was more than twice the size of her little terrace house, and she could see that the garden stretched way back to the woods beyond. Xander had chosen well, though it galled her to admit it.

But I won't be rushed—I won't! He can't just bulldoze me. I won't let him!

She knew, bitterly, that if it came to a legal fight over Dan, Xander would be a terrifyingly powerful opponent. She couldn't risk it, she just couldn't. So surely this way, galling though it was, was preferable? Cooperating, though it choked her—but never just giving in across the board.

Determination filled her as she followed Dan upstairs. Xander was leaving them be, and she was grateful for that at least. Upstairs were three bedrooms, a master with an en suite, plus a very fancy bathroom for the other two bedrooms. Dan made a beeline for the one that looked out over the garden.

"Can I have this one, Mum?" he asked. She could hear eagerness in his voice and felt her heart constrict. It wouldn't take him long to want to live here all the time. Or go to the

He himself already had, with the estate agent when he'd signed the tenancy, just as he'd already looked around the excellently well-equipped fee-paying school Dan would—he fully intended—be going to next term, reserving a place with the headmaster. But these weeks of the Easter holiday before term started were going to be essential to help get Dan used to the new life he'd be living now. Getting him to accept it as his new life. Whether Laurel accepted it he couldn't care less. If she didn't, then he'd make a formal application for joint custody. Drag her into court if he had to, to get his rightful share of the son she'd deprived him of.

As he cast his eye over the neat, spacious, well-kept cottage in this clearly affluent village, a cynical expression fleeted in his eyes. What possible reason would Laurel have to object to living here, completely free, in all this affluence, rather than that cramped terrace house in that urban street in North London?

After all, she took to life with me on my yacht easily enough—enjoyed the luxury I could afford.

His expression darkened. Yes, so much so that she'd tried to take a pricey little souvenir of it back home with her once she realised it was all ending...

He opened the car door and Dan clambered down, looking about him. Laurel got out, and took Dan's hand.

"It looks nice," she said. Her voice was back to bright, and she headed to the front door with Dan. Xander followed with the house keys and her suitcases. When he'd got her to accept that this move was permanent he'd make arrangements to get all of his son's things here. That was all that would be necessary. The house came move-in ready, fully equipped. What Laurel did with her own house and its contents, he didn't care.

All he cared about was Dan.

He opened the front door and ushered them in.

milkshake and a bun Dan had visibly started to relax more, getting used to him, chatting to him, telling him what he'd been doing at school, telling his father more about himself under Xander's obvious interest in him. Xander had taken things slowly, just wanting Dan to feel at ease with him. He continued that now.

"Not far to go," he said cheerfully. "We come off at the next junction."

"It's coming up!" Dan pointed to the sign.

"Well spotted," said Xander, and moved into the slow lane.

Once off the motorway they took an A road, shortly driving though a prosperous-looking market town with an old church and a town square. On the far side they went past a school set in its own grounds.

"That's the school I told you about," said Xander. "You can go there if you want to," he went on, keeping his tone of voice casual.

He saw Dan's head turn to look in the rearview mirror.

"We'll have to see," said Laurel. Her voice was not bright but compressed.

For a second Xander's eyes met hers in the reflection. Clashed hostilely.

His eyes went back to the road. The village with the house he'd rented was a few miles further on, in open countryside. It was as prosperous-looking as the market town, with a village green, a well-kept pub, a smart village shop declaring itself to be a delicatessen and artisan bakery, all neatly manicured and well-heeled. He drew up at one of the several large cottages set a little way off from the green. Detached, made of brick and flint, it had a small white-fenced garden, a front porch and a separate garage to the side. He turned into the driveway in front of the garage and cut the engine.

"Here we are," he announced. "Let's take a look."

Because from now on, everything in Xander's life would be for his son's sake.

Xander's eyes glanced to the rearview mirror as he merged onto the motorway heading out of London. Laurel's head was turned towards Dan, pointing out the road signs to him, telling him where they were headed.

But where they were headed was crystal clear to Xander. Into the future. A future he would decide for his son from now on.

Not the woman who'd stolen him from him…

Who could go to hell and stay there for all he cared…

His eyes snapped back to the road. He might wish Laurel to hell, but he could not despatch her there. For Dan's sake.

She's his safety, his sense of security. I get that. Have to accept it.

Memory bit suddenly, of his own mother. She'd been, so he now could see, with his adult eyes, a foil to his father's strong personality. She'd been calm, placid even. Quiet, unobtrusive but always there.

Until she'd died—

He yanked his memory away. Those final few years of her life, ailing steadily, for all the desperate money his father had thrown at her medical care. And when she'd finally slipped beyond all further care, just as he'd finished university, he and his father had known a loss that had united them even more strongly in grief as in love.

His gaze went to Dan. The son he might have lost all his life, had it not been for that moment of sliding doors at the elevator in the department store…anger bit in him yet again.

Deliberately he calmed himself. Refocussed on the present. He'd spent time with Dan twice more during this last week of term, meeting up with his son and the woman who'd stolen him from him after school at a café nearby. Over a

her with any honesty, but to jump to the conclusion he'd already decided on. Guilty as charged. He was judge, jury and hangman, all in one. *Thief*, he had called her, and had stuck with it ever since.

Stealing that bracelet. Stealing his son.
That's what he thought of her.
And it was bitter, bitter gall.

"Okay, in you go." Xander helped Dan clamber up into the car the following Friday afternoon, parked at the kerb of the narrow two-up-two-down terraced house in the North London inner suburb where his son had had to live.

But no longer. I will insist on that!

Laurel could say that the new rental house was only for a holiday, but once Dan saw it he'd be bound to want to live there and go to the new school with the playing fields and swimming pool. He just had to get used to the idea, that was all. And today would start that off. Dan's school term had ended at lunchtime, and they were free to leave London. For good, Xander was determined.

Thrusting Laurel's suitcases into the capacious boot of the SUV he'd hired, he left her to get in while he settled Dan into the booster seat fitted into the rear. Moments later they were setting off. Satnav guided him out on to the nearby arterial road, heading west out of London.

"Are we on holiday now?" Dan asked from the back seat.

"Yes," Laurel answered. She was using that same bright voice as in the restaurant last weekend.

He didn't contradict her. If it helped Dan adjust to his new life, thinking it was only for a holiday, well, he would go along with that too.

For Dan's sake.

"Well, you'll be able to make up for that now." He smiled at Dan. "And when you come out to Greece—"

He heard Laurel inhale sharply. He ignored it.

"—you can swim in the sea too."

Dan looked at him. His expression was more uncertain than eager.

"But that's for later on," Xander said temporisingly. He must not overwhelm Dan with too many changes all at once. However much he wanted to transform his life instantly, he had to take it at his son's pace. Deliberately he changed the subject. "Now, where's our hamburgers? I'm starving! What about you!" he said lightly.

"Me too," agreed Dan, expression clearing.

Fortuitously, the waitress was heading towards them with their orders, and Dan's face brightened. As their burgers were deposited and they got stuck in, Xander felt emotion knife through him.

My first meal with my son—

Had it not been for that fateful glimpse of Laurel that day in the department store, if he hadn't seen the child at her side, hadn't had her checked out...

I would never have known he existed—my own son...

His eyes lanced to Laurel, and the expression in them was murderous.

But for Dan's sake, the sake of the son who had been taken from him, he had to veil all that he felt about the woman who had done so.

Laurel saw his expression, knew what caused it. Her own hardened in response. She could feel, like a tangible force, the anger radiating from him, the steely will to get his own way. Totally ruthless, implacable. She'd felt its ugly force seven years ago, refusing point-blank to believe her, credit

Dan looked puzzled. His eyes went to his mother.

"A holiday home," she qualified. "Your father—" she seemed to hesitate, as if the word choked her, Xander thought with grim anger "—has arranged a holiday for us," she said brightly. "Out in the countryside. We'll be staying in a cottage with a big garden and woods behind it. I looked at it online—it looks good!"

"Holiday?" Xander's growl was a challenge.

She looked directly at him. "For the school Easter holidays, yes," she said.

"I thought I'd made it clear to you that this was to be permanent." Xander's voice was hard.

Laurel looked back at Dan. "If we find we like it, we might decide to live there," she said brightly again.

Dan looked uncertain, and she went on reassuringly. "Only if you want to, Dan. We'll always have our own little house, Grandad's house, if you like that better."

Xander's expression tightened. His son would never again live in that cramped terraced house in North London. "You can go to a new school too," he said, changing tack. "Much nicer than the one you're at now. It's got playing fields. Great for football. Do you like football?" he asked.

Dan nodded.

"It's got a swimming pool too," Xander said. "Do you like swimming?"

Dan looked uncertain again.

Laurel spoke up. "Dan hasn't had much chance to do a lot of swimming. Our local pool is two bus rides away."

Xander felt anger in his throat. That his son should have been deprived of what would have been his birthright, swimming in the Aegean on visits to the beach in the pristine pool he'd enjoyed as a child at the spacious home he himself had grown up in on the well-heeled outskirts of Athens.

there, ready to take their order. She was young, and Laurel saw her unashamedly gaze at Xander. She knew why. It was a familiar, so familiar a reaction to him. It had been her own, after all…once upon a time. A long, long time ago.

A time that could never return. Had gone forever.

Heaviness pressed on her. Then she blinked. That was then, this was now, and it was the now—the difficult, impossible now—that she was dealing with, had to deal with. She listened while Xander gave his and Dan's order, and then, because she was clearly still being totally ignored by him, she added her own. A hamburger too. Then she took over sorting her drink and Dan's. A jug of tap water and a bottle of elderflower juice for her and apple juice for Dan. What Xander wanted to drink, she didn't give a damn. He ordered a bottled beer.

The waitress, casting one final languishing look at Xander, disappeared. With all her heart, Laurel wished she and Dan could too. But that was impossible. Heaviness pressed on her again.

Xander drew a breath. He was keeping his emotions on a leash so tight he could feel it cutting into his flesh. But it was essential. He could not let them loose. He had to play this very, very carefully. Very gently. His glance went to Dan.

My son—

Emotion stabbed, and he made himself control it. His glance slid sideways to the woman who had kept his son from him for six years, all his young life. Emotion stabbed again. A killing, deadly emotion. He made himself control that too. Not for her sake—for his son's.

He looked across at Dan again, his expression lightening deliberately. "So, what do you think about your new home?" he said.

Her eyes dragged from Xander—dragged from the past, the poisoned past, to the present, the present that Xander was poisoning for her yet again—and went to Dan.

She saw it happen, saw him return his father's smile, saw Xander take his son's outstretched hand and shake it solemnly. Then he let it drop, took up a spare menu, and opened it up.

"Okay," he announced, "what are we having for lunch?"

"A hamburger, please," said Dan. Laurel could see him visibly relaxing. Xander seemed to be too, but Laurel knew it was only for Dan, and it wasn't for real. At her he had not even glanced.

"Sounds good," said Xander to his son.

Dan looked at him. "Do they have hamburgers in Greece?" he asked.

For a fraction of a second Xander's eyes went to her—so swiftly it might not have happened. But his answer was only for his son. "Yes, you can get hamburgers in Greece," he said. He paused a moment. "You know, that's where I come from."

Dan nodded. "Mum said."

"What else did your mother say?" Xander asked. It sounded innocuous; Laurel knew it wasn't.

"She said it's why you haven't been to see me."

"It's one of the reasons, yes," Xander said. His voice was tight. The glance he threw—again, so swiftly it might not have happened—at Laurel was murderous.

Then he looked straight at Dan again. His voice lightened. "But I'm here now, Dan. Here for you. Part of your life forever."

For a second, a fraction of a second, that killing glance came her way again, as if daring her to contest his assertion. She said nothing. Then, to her relief, the waitress was

pushing open the door and striding in, seeing them immediately, heading to their table. He was casually dressed, with a sweater under a jacket, but she could see tension radiating from him. It made her feel slightly, infinitesimally slightly, less wound up herself, to see him as tense as she was.

He paused, closing his hands over the back of the chair opposite the banquette. He wasn't looking at her. His eyes were only for Dan.

"Hello, Dan," he said.

His voice was husked. Laurel could hear emotion in it—but emotion as tightly suppressed as if he were crushing it with his weight.

Dan was looking at him. "Hello," he said. There was wariness in his voice. Laurel could hear it, understand its presence. But there was more as well. Anticipation—

Something flickered in Xander's face, Laurel could see, and then he was pulling back the chair, seating himself in it. He held out his hand towards Dan. "It's nice to meet you, Dan," he said.

For a moment Dan hesitated, then he stretched his own hand out. "How do you do?" he said politely. Laurel had been keen on teaching him politeness.

Xander's expression changed. The visible tension in his face—darkening his features, drawing his brows together, tightening his jaw—suddenly vanished. A smile flashed across his face, and out of nowhere a knife went through Laurel. A memory knife—

He used to smile at me like that! A flashing smile, lighting his face, his eyes—

She heard him speak, and his voice now went with the smile.

"All the very better for meeting you," he said to Dan. Said to his son.

"Oh, yes," Laurel answered, hearing a dry note in her voice. Xander would come, all right, like an avenging dark angel, to wreak his vengeance.

But only on her. For daring to deprive him of his son. For stealing him from him…

Just seeing Xander again—after seven years and their bitter, angry parting—had been an ordeal, emotions crashing all over the place, but to face him in his fury over keeping Dan from him…that had been hideous.

And now Xander was going to meet his son. The son he'd never known he had…

Dread filled her, but for Dan's sake she had to hide it. She felt her heart thudding heavily inside her, like a hammer in her chest, her breath tight in her lungs. Several more diners came in, families mostly and some couples. She felt her tension rack higher. The sense of dread mounted. Since Dan was born she'd been safe from Xander. But now—

Oh, God, how am I going to cope with this? Xander, forcing his way back into my life—into Dan's life—invading it, taking it over.

And there was nothing she could do to stop it. She knew that. With his wealth Xander could hire the best lawyers, demand access, even—fear knifed in her—fight her for custody. He would be ruthless. She had proof of that, bitter proof, from seven years ago.

Now that he knew of Dan's existence, all she could do was try and protect Dan, protect herself, as best she could, not to let Xander walk all over her.

I have to fight my corner, not just roll over and give in. I have to think of Dan—only of Dan! What's best for him—only that.

It was all she could cling to. Her heart clenched, and then her gaze fixed on the entrance. Suddenly Xander was there,

CHAPTER TWO

LAUREL GOT OFF the bus with Dan. Her nerves were sky high, how could they not be? But she was doing her best to be casual and cheerful. Dan wasn't relaxed either. When she'd sat him down after that horrendous day, when the life she had so painstakingly built for herself and her beloved son had catastrophically imploded with Xander's confrontation, and told Dan what she'd had to tell him, what she now had no choice but to tell him, picking her words with excruciating care—still reeling from Xander's discovery of Dan's existence, still desperately trying to come to terms with it, with all the implications he was demanding of her—told him that his dad was in England and wanted to meet him, Dan's face had shown such mixed reactions. Confusion, wariness...and excitement. It had been the last that had pierced her heart like a sword.

It pierced her still as she felt his hand tighten in hers as they walked into the restaurant, her heart thudding with nerves. It was a popular family-friendly chain and was familiar to Dan, which was why she'd chosen it now. It was busy on a Saturday lunchtime, but Laurel had reserved a table online, and the waitress showed them to it, depositing menus. She sat next to Dan on the banquette facing the entrance.

"Will he come, Mum?" Dan asked. He sounded anxious.

her. "I expect you would prefer something a little more... straightforward. Diamonds are always so...appropriate."

Her carefully pronounced English hadn't needed a translation: "Appropriate as a pay-off for a female like you when her time is up. As yours is—"

Laurel had retaliated. How could she not?

"Oh, I don't know. I doubt I'd say no to a ruby-and-diamond bracelet like yours!" she'd said lightly. Unthinkingly...

It had been the following day, as they'd entered the Saronic Gulf sheltering Athens from the open Aegean, that Olympia, a troubled expression in her face, had announced at lunch that the bracelet had gone missing. A search had ensued, crew interrogated, Olympia's expression increasingly troubled. Xander's increasingly black.

Laurel had kept out of it. It was nothing to do with her.

Until she'd walked into the state room, and seen her suitcase on their bed, Xander about to lift the lid.

"What on earth are you doing?" Laurel's voice had been sharp.

Xander had looked at her. Said nothing. But there was something in his face that sent a chill through her. Which showed a man she did not know.

"Do you have any objection to my looking?" he'd asked. His voice had been tight.

Her voice was even sharper. "Yes, of course I do! How could you even think to think of looking?"

He hadn't answered, only flipped open the lid. There wasn't a great deal inside, just clothes Laurel didn't deem worthy of a luxury yacht, a pair of walking shoes for rough terrain, not needed on voyage, a couple of books, some toiletries.

And, carefully layered into a folded T-shirt, a ruby-and-diamond bracelet...

However much of a thief you are—

Memory, hideous and ugly, drowned through her.

Xander had been frowning. "It's a nuisance, but I've agreed to pick up a passenger, a...friend...of the family, when we dock at the next island, and drop her off at Piraeus."

Laurel hadn't minded, not at first. But Olympia had been cool and condescending towards her. Towards Xander, in contrast, she was familiar—and possessive.

Xander was moody, tight-faced. Polite towards Olympia, but nothing more. To Laurel herself he was noticeably withdrawn, clearly not emphasising their relationship to the other woman, obvious though it was. But Olympia had been intent on making things clear to her. Very clear. At dinner that night, she'd drawn attention to the ruby-and-diamond bracelet around her wrist.

"I'm wearing your present to me, Xander." She'd held up her forearm. She'd turned to Laurel. "Xander gave it to me for my last birthday." She'd glanced back at Xander, smiling still. "I do so love rubies. Perfect for an engagement ring too!" she'd trailed. Her expression was transparent, her purpose obvious – to imply that just such a ring would be Xander's next offering to her..

Would it? Is that what Olympia was to him? Laurel's eyes had gone to Xander. His face had frozen, his mouth compressed. He'd said nothing, giving her no clue either way. Olympia's limpid gaze had switched to her now, and Laurel felt she must say something...anything. Inside her, a hollow was forming.

"Rubies certainly suit your colouring," she'd said politely, as innocuously as possible.

"Thank you." Olympia had bestowed a gracious smile on

from everything he knows! And I can't—won't!—drop a bombshell into his life by you suddenly appearing in it! For God's sake, I need time—"

There was desperation in her voice, and she gazed at Xander, stricken, total tumult inside her as if a bomb had just gone off. It was impossible, just impossible, to believe that this was happening. Her heart was pounding, lungs constricted, shock ravening through her. Shock, dismay…and emotions beyond those. Emotions she could not bear to acknowledge…

Something changed in his face, and he gave a curt nod. "Very well. For now you can tell him this move is just a holiday, let him get used to it first. As for my appearance in his life—" his voice seemed to catch for a second, then he resumed "—I leave you to tell him about me. You can bring him to meet me when you have told him, and we will take it from there."

She saw him reach inside his jacket pocket and withdraw a card, handing it to her. "My contact details," he told her. "Text me when you have told him about me, and let me know an appropriate place for me to meet him."

She took it with nerveless fingers, faintness—disbelief, dismay—still drumming through her.

"And one last thing." Through the pounding of her heart she heard him speak again. "Do not attempt to cut and run." His night-dark eyes bored into hers. "You stole my son from me once. You will never—" his mouth twisted, and the barely suppressed rage in his voice was audible "—do so again. However much of a thief you are."

Abruptly, he tapped on the glass divide, and a moment later she heard the click of her door unlocking. She stumbled out, and the car moved off into the traffic. For one endless second she could only stare blindly after it. Then she started to shake uncontrollably. His words were knifing in her brain.

"From now on, I will be in his life. To be the father to him that you have denied him."

"No! I don't want you anywhere near him!" she burst out. "Stay away from him! Just stay away!" Panic and desperation fuelled her outburst.

He ignored it completely.

"He will have my name, and—"

"He's got a name! My name, my father's name!"

"He is my son, he will have my name. And," he went on implacably, "I shall provide for him the life that should be his. As my son."

For a moment Laurel saw in his eyes such black fury that she would have reeled from it had she not already been in pieces. Then they veiled again. His voice changed. Still cold but more measured. Brisk and businesslike.

"Accordingly, for the time being, I have rented a house for you, out of London, far more suitable for him than where he lives now. A prosperous village in Buckinghamshire, with excellent schooling, and easy access to Heathrow for me. You will move there immediately and—"

"No!" Laurel's voice broke from her. "No, of course I won't! I'm not uprooting him like that! How can you even think it?"

"I think it," he bit back coldly, "because I wish it. He will live in far more affluence than you can afford! And why—" his mouth thinned, his eyes spearing her chillingly "—should you object? Just what is so preferable about your lives now to what I can provide?"

"I can't... I can't..." Laurel fumbled, emotions reeling, overwhelmed by what he was saying, overwhelmed just by what was happening to her, out of the blue, without warning, without any chance to arm herself...

She clenched her hands. "I can't just wrench him away

the door handle. Locked, it did not yield. Then turned her fire back on him. "This is assault and kidnap! I'll see you in jail for it!"

"And I," said Xander, his voice as cold and hard as his eyes, "will see you in court." He paused. A deadly pause. "For the theft of my son."

Laurel paled, faintness drumming through her. Her hand fell nervelessly from the door handle.

"My son—"

She heard Xander say the words again. Heard them as terror and dismay iced through her. She tried to speak, but nothing came. Xander was talking again. Each word a bullet, a knife thrust, skewering her. Drawing blood.

"For seven years I've known you to be a thief, but this—" He broke off.

Anger boiled up in her. Familiar anger. "I am not a thief!"

His hand slashed upwards in the air. "Enough! We are not here to rehash the past. It is the future that concerns me. The future of my son."

She stared at him. Emotion was pounding in her, panic, but she had to keep it together. He was speaking again, but she could barely hear it through the faintness drumming through her.

"Do not attempt to deny he is my son. To lie to me! He has been fully investigated! The date of his birth fits, and his likeness to me is indisputable. If necessary I will insist on DNA testing to prove my paternity! I will also," his voice hardened, "use to the law to establish my paternal rights, if you attempt to block me. Do not think that I will not—"

She couldn't speak, couldn't answer. He was ploughing on, dictating to her, implacability in his voice, cold dark fire in his eyes.

It was a resolve he put into practice the very next morning from his office, making the necessary call before he could change his mind. Seeking final closure on a past he could only regret.

But when, the following week, the investigative agency got back to him, closure was the very, very last thing possible. And his rage, his fury, knew no bounds.

Laurel walked away from the school gate, having waved Dan in. It was spattering with rain, and her head was bowed as she walked along the busy street. Then, abruptly, her progress was impeded. A parked car door suddenly opened right in front of her, blocking her. As she made to swerve, a hand descended heavily on her shoulder from the back. A figure leant out of the car towards her. A voice spoke.

Deep. Accented.

And familiar.

"Get in—"

Xander shifted back to his side of the wide rear seat of the car as his driver impelled her inside. She was staring at him, horror on her face. His driver closed the door on her, got back into his seat, separated from them by a glass screen.

"We," Xander said to her, "will talk."

He was being calm, very calm. It was necessary to be so. In the two weeks since receiving the report—comprehensive, conclusive, the photos alone convincing him, from the investigative agency—he had been busy. Extremely busy. And now he was prepared.

"We can talk here and now," he continued, and his gaze lasered hers, dark and cold, "or we can do it at my lawyer's office. Which do you choose?"

Her face contorted. "Go to hell!" She levered urgently at

Until it all crashed and burned.

He shifted restlessly, champagne glass in hand as he circulated amongst his father's guests. Into his mind's eye that fleeting glimpse of Laurel in London the previous month intruded again, unwelcomingly—even if it had proved, he reminded himself acerbically, with that little boy half hidden at her side, that she'd moved on in her life after that long-ago summer that had ended so badly. Just as he himself had, marrying Olympia as he had. Yet for as much as he told himself that, something still needled him, all the same, though he didn't want it to. He hadn't been able to see the boy's face, only taken in an impression of dark hair. How old had he been? Younger than seven, obviously, but how much younger? Of course there was no chance, not the slightest, remotest chance that—

No, he didn't even want to put that impossible surmise into words. Because impossible was what it was. Of course it was.

She'd have told me like a shot! Of course she would! Impossible to think of her not doing so!

After all, his expression darkened, his last experience of her had shown him just how much she'd craved what his wealth could provide. Had she found herself pregnant it would have been a meal ticket for life—she'd have rushed to tell him...

So the fact that she hadn't was proof itself. Wasn't it?

Yet it had been unsettling to have seen her, and with that child. Impatiently he silenced it. If he really could be bothered he could always have it checked out—just to dispose of it. He'd get concrete proof that that little boy was nothing, nothing whatsoever to do with him, with a father alive and well. Then be done with it. Put her out of his life again. For good this time. Then he could move on with his life, just as he was trying to do now he was finally divorced.

he could do without his father pressing him now to find yet another bride. His father had taken his divorce hard. Harder even than Xander had. He'd known his marriage had failed even before his wife had left him.

A wave of weariness washed over him. He'd come over from his own flat in Athens to his father's house on the city's outskirts, the house he'd grown up in, which held all the happy memories of his own childhood—happy until the death of his mother while he was finishing university, which had so devastated his father. It had been then, Xander thought, that his father had become so determined, so set—obsessed even—with starting the next generation of the family. Getting his son married, having children. The pressure on Xander had been constant, and relentless. When his father had finally decided that Olympia, the daughter of old friends of his, whom Xander's mother had always been fond of, would prove the ideal wife, she did, indeed, seem to tick all the boxes. They moved in the same circles, she was intelligent enough, attractive enough, compatible enough. Increasingly, it became assumed, including by Olympia—and finally himself—that they would eventually marry. It would be an extremely suitable match...with no reason not to make it, and many to do so.

But Xander had wanted one last summer of bachelor pleasure. He'd commandeered the Xenakis yacht, and taken off, cruising the Aegean, visiting friends, joining island house parties, generally relaxing and holidaying.

He'd felt himself still free. Free to take advantage, when the yacht needed to refuel at one of the tourist islands, of catching sight of that fantastic-looking blonde and decide she would be the perfect way to enjoy the last of his bachelor days. Sail off with her for the last of the summer.

It had been good—very good. Very good indeed. The days, the nights had flown past. The weeks too...

She made no secret of it, nor did he. With carefully apparent casualness she plotted herself in, why she was on her own like this, why she was in Greece at all. At some point names were exchanged—his meant nothing to her, other than that it sounded good to her—and then, at just the right moment, because the guy was obviously a player, and knew just how and when to make the next move, she'd agreed to meet him for dinner that evening.

Because why not? It was only dinner, only a meal, and if she wanted she was quite, quite free to head back to the apartment solo, wait her for pals to emerge from their post-clubbing hangovers and get back. On the other hand—

On the other hand she'd spent a celibate third year at uni, focussing on her looming finals. She and her previous boyfriend from second year had gone their separate ways, having enjoyed their undemanding relationship, which had come to a natural end. Right now, therefore, in this gap time between the end of uni and the start of her responsible adult life, she could, after all, do as she pleased. And if it pleased her to be romanced under the Aegean skies by a guy that looked like he'd walked out of a romance novel, well, why shouldn't she? She was young, free, and over twenty one.

It would make, one day, a wonderful memory to look back on...

Except that "wonderful" had been the last, last word to attach to her memories of Alexandros Xenakis. The very last—

Xander's father was hosting a party. His son knew why. Trying to get him to socialise more. Start dating again. But in London he'd found himself turning down poor Fabia, despite her obvious disappointment. Was it just too soon after his divorce, or had that damned glimpse of Laurel triggered memories he could do without? Just as, he sighed inwardly,

It wasn't something she was unused to, and her usual response was to shut it down as gracefully or ruthlessly, as occasion warranted.

But this time around—

"The Battle of Navarino in 1827," she said. "It's one of the few things I actually knew about, because it comes into British history as well, given we sent ships out here, with the French and Russians, to aid the Greeks fighting for their independence. Overall though—" she made a moue "—I'm very ignorant about Greek history. The ancient stuff, classical Greece, we learnt something of at school, but nothing about modern Greece really. Hence the book."

His mouth quirked. It was a well-shaped mouth, a beautiful mouth, and when it quirked like that with a smile, she could feel her stomach hollow...

"You are very diligent," he complimented. "Most tourists are uninterested." He did not say it condemningly, only casually.

"Well, I'm a historian, so all history interests me," Laurel replied.

His eyebrows rose. They were dark and arched, and it was ridiculous that eyebrows could quicken heart rates, but in this case...

"A historian? Aren't they all old men with beards?" he queried, the quirk at his beautiful mouth coming again.

"Well, a good few of the history profs at my uni were, I admit," she said. Humour was in her own eyes, as well as an appreciation of what was happening that was impossible for her to disguise. Not that she wanted to.

After all, there was being chatted up, and there was being chatted up. And right now it was definitely the latter. Very, very definitely.

They went on chatting—and chatting up. Mutually now.

over had taken off on the ferry to a neighbouring island and were going to stay there overnight clubbing. That had no appeal to Laurel, so she'd stayed put, making a quiet day of it here on this far more peaceful if still touristy island. They were all staying in a couple of cheap apartments, vegging on the beach or by the pool, frequenting the bars and eating out at the plentiful choice of tavernas the holiday spot afforded.

"'A Brief History of Greece.' Forgive me, but 'brief' is an impossible word to use about Greek history! It stretches four thousand years and more!"

She looked up quickly, turning her head. He'd spoken to her, the incredible looking guy whose long legs were stretched out, his eyes—dark, long-lashed and definitely, definitely looking her over, liking what he was seeing—glinting humorously.

He'd spoken to her in English, which was not surprising, given that her book was in English. Her blond colouring was also pretty good evidence she was from northern Europe too.

"It's just modern Greece," she answered, pointing to the subtitle. "The fall of Byzantium to the present day."

"That," he said with mock seriousness, "is more allowable."

His coffee arrived, the traditional small, dark and quite undrinkable brew that Laurel knew was a legacy of the long centuries of Ottoman occupation which had dominated Greece from the fall of Byzantium until freedom had finally been achieved in the nineteenth century.

"So, where have you reached?" he went on, stirring his coffee, his eyes still with that glint in them that Laurel knew, from the quickening of her pulse, had now nothing to do with the subject of her book, and everything to do with the fact that she was, quite obviously, being chatted up.

field. A barren field. There was nothing for crows to feed on here. So they could take themselves off—

Except that they refused to go. Kept diving down to that barren field. Stabbing with their sharp black beaks.

Stabbing for no reason.

I got rid of her seven years ago. I had to. So there's nothing left to stab.

Nothing—

Yet they kept stabbing.

Laurel was trying to focus on her work, but failing. Preparing a briefing note on the causes of the First World War for her students was not enthralling her. Her thoughts were continually distracted. Outside, in the tiny garden, early spring sunshine was streaming. Bright, but nowhere near as bright as the sunshine she was remembering. The hot golden sunshine of that long-ago summer in Greece...

So hot she'd sought the shade of a café table with a parasol, glancing up as someone came by. Glanced up and caught her breath instantly...

Tall, dark and with looks to make her gulp silently as he'd stopped by her table set out on the edge of the stony beach just beyond the harbour. She was taking a coffee, reading her book on Greek history, about which she knew very little despite her newly awarded, shiny bright university degree in history, and he'd sat himself down at a nearby table, ordering a coffee from the instantly there waitress, his voice deep and delicious. She felt her heart rate quicken. She wanted to keep looking sideways at him, but that would have been too obvious, so she focussed instead on the page she was reading. Very, very aware of his presence nearby.

She was on her own today. The group of uni friends who'd all decamped to Greece the moment graduation was

were being pressed forward into the lift. Faintness drummed in shock and panic as they soared upwards.

He didn't see...he didn't see...he didn't see...

She prayed with all her strength that it was so. That Alexandros Xenakis—who had swept her away to paradise, in that blissful long-ago summertime, then thrown her from him—had not seen, standing at her side, the son she'd borne him...

Xander kept walking towards the doors leading out on to the street, but shock was ricocheting through him. It had been Laurel. Unmistakable. Late twenties now, just as he was now into his thirties. He felt something stab inside him, but he ignored it. So it was her, so what? Seven years ago he'd watched her, his expression grim, head across the quayside at Piraeus, never to see her again until this moment now. Never wanting to.

He pushed through to the street, throwing himself into a hovering taxi. But as he sat back, shutting his eyes, he saw her standing beside the lift, instantly recognisable across the years. But there was something else he saw now, imprinted on his retinas. Something his conscious mind hadn't taken in. A small boy had been at her side holding her hand.

An emotion he could not recognise went through him. His own marriage had been childless, but the woman he'd thrown out of his life had not been...

He fought back against whatever emotion it was that he'd just felt.

So, she's got a child, a son. Why shouldn't she? It's been seven years since she knew me, she's bound to be involved with someone else by now. She could be married, damn it! Even divorced, like me. It's nothing to me! Nothing!

The thoughts circled like black crows over a ploughed

He let his hand glide down the length of her golden hair, like a fall of silk beneath his touch. He felt her quiver, her neck arch slightly at the sensation.

"So, so beautiful—" The husk was more pronounced.

He turned her towards him. Her eyes were wide, long-lashed, her tender lips parted. All evening he'd waited for this moment, steered her lightly, skilfully...seductively... towards it, from sipping champagne as they stood on the deck, with her gazing around her in wonder at being aboard a private yacht, through the gourmet dinner prepared by his on-board chef, the vintage wines his steward served, low music playing from hidden speakers, soft lights strung across on high to cocoon them on the deck...all the way through to this moment now, when, all alone with her, crew despatched to their own quarters, he was finally free to do what he had been wanting to do all evening...

Desire creamed in him, and for one moment longer he held it under leash, savouring this moment. Then, as he felt her hands lift to his upper arms, her head fall back slightly as his height loomed over her slender figure, he lowered his mouth to hers. To taste, to take, to explore...and to indulge.

Indulge in full.

In all of her.

For all the night—for all the carefree, pleasure-filled days that followed, and the sensual, desire-sated nights that came, as they drifted from island to island, cocooned in a timeless idyll.

Until the end came. The ugly, sordid end.

And he had thrown her from him, tainted and toxic.

Never to set eyes on her again until this moment.

Laurel shrank back instinctively, pulling Dan against her, shielding him as best she could from view, then both of them

to pay a worry, she would never, never regret her son's existence. He was the light of her life, her joy, her heart's love, and she would do anything for him—

Anything! She squeezed his hand more tightly as they approached the bank of lifts. There were a good few other shoppers waiting, and as the arriving lift opened its doors Laurel drew Dan aside to let the lift empty first.

And as it did, she felt the blood drain from her.

Xander strode forward impatiently. He'd left Fabia, with whom he'd just had a lengthy lunch at the store's renowned rooftop restaurant, and now he was heading back to his hotel to fit in some work and a session in the gym. He'd known Fabia a while, and she was more than keen to help him move on now that his marriage was over. The marriage that had been such a failure—

He pulled his mind away. No point thinking about what was past. Whether it was the wife he'd failed, the children they'd never been able to conceive despite endless medical tests on both of them, or—

He pulled his mind away again, more sharply now. There was a past that was forbidden for him to think about, that he'd ruthlessly banned.

But as he headed out of the elevator that forbidden past rose up like a snake, to bite him in the face…

A full moon was riding over the open sea. The yacht was at anchor, the swell imperceptible in this sheltered bay. They were standing by the deck rail, gazing out over the moonlit water.

"This is so, so beautiful," she sighed.

He gave a low laugh, the husk in it audible to himself.

"But not as beautiful as you—"

nor—and she gave thanks for this every, every day—he knew that she had walked away pregnant.

Her expression softened, glancing down at Dan as they headed towards the lifts. Though he had his father's dark hair and eyes, there was still something of her own father about him as well, including his name, Daniel Peters, and she was glad. Her father had made a home for them in the little terraced house where she'd grown up in North London, his grandson a comfort to him after the death of his wife some years earlier, until his own ill health, a legacy of a lifetime in the building trade, had taken him too soon as well, when Dan was only three. Since then, without her father's modest earnings, money had been punishingly tight. Thankfully, she had a roof over their heads, but even with the help of some state benefit as a single mother, and what income as she could make from her online tutoring working for an agency, there was council tax, and utility bills and all the other costs of living which had to be found. With Dan now at school she at least had the school day to work in as well as the evenings when Dan was abed, which definitely helped, though it brought new concerns as well. She was increasingly worried that he was not thriving at his overcrowded, under-resourced school with large classes, high teacher turnover, children from problem families or newcomers without English as a first language. She did her best with extra home-schooling, but she feared he was falling behind. She knew the value of education—it had got her to university. It was only ironic, she was well aware, that the graduate career she'd been hoping to have, had proved impossible with Dan on the way.

But a career can wait! For now, it is Dan, and Dan alone, who is important! These precious years with him—

Even if endless budgeting was a necessity and every bill

CHAPTER ONE

"This way, stick close," Laurel said, holding on to her son's hand. He was only six, and the department store—one of London's poshest—was crowded. They were heading to the lavish toy department to round off a day spent at the Natural History Museum to see the dinosaurs, a treat for Dan on his school's half-term break this chilly week in February, before taking the Tube back home. Her tight finances would only stretch to a small purchase from the toy department to mark the occasion, and Laurel's expression flickered as they walked past the ground-floor gift counters groaning with expensive goodies, from handbags costing thousands to delicate scarves costing hundreds. Were there really people who could snap such things up without thinking? It was a rhetorical question. She knew there were.

One of them was her son's father.

But she wouldn't think about him. She never did. He'd thrown her out of his life seven years ago, brutally and ruthlessly, ordering her off his private yacht, discarding her on the quayside at Piraeus, the port of Athens, his denunciation of her ringing in her ears. She'd marched off, head held defiantly high, burning inside her at his accusations. Refusing to let her vision blur with tears…

Pointless, useless tears. Angry tears. Worse than angry.

There had been only one saving grace. That neither she

To all fathers and sons—especially JHW and WSW.

HER ENEMY'S SECRET SON

JULIA JAMES

MILLS & BOON

All rights reserved including the right of reproduction in whole or in part in any form. This edition is published by arrangement with Harlequin Enterprises ULC.

This is a work of fiction. Names, characters, places, locations and incidents are purely fictional and bear no relationship to any real life individuals, living or dead, or to any actual places, business establishments, locations, events or incidents. Any resemblance is entirely coincidental.

Without limiting the exclusive rights of any author, contributor or the publisher of this publication, any unauthorised use of this publication to train generative artificial intelligence (AI) technologies is expressly prohibited. HarperCollins also exercise their rights under Article 4(3) of the Digital Single Market Directive 2019/790 and expressly reserve this publication from the text and data mining exception.

® and TM are trademarks owned and used by the trademark owner and/or its licensee. Trademarks marked with ® are registered with the United Kingdom Patent Office and/or the Office for Harmonisation in the Internal Market and in other countries.

First published in Great Britain 2026
by Mills & Boon, an imprint of HarperCollins*Publishers* Ltd,
1 London Bridge Street, London, SE1 9GF

www.harpercollins.co.uk

HarperCollins*Publishers*, Macken House, 39/40 Mayor Street Upper, Dublin 1, D01 C9W8, Ireland

Claimed by the Enemy © 2026 Harlequin Enterprises ULC

Her Enemy's Secret Son © 2026 Julia James

To Have & To Hate © 2026 Caitlin Crews

ISBN: 978-0-263-41824-8

04/26

Printed and Bound in the UK using 100% Renewable Electricity
at CPI Group (UK) Ltd, Croydon, CR0 4YY

CLAIMED BY THE ENEMY

JULIA JAMES

CAITLIN CREWS

MILLS & BOON

Also by Julia James

Vows of Revenge
Accidental One-Night Baby
Marriage Made in Hate
Dimistrios's Bought Mistress

Also by Caitlin Crews

Forbidden Greek Mistress
An Heir for Christmas
Sicilian Devil's Prisoner
King's Heir of Hate

Discover more at millsandboon.co.uk.

Julia James lives in England and adores the peaceful verdant countryside and the wild shores of Cornwall. She also loves the Mediterranean—so rich in myth and history, with its sunbaked landscapes and olive groves, ancient ruins and azure seas. 'The perfect setting for romance!' she says. 'Rivalled only by the lush tropical heat of the Caribbean—palms swaying by a silver sand beach lapped by turquoise water... What more could lovers want?'

USA TODAY bestselling, RITA® Award–nominated and critically acclaimed author **Caitlin Crews** has written more than 130 books and counting. She has a master's and a PhD in English literature, thinks everyone should read more category romance, and is always available to discuss her beloved alpha heroes. Just ask! She lives in the Pacific Northwest with her comic book artist husband, is always planning her next trip, and will never, ever read all the books in her to-be-read pile. Thank goodness.